DEMENTED

Elise Noble

Published by Undercover Publishing Limited

Copyright © 2020 Elise Noble

v4

ISBN: 978-1-912888-14-6

Edited by Nikki Mentges, NAM Editorial

Cover design by Abigail Sins

www.undercover-publishing.com

www.elise-noble.com

Families are like branches on a tree.
They grow in different directions, yet their roots
remain as one.

CHAPTER 1 - IRIS

A WEDNESDAY.

DAY 1,892 of my stay at Lakeview Secure Hospital.

Or perhaps day 1,893... I tended to lose count, and what were a few days between friends? The cocktail of drugs I took turned my brain to mush and made every thought an effort. Sometimes so much of an effort that I didn't even bother.

And just lately? They'd upped the dosages.

Probably something to do with me biting an orderly's ear off, but I wasn't given a lot of choice in that. I didn't *want* to do it, okay?

Didn't, didn't, *didn't*.

And afterwards, as I sat fastened into restraints for the inevitable bollocking, the hospital director had told me I was never getting out. *Never*. I was stuck in this little corner of paradise until I took my last breath. Locked in a room that was really a cell except we weren't allowed to call them that.

Rules.

Rules, rules, rules.

Take your meds, Iris. Quit talking to pigeons, Iris. Get dressed, Iris. Put your damn feet on the floor, Iris.

The orders never stopped.

Sometimes, I wished I'd been a good girl. Wished I hadn't killed a man. The judge had called it murder. I said I was just doing my job.

And Leland Baker had deserved his punishment, just like the orderly.

Maybe it was Thursday?

Footsteps sounded in the tiled corridor outside my room, keys jangled, and the door slammed back against the wall. Oh, fantastic. It was Bobby. Bobby ate salami for breakfast and never brushed his teeth. I held my breath as he got closer.

"Don't start with this nonsense again," he muttered. "You can't suffocate yourself. Do you want to go back on suicide watch?"

No, I didn't, and I wasn't even suicidal. I'd only torn a strip off my bed sheet to make a wrist support after I hurt myself doing handstands, and some idiot had panicked and told the director I was trying to hang myself.

Now they didn't let me do handstands anymore either.

Lakeview was the pits.

My lawyer told me it was the easy option, far better than prison, more of a relaxing little holiday in the English countryside. But with hindsight, I'd rather have taken my chances in the general population. At least with a prison sentence, there was an end date, a goal. Freedom to look forward to. In Lakeview, the only way out was to convince Director Calvert that you were fixed, and guess what? Nobody was ever fixed because the staff preferred us broken. Drugged-up zombies were far easier to deal with than sentient human beings.

And I heard that in prison, you also got to take classes and go outside occasionally. Theoretically,

Lakeview offered occupational therapy too, but in reality, we were rarely allowed out of our rooms. Books from the hospital library were like treasure, and the highlight of my day was often a visit to the shower or a chat with my psychiatrist. Not that Dr. Tillis ever had much to say. No, he had boxes to tick. *Tick, tick, tick*, meeting over, on to the next patient. Sorry, service user. We were *service users*, a handy little term that made it sound like we wanted to be there.

I swung my legs off the side of the bed, and Bobby stood impassive, watching me. He reminded me of a beluga whale. Kinda grey, with features moulded out of putty.

"Are you gonna walk nicely today, Iris?"

"Maybe."

Why commit? I liked to keep the orderlies on their toes.

He patted the canister of PAVA spray on his belt, a reminder of what awaited me if I didn't behave. I'd never been sprayed with it on purpose, but I'd gotten a faceful when one of the idiot jailers accidentally set his off. I was pretty sure Director Calvert didn't hire the best people.

Bobby took hold of my right arm and marched me into the corridor. The place was quiet, as usual. I rarely saw the other service users, and our rooms were soundproofed. Silent. If I had to pick, I'd say the worst part of being at Lakeview was the loneliness, the days that passed without any meaningful interaction at all. The orderlies were overworked and—I suspected—underpaid, as well as being all-around grumpy. Sometimes, Dr. Tillis talked for a few moments as he filled in his forms, gave me a snippet of information on the outside world, and I treasured those facts more than I'd ever admit. They got filed in the sludge at the back of my brain, and as I lay in bed at night, I'd fight my way through the fog to recall them.

The USA had declared war on Venezuela.

Aston Villa won the Premier League.

Another probe just landed on Mars.

Murder rates in England were up, how terrible.

But more murder meant business for Director Calvert and his friends, right?

Bobby opened the door to the meeting room and ushered me inside. The place reminded me of the closet I'd been interviewed in at the police station—stark, bare walls, a one-way mirrored window at the far end, plus a plain metal table with two chairs—except in the police station, they'd brought me bad coffee but at Lakeview, I only got a plastic cup of tepid water.

Hold on a second… Who was this?

"Uh, we're in the wrong room."

I knew Bobby was dumb, but really? Dr. Tillis was fifty-something with grey hair and a paunch, and I made a game out of counting the bits of cornflake stuck in his moustache. The guy sitting at the table was much younger with dark hair and dimples. No moustache, no breakfast cereal whatsoever, just a barely-there smile that quickly morphed into a serious expression.

"Meet your new doctor, Iris."

Bobby backed away, and I tried to follow. "Wait! What new doctor? Where's Dr. Tillis?"

He just shrugged and closed the door, trapping me inside with a stranger. Great. Another person to figure out, and my brain was moving at half speed this morning. When I'd first arrived at Lakeview, I tried to avoid the pills, hiding them in my cheeks and spitting them down the toilet, but the staff soon got wise to that. Now they checked my mouth before they left.

"Hello, Iris. Would you like to take a seat?"

Not in the slightest. "Hi."

"My name's Marcus Hastings."

"Dr. Hastings?"

"If you like."

"You're a psychiatrist?"

"That's what my certificate says."

"Aren't you too young for that? Dr. Tillis told me psychiatrists had to do years of training."

"We do. Twelve years to be precise. So, Iris, do you want to tell me a bit about you?"

"Not really."

"Not really?"

"What's the point?"

"Once I understand your situation better, I can start to help you."

"Funny, that's what Dr. Tillis said in the beginning as well, but he soon got bored with trying."

After he discovered I was a lost cause, that was. Doing the bare minimum was so much easier. A bit of paperwork, some small talk, and he could collect his salary and go home. At first, he'd asked me to be open with him, to tell him the truth, but the truth was what landed me in Lakeview in the first place. No way was I planning to open my big mouth again.

After I got arrested, my lawyer had given me two options—plead guilty or go to trial. But if I picked a trial, it would only be a formality, he said. I mean, there was no doubt I did it. One of the eyewitnesses had been an off-duty policeman. Oops.

Then Mr. Gibbs, who'd been lovingly assigned to me by Legal Aid, began muttering about mitigating circumstances. Sure, I'd taken a life in cold blood, but the man *had* killed my mother. Maybe we could bargain for a lighter sentence if we could convince the judge I'd had some kind of mental breakdown? And I honestly must have lost my mind because when Mr. Gibbs encouraged me to tell him the truth, I did. He'd gotten this gleam in his eye, the excitement of a man who'd just been handed a surprise gift complete with shiny wrapping paper and a big red bow on the top.

Then he'd advised me to plead insanity.

Looking back, the judge hadn't needed a lot of convincing. Explaining that I'd run Leland Baker down in order to release my mother's trapped soul from its resting place beside the B4726 and fulfil my legacy must have seemed crazy to a layperson. And yet it was true.

Wait, wait, stay with me.

Perhaps I should start at the beginning, yes? The way my mum did with me? Ever since I was a little girl, she'd told me that one day I'd be able to see ghosts, but I hadn't believed her, not at first. Not until I turned eight and saw my first spirit, a teenage boy in Victorian dress standing on the pavement right outside the front door. I already knew his name was Cedric because Mum used to say hello to him every time we left the house, but I hadn't been prepared for the dark magenta sheen of the blood running down his cheeks, or his misshapen head, or the dejected expression on his grubby face. As Mum explained, he'd died in a fistfight in 1892, long before the Greenacres housing estate was built, and now he was stuck there until the Electi fixed the problem.

That was us, by the way. The Electi.

Or at least, it was me. Once I got that first little taste of the spirit world, my mother's abilities had gradually transferred to yours truly, and over the next two years while we could both talk to ghosts, she'd told me everything she knew. The Electi had been created an age and a day ago to keep the balance on the earth, to banish black spirits to the netherworld and ensure the good thrived. When a person's life was taken by another, their soul hung out in the spot where they'd died so they could help us to catch who did it. Once we'd found the bad guy and dispatched him, the trapped soul was free to leave.

Except thanks to pesky laws, closed-mindedness, and the general idea that killing people was frowned upon, we'd stopped doing our job quite some time ago. Now the trapped souls were stacking up while the black spirits lived out their natural lives then got reincarnated for another go. No wonder the prisons were all full.

Tell him a bit about myself, Dr. Hastings had said. No thanks.

"What's the weather like?" I asked.

"I'm sorry?"

"Dr. Tillis said we were due for a cold snap. A polar wind or something."

Although I had a window—a window that hadn't been cleaned for my entire stay at Lakeview—it was hard to tell what temperature it was outside. The hospital stayed at a balmy nineteen degrees, and the only time it got warmer was for the three days of British summer when they were too cheap to turn on the air conditioning. Last week, it had rained every day.

"I, er, I guess it's been chilly lately, for mid-August anyway."

"Do you watch football?"

"Not voluntarily."

I couldn't help snorting a laugh. "Dr. Tillis was a Chelsea fan. He went to all of their home games."

"Are you a football fan, Iris?"

"Not even a little bit."

"What sports do you like?"

"Gymnastics. I—" I realised I'd said too much. Let my guard down. Damn Dr. Hastings and his soft brown eyes. He kept watching me instead of looking at his paperwork the way he was supposed to. "What does it matter?"

"We're going to be working together for a while, so —"

"Oh, please. Working together? I'm stuck in a box, and you're..." I paused to yawn, fighting the brain fog again. "And you're part of the system that put me here." I folded my arms. "I'm done."

CHAPTER 2 - MARCUS

MY SECOND PATIENT in my new job, and much as I hated to admit it because his phrasing was distinctly unprofessional, Doug Calvert, my new boss, had been right. Iris McGivern *was* a whole lot of crazy wrapped up in a pretty package.

Dammit, I should *not* have been thinking of a patient that way.

And now she folded her arms, glaring at me across the table with big blue eyes, her long blonde hair tied back in a ponytail. Twelve years of medical training, and this was where I'd ended up—fresh meat at a medium-security psychiatric hospital, and not a particularly well-run one upon first impressions.

Considering the cloud I'd left my last job under, I knew I was lucky to land the position at all. I hadn't thought I stood a hope. But at the end of my interview, which had lasted a whole twenty minutes, Calvert had surprised me and said I'd fit right in. That every man deserved a second chance. And there I was.

So... Iris.

Her previous psychiatrist, Greg Tillis, had asked to be reassigned after an incident last week. Well, what he'd actually said during our brief handover was, "There's no getting through to that girl. She's delusional, she's dangerous, and she's got deep-seated issues I haven't even begun to touch."

Calvert had suggested we restrain Iris for the session today, but I didn't think that would be a great start to our relationship. No, I was just keeping a very close eye on her, as was Bobby in the observation room next door.

"Let's go back to the gymnastics. Did you participate? Or watch it on TV?"

I'd barely had time to glance at her file, but I did recall a note near the end. She'd tried to hang herself, apparently, then claimed when she got caught that she'd only been trying to do a handstand. In the margin, someone had scrawled the words "history of lying."

She hadn't made another attempt on her life since, just somebody else's, apparently. According to the report, an orderly had bent over her to rearrange her blankets and she'd reared up, latched onto his ear with her teeth, and refused to let go until she spat the bloody lobe onto the floor. Doug Calvert was worried about the guy suing the hospital for damages.

Iris didn't answer, and instead of looking at me, she turned her gaze to the table. Still, it could have been worse. My first patient had flicked snot at me.

What else had Iris's file said? Something about ghosts? Ah, yes—she'd come to Lakeview after she ran a man down with her car, then backed up and drove over him again, and when she got caught—after a police chase that took in two counties—she claimed she'd done it to avenge the spirit of her dead mother. That clearly fitted with her diagnosis of schizophrenia. The case had made the newspapers because, in a twist, her victim had been the man who killed her mother three years earlier by hitting her with his car while intoxicated. The media billed it as "an eye for an eye," and some hailed Iris as a modern-day Hammurabi, but no matter—it was still wrong, and she'd ended up where she belonged. In a place where she could get help for her illness.

But I realised I faced an uphill struggle to convince her to accept that help.

And also a battle to give it. A new wing had just opened at Lakeview, and when it filled up, I'd have thirty patients to look after. Daily sessions just wouldn't be possible in the long term.

"I really do want to help you, Iris. Can you tell me how you're feeling today?"

Silence.

"What would you like help with?"

Silence.

"I understand that staying here at Lakeview is difficult for you." Hell, I'd only been at the place for a few hours and I already wanted to run screaming. "But if you'll talk to me, I can try to make things easier."

Silence.

Was this how our sessions were going to be? Me asking questions while Iris ignored every word and picked at her fingernails?

"Do you want to talk about the weather again?"

Nothing.

"Well, I'll tell you anyway." My phone had a weather app. I'd only used it once or twice, mostly to curse when I'd left the washing out as a shower passed over, but now I was glad I hadn't pressed the delete button. "Looks like we're in for a cold, windy week— you were right. But it's not due to rain until next

Tuesday."

Zilch.

"Would you rather start at the beginning? I took a look at your file, and I understand you see ghosts?"

"I wondered how long you'd take to go there," she muttered.

At least she was talking. "I've never met anyone with that ability before." What was the technical term? Necromancy? "Why don't you tell me about it?"

I'd once had a patient who insisted she could talk to machines, and I don't mean Alexa. Her tumble dryer was called Matthew, and her vacuum cleaner... Best not to think about that. But with the right medication plus psychotherapy, she'd learned to cope quite well.

"The ghosts... Yeah, the ghosts." Iris's head lolled to one side, and her eyes closed for a moment. Due to her medication? She was on some hefty doses. "We talk all the time. It's a regular party at my place every night." She giggled, only there was nothing funny about her demeanour. "Wanna come?"

She reached for my hand, and I jerked back. She laughed harder.

"What? You're scared of little old me?"

"I'd appreciate if you could refrain from touching during these sessions."

"Is that a tattoo?"

I tugged my cuff down. Buttons only, no cufflinks allowed.

"Let's focus on you."

"And my imaginary friends? Did you know there's a ghost sitting next to you right now?" She leaned forward again, her hands in her lap this time. "Boo."

Of course, I looked—it was an unconscious reaction

—and Iris found that hilarious. She laughed and laughed and laughed until she fell right off her chair. I leapt forward, but I wasn't in time to stop her head from hitting the tiles. Bloody Nora.

Was she still conscious? I checked her pulse, but there was no reaction when I called her name. I was about to hit the panic button when Bobby walked in.

"Don't worry; it's not the first time she's done this. I'll take her back."

Not the first time? So that made it okay?

Good grief.

***

In a fitting end to a difficult day, I got stuck in traffic for over an hour. Someone had crashed up ahead, and the police closed the dual carriageway to remove the wreckage. With no way to turn around and no way forward, I switched off my Volkswagen's engine and texted Vijay, my dog walker. Could he possibly visit again to let Teddy out for a few minutes?

Then I scrolled through my emails. Top of the list was a missive from my mother wanting to know why I hadn't RSVPed to her birthday party invitation. The big six-oh. How did I tactfully tell her that I could barely afford lunch at the moment, let alone a trip to Spain?

And further down... An email from my lawyer. I didn't want to open it. Every message brought bad news, and I just wanted the divorce to be over. More importantly, I longed for the custody battle to end. And it *had* been a battle. Laurel, my ex, had used every dirty trick in the book to stop me from seeing my little girl, from turning our friends against me to convincing

Cassidy herself that I didn't want her anymore. Lies, all of it. I loved my daughter more than anything. Full custody was going to be an uphill battle, but anything was better than the four and a quarter hours I currently got each week. Fridays after school, a quarter past three until seven thirty, scheduled as if my own flesh and blood were a part-time job, a chore, rather than the light of my damn life. No overnights, no holidays, no special occasions. I'd missed her sixth birthday party three weeks ago because Laurel had taken out a restraining order against me, the vindictive... *Stay calm, Marcus.* Giving myself an aneurysm wouldn't help matters in the slightest.

But frustration got the better of me, and I thumped the steering wheel. My accidental toot of the horn earned me a glare from the woman in the car beside mine, and I closed my eyes to block out her judgement. How much longer could I go on like this?

I forced Laurel out of my mind—she'd already taken up enough of my headspace over the last few months—and focused on today's problem. Iris McGivern. The woman intrigued me, more than any of my other patients so far. She veered from catatonic to lucid, from awkward to oddly pleasant, but I knew from the warnings that she could turn violent in an instant. What made her tick? Why did she act that way? No matter what she believed, I genuinely did want to help her. While some patients never recovered enough to function in society, most could be aided to a certain extent. And that was my job—to aid them. I took my Hippocratic oath seriously, although from what I'd seen today at Lakeview, a number of my colleagues weren't quite so conscientious.

With little else to do, I plugged Iris's name into the search bar. Her file had mentioned newspaper coverage, so surely there'd be something online?

And there she was.

At the time of her arrest, she'd been little more than a child. Eighteen, a slight figure walking between two hulking policemen as they ushered her into court. She'd pleaded guilty to murder by reason of insanity, the murder of a man who'd killed her mother and never shown any remorse. Was that why she'd done it? Why she'd waited three years before getting revenge? The crime showed premeditation, rational thinking... She'd traced Leland Baker to his new address, then ploughed into him as he walked home from the bus stop. Unfortunately for her, an off-duty policeman had driven around the corner just as Baker bounced off the bonnet, then given chase.

During her trial, she'd spun a story about killing the man to free her dead mother's soul, and it seemed as though Iris truly believed that. Locals reported she'd visited the spot where Edie May McGivern died almost every day since her passing, sometimes laying flowers but mostly just talking to thin air. Had her mother's death set off a long-lasting trauma reaction? It was an avenue to explore.

Tomorrow. I'd explore it tomorrow.

Tonight I had to take Teddy for his evening walk and finish painting Cassie's new room. She wanted it pink, and even though she might never sleep in it, I'd promised to decorate it exactly the way she asked. She had me wrapped around her little finger, but I wouldn't want it any other way.

CHAPTER 3 - IRIS

ON WEDNESDAY NIGHT, I dreamed. Which was strange, because I hadn't dreamed for months. Before that, before they changed my medication, I'd had such vivid nightmares that I woke up drenched in sweat and screaming every day in the early hours.

But that Wednesday, I dreamed I was at the beach. Lying peacefully on the sand, watching the gulls soar overhead as waves washed up on the shore. I'd only been to the beach once, when I was ten and Mum took me for a holiday in Devon. That was right after her abilities finally deserted her, leaving me as the only active member of the Electi in our household, and even at that age, I understood money would be tight in the future.

Up until then, Mum had worked as a medium, acting as a bridge between our world and the spirits to offer some comfort to the ones they left behind. People labelled her a charlatan—not her clients, but people who stuck their noses into our business just to complain. The local vicar held a vigil on our doorstep once, and people on the internet... Don't even get me started on them.

Mum *wasn't* a fake, and when her powers transferred to me, she had to quit her job. We moved out of London, away from the wagging tongues and the rumours and the nastiness, and settled in the village of Highcross, not too far from Leighton Buzzard. Mum got a job at Tesco, and I learned about blackberry picking and riding ponies and ventriloquism—a useful skill when talking to ghosts. I even won first prize in a local talent show. Life back then was pretty damn lovely.

And now I was back on Saunton Sands, relaxing under a blue sky while Mum read a book beside me.

At least, I was until I woke up and realised the shushing sound wasn't the sea, it was the flood of water running out of my toilet. Yeuch! I stood on my bed and started screaming, because what else could I do? I wasn't about to paddle through the mess. Who knew what was floating in it? At that time in the morning, with the moon still high in the sky, there weren't many people around, and at best guess—because I wasn't allowed a watch—it took twenty minutes after I pressed my call button for an orderly to turn up with a nurse in tow. Of course, he opened the door without thinking, and a wave of nasty water gushed out into the hallway. He screamed, the nurse screamed, we all freaking screamed.

Welcome to the wonderful world of privatisation and its shoddy maintenance.

Nine o'clock found me sitting at a table with a cup of tepid orange juice, two soggy Weetabix—plastic bowl, plastic spoon—and a cheesed-off Director Calvert leaning forward on his elbows as he glared at me. He'd already complained about me having food in the meeting room.

"What did you do, Iris?" he asked for the third time.

"Nothing. I did nothing. Why is that so difficult to

understand?"

"Cisterns don't just break by themselves."

"Well, this one did. Maybe a pipe got blocked or something. I was fast asleep, and the next thing I knew, I was surrounded by water."

With me, one small survivor sitting on my bed in the middle of a sea of yuck. If that wasn't a metaphor for my life...

He shook his head and tutted. "Do you have any idea how much this mess will cost to clean up?"

"No, but I'm sure you're going to tell me."

He opened his mouth. Closed it again. What? He didn't have his spreadsheet handy? The nurses all complained about him, you know. About his penny-pinching and his cutbacks and the fact that profits always came first. I thought he'd give me a lecture, but instead, he shook his head again and pushed his chair back.

"Has Iris had her medication this morning? This level of aggression is concerning."

Aggression? Seriously? No, sweetheart, that was sarcasm. I'd honed it backchatting the series of foster parents I lived with after my mother got murdered. They hovered over me with their cloying kindness and their "we just want to helps" until they gave up, labelled me as difficult, and sent me on to the next place. Admittedly, the last set hadn't been too bad. Kind of hands-off. Back then, all I'd wanted was to be left alone, but now, I craved human interaction, even the irritating kind. Painful though it was, sitting with Dr. Hastings was still better than being on my own. Funny how things changed, wasn't it?

The nurse beside me shook her head.

"Not yet. We were waiting for you to speak to her first."

"Well, I've spoken to her now. Give her what she needs, then put her in that empty room on the other side of the second floor."

"Not in the new wing?"

"Those rooms have only just been finished. I'm not having her damage one of those as well."

"But—"

"Just do it, okay?"

The nurse looked as though she wanted to argue, but in the end, she bit her tongue until Director Calvert strode out of the room, his lips pressed together in a thin line. Technically, I couldn't see souls while they were still in people's bodies, but I knew his was ugly.

"Can we behave today, Iris?" the nurse asked, half pleading.

I shrugged. It wasn't as though I acted out all the time, but sometimes, being stuck in that place got hard to take. We were supposed to toe the line like good little robots, and I just wasn't made to fit in. My mum had always said being different was a good thing, but she'd never been to Lakeview.

The nurse—Hazel, according to her name badge—wasn't much older than me. How did she end up at the psych unit? I figured working there was better than being a patient, but only marginally. Luckily, I was in a reasonable mood that day, so I walked like an obedient lemming as she herded me towards the elevator. A change of scene might do me good. I'd been stuck in the same room for five long years, and apart from the cracks on the ceiling and the wildlife that occasionally visited the windowsill, there wasn't much to look at.

Yes, I could see the forest out of my window, but that only depressed me more because I'd never get to wander through the trees.

"What's my new room like?" I asked.

Hazel pushed the button to call the elevator. Pushed it again when the elevator didn't come fast enough. Why did people do that?

"It's mostly like your old room, I guess. Just on the opposite side of the building."

"What's outside?"

"What do you mean?"

"Outside the window?"

"Oh. I've never really thought about that."

The car park. It was the car park. If there was one thing that promised to be worse than watching the birds flitting from tree to tree and the occasional squirrel gathering nuts, it was seeing the staff and visitors go home. They had freedom. I had a bed, a tiny washroom, a bolted-down desk, and a plastic chair with no sharp edges. Plus a ghost.

Fuck.

There was a ghost standing on my new bed. Well, *through* my new bed. What the hell?

Lakeview was housed in an old Victorian asylum—three storeys of high-ceilinged corridors and dingy rooms that wouldn't have looked out of place in a horror movie if the lighting was right. If it was on TripAdvisor, it would rate minus five stars. Even the "new wing" wasn't new. They'd just fixed it up from the decaying mess it was before. I guess someone picked the building up for a song and thought they'd make a few quid by bringing it back into use as the modern-day version of hell.

The age of the building and its former use meant it wasn't unusual for me to see the odd ghost. The girl in the hallway on the way to the showers, for example. I didn't talk to her much because the staff looked at me funny, but her name was Maud and she'd been poisoned by a well-meaning doctor in 1897. An overdose of laudanum, apparently. The Victorians used it as a cure-all, but drinking opium like cough syrup was never a great idea.

That was why the Electi existed, Mum had explained. Maud's death was a prime example of an accidental killing, a situation where the Electi wouldn't want to dispatch the man who'd taken her life to face whatever came afterwards. After all, he'd only been trying to help. We were meant to evaluate the testimony of the spirits left behind before deciding on an appropriate course of action. That could mean doing nothing further, or we might consider removal to be the only remedy. Rumour said the black souls we banished flowed with the waters of the River Styx, tumbling through the underworld for eternity, but I couldn't be sure about that. The Electi were just one small cog in the machine that kept the world as humans knew it turning, and information came to us on a need-to-know basis. Or didn't come. We'd been on our own for thousands of years while our creator whatevered.

Meanwhile, I was left on earth with a new problem.

I couldn't let on that I had a ghostly companion, not with Hazel being staff. She'd note any reaction on my file, and Dr. Hastings would probably give me some fancy new medicine to take my "hallucinations" away.

So I smiled and sat on the bed beside my new friend. Her legs disappeared through the mattress, cut off at the knees as she stared at me through unblinking eyes. How had she died? She didn't look injured, and worse, I realised her outfit wasn't the Victorian-era nightgown that Maud wore but something similar to my own regulation pyjamas. They even had the Lakeview logo embroidered on the pocket because what did the powers that be think we were gonna do, steal them?

Shit. This girl had died recently. She'd been *killed* recently. Was it an accident? Or deliberate? What if it was murder and the person who did it was still wandering the halls at Lakeview? I hadn't heard any whispers about a patient dying, and surely there should've been some commotion? What about the police? Wouldn't they have investigated?

Unless, of course, the staff thought it was natural causes. What was the procedure for that? Ship the body off for cremation and hush everything up? It wouldn't have been surprising.

A chill ran through me. What if I was the only person who realised this girl had been killed by another?

"How do you like your new room, Iris?" Hazel asked.

Act normal, Iris.

"It's nice." Apart from the dead person, obviously, and the damp patch in the corner of the ceiling, and the brown stain on the wall that I didn't want to think about.

"Lovely. I'm glad you like it. You'll just feel a little prick now."

Unlikely. I hadn't had a boyfriend in years. Sometimes, I even missed Alfie, the guy who'd taken my virginity under the slide in the park when I was sixteen. *Little prick*. Yup. I choked out a laugh as Hazel injected me with something or other. At least I had drugs, right? I mean, addicts on the streets would pay good money for the cocktail I got every day. Too bad I... The thought skittered away from me as the haze descended. What was bad? Everything? Nothing? I had no idea anymore.

CHAPTER 4 - IRIS

URGH.

WHATEVER DRUGS Hazel gave me had worn off enough for me to lever my eyelids open, and yup, the ghost was still standing next to me, watching through big brown eyes. How long had I been asleep? It was still daylight outside, but I couldn't see the sun. Which direction did my new room face? I needed to know so I could estimate the time.

"You're one of them," she whispered. "An Electi."

What gave it away? Was it the orange glow that only spirits could see? Or the way the air crackled when I got near? Either way, there was no hiding from my destiny. And to make doubly sure I couldn't walk around incognito, whenever someone got killed, a spirit guide showed up sharpish to let them know of our existence. Between you and me, I didn't like the spirit guides much. Over the last century or so, they'd started making snide little comments to the dead regarding our performance, or rather, the lack of it. Didn't they understand about CCTV and forensics and police? The guides had the easy job—show up, murmur a few complacencies and explain what would happen next, then tick the spirit off the list and move on to the next victim.

If they ever decided to change careers, perhaps they

could join the psychiatry team here at Lakeview?

"Yup, that's me. The orange one. I'm Iris."

"I'm Jacinda. What happened to me?"

Funny, that was meant to be my question. "Don't you know?"

"Not really. Everything's super fuzzy. I think I fell asleep, and when I woke up, I was standing here. This was, like, a month ago, and now I can't move."

"Somebody killed you."

"That's what the spirit guide said, but you know..."

"I know what?"

"It sounds kind of farfetched. I mean, I'm in a hospital. How could somebody kill me in a hospital?"

More of a prison, but that was just semantics. "I don't know, but it happened, because otherwise you wouldn't be here."

"But *why* would somebody kill me? I'm a good girl."

I took a moment to study my new roommate more carefully. She was younger than me, maybe twenty or twenty-one, with light brown skin and curly black hair bunched into a topknot. The only indicator that she'd suffered an uncomfortable death was the sheen of sweat that glistened on her skin. And her eyes were weird. Big pupils, too dilated for the light. Had she died at night? Overall, she looked sweet, but why was she at Lakeview?

"Are you? What did you do to end up here?"

"I defeated the Antichrist."

Hoo boy. Did I dare to ask? "How did you do that?"

"I put a stake through his heart."

Wasn't that for vampires? "I thought Jesus was supposed to defeat the Antichrist?"

"Yes, that's right, but he's not here, so he asked me

to help out."

Okaaaaaay. "How did you find the Antichrist?"

"He was living next door to me."

"That was convenient."

"The Lord moves in mysterious ways. Trust in him, and he shall deliver."

"And he delivered you the Antichrist?"

"Yes."

Wow. She sounded so perfectly sincere when she said that. And people thought *I* was delusional?

"How could you be sure? Did the Antichrist come over and introduce himself?"

"Yes."

"Really?"

"Well, he called himself Steve, but I knew his true identity right away. The symbols inked onto his skin, the dead animals he fashioned into clothing, his dark aura... And he played the devil's music all night long."

Translation: Jacinda's neighbour was a goth, and she'd murdered him because she thought she had a hotline to God. I mean, I was no fan of heavy metal, but impaling the guy was a teeny bit extreme. And now I was stuck with her for the foreseeable future. Brilliant. Just when I thought my life couldn't get any worse.

"Can we go back to the person who killed you? I only ask because I'm still alive and I'd quite like to stay that way. If there's a murderer at Lakeview, they should be in jail."

"Jail?" Her brows pinched together, and she looked adorably confused. "But aren't you supposed to kill them? Isn't that your purpose?"

"Officially, yes, but things have moved on. If the Electi go around killing people, we'll end up in prison ourselves."

"But we're all meant to fulfil our purpose. I fulfilled mine, and I've accepted my fate." Her perky smile was totally at odds with her freaky personality. "And you're already a prisoner."

"Technically, I'm a patient."

Gah. Now I sounded like Dr. Tillis.

"Potayto, potahto."

Although I hated to admit it, she did have a point. I was locked up, and Director Calvert assured me I wasn't getting out. What difference would it make if I managed to track down a killer and dispatch them if necessary? Two things made me hesitate. Firstly, they had sort of done me a favour with Jacinda. She was obviously nuts, plus she'd stabbed a guy, and if someone hadn't put her out of her misery, then that would have been *my* job. Also if I freed her, she'd go on to be reincarnated. Secondly? I wasn't all that great at killing people. I mean, I'd screwed up royally with Leland Baker, hadn't I? When I bumped my car over the kerb to hit him, I'd got a puncture, which meant my plan to flee the scene had turned into a bit of a disaster. At the end of the world's slowest police chase, I'd been driving on three tyres and a rim.

And those two points aside, how would I even find Jacinda's killer when she herself didn't know who was responsible?

"Look, I'm confined to a cell. I can't go around playing detective."

"Then why are you here?"

"Because I got caught doing something that's frowned upon."

"No, that's not it. It's fate."

Now she sounded like my mother. My whole life, Mum had assured me that when the time was right, the stars would align or some other bullshit and bring the Electi together again, but the chances of the others finding me in Lakeview were slim. And worse, if I died in there—if I died without having a daughter—my Electi's soul would be randomly assigned to a new girl, one without a mother able to explain why she saw dead people as she walked down the street.

That thought scared me almost as much as kicking the bucket.

"You're crazy. Fate isn't magic."

"Calling me crazy is rude. My lawyer said so. I'm *disturbed*."

Give me strength... "Okay, fine. You're disturbed. But fate still isn't magic."

"God has a plan for everything."

"Really? How do you know? Do you have him on speed dial?"

"We talk."

My eyes rolled so far back in my head I could see my own brain, and Jacinda pursed her lips.

"You should stop being so cynical."

"I'm talking to a ghost. Doesn't that count for something?"

She stared past me, considering. "Yes, it means that you should understand the existence of other astral planes without me having to explain it to you."

Of all the people I could have been stuck in a room with, why did I get Jacinda? She was kind of irritating, and logically, I knew she was insane, but she also made some good points. There *could* be other astral planes. I'd always wondered what happened to non-human souls, and Mum hadn't been able to answer that question either.

Jacinda's smug expression said she knew she'd got me. One point to her.

"I'll concede that other astral planes might exist. But I'm still not convinced about this grand plan. If a plan exists, then why is the world in such a mess? Why did the Electi get split up hundreds of years ago? If we're not together, we can't fix it."

Again, she pondered. "Maybe it's some sort of experiment? To see whether humankind will self-destruct when left to its own devices?"

"I'd say we have our answer, don't you think?"

"We do. Which means your friends will be coming soon."

I only wished I shared her confidence. Inside, I was more nervous than I cared to admit, both for my own future and for humanity's. The Electi were meant to save the world, but stuck in Lakeview with a killer on the loose, I might not even be able to save myself.

CHAPTER 5 - MARCUS

"DADDY!"

CASSIE SCRAMBLED out of the back seat of my soon-to-be ex-mother-in-law's Jaguar and rushed towards me. I crouched down and braced for impact, nearly tipping over backwards when she hit me full pelt.

"I missed you," she mumbled into my chest as I hugged her tight.

"Missed you too, monkey."

Jacqueline didn't bother to approach, just held out Cassie's backpack as if it were poisonous. She'd been perfecting that pissed-off look for years, ever since I began dating her daughter, but now that the divorce was almost final, the laser intensity of her glare had ratcheted up to Bond-villain levels.

"You'll need this," she said. "Cassidy wanted to bring toys from home." *From home.* Those two words cut deep. "I'll pick her up at seven thirty, as usual. Don't be late again."

She wagged a finger, and I forced myself to take a deep breath before I approached. Maiming my mother-in-law would be difficult to explain at the court hearing. Even though my lawyer had sighed and pointed out a hundred times that I stood no chance of getting full custody, I was still fighting.

"It was ten minutes, Jacqueline, and we only stopped on the way back from the park because Cassie wanted an ice cream."

"The judge said seven thirty p.m. sharp, and ice cream's bad for her."

Cassie ran past me and snatched her bag, saving me from having to get any closer to the old dragon. "But I like ice cream, Grandma."

"You can't be a ballerina if you eat junk food, Cassidy."

She was six years old, for goodness' sake. Kids that age didn't need to diet. If Jacqueline kept up with her nonsense, I'd be treating my daughter for an eating disorder before she hit her teens, and that wasn't a possibility I wanted to contemplate.

"I'll make sure she gets a healthy dinner."

I took Cassie's hand and headed for the house, but Jacqueline wasn't done yet.

"Is that a new car?" She wrinkled her nose as she picked her way across the driveway on four-inch heels to peer through the window of my new Volkswagen. And when I said "new," I meant I'd just bought it. Between my recent salary cut and the bills my lawyer was racking up, I couldn't afford the payments on my Audi anymore, so I'd traded it in for an eight-year-old Polo. "Does it have a booster seat? Cassidy needs a booster seat."

Of course it had a damn booster seat. *Stay calm, Marcus. Practise what you preach.* "Yes, Jacqueline, it has a booster seat and an excellent safety rating. Don't you have somewhere to be?"

The sarcasm was lost on her. "Yes, I'm on my way to play bridge with Felicity Rothwell."

"Bye, Grandma." Cassie waved and tugged me towards the house. "See you later."

Saved by my little girl. She shrieked happily as I swung her up onto my hip, Jacqueline's disapproval following us along the path to the front door as it did every week. Jacqueline—never Jacqui—insisted on dropping Cassie off and picking her up each Friday, presumably because she didn't want the philanderer, as she so charmingly called me, going anywhere near her house. What did she think I'd do? Corrupt her maid?

Inside, Teddy bounced around, licking Cassie's face and making her giggle. Cassie had been the one to name the dog, a Staffordshire Bull Terrier that was yet another bone of contention between Laurel and me. Until we broke up, she hadn't paid the slightest bit of attention to Teddy—apart from complaining about hair on the furniture, that was—yet now she was fighting for shared custody out of spite. Teddy had never liked her, and though I was loath to admit it, the dog had proven to be a better judge of character than me.

"I can have ice cream, right, Daddy?" Cassie asked once Jacqueline's Jaguar had roared off into the distance.

"I've got strawberry, vanilla, and chocolate."

"Chocolate!"

"How did I guess?"

"Can I have it now?"

"Pudding comes after dinner, remember? Do you want a snack?"

"Toast with chocolate spread?"

Some you win, some you lose. "Okay, toast with chocolate spread."

"And can I ride a pony again?"

"At five o'clock." I held up my left hand for her to look at my watch. "What time is it now?"

She grabbed my wrist with both hands, focusing hard. She looked so damn cute when she was thinking. Sometimes, I couldn't believe I'd had a hand in creating something that adorable.

"A quarter past three."

"Not a quarter past."

She tried again. "Half past?"

"That's right." Yes, Jacqueline had been fifteen minutes late, but I wasn't about to waste my breath on that argument. "So you have an hour to change out of your school uniform and play, and then we can go to the riding school. Do you want to show me your toys?"

Cassie flung the backpack across the room, where it bounced off the sofa and landed in Teddy's bed. "It's a doll. I hate dolls, but Mummy made me bring it. Can I play in the sandpit?"

"Sure, sweetie, you can play in the sandpit."

***

On Saturday morning, I woke up feeling hollow, the way I always did after a visit with Cassie. I missed the way she used to rush into the bedroom and pounce on me at the weekends. Now, instead of sneaking downstairs to make her toast with Nutella, I got to gulp down a bowl of cereal before heading to Lakeview for another eight-hour shift. Still, I couldn't complain too much—at least I had a job, and working weekends left me those precious hours on Friday afternoons to spend with my daughter. Laurel would never let me have her for a weekend day. She'd made that quite clear during mediation. *Mediation*. What a joke.

A new guard checked my pass as I waited to clear security, but he wore the same expression as the others —boredom with a hint of misery. So far, I hadn't seen a member of staff who looked happy, and I wondered whether that would be my fate too. Did a year at Lakeview suck out your soul? I'd spent Thursday reading through patient files, and they seemed somewhat sparse compared to those at Deane Valley Hospital. Most consisted of tick sheets and scribbled paragraphs about behaviour problems and adjustments to medication. I saw little in the way of actual treatment notes.

The guard buzzed me through the door into the bowels of the hospital. From the outside, the building was imposing, a stunning example of Victorian architecture, three storeys high plus gabled attic rooms that were never used. A tower rising in the middle housed the main entrance along with Doug Calvert's office on the top floor. Gargoyles stared down from the roofline. But inside, the period features had been stripped away, no doubt to save money during renovation, leaving a maze of small dark rooms interspersed with locked doors and the occasional staircase.

I headed for the staff offices, where I'd been assigned what was basically a cupboard, eight feet square with a single window set high into the wall behind my desk. A previous occupant had carved "Help me" into the wood panelling, and I wasn't sure whether the scribe had been a service user or a former colleague.

Greg Tillis's door was open as I walked past, and I

poked my head inside.

"Got a minute?"

He glanced up from his croissant and brushed crumbs off his tie—a clip-on for safety purposes. "Of course, of course. How are you settling in? Got many patients yet?"

"Half a dozen so far. One that was previously yours."

"Miss McGivern?"

"Iris. Yes."

He sucked in a breath, and I swore his teeth moved. "A difficult girl."

"Is that why she's on so much medication?"

And it wasn't only her. Every one of my assigned patients had been prescribed a high-dose cocktail of drugs.

"You've heard what she did to poor Terrence?"

"That's the guy whose ear she bit off?"

Tillis nodded, and a flake of pastry dropped off his moustache and landed on his blotter. The blotter was covered with doodles, and he hastily scribbled out one of a large-breasted lady when he noticed me looking.

"A terrible affair, that was. But even before then, she was unruly. A danger to herself and others."

"What did she do?"

Her file had been spectacularly vague on that. Better to hear it from the horse's mouth, so to speak.

"She'd act out in her room and cause herself injuries. Did you know she broke her ankle?"

"I didn't see that in the file."

"Really? I'm sure I made a note of it."

No, he hadn't. "How did she manage that?"

"She said she was trying to do a backflip and she

landed awkwardly. Honestly, a backflip. What kind of person attempts that in a small room?"

One who was bored out of her mind, probably. "Does she go outside much?"

"Not since she tried to escape."

Something else missing from the file. "How did she try to escape?"

"She knocked out one of our team members with a croquet mallet and climbed over the fence. Thankfully, the guards caught her before the police got involved. Director Calvert banned croquet after that—people like Iris spoil things for everyone. He almost discontinued basket weaving too, but thankfully, we were able to convince him otherwise."

Dare I ask? "What happened with the basket weaving?"

"She almost blinded another service user with a piece of cane."

"Do you have many incidents like that here?"

"No, because we medicate people."

"How about other treatments? Forensic therapy? Cognitive behavioural therapy? Mentalisation-based therapy?"

"Yes, yes, we consider all of those, of course. But some of the people in here simply don't respond to treatment, and there's only so much time available to persevere."

In other words, the bottom line came first. I understood it, but I didn't like it. At Deane Valley, many of my patients had been private referrals, and budget wasn't so much of a consideration. Here at Lakeview, they seemed to take the "chemical cosh" approach, something I'd read about but not previously encountered. Basically, they medicated the patients up to their eyeballs, enough that they couldn't act out even if they wanted to.

That fitted with Iris's disposition. In our previous session, she'd shown sparks of lucidity, but overall, she'd been sluggish. No wonder—some of the doses she was on were so high they bordered on excessive. It was actually surprising she'd managed to converse at all.

"There's a note on the file that she's a suicide risk?"

"Indeed there is. One of the nurses caught her tearing strips off her bed sheet and tying them together."

"An attempt to hang herself?"

"She claimed she was trying to strap up an injured wrist, but..."

"But you didn't believe her?"

"Actually, after the backflip incident, I thought it was probably true, but you can't be too careful, can you?" Tillis's phone rang, and he grimaced apologetically. "I'd better take this. It's my wife."

Good luck, pal. Women in general and relationships in particular were more trouble than they were worth.

And speaking of trouble, I had to meet with Iris next.

CHAPTER 6 - IRIS

"HOW ARE YOU feeling today, Iris?"

He was back. Dr. Hastings, only this time he had glasses on. Did he usually wear contacts? I hadn't bothered to look closely before. And this morning, my vision was kind of blurry, as was my brain.

"What...what does it matter?"

"I'd like to help you, Iris, but I can't if you don't talk to me."

Every psychiatrist, psychologist, psycharlatan I'd ever met had started out exactly the same. Pretended to care, then got annoyed when I didn't respond in the right way—whatever that was supposed to be—and tanked me up on more drugs than ever before. I'd long since learned that keeping quiet was the sensible option.

"Fine. I'm feeling fine."

He surprised me by cracking a smile. "If there's one thing I've learned from the women in my life, it's that 'fine' doesn't mean what we men think it does."

Hmm. That was something none of my previous shrinks had possessed—a sense of humour. But he was still the enemy.

"You have women in your life? Apart from your mother?"

Just for a second, his face twisted into a grimace.

Why? He shifted back to neutral before I could study him further.

"That surprises you?"

"Yeah, I thought you were gay."

"No, Iris, I'm not gay. But we're not here to talk about me."

"Well, I'm not..." My mind went fuzzy again. "I'm not talking about me, so..."

So, so, so... So nothing. *The sound of silence.* Wasn't that an old song? Mum used to listen to it when I was little.

"That's okay. We'll just sit here, then."

And he did. He just sat there. For ten minutes. Twenty. Thirty. I started off by counting the seconds in my head, but they got lost in the brain-sludge, and I had to guess how much time had gone by. What was his game? When I refused to speak to Dr. Tillis, he just got an orderly to put me back in my cell. I glanced at the one-way glass beside us. Was anyone watching?

My legs began to twitch, to go all creepy-crawly inside. You know that feeling you get when you just have to stand up and move around? I wanted to fidget, but I also didn't want to give Dr. Hastings the satisfaction of knowing he was getting to me.

Another five minutes passed, or maybe fifteen. He didn't move a muscle, just watched me, his chin resting on clasped hands. Seriously, this was getting weird. Didn't he have other patients to annoy? I squirmed in my seat, then cursed myself inside because dammit, he was so freaking calm.

Think, Iris. Think! Focus on something other than the admittedly handsome man sitting opposite you.

Okay, so he didn't look bad. For a doctor. But since

most of the doctors at Lakeview got their fashion tips from the seventies, and they weren't too hot on personal hygiene either, maybe my point of reference was skewed. Barely a day had gone past without Dr. Tillis having some sort of food stuck in his moustache. It was hard to take a man seriously when he had a piece of spaghetti just hanging there, wobbling every time he took a breath.

Dr. Hastings had a strong jaw, a straight nose, and dreamy brown eyes with flecks of gold in the irises, and dammit, *I shouldn't be looking at him like that.*

"I thought you were supposed to be helping me," I snapped.

Shit.

"Finally, she speaks."

"Stop looking so bloody smug."

"That's not intentional, I promise. And whether you believe me or not, I do want to help you."

"Yeah, right."

"Do you want things to carry on as they are?"

"Of course I don't. This place is hell on earth, if hell was boring rather than hot."

"I hear you don't get out of your room much?"

I folded my arms. Who had he been talking to? Dr. Tillis? "They keep me caged like a pet freaking hamster."

Except without a wheel, which might actually have been kind of fun. I had a hamster once. Alvin, he was called. I'd wanted a chipmunk, but Mum said they were too difficult to look after. Alvin used to escape once a month or so, and we'd find him living his best life in the kitchen cupboards, snacking on crackers and nuts and raisins. He'd lived to the grand old age of three and a half, and if animal souls could cross the species barrier, he'd probably been reincarnated as a pot-bellied pig.

"From what I understand, there were some incidents when you were participating in group activities. Do you want to tell me about those?"

"No."

He sighed. Caught himself halfway and morphed it into a smile. "Iris, if you won't talk to me—"

"You can't help. Yeah, yeah, I get the message."

Did I want to talk to him? Explaining to the other shrinks what happened had got me absolutely nowhere, and I didn't know this guy. Everyone in authority lied—doctors, lawyers, cops, the staff in this place. And then there was the matter of an unknown killer on the loose... What if Dr. Hastings was evil in disguise? Not for the first time, I wished I could identify black souls before killing a person. That sure would make my days as a member of the Electi easier.

On the other hand, life at Lakeview couldn't get much worse, and even basket weaving was better than staring at the cracks on the ceiling. Or talking to freaking Jacinda.

"The thing in the greenhouse was a mistake, I swear."

"What thing in the greenhouse?"

Oh. He didn't know about that?

"When I used weedkiller instead of fertiliser. All the pills make my brain go funny sometimes, and I got the packets mixed up."

And nobody had been more upset than me. I'd tried to get a hose and rinse the leaves, but two of the orderlies had grabbed me and dragged me back inside. And when I tried to explain that if they just washed the glyphosate off, the plants might recover, they'd injected me with something that turned my insides to mush. They shouldn't have told me to use chemicals on the plants, anyway. It was bad for the environment.

Dr. Hastings nodded once. "Okay. And the eye injury in the basket-weaving workshop?"

"An accident. Honestly. Joey leaned over to get another piece of cane and poked his eye on one of my spokes."

"Spokes?"

"The sticky-up pieces that make the sides of the basket. I apologised, but they still wouldn't let me have another go. And they said I was unsuited to go near the woodwork room as well."

"What about the incident with the croquet mallet?"

"Where I hit George?"

"I'm not sure of the gentleman's name, but yes."

"Okay, so I meant to do that." I only wished I'd hit him harder, the creepy fucker. "It was the anniversary of my mum's death, and I wanted to go and put flowers on her grave."

There was nobody left to do it but me, and even though I knew she was gone, really gone now, I'd still wanted to visit and tell her I was all right. And then I'd wanted to run as far away from Lakeview as possible, although I appreciated the difficulty of that with no money and a bunch of cops looking for me.

"Do you understand why it was wrong to hit George?"

"If you'd spent any time with George, you'd have wanted to do the same."

"But I wouldn't have done it, because I understand it's not acceptable to hit people."

"If George used to spy on you naked in the shower, you'd have punched his bloody lights out, trust me. And it worked because after I whacked him with the croquet mallet, he got reassigned to different duties."

Dr. Hastings looked up sharply. "He watched you in the shower?"

"Every damn time."

"Did you report this?"

"I tried, but nobody believed me. Didn't you read my file?"

"Who did you tell?"

"Dr. Sedgewick. And my court-appointed guardian, who, by the way, is useless."

Apparently, George said I was mistaken and that was that. Done. Finished. Another tick in the box, and everyone except me was happy. Dr. Hastings scribbled some notes on a pad, but his writing was really, really bad, and I couldn't read what it said. Probably "Iris is a liar." I'd literally seen Dr. Tillis write that once, right before he called the orderly to stuff me full of more pills.

But Dr. Hastings gave me a small, tight smile. What did that mean? I had no idea. Unfortunately, I'd always found it easier to talk to the dead than the living.

"Iris, what would it take to make your time here happier?"

"What?"

"You seem surprised by the question."

Of course I was surprised. In five years, nobody had ever asked it before. Happiness wasn't a factor in my stay at Lakeview.

"Uh..."

"Some changes to your room? I understand you

rearranged your furniture last night?"

Oh, crap. I stiffened involuntarily. Why did he have to bring that up? Yes, I'd moved the bed four feet to the right because it was either that or share it with Jacinda, but in the morning, the nurse told me off and moved it back again.

"So?"

"Why did you do that?"

Think, Iris. "Uh, the sun was getting in my eyes this morning, and I don't have a blind."

"So you'd like a blind?"

No, I wanted my bloody bed four feet to the right. But I couldn't admit that because it would only lead to more questions I didn't want to answer.

"I'd love a blind."

"I'll see if there's anything I can do. We have to be careful with the cords, though."

For fuck's sake. "I didn't try to kill myself either. You can write that on your damn pad."

"Actually, I'm inclined to believe you."

Huh? "What? Why?"

"Because nobody as stubborn as you would take her own life." He glanced sideways at the mirrored window, then closed his eyes for a second and sucked in a breath. "I apologise. That comment was unprofessional."

"Is someone watching us?"

He hesitated for so long I thought it was my turn to get the silent treatment.

"Not today, no. But I'm afraid our session's over. We'll speak again tomorrow."

***

"Why can't I lie down?" Jacinda asked as I sat cross-legged on my plastic chair. "Every time I try, I fall right through the bed."

"Because you're a ghost."

"But why can I pass through solid objects? That's super annoying."

"Because that's the system."

"But why?"

"Think about it—if you died in the middle of a road and you couldn't pass through cars, you'd get splattered every ten seconds."

"I guess that makes sense. So I have to stand forever?"

"What does it matter? Your muscles won't ache because you don't have any." Mum had told me she no longer felt pain. Or the cold, and she didn't sleep either, which she found both a blessing and a curse. "If it helps, you can pretend to lie down."

"How?" She tried leaning backwards and fell right through the bed again. I burst out laughing, as much from her indignant look when she righted herself as anything else. "It's not funny."

"Yeah, it is."

"You're the worst spiritual advisor ever."

"That's because I'm not a spiritual advisor. I'm... I'm..." What even was I? "I'm more of a cosmic assassin."

"Who doesn't kill anyone, apparently."

"I killed one person."

"Out of, like, a million."

I was never going to win that argument, so I changed the subject instead. "Look, I've heard that if you kind of imagine yourself in the position you want to be in, your body aligns itself with your mind."

At least, that was what Mum had said. It'd taken her a week to get the hang of it, but after that, she'd been able to do better backflips than me. She said there had to be some advantages to being dead, after all.

Jacinda tried it, her face screwed up in concentration, and managed to float at a passable forty-five-degree angle. "Hey, it works."

She tried again, and her feet ended up in the air. I was still giggling when a nurse walked in. Whoops. And worse, it was Grumpy Glenda on duty tonight. She never smiled, and she was such a fusspot about the rules. If that stick went any further up her ass, the cook could roast her like a pig.

"Time for bed, Iris."

Brilliant. This was gonna be cosy. The only saving grace was that my sleeping pills would knock me right out. I slid under the blankets, propped myself up, and waited for the rattle of the pillbox, the *shoosh* of water as Glenda filled a cup for me to wash the nasties down.

Except she did a quick check of my room and headed for the door.

"Wait! You forgot my sleeping stuff."

She turned back, scowling. "No, I didn't forget. Dr. Hastings made some changes to your medication."

"What? But I *always* have pills."

"You'll have to take it up with him if you have any questions. I'm just a nurse." And her tone said she thought his decision was a foolish one.

"Is he here?"

"Not until tomorrow."

"But—"

"There's nothing I can do tonight. Between you and me, I agree with you. These new people come in and start changing things, and then they realise it's not as straightforward as they thought."

"He's new?"

I hadn't realised he was new to Lakeview as well as being new to me.

"Only been here for a week."

Which meant he definitely couldn't have been the person who snuffed out Jacinda. That was something, at least. One down, eleventy million suspects to go. Hercule Poirot would've been proud of me.

"Can't I just—"

"Go to sleep, Iris."

Click. Nurse Glenda turned out the light, leaving me wide awake with an inexperienced ghost and a bed that wasn't big enough for the two of us. Fuck my damn life.

CHAPTER 7 - IRIS

"WHY DID YOU stop my sleeping pills?"

Dr. Hastings faced me across the table, hands folded in front of him. Where were his tick boxes? Dr. Tillis always had tick boxes, and he also never ticked those damn boxes more than once a week. So far, I'd had three sessions with Dr. Newbie, and the experience left me drained.

"Because I think you take too much medication, Iris."

"Then cut something else. I like the sleeping pills."

And I also liked sleep. Last night, Jacinda had spent half the night babbling away, and I didn't care two hoots that she'd managed to float cross-legged, or that she couldn't stand Nurse Glenda, and I definitely didn't want to hear her thoughts on the second coming at three o'clock in the morning. Eventually, I'd resorted to stuffing toilet paper in my ears, and then Jacinda had accused me of being rude again.

"I'd rather address the root of the problem than mask it with drugs. Why do you have trouble sleeping?"

"I just do, okay?"

"The nurse said she heard you talking in the early hours. Can you tell me more about that?"

Glenda snitched on me? Why was she even around at that time? In that case, I'd have to agree with

Jacinda's assessment. Nurse Glenda wasn't very nice. "I was counting sheep."

"Out loud?"

"It helps. I used to watch TV when I couldn't sleep, but they took that away."

"Your file says—"

"I know, I know, it says I broke it. But it was an accident. I was trying to catch a spider, and it ran behind the TV, and then the TV fell off the shelf." It was a big spider too. An eight-legged bloody freak, and Lakeview was full of them. "They should have screwed the TV down. For safety."

"Yes, they probably should have."

"So can I have my sleeping pills back?"

"Not right now. Today, we're going to run through a breathing exercise to help you fall asleep."

"A breathing exercise?" No, that wasn't gonna be much help, not unless it stopped Jacinda from breathing, and she wasn't really breathing anyway since she was dead. "Why are you doing this to me?"

"Doing what?"

"Pretending to care. Don't you have other patients to see?"

"At the moment, I don't have a full caseload. Which means I'm able to spend some extra time working with you."

Oh, brilliant. *Come back, Dr. Tillis, all is forgiven.*

"And what if the breathing thing doesn't work? Then can I have the pills?"

"We'll see."

We'll see? No, that just wasn't good enough. "But I'm crazy. Everyone says so." Even if, ironically, I felt less fuzzy that day than I had in years. "I need pharmaceutical help, not some psycho-mumbo-jumbo."

Because honestly, the only thing worse than spending the rest of my life at Lakeview stoned out of my mind was being stuck there with a clear head. Being able to focus and think and reflect on my poor choices was a horrible, horrible prospect.

"How long have you been taking your current medication? Do you remember?"

"No, I don't remember anything. My brain's fried. Fried like an egg." I threw in a giggle for effect. When all else failed, act loopy-lou. For a brief moment, I envied Jacinda. Not because she was dead, but because there was no way Dr. Hastings would ever have cut *her* meds. "Did I mention I talk to the Antichrist? That's who I was chatting with last night. Not sheep. Baaaaaaaa." Was that cuckoo enough for him? I began singing. "Baa baa black sheep, have you any wool? Yes sir, yes sir, three bags full..."

I risked a glance at him. Was he buying it? Dammit, I couldn't take another night of Jacinda's nonsense. I *needed* those sleeping tablets or I really would go insane.

CHAPTER 8 - MARCUS

FOR A MOMENT, I was inclined to agree with Iris because she sure was acting crazy. But then she glanced up at me from under her thick eyelashes, and just for a second, I saw something different. Those eyes weren't vacant or glittery or confused like I'd seen in so many other patients. No, they were calculating.

So far that Sunday, I'd spoken with two other patients. The first had been happy at the prospect of joining a craft workshop, and with the second, I'd had a constructive discussion about linking thoughts and behaviours. I wanted to start a group therapy session, which was an idea I'd need to discuss with Doug Calvert. Beyond my interview, I'd had little interaction with him, and I hadn't got a read on the guy yet. His management style seemed rather hands-off, and I wasn't yet sure whether that was a good thing or a bad thing. At Deane Valley, I'd had weekly meetings with my supervisor whether I wanted them or not, although his support had come to an abrupt end when I split up with Laurel.

Since Laurel's father was the chief executive at Deane Valley, the fact that I got shafted shouldn't have come as a surprise, but losing the career I'd worked for over a decade to build still hurt. They didn't have to fire me—I'd have left anyway. But I guess vindictiveness ran in the family.

All of which left me sitting opposite Iris, trying to work out if she genuinely had a mental illness I could try to treat or whether she was faking the severity of her problems for an as-yet-unknown reason. Although I'd only recently qualified as a psychiatrist, I'd seen hundreds of patients under supervision while I trained, as well as working through my formal studies. But somehow, I still felt underprepared.

Should I put her back on the sleeping pills? I didn't want to cause her distress, but I also wanted to get to the bottom of whatever was preventing her from sleeping. Long-term use of the pills came with its own risks, and a check of her notes revealed she'd been taking them for far longer than the twenty-eight-day maximum recommended by the manufacturer.

"Iris, you've been taking a high dose of zolpidem for over a year now. Do you recall why you were prescribed the pills?"

"Because I kept walking around my room at night. And I'll start doing that again, I swear."

"You're also taking lorazepam and haloperidol." Which could have a dangerous effect on the heart. Plus I'd noted injections of zuclopenthixol acetate, a fast-acting antipsychotic used to treat acute schizophrenia. It knocked patients out in minutes, but what I didn't see in Dr. Tillis's notes were any accompanying details of the symptoms that had led to its prescription. Which led me to believe that perhaps there weren't any. "I'm going to wean you off the haloperidol."

"Is that what I take in the mornings?"

And there we were—back to lucid.

"Yes."

A shrug.

"Does that bother you?"

"A bit."

"But not as much as the sleeping pills."

"If you won't let me have two each night, can't I at least have one?"

"How about we try with the breathing exercises for a week or two first?"

Iris folded her arms. Stared right at me. "They won't help."

"How do you know until you've tried them?"

"I just do. Can't you speak to Dr. Tillis? He never had a problem giving me pills."

"I'm your doctor now, Iris."

"Please?"

This time she spoke quietly, pleading. She'd gone from brash and argumentative to defeated, and in that moment, I was all too aware of who held the power in the room. And I felt guilty as hell for making her suffer, even though my job was to do what was best for the service user when they weren't in the best position to make that judgement for themselves.

But dammit, I still wanted to understand Iris.

"Why do you want the sleeping pills so much? Do you get nightmares?"

"Yes." She sounded sulky, and she was also lying.

"The truth, Iris."

"If I tell you, can I have pills?"

"That's not how this works, Iris. I can't bargain with you for drugs. But if I fully understand the problem, I'm in a better position to make appropriate decisions for your care."

"I hate this place. I hate you."

That stung more than it should.

"My goal is the same as yours—to help you to get well enough to be released."

"I'll never be released."

"That isn't necessarily true."

"Yes, it is. Director Calvert told me."

"I'm sure he didn't—"

"He did! Right after I bit Terrence's ear, he sat in the same chair you're sitting in now and said, 'Iris, after that stunt, you're never getting out of here.' And then they started giving me that stuff in needles again."

Could Doug Calvert really have said that? Logic said it couldn't be true—speaking to a service user in that manner would violate more rules than I could count—but Iris was strangely convincing.

"Why did you bite Terrence?"

Another shrug. "Because he tried to rape me."

Few things in my professional career had left me speechless, but her words, coupled with the offhand delivery, hit me like a punch to the gut.

"What?" I managed to utter before I quite got my thoughts under control.

"You said you wanted the truth. Can't you handle it?"

If there'd been an allegation of that kind, there would have been an investigation. Paperwork. Notes on Iris's file. The staff handbook detailed a specific grievance procedure to be followed. But there was nothing, and I'd heard Terrence was still employed at Lakeview, although he was on sick leave. Rumour said he'd got one of those "no win, no fee" solicitors involved.

"That's a serious accusation, Iris. Why didn't you

report this at the time?"

She just looked at me, head tilted to one side. Her expression said, *Seriously?*

"*Did* you report it?"

"To Director Calvert."

Shit. What was I meant to do? I could hardly go steaming into my new boss's office and ask him if he'd ignored a rape allegation. But at the same time, I couldn't simply ignore what Iris was telling me. Was it too late to quit medicine altogether? A career as a cab driver had never looked so appealing—no awkward conversations, no moral quandaries, and when you dropped your last passenger off, you were done for the day.

"What did he say?"

"Apart from informing me I'd be here for the rest of my life? He told me off for trying to ruin Terrence's good name."

I was still on probation at Lakeview. If I rocked the boat, they could let me go quietly with no comebacks. Deane Valley had a whistle-blower hotline for issues like this, but not Lakeview. As a private facility, it didn't need to. Less than a week into the job, and I faced the most difficult dilemma of my adult life. If I lost this salary, I'd lose my house and any prospect of getting custody of my daughter. With no references from Deane Valley or here, the chances of me finding another position in the near future were slim.

"You're not going to do anything, are you?" she said. "I can see it in your face. You don't want to make waves."

"I need to look into the procedures here."

"You're scared you'll get fired, and you'd rather save

your own skin."

Was I that transparent? And more to the point, was I that transparent to Iris? Her file said she had limited social skills and struggled to interpret body language. That wasn't what I was seeing here.

"I'm saying I need to tread carefully. Can you tell me exactly what happened?"

She glanced at the mirrored window, and I shook my head. Nobody was there. Apart from the first few sessions when I was still finding my feet, I'd been told observation was by request only. Lakeview didn't have spare staff to go around.

Iris closed her eyes and leaned back in her chair. "It was late. Terrence did the final evening check, and I thought he'd gone downstairs, but then he came back."

"Was that usual?"

She shook her head. "Once they're gone, they're gone until the next morning."

"He just walked in?"

"Yes. I pretended to be asleep, and normally I would've been comatose, but when Terrence gave me my meds earlier, he got distracted by something in the hallway and I managed to spit one of my sleeping pills into my hand. So I was half-awake." Her voice dropped, and a tear rolled down her cheek. "And I knew what was going to happen because it'd happened before. I'm sure it did. When I woke up, I hurt...you know...*there*, and I remembered him leaning over me in the dark. His weight, pressing me down."

Son of a bitch. I pulled a handkerchief out of my pocket and passed it to Iris. She wiped her eyes before continuing.

"That night, he came across the room really quietly.

Didn't say a word. And I heard..." Her voice hitched. "I heard him fiddling with his belt. Then he pulled the blankets off me and lifted my nightgown up." Fear morphed into anger. "He came prepared. That fucker came prepared with a condom."

I'd counselled assault survivors in the past, but never before when they'd been assaulted in a supposedly safe environment. I clenched my hands under the table to control my own anger. Anger at Terrence. Anger at Lakeview's management. Anger at the situation. Because either Iris was worthy of an Oscar or she was telling the truth.

But one thing didn't quite add up, at least. If Iris had been so clever about spitting out a sleeping pill the night she bit Terrence, why was she so desperate to take them now? Were the nightmares bad enough that she'd risk another attack to avoid them?

"Is that why you can't sleep? Because you're remembering?"

She cast her eyes down at the table. "Yes."

I took a deep breath. Bargaining with service users was a dangerous game, and one I didn't want to start, but I needed to do something for Iris. "One sleeping pill each night. The dose you were on before was too high. Can you cope with that?"

That earned me a small smile, the first genuine one I'd seen from her. "Yes."

"I'll speak to the nursing team."

***

Traffic was murder on my way home. Roadworks ahead, according to the signs. At least I'd arranged for

Vijay to come and give Teddy an extra walk.

Before I left, I'd spoken to the nurse manager and adjusted Iris's medication—again—and also explained that we'd uncovered some historic trauma during our last session, so she'd need to be attended by only female nurses until we worked through it. If Terrence returned to Lakeview, I didn't want him anywhere near her until I got to the bottom of this mess, and the thought of another George watching her in the shower didn't sit well either. That wouldn't be a problem, I'd been assured, so at least I'd managed to help Iris in a small way today.

Tomorrow, I'd speak to Doug Calvert. I didn't have a choice, not after what Iris had told me. Why hadn't he acted at the time? Was there more to the situation than I knew? As I crawled along behind a Honda, I decided to take the softly-softly approach. Rather than accuse him of brushing the problem under the carpet, I'd go in with an open mind and ask for his side of the story. Perhaps there truly had been a misunderstanding somewhere along the line?

I was nearly home when my phone rang, unusual in itself because few people called me nowadays, not since Laurel had turned our mutual friends against me.

"Vijay? Is everything okay with Teddy?"

"She... She..." He paused, gasping for breath. "She was in the park!"

"Who?" Even as I voiced the question, I knew there was only one answer. "Laurel?"

"I let Teddy off the lead to do his business, and she lured him with those bacon treats he likes. She laid a trail all the way to her car."

My heart seized. I loved that damn dog, and if

Laurel had got her claws into him, I'd face the mother of all battles to get him back.

"Did she take him?"

"I caught him right before he got into the back seat, and she started screaming at me. Man, she's crazy!"

I let out the breath I hadn't realised I'd been holding. At times, Laurel made Iris look positively balanced. "Tell me something I don't know. Are you at home now?"

"No, I ran, like, a mile. I'm by the pub, and I'm going in for a drink."

"You know what? I think I'll join you."

CHAPTER 9 - IRIS

"WHY WOULDN'T YOU speak to me last night?" Jacinda asked.

"Because you're really annoying, and I was asleep."

"There's no need to be insulting."

"There is when you won't be quiet."

"But I'm bored, and I've got nobody else to talk to. Why don't you have a TV?"

I didn't bother to answer, just grabbed my things and got ready to go to the shower. The nurse would be along soon. I'd heard people on the first floor had showers in their cells, but since I'd been banished to one of the crappier rooms upstairs, all I had was a tiny sink and a toilet in a glorified cupboard. There was no escape from Jacinda because the door didn't even close properly.

"Dammit, shit."

I cursed when I bashed my elbow off the wall as I got dressed in my regulation tracksuit. No drawstrings, no buttons we could swallow, no zippers. Everything was elasticated, and my shoes fastened with velcro. Last year, after they changed my medication, I'd started to put on weight, so I'd come up with an exercise routine I did every afternoon now, in between my morning meds wearing off and the afternoon fix. Jumping jacks, squats, lunges, crunches, jogging on the spot. I saw the nurses sniggering when they looked in and found me standing on my head, but I was beyond caring anymore. I'd do whatever kept me sane.

Today, I had Nurse Sandra escorting me to the shower room. Sandra didn't give a shit about her job, which was nice because it meant she spent most of the time looking at her phone instead of bugging me to hurry up. Sometimes, she just locked the door and went off to get a cup of coffee and a donut. Never offered me one, mind you. This morning, I could hear the *beep, beep, boop* of whatever game she was playing while she sat on the bench outside. Taxpayers' money hard at work.

I turned the water as hot as I could stand and let it cascade over my shoulders. Without George "helping," the shower was my favourite place, even more so now that I had a new roommate. I never thought I'd say it, but I missed being on my own. At least I had my sleeping pills back, even if I did feel kind of guilty for telling Dr. Hastings a little white lie yesterday. Most of the story was true—Terrence *had* attacked me—but better to pretend I had nightmares about a would-be rapist than explain details of the dead girl who wouldn't shut up.

Would Dr. Hastings truly speak to Director Calvert? I had my doubts, but at least he hadn't written my story off as lies like every other person at Lakeview. Maybe having a new doctor wouldn't be the disaster I feared? My head didn't feel as cotton-woolly this morning, and he'd kept his word about the sleeping pills. Could I blame him for keeping his head down in a new job? Not really. I'd probably do the same in his position.

"Iris, you've been in there for half an hour," Nurse

Sandra called. "You'll be late for your session with Dr. Hastings."

Should I thank him for the pills? That would be polite, wouldn't it? Weird. I hadn't considered being polite in years. What was wrong with me?

***

"How are you feeling today, Iris?"

"Do you ever start with anything else?"

His lips twitched into a half-smile. "Standard opening, I'm afraid. Psychology 101."

"I'm... I'm feeling...funny."

"In what way?"

"Like my brain's working again, but I keep shaking." I held out a hand to show him the tremble I'd noticed as I towelled myself dry. "What's wrong with me?"

"It's most likely withdrawal symptoms from the haloperidol. We'll monitor it, but it should pass."

"It's normal?"

"Entirely normal."

"Hmm."

"What's hmm?"

"I'm so used to being not normal, I just assumed I was having a breakdown or something."

This time, I got a proper smile, and I wasn't prepared for my heart to skip the way it did. Stupid withdrawals.

"You're not that special, Iris."

Ooh, ouch. If only he knew. But shh... I couldn't tell him. "Thank you for the sleeping pills."

"It's the best thing for you at this time. I should also

mention that I tried to speak to Mr. Calvert, but he's gone on holiday. I've made an appointment to see him on the second of September."

Really? Dr. Hastings *had* done something? "What's today?"

"The nineteenth of August."

"What day?" I was pretty sure it was Thursday or Friday, but every day was the same at Lakeview.

"Monday."

"Oh." So yesterday had been Sunday. "You work at weekends?" That sounded kinda sucky.

"Saturday through Wednesday, which means we have sessions scheduled for the next two days as well. Is there anything you want to talk about? I realise yesterday must have been difficult for you."

The last thing I wanted to do was relive the past. That had been the one advantage of being tanked up on drugs all the time—I'd had no trouble blocking out the parts I didn't want to remember.

"Can we talk about the world?"

"The world?"

"What's going on out there? I have no idea what's happening beyond these walls."

He grimaced. "You probably don't want to."

"Why?"

He paused, as if he was undergoing an internal struggle over how much to tell me.

"Come on, I'm not some delicate flower."

"But you are." His words were sweet, but his shocked expression said he regretted saying them the instant they left his mouth. "Sorry, inappropriate. I just meant your name... Iris... It's a flower."

It was funny when he got flustered, as if he were

twelve rather than, what? Thirty?

"I know. Irises were my mum's favourite." This time, it was my turn to shut up in a hurry because I didn't talk about my mother. "Never mind."

"Tell me about—"

"No. Don't go getting all psycho on me again."

"Isn't that my line?" He smacked his forehead. "Dammit. I apologise. Profusely. You make me lose my mind."

So he did have a sense of humour lurking. "Now you're stealing *my* lines. But don't worry; I won't tell if you don't."

He sat up straighter and rearranged his stuff. Pen, pad, coffee cup. As he tugged his cuffs down, I caught a glimpse of ink again, and this time, I resisted the urge to reach out. He hadn't liked that the last time I tried it.

"Can we start this conversation again?" he asked.

"Sure. So, Dr. Hastings, tell me what's going on in the world?"

"I'm guessing you don't want to hear about football?"

"Please, spare me."

"I'm afraid I don't keep up with gymnastics."

"But you'd look so good in a leotard." I mimed shock, hands on my cheeks. "I'm so sorry. Inappropriate."

"Iris..."

"Okay, okay, I'll behave. Brownies' honour."

"Were you ever in the Brownies?"

"For two weeks, then I got asked to leave. I swear the fire was an accident."

"Dare I ask?"

"It was a cookery lesson. I mistakenly turned on the

wrong gas ring, and there was some kitchen roll hanging over the edge, and then the village hall caught on fire. But I put it out really fast. Mum taught me how to use a fire extinguisher when I was seven."

"Because you were always a terrible cook?"

"No, because she was. I got used to scraping the burnt bits off." *Shut up, Iris.* "Uh, can we go back to you talking?"

I couldn't help smiling when he laughed. It made him seem like a friend rather than a doctor, which was stupid because he was one of *them*. I wasn't meant to *like* him.

"The world? Where do I start?"

"Is Viner still prime minister?"

"No, he got voted out, but the new guy's worse. He came in with a screed of promises—an overhaul of the education system, improvements to healthcare, a crackdown on crime—but he hasn't delivered."

Because he *couldn't* deliver, not with so much negative energy from the spirits permeating the atmosphere. Things would only continue to get worse. It was why Mum had thrown our TV out when I was twelve. She'd hated watching all the destruction. But me? I said better the devil you know.

"No surprises there. What about movies? How many Mission: Impossible films are we up to now?"

"I have no idea."

"You don't go to the cinema?"

"The last film I watched there was something Disney. There were dancing ponies and rainbows. That's all I remember."

"Disney? Why did you—" Oh. Right. Duh, of course. "You have kids?"

"A daughter."

A daughter. Which meant he had a wife or a girlfriend. I glanced at his left hand. No ring. A girlfriend, then. Why did that make me feel so stupidly disappointed? Dr. Hastings was my *psychiatrist*. Just a man doing his job.

A job that none of his predecessors had been particularly successful at. Perhaps my future therapy sessions wouldn't be so bad after all?

***

By the weekend, I had a TV, and on Saturday, after I confessed the details of my exercise routine to Dr. Hastings, a gym mat appeared. Nurse Glenda cursed under her breath as she dragged it into my cell.

"Dunno what you've done to get this," she grumbled. "I heard it was a special order."

Really?

"It's probably because I'm not allowed outside."

"And whose fault is that?"

I thought nursing was meant to be a caring profession? When nine-year-old me spent a week in the hospital getting my arm pinned—the cat I tripped over just came out of nowhere, okay?—the doctors and nurses had all been lovely, some of the kindest people I'd ever met. It seemed as though Lakeview hoovered up the worst of the profession and set them to work making our lives miserable. Which begged the question, how did Dr. Hastings end up working there? From what I'd seen so far, he certainly wasn't a typical recruit.

And I'd begun to enjoy my psych sessions,

something I never thought would happen. The channels on my TV were restricted, and I wasn't allowed to watch the news, so each day, he'd start with an update on current events. The world really was going to hell in a handbasket, as my mum would have said.

Every so often, he tried to ask about my past, but I'd gotten good at changing the subject, the same way he did when I mentioned his life outside of Lakeview. I got the impression it wasn't all that rosy, though. On a couple of days, he looked kind of rumpled, as if he hadn't slept much the night before. And he was developing frown lines. Hadn't he heard of moisturiser?

"Did you watch *Survival Island* last night?" I asked.

He raised one eyebrow. "*Survival Island*? I'm not sure I want to know."

I told him anyway. "It's a show where they put a bunch of—well, they call them celebrities, but they're not really—onto an island with a survival manual, and they have to solve a bunch of clues to escape. Last night, they tried to make soup and set fire to their shelter."

The shelter they'd spent the whole day building. Jacinda thought it was hilarious.

"That sounds like something you would do," Dr. Hastings said. "Based on past form."

"Nah, I'd sleep in a cave and live on salad."

"Hmm. So you're enjoying the show? I'd never pictured you as a reality TV fan."

I wasn't. *Survival Island* was Jacinda's choice, not mine, but if it kept her from talking, I'd put up with it.

I shrugged. "It's okay. There are a thousand other

things I'd rather do, but it's not as if I can go out for a walk or potter around in the garden, is it?"

"I never saw you as a gardener either."

"Yeah, well, I used to work in a garden centre."

Before Mum died, I'd planned to go to university and study criminology since I figured it might come in handy at some point, what with my destiny and all that, but when I turned eighteen and the state washed its hands of me, I hadn't been able to afford it.

And I'd always had green fingers, accidents with weedkiller notwithstanding. In London, I'd started out by sowing mustard and cress seeds on sheets of damp kitchen roll and graduated to a full-on herb garden that took up every windowsill. When we first moved to our cottage in the country, the garden had been a wilderness of stinging nettles and brambles, but over the five years we lived in Highcross, we transformed it into a lush paradise that won first prize in the Best Kept Garden competition. Even in winter, we liked to sit out there in the evenings, bundled up in coats and scarves, our hands wrapped around mugs of hot chocolate to keep warm.

I tried not to think of my old home too much because it hurt. The new owners had probably filled in the pond and paved over my vegetable patch.

"A garden centre. Hmm."

Another hmm. "Do you have a garden?"

"Yes."

"What do you have in it?"

"Grass. Plus a sandpit and a swing."

"Grass? That's it?"

"I haven't done much with it."

"You should make the effort. It might help you relax

more."

"I'm not sure growing a few flowers would help."

"Want to talk about it?"

"We're here to talk about you, not me."

"You're right." My lips twitched as I fought a smile. "Have you considered seeing a psychiatrist?"

"Iris..."

"I meant do you want to talk about your garden, okay? It's what I used to do—advise people on layouts and plants and stuff. Water features, if you fancy being one of those posh wankers off the telly."

I might have watched the occasional episode of *Garden Force* on iPlayer after Mum declared us a television-free household.

Now Dr. Hastings was fighting a smile too. "I'm not sure I'm a water feature sort of guy."

"If you give me a pen and paper, I can draw you some ideas. Please? I'm so bored. I promise I won't stab anyone in the eye with the pen."

Dr. Tillis wouldn't even let me have crayons after I accidentally left one on the floor and a nurse skidded over on it.

Dr. Hastings rested his chin on his intertwined fingers, elbows propped up on the table as he regarded me. I crossed my fingers in my lap because I *really* wanted a pen, dammit. Finally, he tore off the used pages of his notepad, then slid the remainder in my direction along with his fancy silver ballpoint.

"Don't make me regret this, Iris."

"You won't, I promise. How big is your garden?"

***

Another week passed. I'd begun keeping track of the days now so I knew when Dr. Hastings would be in. Sometimes, we only talked for twenty minutes, and I wondered how many other patients he had to fit in. Did he see all of them so often? He'd started looking at his watch more.

Mostly, we discussed easy stuff—current affairs, TV, that old British favourite the weather. It was meant to warm up next week. Both of us remained cagey about our personal lives, such that they were, but after I'd presented Dr. Hastings with my first garden design, set around a sunken seated area, he told me his house was rented so he couldn't do much to the topography. And after my second—admittedly high-maintenance—suggestion, he'd confessed that after five days a week at Lakeview and Friday afternoons spent with his daughter, he didn't have much spare time for plants.

Only Fridays with his daughter? Did that mean he didn't live with her mother? That... That made me happier than it should have.

I liked him. There, I said it. Happy now? It was stupid and pointless and possibly even Helsinki syndrome or whatever it was called. Something Scandinavian, anyway. You know, that thing where you get brainwashed by your kidnappers? But the only high point in my time at Lakeview was those hours spent with him.

Which meant I had something important to ask Dr. Hastings on that Sunday.

"Pots," he said as he studied my latest idea. "That's a lot of pots."

Yup. Big pots, little pots, shallow pots, deep pots. "If you move house, you can take everything with you."

"What about watering?"

"You can automate it with a simple irrigation system. Just turn the tap on, and it's done. You could even use a timer. Plus there's less weeding with pots, and if something dies, it's easy to swap it out for a new plant. And the pots are a feature in themselves."

"Won't that get expensive if I have to buy pots as well?"

"It depends on which pots you use. The pretty ones are pricey, but if you wanted to use plastic, I could tweak the design to hide any ugly bits. Plastic retains water better, so it does have advantages."

He gave me a tight smile. "Let's assume I'll go with plastic."

Because he couldn't afford terracotta? But I thought doctors made good money? And he didn't have a massive garden, which made it unlikely he was renting a palace. How much did children cost? I had no idea, and since I was stuck at Lakeview, it wasn't as if I'd ever need to find out.

I had a million questions, but I smiled back and nodded. "Okay, plastic. I'll do another design with plastic. Uh, can I talk to you about something?"

The warmth came back into his voice. "Of course. That's what I'm here for."

"Tomorrow's Monday."

"Yes, it is."

"You said you were going to speak to Director Calvert on Monday."

"I have an appointment to see him at nine."

"Could you not?"

"Not what?"

I took a deep breath. "I don't want you to talk to

him about Terrence."

"Why not, Iris? The allegations you made deserve to be taken seriously."

His unspoken words? *If they're true.*

The doubt hurt, but with Jacinda occupied by the contestants on *Survival Island*, I'd thought long and hard about the situation. I knew my reputation at Lakeview, and I also knew Director Calvert would do everything he could to bury the story. He'd already ignored me once. If Dr. Hastings rocked the boat, he'd be reassigned or maybe even pushed out for good.

And I needed him.

I just didn't want to admit that.

"I lied," I whispered.

"You lied? About Terrence?"

"Yes."

"Why did you lie, Iris?"

Now I heard the disappointment in his voice, but it was better than not hearing his voice at all.

"Because I wanted attention."

"You realise you could have ruined a man's career over this?"

"I'm sorry." I couldn't look at him. "Can I go back to my room now?"

The screech of his chair legs on the tile tore right through me.

"I'll call an orderly."

CHAPTER 10 - MARCUS

ON MONDAY MORNING, I sat on a hard plastic chair outside Doug Calvert's office, waiting for him to finish his phone call. It was a quarter past nine already, but his time was clearly more valuable than mine.

As I waited, I mulled over the woman who'd taken up far too much of my headspace over the past fortnight. Iris McGivern.

Why had she lied to me? And I didn't mean about the night Terrence attacked her, I meant yesterday when she told me she'd invented the story.

It wasn't her first lie, either. She told me she'd moved her bed because the sun was getting in her eyes, and yet her room faced west. The sun wouldn't have been visible through her window in the mornings. But that had been at the beginning, and I thought we'd made progress the way she'd been opening up and talking more, but now it seemed that she still didn't trust me with her problems. Was she scared of facing Terrence? Or of the manner in which Doug Calvert might choose to handle the situation?

Either way, I couldn't take it further without her say-so.

"Mr. Calvert will see you now," his PA told me, smiling as she motioned me towards his door. "Can I bring you a drink?"

"Coffee, please. White, no sugar."

Calvert rose to greet me as I walked into his office, and he'd been somewhere sunny judging by his tan. A golf course? Displayed on the wall behind him was a trio of golf pictures, one of him taking a swing, another of him holding up a trophy, and the third with a group of friends, all holding clubs.

"Good holiday?" I asked.

"Not bad, not bad. Take a seat, won't you? The Algarve's always nice at this time of year."

Apart from the fact that Laurel's parents owned a villa in Vale do Lobo and I'd therefore vowed to avoid the whole of Portugal, it was lovely, yes.

"A golfing trip?"

"Yes, do you play?"

Not since I'd stopped trying to impress my father-in-law several years ago. I'd gotten down to a reasonable handicap, but sitting around in the clubhouse for hours afterwards while a bunch of buffoons compared the size of their stock portfolios quickly wore thin.

"No, never have."

"You should give it a go. A group of us play every Saturday afternoon."

"I work here on Saturdays."

"Right, you do. So, what was it you wanted to talk to me about? You're settling in okay?"

"Everyone's made me feel at home." Put it this way, nothing could be as bad as the last year I'd spent living with Laurel. "Now that I've had a chance to meet my first patients, I was hoping you'd be amenable to me setting up some group therapy sessions."

"Instead of the individual sessions?"

"No, in addition."

"How many sessions are we talking?"

"Let's say one a day?"

"Once the new wing's full, you won't have the time. That's five less individual sessions you'd be able to run each week."

"But with more intensive treatment, service users could potentially be released faster."

"Dr. Hastings, you worked in the public sector before you came here, didn't you?"

"I had a mix of NHS and private patients." As he'd know if he'd bothered to read my CV.

"And your private patients were billed by the hour?"

"That was standard."

"Here at Lakeview, we have to be mindful of our bottom line. We receive a set amount for each day a service user stays with us, and in order to keep our margins up, we can't afford to provide them with extra services when we're running at capacity."

"But isn't our goal to rehabilitate these people?"

"Well, yes, but this is a business, Marcus. We also need to provide value to our shareholders. How about this—while you've got some unallocated time, you can run these extra sessions, but you'll need to cut back when we get more guests."

"You can't start treatment and then just stop it."

"I guess you could use your lunch breaks if you feel continuing is important. As long as you're up to date with your paperwork, of course."

Inside, my blood heated. Calvert saw our service users as a commodity. Interchangeable units. The principled part of me wanted to quit on the spot, but my bank account reminded me not to be too hasty. And then there were the people I was there to treat. If I didn't act in their best interests, who would?

Calvert's attitude explained a lot about what I'd seen at Lakeview over the last three weeks. The staff weren't expected to care, and the few that *did* care couldn't afford to make waves because we were a commodity too. Easily replaced.

I gritted my teeth. "Understood."

I'd wanted to speak to him about running additional workshops too, but I realised that was pointless. Extra workshops would cost in terms of staff and materials, and his precious bottom line would suffer. Calvert would rather the service users suffered.

"Are we done here?" he asked.

"Actually, I do have one more thing. Iris McGivern —I've been working with her for the past fortnight, and I believe she'd benefit from time spent outside. I see the note on her file—"

"Ah, young Iris. She's a troublemaker. Caused us no end of legal problems with her recent antics. No, I'm afraid letting her outside is out of the question. You know she tried to escape?"

"Having spoken to her, I believe there may have been some misunderstandings."

"She's brainwashed you too? She did the same to Greg Tillis when he first arrived. He insisted she be allowed to join a cookery class, but he soon realised the error of his ways when she threw food all over the kitchen."

"*Threw* the food?"

"Oh, she claimed she dropped it, but she rarely tells the truth. The girl's disruptive and she's dangerous."

"What if—"

"Marcus, don't worry. Iris doesn't have any family, so nobody's going to complain if she doesn't get to join our activity program."

"I'm more concerned about her well-being."

"You just haven't seen her bad side yet. Trust me on this one—she's better off out of everyone's way, including yours. Now, if you'll excuse me, I have a conference call to join."

That was it: dismissed.

Calvert's PA gave me a wan smile as I stepped outside his office.

"Did it go well?" she asked.

"Does he ever listen to anyone but himself?"

The man was an administrator, for crying out loud, not a medical professional. Who was he to judge what was best for the service users?

"No, not really. Welcome to Lakeview."

***

"I thought you might like this."

I slid the plant across the table towards Iris, and she rewarded me with a wide smile. That alone made the detour on my way to work this morning worth it.

"An orchid?"

"The lady at the garden centre assured me it would do well on a west-facing windowsill."

I'd hoped to have better news for Iris—the promise of time outside—but my conversation with Calvert yesterday had scuppered that idea. The more I thought about it, the more annoyed I got. It was me who'd had to resort to breathing exercises to get to sleep last night.

"It definitely will. I love it." A hesitation. "Thank you."

She wasn't accustomed to thanking people, was she? "Perhaps I should get one of those for my garden?"

"A phalaenopsis? No, it won't do well outside, not in winter. The cold'll kill it. There are some smaller orchid varieties you could get, but they're not as flashy. A pleione, perhaps, or a cypripedium. They call those slipper orchids because their flowers look like... Well, it's pretty clear, isn't it?"

"Did you used to grow orchids?"

"A few, but I couldn't afford the fancy ones. When Mum was alive, the garden was full of fruit and veggies, and when I was in foster care, it wasn't easy to cart plants around between each home."

"How long were you in foster care?"

"Long enough. Could you get food for the orchid? It'll be okay without for a few weeks, but after that..."

And there it was again—the not-so-subtle change of subject Iris had become so proficient at. She hated to discuss her past, even the more mundane aspects. And as for the ghost thing that had led her to Lakeview in the first place... I'd read through the entire court transcript twice. What had planted the seed for a delusion like that? She'd stuck to the story for the whole trial and been convincing enough for the judge to send her to a secure hospital instead of a regular prison. A carefully planned but poorly executed revenge killing dressed up as a need to free her dead mother's trapped soul from earth. Fascinating.

Yet apart from her snarky comments on the first

day we met, Iris hadn't mentioned ghosts once, and I didn't want to risk her shutting down by broaching the subject myself. Being honest, she was easier to deal with than any of my other patients, no matter what Calvert said about her.

Days like today, she seemed as rational as you or me.

"I'll get the plant food. Just tell me what you need."

***

"How are you feeling, Iris?"

She mirrored me, chin resting on her hands. "Shouldn't that be my line today? You look like shit."

Unfortunately, she was right. Yesterday, Cassie had been quiet all evening, and when I'd pressed her to tell me what was wrong, she'd mumbled that Laurel had a new boyfriend and he'd told her off for making too much noise. There'd been the quivering bottom lip. A plea not to make her go back home. Tears when Laurel's mother arrived to pick her up. And the worst part? I couldn't do a damn thing about it. Jacqueline informed me that Rupert Horton was a fine man, a stockbroker in the City, and far better for her daughter than I'd ever been.

"Cassie doesn't like him," I told her.

"So? Cassidy doesn't like avocados either, but that doesn't mean they're bad."

I begged to differ. Avocados were evil little suckers. "She's perceptive."

"She's a child. And Laurel's relationship is none of your business. You lost the right to have any say in her life when you cheated on her."

"I didn't—"

"Be quiet. I don't want to hear any more of your lies. Come on, Cassidy, it's time to leave."

The look my little girl had given me through the car window as Jacqueline drove off... It felt as though I'd been stabbed through the heart. And then this morning, one of my patients had decided he didn't want to go back to his room and lashed out. It was always a risk, but the episode still left me more shaken than I cared to admit. Statistically speaking, mental illness was rarely associated with violence, and sufferers were more likely to harm themselves than others. But in every sample, there were anomalies, and a number of those anomalies had ended up at Lakeview.

"It's not been a great twenty-four hours." I moved my hands to the table and resisted the urge to fidget with my pen. Truth be told, I wanted to go home and pour myself a stiff whisky, and I hadn't touched alcohol since the night I left Laurel.

"Want to talk about it?"

"Which one of us is the psychiatrist?"

"You got hurt?" She spotted the stains on my shirt and pushed the cuff back to reveal a row of scratches. I'd tried to scrub the blood off the fabric, but I clearly hadn't done a good job. Tomorrow, I'd bring a spare shirt to keep in my locker. "What happened?"

"Another service user. It's nothing."

"Looks sore." She pushed my sleeve up further. "You *do* have a tattoo."

"Ten out of ten for observation, Miss McGivern."

"What is it?"

"A sound wave."

"Really?"

"You can play it back with an app."

"And what does it sound like?"

Should I tell her? I was well aware of the need to maintain a professional distance from my patients, but at the same time, I needed to gain Iris's trust. Would she open up if I did? Sometimes, I needed to take a chance. I took my phone out of my pocket.

"Love you, Dada." Cassie's sweet voice filled the soulless room.

"That's your daughter?" Iris asked.

"It is."

"And you love her enough to have her words permanently inked onto your skin."

"I do."

Iris fell silent for a long while, and I waited her out. Finally, she spoke again.

"I wish I had a father who cares as much as you do."

"Do you want to tell me about your father?"

"What father? He was never in the picture. It was always just me and Mum." A tear rolled down her cheek. "I miss her so, so much."

"Do you have any other family? Any friends who come to visit?"

She shook her head, and the tear plopped onto the table, a tiny Rorschach of pain that hit me unexpectedly hard.

"Nobody. The only person who's come to see me since I've been here is the court lady, and she stays for five minutes to fill in her forms then disappears for another three months. Tick. Another name off the list. It's just me, myself, and I."

And now me. Hearing Iris reveal little snippets

from her past was painful, but it was progress.

CHAPTER 11 - IRIS

"WHY CAN'T WE watch *Star Makeover*?" Jacinda whined.

"Because I'm watching the Garden Channel."

"Why? Plants are dumb. It's not as if they can talk."

"You say that like it's a bad thing. Does your overlord approve of you watching celebrity trash?"

She folded her arms. "He hasn't expressed an opinion on that one way or another. You're literally the most boring roommate ever. What are you drawing? Another garden you'll never get to plant?"

"It's for Dr. Hastings. He might plant it."

"Did he say that? Because doctors lie. Like, all the time. Lie, lie, lie, whatever it takes to get you to take your meds and be quiet and do what they say like a good little sheep. Moo."

"Sheep don't moo." Idiot.

Jacinda giggled. "Oh, yeah."

"Look, if you want to do something useful, perhaps you could focus on remembering who killed you rather than constantly moaning."

"I tried. Everything's still fuzzy. I think there was a person sort of leaning over the bed?" She shrugged. "If you won't watch *Star Makeover*, can't we have the news on?"

"We're not allowed the news." Or movies that

weren't PG-rated, or detective shows, or anything remotely dirty. Basically, we got children's cartoons, home improvement programs, reality crap, game shows, and the nature channel. Seeing a gazelle ripped apart by lions was okay, apparently. "And you've put your hand through my leg again. Can you move it, please? You know it makes me uncomfortable."

Not for the first time, I considered trying to flood my new cell to get away from Jacinda, but not only did I lack the appropriate tools, I figured they'd probably sling me into a dungeon if I made another big mess so soon after the first one. Even if the first mess hadn't been my fault.

Keys jangled, the door opened, and I'd never been so happy to see Nurse Hazel in my life.

"One second, I'm just coming."

She laughed as I ran to the washroom to grab my towel and my basket of shower stuff. "Someone's a bit eager today. Got bedbugs?"

"You don't know the half of it. I'm running out of shampoo—can I get some more?"

"I'll see what I can find."

Most of my fellow inmates had an account at the hospital commissary that they used to buy personal items like snacks and toiletries. But I didn't have any friends or relatives to fund an account, and I wasn't deemed responsible enough to hold a hospital job, so I relied on Lakeview to provide me with the basics. If I was lucky, I got the leftovers from other patients who'd been transferred, but more often I got a bottle of shiny pink off-brand soap that I had to use for everything. I really, really missed hair conditioner.

"I'll need toothpaste soon too."

We reached the shower room, and Nurse Hazel looked at her watch. "You've got twenty minutes, and then I need to get the next person."

Twenty minutes of peace was better than nothing. And that's what I usually got—peace—but not today.

You've got to be bloody kidding.

The dead girl turned to look at me the moment I walked through the door, blood dripping down her face from a gash on her forehead. Her mouth formed into an O as she realised who, or rather what, I was.

"Are you...are you...?"

Someone up there had to be playing a joke, surely? My only sanctuary had been invaded. Was this Jacinda's doing? Did she really have a hotline to the big boss?

"A member of the Electi? Yes." I kept my voice down since Nurse Hazel was right outside. She didn't tend to get distracted like Nurse Sandra. Fear pooled in my belly as the true horror of the situation set in. Another girl had been killed at Lakeview? Could it have been an accident? "Who are you?"

"Rylie. Like Kylie, but with an R."

"I'm Iris. What the hell happened?"

"I was just taking a shower, the same as always, then I felt somebody behind me, and before I could turn, I got shoved forward. The last thing I remember is seeing the button coming towards me."

Lakeview didn't trust us to use regular taps in case we forgot to turn them off. Instead, we had push-taps that gave us water for ten seconds at a time, and now that I thought about it, the shape of the knob thingy did match the dent in the girl's forehead. Fuck. The room only locked from the outside, and there wasn't anything in there I could use to block someone from walking in.

"Didn't you hear the door open?"

"Not above the noise of the water."

I pushed the button and stepped back as water splattered on the tiled floor. Yes, that would easily cover up a *click* from the door. The room was small, with just a shower at the far end, a tiny window set high in the wall above it, and a narrow wooden bench by the door to leave our clothes and towel on. I paced it out— four steps from end to end. A person could cross that in a second. The girl's face shimmered through the stream until the water stopped.

"You're sure someone pushed you? They couldn't have tripped and, I don't know, fallen into you by accident?"

"I guess it's possible, but why did somebody come in while I was showering? And why didn't they say anything?"

I saw her point. An accident seemed less likely. Even when George had watched me lathering up, he'd done so through the little window in the door rather than standing inside the room.

"Who brought you to the shower? It must have been them who did it, because how else would someone just walk in here? They'd have to go right past." Unless...

"Sandra. You know, the nurse who never puts her phone down?"

Of course it was Sandra. She wouldn't notice if a herd of elephants thundered down the corridor. Chances were, she'd nipped off to go to the loo or get a cup of tea instead of doing her job anyway.

"Yeah, I know her."

"I must've blacked out for a bit because when I opened my eyes, whoever came in had gone and I was standing in my body. Like in my body. I was lying on the floor and standing up at the same time, and my blood was running down the drain. Then this *thing* arrived..."

"The spirit guide?"

"Yes, her. She said you'd be along at some point to avenge my death, but I didn't think you'd get here so quickly. She said you people were pretty slow."

Gee, thanks. The spirit guides got the easy job. And their patter was hopelessly out of date. Even in the twenty-first century, they still implied we went around killing people. Mum happened across one after a car accident and tried to tell her otherwise, but apparently, the guide just shrugged and said she'd take it into consideration. And they called *us* lazy?

"Well, I'm here. Could you just...I don't know, lean to the side or something? I need to take a shower."

"A shower? Aren't you meant to be helping me?"

"Technically, yes, but I only have twenty minutes in here, so you'll have to talk while I wash. And I can only avenge your death if you tell me who did it. In case you haven't noticed, I'm locked up in here just the same as you were, so I can't exactly run around playing detective."

"But I don't *know* who did it."

"No idea at all?"

"I'm fairly sure it wasn't Bobby. I would've smelled him coming."

That didn't exactly narrow it down much. "Any other clues?"

She shrugged helplessly. "Sorry. When Director

Calvert arrived, he said it must've been an accident. That I'd slipped over and hit my head. But I didn't, I swear."

"I know. You wouldn't be here otherwise."

"Unless you do something, whoever killed me will get away with it."

"Thanks, I had realised." No pressure or anything.

"Or maybe they'll kill you next. Unless you're immortal. Are you immortal?"

"No, I'm not immortal."

"Really?" She reached out to touch me, and her hand went straight through my arm. "Whoa! That's weird."

"Can I take a shower now?" Time was running out, and Nurse Hazel would make me walk back to my room with soap suds in my hair if I wasn't careful. "Do me a favour and warn me if anyone comes in, okay?"

With Rylie acting as lookout, I set about washing my hair as fast as I could. It would've been quicker if my hair weren't so long, but getting a trim in that place took months of begging, and having my own scissors was out of the question.

Over the past few weeks, I'd managed to push the manner of Jacinda's death to the back of my mind. With little chance of solving the mystery, I'd begun to hope an accidental overdose might have been the cause, but now that a second person had been killed... Two months, two bodies, two trapped souls—was it a coincidence, or were the deaths connected?

Jacinda certainly seemed to think so when I mentioned the problem.

"Rylie's dead? As in R-Y-L-I-E?"

"That's her."

"Oh, that's so sad. She was in my pottery class."

"How come you got to do pottery and I didn't?"

"I think my parents paid extra." So there was no hope for me, then. "How are you gonna solve these murders?"

"How *can* I solve them?"

"Isn't that what I just asked?"

"I meant I have no idea where to start."

"Don't they train you for this?"

"No."

"They really should."

"Thanks for your input, Agatha Christie."

"You should take your destiny more seriously. Before I faced the Antichrist, I watched a lot of detective shows, and I even took an online class in forensic science."

"And yet you still got caught."

"Only because a homeless man saw me disposing of my stake in a dumpster on the other side of town." She shook her head. "Damn busybody."

"Perhaps he was just hungry?"

"There was a soup kitchen literally one block away. Why didn't he just mind his own beeswax and go there?"

Every time I began to feel a modicum of sympathy for Jacinda, she provided me with yet another reminder of why I shouldn't. But unfortunately, I needed her help because unless I could conjure up a private investigator, she was the only sidekick available.

"Can you try not to be a bitch? Just for a few days?"

"Hey, I *donated* to that soup kitchen. What was the point if nobody used it?"

Shame it wasn't possible to murder a ghost. "Why don't we stop talking about the whole stake thing and stick with our current problem? Since we don't have a forensics lab, how do we find the culprit?"

"Somebody must know something. Maybe there's rumours going around? You should ask people."

"I'm only one step away from solitary here."

"And perhaps there's circumstantial evidence. It probably wasn't a patient because we're always escorted, so it must've been a staff member. If we can find out who was working on the day I died, that would narrow down the list of suspects."

Ah, that made sense. "And we could cross-reference that with people scheduled to work the day Rylie died too."

"Exactly. Maybe it's a serial killer."

"Can you call them that if they've only killed two people?"

"Two people *that we know of*. What if there are more victims?"

Shit. That didn't bear thinking about. Of course there could be more victims. It wasn't as if I'd wandered around the hospital to check, was it?

How could I find out for sure? There had to be a record of deaths somewhere, but my psychic abilities didn't extend to communicating with Lakeview's computer system. There was only one person who might be able to help with that. My slightly uptight psychiatrist.

A clock began ticking in my head. I was the same age as Jacinda and Rylie, nobody would miss me if I disappeared, and I spent most of my time alone. How did I broach the subject of murder with Dr. Hastings before I became a victim myself?

CHAPTER 12 - MARCUS

I'D BEEN FORCED to cancel yesterday's appointment with Iris due to mandatory staff training, but I hadn't expected the missed session to have quite such an impact. On Monday, she'd been reasonably talkative. Not about herself, despite my best efforts, but she'd chattered happily about her plants. I'd bought her a fern plus some seaweed fertiliser that shouldn't harm her if she decided to try drinking it. I hadn't forgotten the "attempted suicide" notation on her file.

She'd seemed absurdly thrilled with the new plant, and for a moment, I thought she was going to try and hug me. Thankfully, she'd chosen to back off before I had to stop her. That she should be pleased by something so trivial was a novelty for me—Laurel hadn't been happy with anything less than a designer handbag.

But this afternoon, Iris had gone quiet, nervous even. I hadn't seen her look worried before. Or so vulnerable. Wet hair dripped around her shoulders, and the effect was a little creepy.

"Did something happen to you, Iris?"

My first thought was that George had got to her again. Terrence was still off work—I'd been keeping an eye on the situation.

"Happen to me? No, I'm fine."

Fine. Fine was a dangerous word.

"Is there anything you'd like to talk about?"

I couldn't bargain with Iris in this instance. Either she'd tell me or she wouldn't. Greg Tillis mentioned that he'd once tried to barter dessert privileges in exchange for her cooperation, and she referred him to the response in Arkell versus Pressdram.

Iris was a smart girl.

And today, she was also twitchy. The way she chewed her bottom lip, those quick glances... She had something she wanted to say, but she wasn't yet sure whether she wanted to say it. In that moment, I grew desperately sorry for her. Who had screwed her up so badly that she felt she couldn't trust anyone?

I wanted to reassure her, to promise I wasn't like the others, but why should she believe me? All I could do was hope that my actions spoke for themselves. It was early days, but I'd given her no reason not to trust me. Whether she confided or not would depend on how desperate her situation was.

What the hell had happened in those forty-eight hours?

Finally, she spoke in a whisper. "I heard a girl got killed this week."

A spark of elation lit inside my chest. She *had* trusted me enough to share.

But how had she found out about Rylie Draper's death? During the training session yesterday, which was actually more of a chewing out, truth be told, we'd been warned that under no circumstances were we to mention what had happened to any of the service users. The staff member at fault had been disciplined, and that would be our fate too if we talked.

Much as I disliked being lectured by Doug Calvert, I did see his point. Knowing that one of their fellow patients had passed away at Lakeview could leave service users feeling anxious and confused, and if the reaction I saw in Iris was any indication, Calvert's fears had been well-founded.

"Where did you hear that?"

A shrug. "Is it true?"

If Doug Calvert had been sitting on my shoulder, he'd have whispered in my ear to lie. No, actually, he'd have shouted. But I knew the observation room was empty, and I also knew that if I lied to Iris, it could set our relationship back months. Trust went both ways. I'd have to trust her not to drop me in it with my boss.

"Yes, a girl died, but it was an accident." A tragic accident with an outcome that could perhaps have been avoided if a particular member of staff had followed the rules. "And you're not meant to know about it. Who told you?"

"A nurse. I overheard her talking to someone."

"Which nurse?"

I wasn't sure I'd give their name to Calvert, but a reminder about discretion wouldn't go amiss. If Iris had overheard the news, how many other service users were aware?

"I forget. They all look the same."

"You don't recall a hair colour? An accent?"

"Maybe brown? Or blonde? I'm still taking pills, remember? They mess with my mind."

I'd taken her off the strong stuff. A low dose of lorazepam could cause forgetfulness, but Iris had remained remarkably cognisant over the last few weeks.

Which meant she was most likely fibbing again. I swallowed a sigh. Getting annoyed wouldn't help matters, and the most important thing was for me to reassure her that it had been a one-off.

"Okay, it's not important. The girl who passed away slipped in the shower, and unfortunately, the member of staff who was meant to be supervising her had stepped away for a break." An unsanctioned break. Sandra, the nurse in question, had apparently sworn that she'd only been gone for two minutes to get a glass of water, but I'd heard she was in the break room for long enough to microwave a cheese pasty and eat it too. Unfortunately, it seemed the cameras in that part of the building had malfunctioned, which meant nobody could prove or disprove either story. "We've all had a strong reminder not to leave any service user on their own, which means that if you have a fall, someone will be around to help right away."

"How do you know she fell?" Iris asked. "Did somebody see?"

"No, but she was in the shower room by herself."

"What if somebody pushed her?"

"The door was locked."

"What if somebody with a key unlocked it?"

"Why would they do that?"

She paused. "I don't know."

"Iris, I care very much about your safety in here, and I've got no reason to believe that my colleagues would feel any different."

"Rylie's the second person to die here in the last few months, so excuse me if I don't share your confidence."

Really? How did Iris manage to stay better-informed than me? "Who else died?"

"Jacinda Warren."

The name was new to me. "Another accident in the shower?"

"No, she fell asleep and never woke up."

"There must have been an underlying cause."

"Try a drug overdose."

"That's unlikely. Service users aren't allowed to self-administer."

"Exactly my point."

"You think someone *gave* Jacinda an overdose? That's... That's..."

I wanted to say "preposterous," but in truth, it wasn't. Back when I was a junior doctor, overworked and underpaid, I'd come close to screwing up myself on occasion. Long hours, lack of sleep... It was all too easy to misread someone else's scribbled notes. Fortunately, I'd always caught myself in time, but I recalled a colleague who'd accidentally given a cancer patient a massive overdose of cyclophosphamide. The notes had said "40 mg/kg over 4 days" with the intention that the lady receive ten milligrams per kilogram for each of four consecutive days, but a misunderstanding meant that she got forty milligrams per kilogram *each* day. The wrongful death lawsuit had cost the hospital millions, and the doctor involved had quit medicine for good. So it happened.

"That's unlikely," I finished up.

"Unlikely, but not impossible, yes? And how many other people have died?"

"None that I know of."

"That you know of. You hadn't heard about Jacinda either." Iris looked me right in the eye, and it unnerved me. "Dr. Hastings, forget what you've read in my file—I don't want to die."

"Iris, you won't die. As I said, shower procedures have been tightened up, and you're on minimal medication now. Just two pills per day, and one of those is by your own choice."

My words did little to soothe her. Her worry had turned into something more. She was scared.

"Could you find out if anyone else has died?"

"Iris..."

"Please?"

I had to admit, she'd piqued my curiosity. And if service users were getting hurt due to slipping standards, something needed to be done. Surely Doug Calvert wouldn't want to invite a lawsuit? His shareholders wouldn't be too happy with that.

"I'll ask around. Now, is there anything else you want to talk about today?"

She shifted, settling herself into her seat. "Not really. Did you buy any pots yet?"

CHAPTER 13 - MARCUS

AFTER I'D FINISHED the rest of my sessions that afternoon—I had ten patients on my list now—I headed to the nurse's station to check the shift schedule. Rylie Draper had fallen the day before yesterday, and according to the rota, only two nurses had attended to Iris since. Some orderlies may also have had contact, but she'd definitely said it was a nurse she'd heard speaking about Rylie.

Glenda was busy cursing out the vending machine. Her packet of Twiglets had got snagged on a flapjack halfway down the window, and as I approached, she kicked the machine and swore louder. Anger-management issues?

"Allow me." I rummaged through my pocket for a pound, then punched in the code for a flapjack. The Twiglets dropped down with it. "Here you go."

"Oh. Thanks."

"You're very welcome. While we're here, could I have a quick chat about Iris McGivern?"

"What about her? Is she being difficult again?"

"On the contrary—we seem to be making progress." Albeit slowly. "But she seemed a little distressed today, and she mentioned that she'd heard about the incident with Rylie Draper."

Glenda squared up to me, hands on hips. "And you

think I told her?"

"I didn't—"

"Let me tell you, *Doctor* Hastings, I take my job very seriously. Mr. Calvert told us not to tell the prisoners anything about the girl dying, and I kept my mouth shut, unlike some people."

"The correct term is 'service users,' and I'm sure you—"

"I don't like unfounded allegations being made against me."

"I'm merely trying to—" Finish a sentence.

"It was probably one of the orderlies who blabbed. They never can keep their mouths shut. Now, if you'll excuse me, some of us have work to do."

She turned on her heel and marched off, Twiglets in hand. So, the culprit probably wasn't Glenda, then. Her attitude made Iris look positively rosy. I was tempted to stir a tablet or two of diazepam into her tea to mellow her out a bit.

Marcus, you did not just think that.

"Picture of happiness, that one," an orderly muttered from behind me. Bobby, judging by the whiff of halitosis. The man never seemed to use a toothbrush.

"I'd have to agree with you there. Want a flapjack?"

"Aren't you gonna eat it?"

I'd only bought it to free Glenda's Twiglets. I'd hoped it might endear me a little, but no such luck.

"I meant to buy crisps, but you know what that machine's like."

Bobby nodded as he took the flapjack. "Ta, pal. Bloody thing doesn't give change either."

Where was Hazel? Her schedule said she had another hour to work, and I often saw her come into the break room for coffee around this time. Lakeview charged fifty pence for it from yet another vending machine. There was no kettle, and Thermos flasks were banned, ostensibly for safety reasons, but having met Doug Calvert, I suspected he was more concerned with making a margin on every cup of terrible coffee the machine spat out. I tried to avoid it whenever possible —my lawyer charged two hundred pounds an hour, and all those fifty pences added up.

But today, I bit the bullet and fetched myself a cappuccino made with fake milk and hardly any froth while I checked through the emails on my phone. Lakeview didn't provide us with company phones either, merely sent someone from the IT department— which was actually just two overworked twenty-somethings in a very small basement office—to put the email program on our own devices. That way, they could contact us twenty-four-seven whenever there was a problem. Luckily, I hadn't had an emergency call yet, but I'd heard tales of staff members being dragged away from birthday parties and even a wedding in order to attend to service users.

I'd almost given up hope for the day when Hazel hurried in, wiping at a stain on her scrubs. Blood? No, it wasn't dark enough. I shoved the phone into my pocket and grabbed a handful of paper towels from the dispenser.

"Here, these might help."

"Thanks. A new guy threw his drink at me. Normally, I'm quite good at ducking, but it's been a long day."

"Isn't every day?"

"That's true enough. How are you settling in?"

"It's quite a change from my previous job, but I've always enjoyed a challenge."

"Aye, I suppose that's one reason for working here. What made you choose Lakeview?"

It was the only place that would have me. "It's convenient for my new home. How about you? Why do you work here?"

"I like seeing the difference I can make. As my mum always used to say, it's not a job, it's a calling."

Funny, my mother had said that too, but I wasn't sure it was *my* calling. Originally, I'd gone to medical school to please my father, only for him to die from a heart attack right before I graduated. If I'd been thinking straight at the time, which I hadn't, I'd have taken my degree and used the piece of paper to get a job that didn't involve being on call at all hours of the day and night, but I'd still been trying to honour Dad's memory, so I began work in the ER instead. The move to psychiatry came when I realised my favourite part of the role was talking to people rather than stitching them up. Then I met Laurel, and on the odd occasion in the early days when I'd voiced the possibility of changing career, she'd acted so horrified that I stopped mentioning it. And so there I was. Thirty-one years old with a rented house too big for one person, a pile of legal bills, and a reasonably well-paid job I couldn't afford to quit.

But I had made a difference to at least one person in my time at Lakeview. Iris. She'd gone from sullen and snarky to chatty and, well, still slightly snarky, but she seemed happier. My other patients were presenting me with more of a challenge, but I had hopes that we'd get there someday.

So I nodded and agreed with Hazel. "I know what you mean. Do you need more paper towels?"

"I'll just put the top in the wash when I get home. Thanks again."

She made to move off, so I spoke quickly. "Do you have a moment?"

"I need to grab a coffee and get back to work."

"It'll only take a second. Let me buy you that coffee." While the machine clunked ominously, I broached the subject of Iris and her overly sensitive ears. "One of my patients overheard a member of staff mention Rylie Draper's death. I was just wondering if you'd heard Rylie's name being mentioned anywhere in the hallways? I'm somewhat concerned about sensitive information reaching the service users."

"No, I haven't heard a thing. Which patient?"

"Iris McGivern."

"She never mentioned it to me, and I did her late check yesterday. Maybe it was somebody talking this morning?"

"It could well have been."

"I'll let you know if I hear anything."

"That'd be much appreciated."

"Hey, I heard someone talking about it." Bobby again, this time with his mouth full of flapjack. "Doug Calvert and that girl who does the PR. They were in the lift."

Hazel backed away, and I didn't miss the slight wrinkle of her nose. "Uh, see you around."

Nice timing, Bobby.

"Reckon they're having an affair," Bobby continued. "Jim saw them coming up the stairs from the basement the other day, and why else would they have been down there?"

"Who?"

"Calvert and the PR bird. He was messing around with his last secretary too. Dunno how his wife puts up with him."

"Fascinating, but—" On second thoughts, Bobby seemed to be a bit of a gossip, didn't he? I lowered my voice and willed myself not to gag as I stepped closer. "Did Calvert say anything else about the girl who died? I heard it wasn't the first fatality here in recent months."

"Nope, we've had a right spate of them, it seems like. That's probably why Calvert's griping so much about Rylie Draper. Wouldn't look good if the news got out that another prisoner carked it."

"How many are we talking?"

Bobby began counting on his fingers, and I sucked in a breath when he started on the second hand.

"Six in the last year. And there was another one the summer before that too. Young Mandy Horner fell down the stairs and broke her neck, up on the second floor by the prayer room. That was what started it. If my mum was alive, she'd say this place has bad vibes."

"How did the others die? All accidents?"

"It was hardly likely to be murder, was it? Not in here. Everyone's locked up."

"What happened, then?"

"I forget the details now. One girl got hold of some sort of drain cleaner and drank it, that one I do remember. Claire Welby, her name was. Terrible for the nurse who found her. The stuff ate right through her throat. A nasty way to die, although I'd be tempted to top myself too if I was stuck in here."

Six deaths in the last year and a seventh before that? It seemed a high number for a single facility, especially a facility whose service users tended to be on the younger side. All my patients were under forty.

"Do you recall a girl called Jacinda?"

"Ah, yeah. Jacinda. She had heart problems, or so I heard. Her ticker gave out one night."

"How old was she?"

"Twenty-something. Pretty little thing, but mad as a March hare. Thought she was the Antichrist or summat."

And her heart failed? "Where can I find more information on this?"

"Doubt you can. Calvert hushes everything up. And why would you even want to?"

"Just curious, I guess. Being new and all that."

"Take my advice—keep your head down and do your job. The powers that be don't like troublemakers around here."

Of course they didn't, especially if they were trying to cover up atrocious mortality rates.

"Understood. Well, I should get back to work." But not before rummaging around in my trouser pocket. "Stick of gum?"

I held out the packet, but Bobby shook his head.

"Never touch the stuff. Like chewing old tyres, it is."

Well, I tried.

***

On Thursday, I spent an hour of my time off searching the internet for any reference to the tragedies at Lakeview, but Bobby was right—Calvert liked to keep things quiet. The only mention I found of a death was a small article in the *Lincolnshire Herald* detailing how Lee Sorensen, beloved son of Mary and Arthur, had taken an overdose during a brief stay at the facility and passed away three days later in St. Anthony's Hospital. And as I said, overdoses weren't entirely unknown. Not only were there occasional errors, but residents in psychiatric wards could be surprisingly resourceful when it came to finding ways to harm themselves.

But still, seven deaths...

I pushed work out of my mind on Friday as I waited for Cassie to arrive, and when she ran up the driveway with a huge grin on her face, I relaxed for the first time in a week.

"Hey, sweetie, how have you been?"

In the background, Jacqueline tapped her watch. "Seven thirty."

How had I ever married her daughter? It was scary how Laurel had turned into her mother over the years. Genetics at work. I just had to hope that Cassidy took after my side of the family, which would be a challenge given how little I saw of her.

"Rupert's going to buy me a pony!" Cassie squealed. "Isn't that awesome?"

Laurel's new boyfriend had only known Cassie a matter of weeks, and he was already trying to buy her affections? What a dick. It shouldn't have surprised me, given who he was dating, but my heart still dropped into my stomach. How was I meant to compete with a pony? I could barely scrape together enough cash to pay for Cassie's riding lesson each week, let alone a four-legged friend that would basically eat money.

But I couldn't rain on Cassie's parade. Above all, I

wanted her to be happy.

"That's great, Cass. Where are you gonna keep it?"

"At his house. He's got stables and everything."

Of course he did. Not for the first time, I wondered whether I was right pursuing custody of Cassie against the odds. Could I really offer more than Laurel and her family? Jacqueline looked after Cassie in the mornings while Laurel worked, whereas I'd have to use a childminder. And Rupert, it seemed, would cater to her every whim, even if she didn't like him much as a person. But she was my flesh and blood, dammit. I was her father, and I loved her.

I'd fight for her, even if I knew I'd lose.

CHAPTER 14 - MARCUS

"DID YOU ASK around?"

On Saturday, Iris didn't bother with the preliminaries, just came straight out with the question. I was still feeling somewhat fragile after having my ego bashed by Rupert the day before, and the thought of another challenging conversation with Miss McGivern left me drained.

"First, let's talk about—"

"How are you feeling, Iris?" she mimicked. "I'm fine. Still alive, thanks. Did you ask? Has anyone else died here?"

I had to smile. Iris was sharp, but not in the calculating, manipulative way Laurel had been. No, now that she'd started talking to me, Iris didn't like wasting words. Her determination left me in a tricky position because I wasn't supposed to be discussing Lakeview's problems with anyone, let alone a service user, but she had an effect on me that I struggled to explain. I couldn't walk away. Answering her would be playing with fire, but I must have been feeling particularly masochistic that day because answer I did.

"You were right," I said, and she grinned triumphantly for a second before a hint of fear flashed in her eyes. "Rumour says there've been seven deaths here recently. But from the details I've heard, they were all accidents or suicides. There's no reason for you to worry about your time in here."

"But—"

She fell silent, and the way she folded in on herself reminded me of our first days together.

"Iris, please—"

"You're wrong," she muttered.

"Wrong about what?"

"They weren't all accidents and suicides."

"Why do you say that?"

Another long pause, and I waited silently. Gave her space. Pushing wouldn't work with Iris, and I didn't want to take a huge step backwards.

"What's the point? You won't believe me."

"I'm not here to judge you, Iris. Anything you want to tell me, I'll treat as confidential, and I promise I'll give it due consideration."

She took a deep inhale and closed her eyes. Whatever she had bottled up in there, it was difficult for her to speak about.

"Jacinda and Rylie were killed by somebody. There needs to be an investigation."

"Killed by who? How do you know? From what I've heard, Jacinda died of heart failure and Rylie tripped in the shower."

"I don't know who. If I did, I'd tell you. That's what the investigation's for."

"I can't just start an investigation."

"Well, somebody needs to. There's a killer walking around Lakeview, and the only person I know it's not is you." I guess I should have been flattered by that. At least she had a modicum of trust in me. "Because you didn't start working here until after Jacinda died."

Ah. Not so much trust as logic, then. But slightly flawed logic.

"And how do you know the same person killed them both?"

"I don't. Aw, dammit." She screwed her eyes shut, then opened the left one. "Did you kill Rylie?"

"Of course not." Good grief. "Iris, nobody killed Rylie."

"They did!"

"How can you be so sure?"

"Because she told me so, okay?" Iris clapped both hands over her mouth and stared at me, wide-eyed. "Oops."

Oh boy. I guess this was why she'd ended up at Lakeview. *Tread carefully, Hastings.*

"Did you...speak to Jacinda as well?"

Now she folded her arms. "Stop looking at me like that!"

"I'm not looking at you in any particular way, Iris."

"Yes, you are. You're judging, just like you said you wouldn't. Right at this moment, you're thinking that all the rumours were right, and trying to decide exactly which drugs you should stuff me full of after the orderly's taken me back to my cell."

Delusional or not, Iris wasn't a bad mind-reader.

"It's a room, Iris, not a cell."

"It's got a lock on the door. It's a damn cell. And stop being so sanctimonious."

"Iris, calm—"

"Never in the history of the world has anyone calmed down by being told to calm down, asshole. And if something happens to me, you'd better investigate then. Because I'm telling you, my heart's fine, I'm not suicidal, and I'm too careful to trip in the fucking shower."

It was all I could do to refrain from putting my head in my hands. How had we gone from chatting about potted plants and decking to this? It wasn't the first time I'd had a setback with a patient, but nevertheless, it was disappointing. Until today, Iris had been reasonably easy to deal with, and against my better judgement, I'd actually begun to like her.

Actually, perhaps this blow-up was for the best. Because I wasn't *meant* to like the people I was treating.

Not in the way I'd been starting to like Iris.

"Nothing'll happen to you, flower." Flower? Now it was me who was losing my fucking mind. "We can talk about this."

"Talk? *Talk*? What's the point? Jacinda died in my room, do you know that? In my *bed*. Why do you think I moved it? She won't shut up, and all she wants to watch is reality TV. I don't care who Jordan shagged on *Survival Island*!"

What should I do? It was tempting to give Iris a little something to take the edge off, but if there was any trust left between us, that would destroy it completely. And no matter what might have happened in the past, at no point did I feel threatened by her.

"Tell me more about the ghosts, Iris." She obviously believed in them, even if I didn't. If I understood what she was thinking, perhaps I could work out the best course of action?

"What's the point? You'll just go and laugh about it with your friends, which is mean, and it'll also put me in danger because if whoever killed the others gets to hear what I said, they'll know I'm not lying."

"Unless someone's in imminent danger, anything that happens in our sessions is absolutely confidential. There's nobody in the observation room, and I'm bound by a code of ethics."

"What if *I'm* in imminent danger?"

"Then I want to help you to stay safe."

"Then work out why people keep dying here!"

"Can I speak frankly?"

"Why not? It's better than bullshitting."

A sigh escaped. Situations like this made me want to walk out the door and just keep...on...walking... "Doug Calvert's an asshole. He doesn't want the bad PR that would come with an external investigation, and he certainly isn't going to open an internal one when the deaths have already been ruled accidental. The only way I could possibly take this further would be if I had the evidence to do so, and the word of a service user channelling two ghosts just doesn't cut it."

Weirdly, she thought about that for a few seconds and calmed down a bit. "I guess I see how it could be difficult."

Thank you. "The question is, where do we go from here?"

"Well, it's obvious, isn't it? We have to investigate ourselves."

Oh, hell. "That wasn't quite what I meant. I can't just start asking questions. As you said yourself, that could tip off the wrong people."

Iris tugged at her hair. "This is impossible."

At least we shared the same opinion on that. "Let's make a plan to help with your anxiety."

"More pills, you mean?"

"Medication could be a part of it if that's appropriate."

A sob burst from her mouth, and I felt like a shit for contributing to her distress.

"I'm not crazy. I'm *not*." She took one deep breath, two, trying to steady herself. Then a change came over her. She sat up straighter and looked me in the eye. "I've got a plan. Forget I mentioned the spirits. Forget today ever happened. Take me back to my *room*, and tomorrow we can go back to how things were before."

Well, that was interesting. The sudden switch was indicative of dissociative identity disorder, the emergence of an alternate personality. Was that a possibility? Or was she just battling hard to control her emotions and winning? Instinct and experience made me believe it was the latter, although I was by no means sure.

"Yes, Iris, you can go back to your room. If at any time you want to talk, just ask one of the nurses to call me, okay? I'll keep my phone with me, so even if I'm not here, I'll be available."

I'd also ask for a nurse to check on her hourly, including throughout the night. She might have assured me she wasn't suicidal, but I didn't want to take any chances.

Rather than calling an orderly to take Iris upstairs, I decided to walk her there myself. No sense in making her ordeal any worse than it was already. Except when I tried to guide her out of the room, she snatched her arm away.

"Get off! I can walk by myself."

I took a step back, only for her to trip over a chair leg. Her arms flailed, and I barely caught her before she hit the deck. This time when I took her arm, she didn't protest.

The ride up in the lift went more smoothly than I'd expected, and in Iris's room, my gaze lingered on her bed for a beat too long. A ghost? Impossible.

Wasn't it?

A part of me still found it odd that she'd gone to the effort of moving her bed all those weeks ago and then lied about her reason for doing it.

"I'll see you tomorrow morning," I said.

Nothing. She lay down on top of the blankets and stared at the ceiling.

Out in the hallway, Bobby walked past pushing an empty wheelchair as I locked Iris's door and checked it was secure.

"Iris have another meltdown?" he asked.

"What makes you think that?"

"I used to see that look on Dr. Tillis's face."

Perhaps that should have made me feel better, that I wasn't the only psychiatrist she'd done this to, but it didn't. And I had no desire to discuss Iris's issues with a man I suspected to be the biggest gossip at Lakeview.

I made a non-committal noise, then on impulse, turned back to ask another question. "Which room was Jacinda Warren in?"

Bobby pointed at Iris's door. "That one. Why?"

"It doesn't matter."

Or did it?

***

"Teddy? It's too late for this."

After the day I'd had, the last thing I needed was

the dog refusing to come in after his evening potty trip. I squinted into the darkness, wishing I'd had the time to install some sort of light in the back garden. Nothing moved. I grabbed the torch from beside the microwave and changed my slippers for a pair of trainers since it'd been raining earlier. Despite Iris's best efforts, the garden was still a soulless patch of grass with a moss-flecked patio at the house end. Cassie's sandpit and swing were the only things in it apart from the dustbins and a twiggy bush I very much suspected was dead.

"Teddy?"

I shone the dim beam around, then cursed as I spotted the open gate in the back fence. Had I forgotten to close it when I took the rubbish out this morning? The service alley was deserted at that time of night, but a stiff breeze blew through my neighbour's trees, making shadows dance across the wooden slats. Something small and dark skittered across the ground to my left. A rat? It wasn't big enough to be a dog, and besides, Teddy was white. He should show up against the blackness.

"Teddy!"

I kept calling as I walked towards the road, thankful I lived in a cul-de-sac rather than on a busy main street, but there was no flurry of paws, no answering bark. Where the hell had he gone? He'd only been outside for a couple of minutes.

As I searched, I cringed inwardly at the thought of Laurel's inevitable "I told you sos" if I'd lost the dog. She'd told me many times I was incapable of caring for anything by myself, and this would only add weight to her argument. And Cassie would be devastated if Teddy didn't return home. She loved that mutt, and so did I.

Fuck.

"Teddy! Come here, boy!"

CHAPTER 15 - IRIS

I BUNCHED THE cuffs of my sweatshirt up in my hands as an orderly led me into the meeting room the day after I lost my damn mind. Why had I ever let my guard down with Dr. Hastings? The friendly smiles, the easy-going manner... For a moment, I'd thought he might actually have been different.

Stupid, stupid Iris.

I was right back where I'd started—stuck in hell with a psychiatrist who thought I was a lunatic—except now there was a reasonable possibility a genuine maniac might try to kill me. What had Dr. Hastings said? Seven victims? With two hundred beds, according to the corporate propaganda plastered to the walls in the guise of art, that gave me roughly a three percent chance of dying.

I'd rather have backflipped across a minefield than sat around, waiting for my fate. At least that way, I'd know the outcome faster.

For the first time, the room was empty when I arrived. Empty except for the tired furniture. I'd seen psychiatrists' offices in the movies, and they always had a comfortable couch, potted plants, and abstract paintings on the walls. Seemed Director Calvert wasn't a film buff because in the whole time I'd been at Lakeview, Meeting Room Three had been furnished with the same scratched metal table and a pair of chairs that looked as if they came from a yard sale. We didn't even have carpet. I took a seat opposite a framed list of rules.

> *No touching.*
> *No spitting.*
> *No shouting.*
> *No smoking.*
> *No eating.*

At the bottom, someone had added another item in black marker: *No urinating.*

Wow, Director Calvert really knew how to spoil our fun.

"Where's Dr. Hastings?" I asked the orderly.

"Running a few minutes late. I'll wait with you until he arrives."

I began counting in my head, and "a few" minutes turned out to be almost ten. Not that I was impatient or anything. After yesterday's chat, I'd gladly have waited forever for my next appointment. Although I would've missed Dr. Hastings's company. Over the last month, he'd helped to take the edge off the loneliness in a way Jacinda never could.

Last night, once I'd got Jacinda settled with *Reality Bites*, a gem of a show about the trials and tribulations of trainee dentists—who all seemed to shag either the dental nurses or each other—I'd had plenty of time to think. Never again would I mention ghosts in front of Dr. Hastings. The word was forbidden. *Verboten.* As were spirits, phantoms, demons, spectres, and dead, twisted souls.

I'd take my chances with Lakeview's resident serial killer. Maybe dying wouldn't be so bad? Since I was an active member of the Electi, my soul couldn't be trapped on earth like Jacinda's because the rules said there had to be four Electi on duty at all times. My spirit would find its way into a new girl, although she wouldn't have the faintest idea what to do with it. She'd just have to wait for fate to take its course. For the other Electi to find her, assuming they were still part of the original line and carried the legend with them. Otherwise, we were fucked. The whole world was fucked.

But at least in the meantime, I'd have someone to talk to.

I'd drawn Dr. Hastings another garden. This one had helianthus and daffodils and golden chamomile because I was just a regular ray of fucking sunshine.

The door opened, and Dr. Hastings traded places with the orderly. Boy, he looked like shit again. Dr. Hastings, not the orderly. The orderlies merely looked untidy. Theoretically, there was some sort of uniform code, but none of them ever followed it. Dirty white trainers seemed to be the fashion right now. Dr. Hastings set his coffee and a plastic-wrapped flapjack on the table beside his notepad, then lined up a pen just so beside it.

"Good morning, Iris. Where would you like to start today?"

Where to start... Where to start... Was it me who'd given him a sleepless night? I mean, I hadn't gotten much shut-eye either. When I'd checked myself in the mirror this morning—polished metal, not glass—my eyes had been bloodshot with dark smudges underneath them. Dr. Hastings looked as if his eye-bags had been drawn on with charcoal.

"Uh, I'm sorry about yesterday. I just get silly sometimes."

"It's not a problem."

"Well, it clearly is. I mean, you look terrible."

He hadn't even ironed his shirt. Dr. Hastings always ironed his shirt.

"Do I?" He gave his head a little shake. "Shit."

"Are you okay?"

"I'm fine."

"'Fine' doesn't mean what you think it does."

"My dog escaped yesterday evening, that's all. I spent most of the night looking for him. My apologies if I'm a bit tired today."

"Did you find him?"

Another shake of the head, and his shoulders slumped.

"I'm so sorry. Has he run off before?"

"No, but I've never left the back gate open before. I'm usually careful. And I haven't lived in the new house long, so Teddy doesn't know the area very well."

"Did you try calling the dog warden? The pound? Local rescues?"

"As many as I could, but some of them aren't open yet. I'll try again at lunchtime."

"There's a website—Lost Dog, I think it's called? When Jean from the garden centre where I used to work lost her poodle, they helped her out."

"DogLost. I've already emailed them. They promised to alert their volunteer network, but I'm not sure it'll do much good. I'm beginning to suspect he's been stolen."

"Then you should call the police."

"I did. They basically said they're far too busy

catching murderers to search for a dog." He met my gaze for a second. Glanced away. "Sorry."

Why was he sorry? The fact that I'd killed a man was inescapable, as was Lakeview.

"How about a private investigator?" I asked.

He still didn't look at me. "I can't afford a private investigator, Iris."

Really? I still couldn't work out why he was so short of money. Expensive holidays? A gambling habit? What did he spend his cash on? I figured if his daughter didn't live with him, there was probably child support. And rent. When I moved out of my last foster home, I'd shared a house to save money. My roommates had been three guys, and I spent most of my life picking up dirty laundry and dumping it in front of the washing machine. And don't even get me started on the washing-up.

If I'd had money myself, I'd have offered it to Dr. Hastings, but the only thing I owned of any value was my gold necklace, and I couldn't sell that. It was part of who I was. Each of the Electi had one, and when we put them together, great things would happen, although Mum had been slightly hazy on exactly what those things were.

"Someone might be feeding him. It turned out Jean's poodle had wandered into a lady's house three streets away, and she thought he was a stray. She'd bought him a new bed, half a dozen squeaky toys, and the expensive brand of dog food. When Jean went to pick him up, she had a hell of a fight to get him to leave."

"Thankfully, I think you're right. The most likely culprit is my wife, and she'll be feeding him all right.

Probably steak and bloody caviar."

He was still married? "Your wife? I assumed you were divorced."

"Separated. The divorce is taking longer than I'd hoped." He seemed to give himself a mental kick because he straightened his cuffs and faced me again. "But we shouldn't be talking about my problems. This is your session."

"I'm fine with talking about your problems. It's better than talking about mine."

"That wasn't quite the point I was trying to make."

He began unwrapping his flapjack, and I pointed at the sign above his head. "You're such a rebel."

Finally, he cracked a smile. Just a small one, but it was a start. "Sometimes, rules are made to be broken. Want a piece?"

I met his smile with one of my own. "I'd love a piece."

CHAPTER 16 - MARCUS

"YOU'VE GOT TO be kidding me."

I stared at Doug Calvert across the vast expanse of glass and chrome he called a desk, not that he seemed to do much work at it. Between screwing around with the PR lady and playing golf, he didn't have the time. Perhaps I shouldn't have reacted quite so rudely, but what he was suggesting was ridiculous.

"Now, now, Marcus. No need to get upset. It's just a little chat and maybe a few tests."

"Iris is a patient, not a lab rat."

"A patient, precisely. And we want to *cure* our patients, don't we?"

"Yes, but we do that using proven treatments that have undergone proper evaluation, not by allowing scientists to experiment on them."

"How do you suppose these treatments get evaluated? I'll tell you—by experimentation just like this."

No, not just like this. I'd been part of trials in the past, for cognitive stimulation and neurofeedback, and we'd had protocols to follow. Patients were carefully assessed prior to treatment, and every step of the process was recorded and analysed. Simply letting some American geneticist walk into a hospital and start poking and prodding the patients was a diabolical idea, no matter how good his credentials were. The chances of Iris having a genetic disorder were slim in any case. There was no evidence to support that.

"Why Iris?"

"Because this doctor's researching a link between paranormal delusions and the human genome, and since Iris claims to see ghosts, that makes her the perfect candidate, don't you agree? The only other possible candidate is Terri Foyel, but she insists she talks to pixies rather than ghosts, which I don't think is quite what Dr. Bordais is looking for."

"Outside interference could set Iris's treatment back months."

"She's one of our long-stayers anyway. I doubt she'll be getting out anytime soon."

"You can't know that for sure. She's been showing improvement."

"I heard she had an episode on Saturday?"

"A minor setback. Nothing significant."

At least, I hoped so. Iris had seemed much better yesterday, even if I groaned inwardly every time I thought of the way I'd unloaded on her about Teddy. She didn't need to hear my troubles, and I shouldn't have mentioned them. I'd spent three hours last night pinning posters around the neighbourhood just in case, then risked driving over to my old home to snoop. I felt like a damn burglar creeping around the garden, but there'd been no sign of Teddy, and when the security light came on, I'd panicked and run, twisting my ankle as I jumped over the back fence. Even after an ice pack and a couple of ibuprofen, the pain pulsed and throbbed, and I'd resorted to sleeping pills in order to avoid looking like a zombie at work again.

"I took a look at your notes, and the girl's clearly still deranged." Calvert glanced at his Rolex. "Don't worry—you've got three hours to explain the situation to Miss McGivern before Dr. Bordais arrives."

"He's coming *today*?"

"She, actually. I've checked, and she has an excellent reputation. She works with Professor Fairchild at the Institute of Human Genetics in San Francisco."

I didn't care if she worked with Watson and Crick themselves. She should have been ashamed of herself for running a study in such a cavalier manner.

"For the record, I think this is a terrible idea."

"Your concerns are noted, Dr. Hastings. Now, if you'll excuse me, I have calls to make."

Outside his office, Calvert's PA glanced up from her computer as I stormed past.

"How did it go?"

"I'll give you three guesses."

"Was it about the scientist?"

"He told you about that?"

"I have access to his emails."

I'd have to remember that if I ever sent a scathing resignation letter. "Yes, it was about the scientist." An exasperated sigh escaped. "It's a crazy scheme."

"You're not the first person to say that."

"He's done this before?"

"Not with Dr. Bordais, but other studies, yes. For universities and stuff. Anyone who's willing to pay the admin fee, basically." There was a fee? How did I guess? Money definitely talked with Doug Calvert. He had to buy that expensive watch somehow. "But who knows? One of the studies might find a miracle cure.

It's not as if Iris McGivern will ever get out of here without one."

"We can't say that."

"Mr. Calvert did."

"He discussed a patient with you?"

The girl snorted. "Of course not, I'm *just* a PA. Get the coffee, Becca. Fetch my dry cleaning, Becca." She pointed at the intercom. "He was talking to Greg Tillis. Said she was a lost cause."

That was a strong statement, especially from a man who was essentially a glorified administrator. In my years as a doctor, I'd seen few patients who showed no improvement whatsoever from treatment, and in my opinion, Iris was *far* from a lost cause.

"Did the other studies go smoothly?" I asked Becca, making a mental note never to discuss anything with Calvert that I didn't want spread all over the hospital. Between her and Bobby, Lakeview's gossip tree was watered, fertilised, and thriving.

"For the most part, yes."

"For the most part?"

"One girl didn't do so well, but she died without finishing the course of treatment, so..."

She died? "What kind of treatment?"

"Something to do with electricity? I didn't really understand the details." She glanced at Calvert's closed door. "Shh. We're not supposed to talk about that."

I bet they weren't. I was beginning to suspect Lakeview had a real problem.

***

I debated whether to tell Iris about the scientist's visit

right away, but in the end, I opted to leave it until just before Dr. Bordais arrived. Otherwise, it would only give her time to stew. Iris was a worrier.

A worrier, but perhaps not as paranoid as people thought. Her concerns over Lakeview's death rate may well be valid, even if the underlying reasons for her beliefs were way off.

Which Iris would we get today? The nervy girl who saw murderers and ghosts around every corner? Sweet Iris who'd tried to comfort me about Teddy yesterday? Or the young woman brimming with snark and sarcasm? Only time would tell. Even though I knew superstitions had no basis in reality, I still pressed my fingers to the doorjamb before I walked into the meeting room. Touch wood.

"How are you feeling today, Iris?"

"Hungry. Why are we having this session at lunchtime?"

Because Calvert had insisted. "I brought you a flapjack."

"Thanks. They taste better than the bland crap the kitchen here serves up."

The flapjacks from the vending machine were a mix of old tyre rubber and overly sweet syrup that left a furry layer on the roof of your mouth. Whatever Iris ate must be truly terrible, which didn't exactly shock me now that I'd worked at Lakeview for over a month. She tore at the wrapper with a need that bordered on desperation.

"Let me know if you want anything else, and I'll see what I can do."

She answered around a mouthful of flapjack. "You didn't answer my question. Why are we meeting at lunchtime? We never meet at lunchtime. Aren't you hungry?"

Not in the slightest. "Iris, you're going to have a visitor this afternoon."

"A visitor? Who? Is it that woman the court appointed? Because you might as well tell her it's a waste of her time and mine and save us both the bother."

"No, it's not your court-appointed advocate. Mr. Calvert's arranged for you to participate in a scientific study."

Iris dropped the flapjack and leaned forward on her elbows, curiosity piqued. "What kind of a study?"

Here goes... *Please don't have another blow-up.* "It's some sort of research into a possible link between genetics and paranormal delusions. I've informed him that I don't think it's in your best interests, but unfortunately, he's decided to go ahead with allowing access."

"Of course he has."

Hmm, she was staying remarkably calm.

"You don't mind?"

"Why would I? I don't have paranormal delusions. I just made all that stuff up, and I'll tell this person so."

Was it possible to be delusional about delusions? It certainly seemed that way.

"I'd advise just answering her questions as best you can, and there may also be a few tests. I'm sure it won't take long, and I'll stay with you the whole time."

"Her? The scientist's a woman?"

"That's my understanding, yes."

"Do you know her name?"

"Dr. Bordais."

Iris mulled that over. "Nope, never heard of her. When will she be here?"

"Any minute now."

"Do I look okay? I didn't get a shower this morning."

"Radiant."

My tone stayed light, jokey even, but I wasn't kidding. Iris always looked beautiful in an ethereal sort of way. A century ago, she'd have been an artist's muse, her delicate features immortalised in a hundred oil paintings for the bourgeoisie to salivate over.

A knock at the door signalled the scientist's arrival, and I said a silent thank you to the heavens that Iris hadn't yet lost the plot. All she had to do was keep her head for an hour or two, and this would be blessedly over.

Calvert had accompanied Dr. Bordais personally, which now that I saw her, didn't surprise me in the least. Nor did it surprise me when I caught him staring at her backside as he motioned her to go first through the door. She reminded me more of a model than a lab geek.

"Marcus, this is Nicole Bordais. She just arrived on the red-eye this morning."

I forced a pleasant expression. "Pleased to meet you."

Just hurry up and get this finished.

I glanced back at Iris to check she was okay, then swivelled to take a longer look. Her mouth had dropped open, and she was staring at Dr. Bordais with the strangest expression on her face. Thankfully, Doug Calvert was too busy checking out the good doctor's chest to notice.

"And this is Iris McGivern." Calvert waved vaguely in her direction. "She looks forward to cooperating *fully* with your research."

Nicole gave him a smile that didn't reach her eyes. Yes, she had him nailed already. "I appreciate your time." She nodded towards the mirror-window at the far end of the room. "Will you be observing?"

"Oh, I don't get involved in all that, but Marcus here will be on hand to assist in any way you need. We must get together for a coffee before you leave."

"I'd love to, depending on time. I'm due to meet some friends for dinner later." Her tone said she'd be running late for that meeting no matter how quickly she finished with Iris. "Shall we get started?"

The way she dismissed Calvert as he'd done several times to me brought a smile to my face. Her attitude gave me hope that this session wouldn't be as difficult as I'd feared.

But Iris still seemed out of sorts. She hadn't taken her eyes off Dr. Bordais, and as Calvert backed out of the room, a tear rolled down her cheek. *Oh, hell.*

Whatever was about to happen, it made me very nervous.

Chapter 17 - Iris

MY KNEES TREMBLED as Dr. Bordais turned back to me, and I gripped the edge of the table to steady myself. She'd come. One of the Electi had found me! Mum had been right, and fate was finally showing its hand.

The air glowed blue around her, shimmering and pulsing as she moved. It was beautiful. So beautiful. Ghosts had told me I did the same, except my aura was shades of orange from pale peach to Fanta, and of course I'd never seen it.

"Hi," I choked out.

Dr. Bordais glanced sideways at Dr. Hastings.

"It's good to meet you, Iris. Thanks for agreeing to participate today."

"Okay. I mean, yes, you're welcome."

Dr. Hastings was looking at me funny, and I gave myself a mental kick. This was too important for me to screw up by doing something stupid. Something like breaking down in tears or whooping with joy. I swiped at my damp cheeks with my sleeve and plastered on what I hoped was a neutral expression.

"Where do you want to start, Dr. Bordais?" he asked. "Iris tires easily, so…"

It was nice of him to give me an excuse, but I didn't need it. Not today. "I'm absolutely fine, honestly. I slept really well last night."

"Great. That's great. I thought we'd start with some background information. My name's Nicole, and I'm running a genetic study in conjunction with the Institute of Human Genetics at the University of San Francisco." Sure she was. "A little research told me you might be a good candidate, and it seems I was right." Her eyes shone. "You're exactly the person I was looking for."

"And you're really a doctor?" She'd worn a suit, but she still looked kind of casual. And young. She wasn't much older than me. Maybe twenty-five or twenty-six?

"Yes, I really am. Not a medical doctor, but I have a PhD in genetics."

Wow. My sister was smart. And I say she was my sister because it was true. We weren't related by name, and not by blood either, but in spirit, I was her and she was me. Our souls had been split from one thousands of years ago.

"That sounds like a lot of work."

"It was, it *is*, but I enjoy it. Understanding the human body on a molecular level is fascinating, and there's so much left for us to learn."

"Like how DNA interacts with your psyche?"

She gave me a pleased smile. "It's still something of a mystery."

"And that's where I come in?"

"Exactly."

A shiver of fear ran through me. What if she genuinely did just want to use me as a human guinea pig? Although I felt a connection to Nicole, a weird energy I couldn't explain, I didn't *know* her. Was she here to help me, or just to observe?

"Mr. Calvert shared an outline of your clinical history, Iris... Can I call you Iris? Or would you prefer Miss McGivern?"

"Iris."

"Iris, good. So, I know the basics, but I'd rather hear some of this in your own words. Could you tell me about the ghosts?"

"Uh..." I shot a glance towards Dr. Hastings, who'd settled into a third chair at the head of the table. He was watching me closely, arms folded. "Uh, do you mean the stuff I said in court?"

"Yes."

"I, uh, I made all that up. My lawyer said if they thought I was insane, I'd get to come here instead of a regular prison." And like an idiot, I'd gone along with it —a decision I'd regretted almost as soon as I arrived at Lakeview.

"Interesting. Perhaps you could tell me about your thought—"

Nicole went into a coughing fit, and I wasn't sure whether to stay put or thump her on the back. The "No touching" rule glared back at me. For his part, Dr. Hastings didn't seem to have a clue what to do either. Finally, her coughs subsided, and she waved a hand.

"Excuse me. The air on the plane was so dry. I don't suppose I could get some water?"

"Yes, of course." Dr. Hastings got halfway to the door before he stopped. "I shouldn't really leave you alone with Iris. She...er..."

I smiled sweetly at him. "I promise I'll behave."

"We'll be okay," Nicole assured him. "I'm used to this now. Iris is the sixth participant in my study."

"If you're sure."

"We're sure," we both said.

"I'll be one minute. The water cooler's just along the hallway."

The door clicked behind him, and for a second, Nicole and I just stared at each other. Then she leapt up, ran around the table, and squeezed me in the tightest hug I'd ever had.

"Oh my gosh," she gasped. "I can't believe we finally found you."

"I can't believe you're here."

"And I can't believe that asshole Calvert let me in. I have no idea what I'm doing."

"Then you're *not* a doctor?"

"I'm a PhD, not a freaking psychologist! This study's total baloney. I'm making it up as I go along, but we didn't know how else to see you. They're really weird about allowing visitors who aren't family."

"Just don't make me talk about the ghosts. Please? I'm trying to convince them I'm not crazy."

"How's it working out?"

"Uh, not very well so far."

"Shit. Well, we have to say something about the ghosts because otherwise I have no reason for being here, and I need to come back. I'll try to follow your lead, okay?"

Footsteps sounded in the hallway outside, and Nicole hurried to her seat.

"Okay," I mouthed just as Dr. Hastings walked back in.

We both turned to look at him, and I hoped to goodness I didn't look as guilty as Nicole.

"Everything okay?" he asked.

"Fine," we answered in unison.

Shit, shit, shit. Now what? On the plus side, I knew Nicole was here to help me, but if I wanted to keep seeing her, we'd need to convince Dr. Hastings her study was real. Which meant admitting what I'd sworn to myself I'd deny.

That I saw ghosts.

He'd think I'd lost my marbles, but when the alternative was not seeing Nicole again... I had to do it, didn't I? It wasn't as if I'd be getting out of Lakeview anytime soon.

I opened my mouth to speak, but when Dr. Hastings focused on me, the words stuck in my throat. He was the only friend I had in here. Nicole wouldn't be able to keep the pretence up forever—how long did genetic studies take, anyway?—and over the next few months or even years, Dr. Hastings was the person I'd see day-to-day.

Short-term gain versus long-term pain. Which should I choose? Nicole had said she'd follow my lead. Did I deny, deny, deny? Or speak the truth, no matter what it cost me?

More than anything, I wished my mum was around. She always gave the best advice. I mean, she'd told me not to kill Leland Baker, but I thought I knew best, and look where that got me.

Dammit.

Nicole had to come first. She was my soul sister.

"Iris, are you all right?" Dr. Hastings asked.

Not even a little bit. "Uh, please don't be mad, but I fibbed again."

He took a deep, steadying breath and closed his eyes for a brief moment. "When?"

"Earlier, when I said I lied in court. About the

ghosts."

"I'm getting a bit confused. Do you think you saw them now or not?"

"I did see one or two, yes."

"Right. One or two."

His slow nod said he didn't believe a word I said, which I guess I couldn't blame him for. But his attitude still annoyed me.

"There's no need to be so patronising."

"I apologise—I'm not trying to be. I admire you for opening up. We can work together on this."

"I'd prefer to work with Nicole. Dr. Bordais, I mean. Her study sounds really interesting."

If I didn't know better, I'd have said that was hurt in his eyes.

"I'm not sure..."

"DNA is the building block of life, so it stands to reason that it can impact our minds." I smiled brightly. "And I've never participated in a study before. I might learn something."

"I'm not saying there isn't a genetic element to psychosis, but research shows that your illness is far more likely to be psychosomatic."

"I don't even understand most of what you just said."

Nicole stepped in. "He thinks that the ghosts you saw may have been your mind's reaction to external stress, such as your mother passing away."

"See?" I said to Dr. Hastings. "She speaks English rather than science."

"I'll make sure I simplify things in the future too," he promised.

"Great. You can start after the study's finished."

"You're certain you want to participate?"

"Why not? It'll be fun." I turned back to Nicole. "Where do we begin?"

CHAPTER 18 - IRIS

NICOLE UNCAPPED HER pen and made a show of writing the date and my name in her notepad. Her neat printing was far easier to read than Dr. Hastings's scrawl.

"How about we start at the beginning? Do you want to tell me when you first began seeing ghosts?"

Okay, here goes. I took a deep breath and jumped off the diving board, metaphorically speaking, since I hadn't seen a swimming pool in years.

"The first time was right after my eighth birthday. There was a boy on the pavement outside our house, and when we got close, he started yelling at me." Of course, I'd known it was coming. Cedric had been bitter since the day he died, and no amount of pleasantries from my mother could entice him into a pleasant conversation. "I ignored him, but over the next year, I began to see more and more spirits."

The ability faded in and out at first. Sometimes I could see the other world, and sometimes I couldn't. At the same time, Mum's powers diminished. Some days, we both saw the spirits together, and other days, there was nothing at all. Those were the best days. We'd make the most of the peace and go to visit the Tower of London and Marble Arch and Cheapside, the kind of places we usually avoided. Who wanted to see the spirits of headless noblemen or corpses swinging from the old Tyburn gallows or burned victims of the Great Fire? And we rode on the Tube instead of walking. The Tube had far too many spirits for us to face on a regular day, although they tended to be more modern. People pushed off platforms, stabbing victims with knives sticking out of their chests, a few mangled souls who'd died during the bombing and were now destined to spend eternity in darkness unless we could set them free.

"Same," Nicole muttered, then quickly corrected it to, "Yes, that's the same as I've heard from others."

Dr. Hastings looked at her funny, and I quickly continued.

"And it wasn't really a problem until a man killed my mother. I could deal with all the nameless ghosts as long as I didn't stop to talk to them, but then she was there too, stuck unless I did something about it."

"It must have been difficult for you."

"Yes, I mean, she told me she'd be okay, that I should forget her, but how could I? Every night, I went to sleep thinking of her by the side of the road, and by the time Baker got out of prison, I just couldn't deal with it anymore. Did you know he spent less time locked up than I have?"

"Justice isn't always fair."

"Exactly. And there he was, walking around, getting on with his life. My mum *had* no life. And worse, it should have been me killed that day. Every Friday, I walked to the fish-and-chip shop to get us dinner, but that week, she offered to go because I was busy planting asparagus crowns."

I'd never eaten asparagus again.

"So you...ran him over?" Nicole asked.

"Yes, and now she's free."

"How do you know she's free?" Dr. Hastings asked, and Nicole glared at him.

"That's not important for the study. What's important is that Iris believes, which makes her a perfect candidate. Maybe we could take some DNA samples now?"

Absolutely. Being poked with a needle was more fun than having my life torpedoed.

"Sure."

Except she didn't use a needle. Instead, she wiped around the inside of my mouth with a fancy cotton bud and sealed it into a plastic tube.

"I'm borrowing some lab space in the UK, so I'll get this analysed as soon as I can."

I worked my jaw around. "That thing tasted funny."

"There wasn't anything on it."

"There definitely was. Something kind of bitter." Was it me, or was I getting better at the lying thing? "Dr. Hastings, can I have a drink? And you said you'd get me more food if I was hungry. I'm starving."

Nicole gave him an encouraging nod and drained her cup of water. "I wouldn't mind a refill either."

"I can get an orderly to step in."

"No need. We'll be fine here for a few minutes."

"We're not really supposed to—"

"Mr. Calvert told me you were short-staffed at the moment, so I completely understand that it's difficult. We'll just sit here and chat. I'll save any study-related questions for when you come back."

"I won't be long, but I'll have to go to the vending machine in the break area."

"Here..." Nicole rummaged in her handbag and handed him a twenty-pound note. "Could I get a snack too?"

The instant the door closed, Nicole slumped in her chair. "This is so hard. Thank goodness I'm not speaking to someone who's genuinely ill. I'd set their recovery back months."

"You're doing great. Nice touch with the twenty-pound note, by the way. He'll have to go and find change."

"I didn't even think..."

"Then you're a natural." We both giggled, and I reached out to touch her aura. My hand went straight through the haze, and it didn't feel any different. No fizz, no crackle, nothing.

"You're blue," I told her. "It's so pretty."

"You kinda look as if you're on fire."

"So I've heard. I never saw the aura when my mum had it."

"Me neither. It's weird that we can't see our own colours."

"That's just the tip of the iceberg when it comes to our weirdness, though. Will you genuinely use that cheek-swab thing?"

"Hopefully. I really am doing a research project, but the small sample size makes it difficult to draw conclusions. Technically, you're not meant to eat for at least half an hour beforehand, but if the swab doesn't have enough cells, at least that gives me an excuse to come back. Or I could take a blood sample, but I'm more used to doing that with rats and the occasional monkey. Professor Fairchild's been helping me to prepare, and my boyfriend too because he's used to doing undercover work, but..."

"Professor who?"

"Professor Fairchild. My supervisor. He was the first person I confided in about the ghosts."

"And he believed you?"

"It's a long story. Basically, his wife got murdered, and now I have to relay messages about dry cleaning and remind him to pay the household bills. Darlene's a sweetheart—she's been helping me to improve my cooking skills. I'd only mastered the basics before."

That all sounded so...normal. And Nicole was dating somebody? "I'm not the best cook in the world, but I can do apple crumble and cupcakes. Does your boyfriend know too? About your abilities?"

She nodded. "Can you believe he thought I was the sceptical one? There I was, doing my best to act normal around dead people, and when I tried to deny the afterlife existed, he told me I should be more open-minded."

"Wow."

"Exactly. Until I met him, I'd only had the professor to talk to, but with Beck... It's different, but a good different."

"I found talking about ghosts caused more problems than it solved. How do you think I ended up in this place? My roommate's a freaking dead girl, and the only way to stop her jabbering is to put reality TV on twenty-four-seven. It's frying my brain."

"We're gonna get you out of here."

"How? I tried escaping once, but I got caught, and now I'm not allowed outside."

"I don't know yet, but we'll bust you out if necessary."

"'We'? You mean you and Professor Fairchild?"

She choked out a little laugh. "No way, not him. Me and the others like us. And my boyfriend'll help. He used to be an Army Ranger, so he's used to getting in and out of places he shouldn't."

I froze. Every atom in me stilled for a second. "Wait. Wait! The others? You found them?"

"Earlier this year in Las Vegas. They were on vacation, and I was searching for my ex-boyfriend because he'd stolen my gold necklace, and—" Her turn to stiffen. "Do you still *have* your gold piece?"

"Not here, but it's safe."

"Thank goodness." She let out a long breath. "We know they're important, but we don't know why."

"My mum said when they're put together, they activate additional powers."

"What? What powers?"

"That's a bit of a mystery. Original me forgot some stuff when I was running for my life."

"Running? Why were you running?"

"Death squads... Persecution... You don't know any of this?"

"No! All we know is the basics—that we're supposed to kill killers to set souls free."

"Flippin' heck. Your past self had worse memory problems than mine. Okay, so when the Judge got murdered—"

"The judge? What judge?"

"You don't even know who the *Judge* is? But you said you found the others?"

"I found the other two Electi, but—"

Footsteps sounded outside. Two sets, but one carried on along the hallway. I'd gotten good at listening to footsteps over the last few years. Orderlies dawdled in rubber-soled shoes. Nurses walked with more purpose. Doctors preferred fancy footwear that clicked rather than squeaked. Dr. Hastings favoured brogues, and unless I was very much mistaken, it was him outside the door.

Never in my life had I wanted to be wrong more.

But I was right. Dr. Hastings balanced the tray on one hand while he opened the door, then set it on the table with a flourish. Had he been a waiter in a past life?

"Sorry, the water cooler's malfunctioning, so this is slightly tepid. I wasn't sure what flavour crisps you both liked, so I got ready-salted." He dumped a pile of coins onto the table. "And here's your change."

I was almost too fidgety to eat. A mixture of excitement and fear bubbled through me as Nicole turned the conversation back to the mundanities of DNA. Excitement because Nicole was there, and she'd also found two out of the three missing pieces. That the Judge was still AWOL was a disappointment but not a surprise. It was *his* soul that'd been reassigned to a new line. Chances were, he didn't realise who—or what—he was.

The fear? Now I was more scared than ever about being stuck at Lakeview, not just because a killer was roaming free, but because I might miss out on whatever my sisters were doing without me. Knowing that they were together and happy was almost harder than remaining in the dark.

And now I had to sit and fill in a bloody questionnaire about my background. Was this Professor Fairchild's idea? Had I suffered from any childhood illnesses? *No*. Did I have a family history of high blood pressure? *No*. Could I be pregnant? I had to laugh at that one.

I hoped Nicole would come up with another excuse to get rid of Dr. Hastings, that we'd have a chance to talk further because there was so much we needed to say. But as I reached the bottom of the sixth and final page of questions—Had I ever knowingly been exposed to radiation? *No*.—he looked at his watch. A cheap digital one, I'd noticed. He might have dressed smartly, but he wasn't pretentious.

"I think we'd better call it a day, Dr. Bordais."

"I actually have a few more things I'd like to discuss."

"I'm sure you'll understand that it's not good to tax the patients. It's been a difficult session for Iris."

"No, it hasn't," I told him. "I'm perfectly all right."

"As your doctor, I need to act in your best interests, and we've done enough for this afternoon."

"Why do you have to be such a party pooper?"

"It's important for you to get enough rest. If Dr. Bordais feels she needs a follow-up session, she can apply for one in the normal way."

"But—"

"I'm afraid I also have other commitments I need to attend to. Dr. Bordais, I'll arrange for somebody to show you back to Mr. Calvert's office."

No, no, no. I still had so much to say to Nicole. She had gaps in her knowledge, that much was clear, and I could help to fill some of them in. And she needed to know about Jacinda, and Rylie, and—oh, yeah—the person who'd freaking killed them.

"Can I please have another cup of water?"

"We can stop at the water cooler on the way up to your room."

Why was he being so pushy? Normally, Dr. Hastings didn't clock-watch or hurry me. Was it these other commitments he'd mentioned? What if he'd heard something about his dog? Obviously, I wanted him to find Teddy, but not if it meant losing the chance to spend time with Nicole. I kicked at the table leg in frustration, then bit my lip because my toes hurt.

"I'll see you soon," Nicole whispered as an orderly escorted her from the room.

"Okay," I choked out, my throat dry. I hadn't been joking about the water.

As Nicole disappeared in one direction, Dr. Hastings led me in the other, back towards the lift. He paused long enough for me to gulp down a cup of lukewarm water.

"Dr. Bordais seems interesting," he said.

"Of course she's interesting. She's a scientist. Talking to her beats watching a bunch of Z-list celebrities cavorting around an island."

"You seemed a little...fidgety."

"If you want me to stop fidgeting, get me a cushion. Have you ever tried sitting on one of those stupid plastic seats for longer than half an hour?"

"Unfortunately, yes. Iris, I'm not sure she's a good person for you to be around."

"Was that why you shooed her out of the room?" I realised I was taking my upset out on the wrong person, and a twinge of guilt hit me. "I appreciate your concern, honestly, but I can pick my own friends. Researchers, I mean."

I didn't even get a smile as he held the door to my

room open for me. "We can discuss this further tomorrow."

"Did you find your dog?"

"No, not yet."

CHAPTER 19 - MARCUS

WHAT THE HELL was Dr. Bordais playing at? *Was* she even a doctor?

There was a Dr. Nicole Bordais listed on the University of San Francisco's website, alongside a Professor Fairchild—I'd checked on my phone while I waited for her to come out of the building—but there was no picture, and therefore no guarantee that this was the same person. Why would she impersonate a renowned geneticist? And what did she want with Iris McGivern?

Dr. Bordais didn't notice me as she walked towards her car, a silver Prius with a sticker from a rental agency in the back window. I'd found the registration number in the visitors' book, and she was too busy looking at her phone to see me standing next to the vehicle. Checking in with these mysterious "others" she'd mentioned?

"Oh, I'm sorry." She got a foot from treading on my toes, then looked up abruptly. "Did I forget something?"

"I think that's my question?"

"Huh?"

"Did you forget to tell me why you really wanted to speak to Iris McGivern?"

She tried to sidestep me, but I moved too and

blocked the door. The part of me my mother had brought up to be a gentleman hated intimidating a woman, but needs must. Nicole Bordais wasn't who she claimed to be, and I intended to get to the bottom of the mystery before she did lasting damage to Iris.

"I explained about the study. It's to do with the genetics of—"

"I know what you *said*. But I want the truth. Is your real name even Nicole Bordais?"

"Of course it is! Look..." She rummaged around in her handbag and thrust a Vermont driver's licence at me, plus an ID card for the University of San Francisco. Hmm. She *was* Dr. Bordais. "See?"

"Yes, I see. Then why are you trying to make my patient lose her mind? Is that part of your 'study'?"

"I don't know what you're talking about."

"Let's see, shall we? Your boyfriend's going to break Iris out of Lakeview, there's a gold trinket involved, death squads, persecution, and something about killing killers. Did I miss anything out?" Nicole had a California tan, but somehow she managed to pale to an interesting shade of porcelain. "I don't know what your game is, but you're not coming near Iris again, no matter how many times you flutter your eyelashes at Doug Calvert."

Even as I said the words, I knew I was lying. I couldn't overrule Calvert, not if she kept paying his "admin fees," which I strongly suspected was a euphemism for "golf-club membership fees." My only hope was that Dr. Bordais would believe I had more power than I did.

"How did you...? But you left...?"

"There's an observation room, remember? After I

nipped out the first time, Iris seemed remarkably unsettled. So when an orderly offered to help out with the refreshments, I thought it'd be a sensible idea to see what you were up to, and it's a good thing I did."

Dr. Bordais slumped back against the car and sort of slithered down the side. I couldn't exactly let her hit the deck, so I caught her and helped her awkwardly into a sitting position, propped against a wheel. Honestly, this case had me perplexed. If it wasn't Iris herself doing the unexpected, it was a connection doing something downright inexplicable. From the way the two women had spoken in the meeting room, I could've sworn they knew each other, but Iris herself had told me she had no family or friends left. And I'd checked the visitors' log in her file. She hadn't lied about that—nobody had been to see her apart from the court-appointed advocate. Or rather, advocates. She'd been through three during her stay, and all of them appeared to have done the bare minimum.

Iris had been forgotten by just about everyone.

Except, it seemed, Dr. Nicole Bordais.

Who closed her eyes and groaned. "I'm sorry. I'm so sorry. Hell, I've messed all of this up."

I'd expected her to deny everything, at the very least. To tell me I'd been mistaken in what I saw. She'd been so cool inside, so composed, but now... It appeared that Dr. Bordais was as unpredictable as Iris. She opened her eyes again, but this time she focused on her knees rather than meeting my gaze.

"What's going on?"

"Where do I start?"

"How about at the beginning?"

"I don't even know the beginning. That's part of the

problem."

"You didn't turn up here today by accident."

"No, of course not. There were months of research, and a few false starts, and... I feel sick."

Excuse me if I didn't break out the sympathy. "Why Iris?"

"I... I think we're related. Sort of."

"How can you be sort of related? Are you adopted?"

"It's complicated."

"Luckily for you, my speciality is complicated."

And also maintaining composure in difficult situations. Underneath, my blood was boiling. Although Iris had seemed calm when we walked up to her room, who knew what long-term effects this afternoon's meeting would have on her? I'd only caught part of the conversation, and that had been bad enough. Shocking, in fact. Shocking that a so-called professional would have so little respect for a vulnerable young woman. And shocking that Doug Calvert would have allowed her to visit in the first place. How many other patients had he sold access to?

"I'm not sure where to start. It's a really long story."

One that I needed to hear, but I wasn't due to finish work for another hour. I didn't have any more patients to see, but there was a ton of dreaded paperwork to do.

"Is everything okay?" a voice asked from behind us. I swallowed a groan as one of the nurses came into view. Monica? Anneka? Something like that. I'd only spoken to her a handful of times, small talk in the break area.

Dr. Bordais smiled up at her. "I just felt faint for a second, but I'll be okay."

"You should sit down, love. Not on the ground, I

mean. It's about to rain."

I saw an opening, and I took it. "Excellent point. Why don't you come and sit down in my office?"

"Oh, no, I'll be just fine. I really need to leave."

Monica/Anneka swooped in and took her arm. "That's not a good idea. You shouldn't be driving if you're feeling faint. Here, I'll help you inside, and we can get you a hot drink with some sugar in it. When did you last eat?"

"Around a half hour ago."

"Have you had an episode like this before?"

"No, never."

"Hmm... Maybe we could get a doctor to check you over? You're not pregnant, are you?"

"What? No!"

"I'm a doctor," I pointed out. "I'll take care of our visitor."

"No, I—"

"Now, now, safety first." Monica/Anneka half lifted Dr. Bordais to her feet and wrapped an arm around her waist. "Let's get you somewhere more comfortable. Lean on me if you don't feel steady."

Dr. Bordais was soon settled into the visitor's chair in my office. She'd recovered from her shock, it seemed, and now her eyes were sharp, assessing as she studied my bookshelf.

"I'll be right back with that drink," Monica/Anneka said.

Don't hurry. "Thank you, Nurse."

"Ooh, call me Jennifer." Well, I'd been close.

She left, and I leaned my chin on my hands as I studied our duplicitous friend from the other side of the desk. "So, let's talk."

"I'd rather not."

"Why? You seemed keen enough to chat with Iris earlier."

"Because once you've heard what I have to say, you'll probably lock me up in here too."

"Will you *please* just tell me what's going on?"

"I'm not sure there's much point. Iris already tried, and it's clear you don't believe her."

"Iris has a history of lying." Whoever wrote that note in the margin of her file had been absolutely correct.

"No, Iris backs off the truth when she thinks it's something you don't want to hear."

"How can you possibly know that? You only met her an hour ago. Or did you?"

"I did. I swear we've never crossed paths before. If we had, she probably wouldn't be in this situation."

"The situation you blithely promised to get her out of. Giving her false hope like that borders on cruel."

"We *will* get her out of here. Maybe I was a bit gung-ho with my breaking-her-out comment, but this isn't where she belongs."

"I'm afraid I beg to differ. Iris shows evidence of a mental illness that I'm not at liberty to discuss the details of, no matter what Mr. Calvert may have told you."

"She told you she sees ghosts? That's not a mental illness. It's just part of who she is."

"Seeing things that aren't there is an indicator of a schizo-affective disorder."

"Not necessarily."

"With respect, Dr. Bordais, your expertise is in genetics, not psychiatry, so you may not be the best person to make a diagnosis."

Especially on my damn patient. I'd spent over a decade training, yet some jumped-up scientist from California who might have read a book or two thought she knew better?

"In this case, I'm absolutely the best person to make a diagnosis."

"How on earth can you claim that?"

Dr. Bordais shrank back, and now that I'd asked a difficult question, a little of the steam seemed to go out of her. She considered for a moment before taking a deep breath. Preparing for another lie?

"Because... Because I see ghosts too."

She sat back, arms folded, and I imagined I resembled some sort of fish the way my mouth gaped. How on earth was I meant to respond to that? Now I had two delusional women to deal with, and this one had a PhD.

Shit.

What should I do? Recommend a good psychiatrist?

"That's... That's not what I was expecting."

"Of course it isn't. People like you want to believe they're open-minded, but in reality, you're closed off to anything you can't see with your own eyes or read in peer-reviewed journals."

"There's no evidence ghosts exist."

"On the contrary. There's evidence, but the world isn't ready to see it."

"What evidence?"

"So far? We've found they emit low levels of high-frequency electromagnetic radiation that concentrates when they're in groups, and there's also a possible DNA link."

Ah, now we were getting somewhere. "That's why you needed Iris? To be part of your little experiment? Is the University of San Francisco even aware you're doing this?"

"Uh, this one's kind of off the books. Mostly, I do research into the ageing process."

"And who's 'we'?"

"Huh?"

"You said '*we've* found.' Who's 'we'? You and this Professor Fairchild?"

"Yes, and some others."

Good grief. This was turning into a full-blown conspiracy theory. Next thing, she'd be telling me they lived in a former fire station, had a pet ghost named Slimer, and designed proton guns in their spare time. Probably accessorised with tinfoil hats too.

What was I supposed to do? Much as I thought Dr. Bordais belonged in the room next to Iris, I couldn't lock her up. Lying to Doug Calvert wasn't a crime, and it wasn't her fault he was stupid enough to believe her. Should I inform the university that one of their researchers was performing unsanctioned studies? That was a tricky one. Dr. Bordais had the feel of Iris about her—smart and determined yet also fragile. Losing her job could have a detrimental effect on her mental state, and as long as she stayed in her lab where she belonged, she probably wasn't going to do much harm.

"I suggest you and your friends make sure that in future, you keep well away from people like Iris. You may also want to consider seeking therapy for yourself. Now, give me whatever samples you took, and if you promise not to come back, we'll draw a line under this."

"I already told you, we can't leave her here. She's not crazy, and if you were as smart as you seem to think you are, you'd already have realised that."

Ouch.

Although when I put my feelings aside, there was an element of truth to her comment. Iris had issues, certainly, and she needed ongoing support, but she wasn't the lost cause Doug Calvert claimed. Part of me wanted someone to fight for her. And then there was the added issue of people dying at Lakeview. I didn't want Iris to be next.

"What do you plan to do?"

"Get her a good lawyer to start with."

"Lawyers are expensive." I knew that first-hand.

"We have money. Hey, maybe we'll get her a new psychiatrist too."

Another jab to the ribs. "She doesn't need a new psychiatrist."

"She needs someone who'll fight for her rather than against her."

"I'll do whatever's best for Iris. If transferring her into a low-security facility or even supported housing is the most appropriate option, then that's what I'll recommend."

"So you'll help?"

"I'll help *her*. But I can't do that if you're working against me."

"We don't want to work against you, honestly. But if you keep on thinking we're delusional, it'll make everything a hundred times harder."

"You're asking me to believe in ghosts?"

"I'm asking you to believe in Iris." Dr. Bordais sat

up straighter, head tilted to one side as she thought. "Hey, we're both doctors, albeit different kinds. We both believe in testing, don't we?"

"We do."

"So test Iris."

"Test Iris? How?"

"There's a ghost in her room."

"Ah, yes. Jacinda."

"She's told you about her?"

"She did, and then she retracted the story."

"Exactly. Telling you what you wanted to hear. But Jacinda's real, I assure you. Although..." Dr. Bordais rubbed one eye as she paused again. "Although I don't understand why Jacinda's there. I guess she must've died back before this building was modernised. Sometimes, the older spirits are difficult to communicate with. You have to speak slowly and carefully and avoid slang. Well, usually. Iris said Jacinda watches a lot of TV, which is weird."

"Jacinda died recently," I offered. It seemed as though the two women had discussed more than I thought before I slipped into the observation room. "Not long before I began working here, in fact. I'm sure she understands slang just fine."

I gave my head a little shake, checking myself. By talking about a ghost as if she were a real person, I was only feeding into Dr. Bordais's fantasies. Which was dangerous. How dangerous was quickly revealed when she paled once again. Her knuckles turned white as she gripped the arms of the chair.

"Who killed her?"

"Nobody killed her. She died of heart failure in her sleep."

"No. No, no, no. If she died of natural causes, her spirit wouldn't be there."

"Did Iris tell you that?"

"No, she didn't. There are rules. Rules that the spirit world has to follow. The only way a person's ghost can stay on earth is if they were killed by another. And if everyone here believes Jacinda died in her sleep, then that means her killer's still free because nobody's even looking for them." She locked her gaze onto mine. "What? No condescending comeback?"

Her story was disturbingly similar to Iris's. Was she being honest when she said they hadn't discussed it beforehand? Because that meant... No. Ghosts couldn't possibly be real. But the part about a woman being murdered... Perhaps there was a grain of truth in it. A spidery chill ran up my spine.

"I'm trying to remain professional here," I told Nicole.

"Then do your job. Test Iris. Prove that what she says is true."

"How?"

"Simple. When Iris is out of her room, go in there and tell Jacinda something Iris couldn't possibly guess. Jacinda will relay the message, and then you can ask Iris what you said."

Much as I hated to admit it, that was a simple, straightforward protocol. And Iris would leave her room to take a shower tomorrow morning. If nothing else, participating in Dr. Bordais's experiment would prove I wasn't losing my mind, because at times, she was so convincing I began to doubt myself.

"Fine. I'll do it."

"Quickly. You need to do it quickly. There's a killer

on the loose, which means Iris is in danger, and we don't have any time to lose."

CHAPTER 20 - MARCUS

ALTHOUGH IT WAS well within my rights, it seemed decidedly underhanded being in Iris's room without her present. I felt stupid too. Even stupider than I'd felt yesterday when I walked around the neighbourhood for the third night in a row, calling Teddy's name and waving a bag of particularly pungent cheese in the hope that he'd smell his favourite treat and come bounding up to me. An elderly neighbour had passed me a cup of tea out of the window and wished me luck, but her tone suggested I was wasting my time.

Perhaps I was *still* wasting my time.

First, I checked Iris's room thoroughly for a recording device. How was I to know whether or not this was some sort of elaborate plan cooked up by her and Dr. Bordais to trick me? Iris may not have had visitors, but it wouldn't be beyond the realms of possibility for Dr. Bordais to bribe a member of staff to sneak a dictaphone inside. Rumour—Bobby—said that one of the patients had been caught with cannabis not so long ago.

But there was nothing besides the most basic of possessions. A handful of dog-eared paperbacks, none of them hollowed out, three sets of hospital-issue clothes, and the remote for Iris's new TV. That still had the factory seal on it. The plants seemed to be thriving, at least, and the orchid was in full bloom.

Outside, black clouds darkened the sky, and rain splashed onto the windowsill. It'd been pouring since Dr. Bordais left yesterday, which seemed about right given the current state of my life.

"Uh, Jacinda? We never actually met, but I'm Marcus Hastings—Iris's doctor—and I was wondering if you'd be able to pass a message on?"

Good grief, I was talking to thin air. If anyone caught me...

"This is demented," I muttered, making sure to face the bed. That was where Iris had said Jacinda hung around, wasn't it? "Er, could you tell her my favourite movie is *The Matrix*, and I detest avocados. Thanks."

I backed out of the room, grateful to find the hallway empty. The sound of the shower came from around the corner, and I strolled in that direction to find Glenda standing guard outside the room, her back to the door. Much as I hated to admit it, she scared me a bit. A ball-buster, Bobby called her.

"Yes?" she asked, challenging.

"Iris has a counselling session at two. You won't forget to bring her?"

She stared me down, hands on hips. "Have I ever forgotten a session before?"

"No, I was just checking..."

"It's on the schedule."

"The schedule. Yes. Got it."

I practically ran back to my office.

***

Stop tapping your foot, Marcus. I'd arrived in the

meeting room at five minutes to two, and despite Glenda's earlier assurances, she was running late. Was I going to chastise her for it? Of course not. I liked my testicles where they were, thank you very much.

Finally, the door opened, and I forced myself to look at Iris. How was she holding up after yesterday's examination by Dr. Bordais?

"*The Matrix*? Really?" Her eyes gleamed as she sat. "The first part was okay, but two and three were a let-down."

Quite honestly? I felt as though someone had attacked me with a defibrillator. I froze, and she laughed.

"You shouldn't relay messages if you don't want to hear them. I'm with you on the avocados, though. Slimy balls of mush."

"How did you do that?" Had I missed a microphone somehow?

"You know how." She reached across and patted me on the hand. "You're just in denial, but don't worry, I get that it's difficult for you. It's not every day you realise there's a whole other world out there that you can't see."

"There has to be a logical explanation for this."

"Oh, sure, like I wired my room for sound? You already checked. Jacinda told me that too."

"This can't be..."

"You know, for a man who allegedly listens to people for a living, you're not very good at hearing."

Have you ever had a moment where your whole world flips on its head? Where up becomes down and down becomes up? How could we have missed this for so long? That humans weren't the only ones walking the earth? That souls existed independently of their bodies? If what Iris and Dr. Bordais were telling me was true, everything we knew about people and matter and life itself needed to be re-evaluated.

"Ah, now you believe it." Iris nodded, grinning. "Poor old crazy Iris isn't so crazy after all. But I'm curious—what made you speak to Jacinda in the first place?"

"Dr. Bordais," I blurted out.

"Really? After you practically shoved her out of the room yesterday, I thought you'd decided she was bad news. I'm not sure whether to be happy you spoke to her or insulted because you believed her when you didn't believe me. Just because I don't have a fancy title doesn't mean I'm stupid."

"I never thought you were stupid, Iris. Not for a minute."

"But you thought I was a liar and completely cuckoo."

She sang the last word, whirling two fingers by the side of her head, and I realised we might have a bigger problem. If ghosts existed, then Iris was totally sane. And if she was sane, that meant she was quirky and outspoken and also a cold-blooded murderer. She'd killed Leland Baker in a quest for revenge, not because she'd been hallucinating. A sliver of a memory came back to me. Hadn't Dr. Bordais mentioned something about killing killers?

Shit.

Now I was forced to look at Iris through different eyes. So many lies became truth, and I didn't quite know what to make of it. I needed help, but not the kind I could find amongst my colleagues at Lakeview.

Before she left yesterday, Dr. Bordais had given me her card, together with a promise that she'd assist in any way she could once Iris had been proven right. I needed to call her straight away.

"We'll need to cut today's session short, I'm afraid."

"What? Why? But we have stuff to talk about now. Like these stupid pills you have me on, and Nicole's study, and what about all the dead people around here?"

"Iris, please. I need to process this."

"Can't you multitask? When's Nicole coming back?"

Soon. It had better be soon because I wasn't sure I could deal with this alone. "I'll call her."

"Good. Go do it. Can I have another flapjack?"

"I'll see what I can find."

"You know, you were right about one thing when you spoke to Jacinda. This *is* demented."

CHAPTER 21 - IRIS

WHEN I GOT to the meeting room on Wednesday afternoon, there were three chairs at the table again, and my heart jumped. Did that mean Nicole was coming too? I wanted Nicole to come. She'd managed to talk sense into Dr. Hastings once, and I needed her to do it again. People were dying. We didn't have time for him to mull things over and analyse every damn word I said.

The door opened, and I only just managed to stop myself from rushing forward to hug Nicole. The relief that she'd come back... My legs turned to jelly because until that moment, I'd harboured a niggling doubt I'd ever see her again.

"Is anyone watching?" she asked, and Dr. Hastings shook his head. Nicole took that as a sign and hugged me, even as he muttered, "We're not meant to have physical contact."

"Rules, schmules," I told him. "Not crazy, remember? Therefore I can make up my own mind about who I want to touch."

He didn't have a lot to say to that. Good. We took our seats, and he placed a tray with three plastic cups of water onto the table. I reached out and touched mine. Lukewarm again.

"Where do we start?" he asked. "I'm afraid this goes

well beyond my usual remit."

Excellent question. There was so much to say, and Nicole and I had barely scratched the surface yesterday. How much should we discuss in front of Dr. Hastings? Not the really freaky stuff, for sure. He might have grudgingly accepted the existence of ghosts, but the whole Electi thing would most likely blow his oh-so-academic mind. Right now, I had two goals. The first was not to die, and the second, the one I wasn't sure was even possible, was to get the hell out of Lakeview. Nicole's offer to break me free was sweet but not particularly realistic. I'd heard that since my last attempt, they'd increased security somewhat.

"I want to leave here alive," I said.

"We're working on it," Nicole assured me. "While I'm here, the others are finding you a decent lawyer. From what we've seen, yours didn't do a great job of representing you."

"He was rubbish, but I couldn't afford to hire a better one."

"Could we just clarify 'others' here?" Dr. Hastings asked. "Who are we working with?"

Nicole listed them out, counting on her fingers as she went. "Me, Kimberly, and Rania. We're the others like Iris."

Kimberly and Rania. I knew their names now. Not their faces, but their names. Where were they from? "Rania" sounded kind of unusual.

"My boyfriend, Beckett, and Kimberly and Rania's guys, Reed and Will," Nicole continued. "Plus Will's friend RJ, Reed's sister, Emma, and her boyfriend, Wyatt. They all got involved during some previous, uh, incidents. And then there's Professor Fairchild that you already know about."

"So only four of you see ghosts?" Dr. Hastings asked. "That's all?"

Nicole nodded. "Rania calls it a curse, Kimberly calls it a gift. And yes, I always thought there were only four of us, but now... Iris mentioned another person."

"The Judge?"

I looked sharply at him. "How do you know that?"

"He eavesdropped on our conversation," Nicole said. "From the observation room."

He what? How many times had Dr. Hastings said he wanted to help me? I'd lost count, and to think I'd actually begun to trust him! Instead of helping, he'd betrayed me.

"You're such an asshole," I told him.

"I was worried about you. After I came back into the room the first time, you looked distinctly uncomfortable."

"Yes, because you were there and I wanted to talk to Nicole."

"Well, I didn't know that."

"Perhaps you should have asked?"

"Would you have told me the truth?"

No. "Maybe."

Nicole stepped in to mediate. "It's in the past now. We should move on and work together."

She focused on Dr. Hastings as she said that. Work *together*. Did she consider him part of the team? Or a potential spanner in the works?

"Yes, quite," he said. "We're all on the same side here. I don't want to see anyone else get hurt, but my hands are somewhat tied if you two are working from a different agenda."

I got his point. I didn't want to see anyone else get hurt either, especially me.

"Fine, okay, we'll share." Some stuff, at least. Information for Dr. Hastings was on a need-to-know basis only. "The judge... He's sort of like us, but not exactly the same."

"You're going to have to elaborate."

"Like, we have one, uh, purpose, and he does something slightly different but similar."

"You've lost me."

Nicole sighed. "We have to tell him."

Had she lost the bloody plot? Was Lakeview contagious?

"You think? He's barely on board with the ghosts."

And he kept giving me odd looks, which was kind of annoying since it wasn't my fault I could speak to the dead.

"Tell me what?" he asked.

Nicole took over, and I might have rolled my eyes. On her head be it. Dr. Hastings was a sceptic temporarily inhabiting a believer's body.

"Me, Iris, Rania, and Kimberly are called the Electi. Thousands of years ago—we don't exactly know how many—we were created to maintain order on earth. Our job is to hunt down people who've taken the life of another, and if we decide they're not good at heart, we're meant to kill them so their rotten souls can't be reincarnated. But we totally don't do that," she added hastily. "Well, except Iris, but that was only the once. And Rania, but she's stopped now. And there may have been a couple of other little accidents."

Judging by Dr. Hastings's expression, he didn't know whether to run from the room or reach for a syringe of the good stuff. He couldn't lock Nicole up, could he? I mean, there was a legal process to follow, and she didn't say *she'd* killed anyone.

"I-I-I don't really know what to say to that."

"It's not the easiest concept to understand, but it's true. Just like it's true that ghosts exist."

Oh, in for a penny, in for a pound. "That's why there're so many ghosts around," I said. The Electi should stick together, right? "They're supposed to help us to solve their murders, and once we dispatch the bad guys, the ghosts are free to leave. Except they're all still here because we haven't been killing people. Apart from my mum—she's not here anymore. At least, I hope she's not. I was never able to check on account of I got arrested. But I couldn't risk leaving her by the side of a road for eternity—I just couldn't—and Leland Baker never even said he was sorry. He was still drinking and driving too. I know because I followed him for weeks before I ran him over. It was only a matter of time before he murdered someone else."

"I... Well..."

I tried not to smile because there wasn't anything remotely funny about the situation. It was just weird seeing a man who specialised in talking speechless for once. Dr. Hastings looked like a guppy. When I was a kid, the orthodontist had a tank of guppies in the waiting room. He started off with half a dozen, but they soon multiplied into hundreds, and then the tank was gone and Mum told me they'd gone to guppy heaven. I cried and cried, and then I yanked my removable brace out and threw it in the bin. That was why my front teeth were still a bit wonky.

"The Judge?" Nicole prompted. "What does he do?"

Oh, right. The Judge.

"He judges us." Wasn't it obvious from the name?

"Judges *us*?"

"If he believes we've done everything we can to find a killer and either failed or decided the person should live for whatever reason, he can release the trapped soul."

"Oh my gosh." Nicole's eyes shone with excitement. "We thought they were stuck here forever. But how do we find the Judge?"

"I'm not totally sure. I only know that when the four of us are together, it should be possible. Maybe fate'll lend a hand? After all, we've found each other now, even if I'm locked up in here."

"That has to be our first priority—getting you out."

"There's actually a slightly more pressing problem. People keep dying."

Nicole's hands flew to her cheeks. "I know, I know. You're right. Dr. Hastings told me about Jacinda yesterday."

"And Rylie?"

"Who's Rylie?"

"Rylie Draper," he said. "And there's also Mandy Horner, Lee Sorensen, Claire Welby, plus two others whose names I haven't managed to find out yet."

The three of us stared at each other.

Holy fuck. Dr. Hastings had mentioned seven possible victims, but now some of them had names, identities, that made it all the more real. I'd been nervous when it was just Jacinda and Rylie, but five others? I'd never felt quite so helpless as I did at that moment, knowing I was a sitting duck. Was this how ghosts felt too? Trapped in one place, totally reliant on others to spare them from their fate?

Guilt lapped at the edges of my fear. Maybe I *should* have tried harder to do my job.

"Were they all killed by others?" Nicole asked, a tremble in her voice.

"All accidents, apparently, but so were Jacinda's and Rylie's deaths according to management, and now you're telling me otherwise."

"Why would they lie?"

"Trying to avoid a scandal, I expect. Lakeview's a private facility. They have shareholders to answer to."

They were covering up murder for money? I felt sick.

"I *really* need to get out of here. I never did karate or judo or any of those things as a child. Well, apart from one self-defence course when I was fourteen or fifteen, but I didn't even finish it."

Day two, the instructor had tripped over my foot and broken his arm, and that was the end of that.

"We'll make a plan," Nicole said. "Dr. Hastings—"

"I think we've gone beyond Dr. Hastings now," he muttered. "Call me Marcus, for goodness' sake. I can't even begin to pretend that this falls under my professional responsibilities."

"And you'd better call me Nicole. Marcus, can you restrict access to Iris?"

"I already did so. After she told me she was attacked —"

Nicole gasped. "You were attacked?"

"She later said that she wasn't."

"I was."

Dr. Hastings—Marcus; was *I* supposed to call him Marcus?—nodded. "I thought as much. Iris, if you want my help, you have to stop lying. Trying to follow your thought processes is giving me whiplash."

"Sure, I can do that. Now that you know my big secret, I've got nothing to hide."

But I still kept my fingers crossed under the table, just in case.

"Who attacked you?" Nicole asked.

"An orderly, but don't worry. I bit his ear off."

"Wow, well done."

"Thanks."

"Can we get back to the plan?" Marcus prompted. "I appreciate this is important, but I've got other patients to see, and I'm an hour behind on paperwork thanks to yesterday's distractions. As I was saying, I requested only female nurses should attend to Iris. I'm not sure I can narrow it down much further without arousing suspicions, and even if I did, there must be fifty people with universal key cards. Any one of them could get into Iris's room, and short of standing guard outside, I've got no way of stopping them."

Nicole didn't look pleased by that. "I guess standing on guard isn't feasible?"

"Not in the slightest."

"Could you schedule extra therapy sessions?"

"Perhaps one or two, but I can't neglect my other patients. Nor can I afford to lose this job."

"Why?" I asked. "You're not a bad psychiatrist, way better than Dr. Tillis anyway, and no offence, but this is a pretty crappy place to work. Surely you could go somewhere better? Not that I want you to leave or anything," I added.

"That's not an option, unfortunately."

"Why?"

"It's a long story."

"I've got all day."

"But I don't."

"How about overtime?" Nicole asked. "Could you work overtime?"

"Some unpaid, possibly. But definitely not Fridays, and I also have a missing dog to look for."

"Why not Fridays?"

"He sees his daughter on Fridays. Right?" I looked to him for confirmation.

"Yes."

Nicole did sympathy much better than me. "You're not with her mother anymore? I'm so sorry."

"I'm not sorry." He grimaced and, unusually, didn't even try to hide it. "It's all part of the long story. But I do need to see my daughter. I don't get enough time with her as it is."

"Okay, so Fridays are out. But the other days? We can help to look for the dog."

"Maybe you could hire him a private investigator?" I suggested.

"Rania, Will, and Reed *are* private investigators, although they normally work murder cases for obvious reasons. And they've already started digging into Jacinda's background. I'll get them onto the dog hunt right away. The overtime?"

Marcus slumped back into his chair. Was it me, or had he aged markedly over the last week? This thing was taking its toll on both of us.

"Okay, I'll do the overtime."

"Thank you," I whispered.

Chapter 22 - Marcus

WHAT THE HELL had I just got involved with?

Not only had I agreed to cover for Nicole with regard to her bullshit study, but now I needed to spend my days and apparently part of my evenings watching over Iris, all without raising my colleagues' suspicions.

That shouldn't be too hard with Doug Calvert, at least—he spent most of the time skiving, and according to Nicole, he'd promised her access for two hundred and fifty pounds a session, transferred to an unnamed bank account. I didn't know who was bankrolling this enterprise, but she hadn't batted an eyelid at the cost.

"Will you come in tomorrow?" Nicole asked as I walked her out to her car.

"For a few hours, yes. I'll say I need to catch up with paperwork, although people around here seem remarkably lax about following the proper procedures. Iris's file— Actually, you don't need to know any of that."

"Can you meet with her?"

"I'll think of something."

Some sort of intensive short-term treatment, possibly. In my old job, that would have required approval, but at Lakeview... I got the impression Calvert didn't care what his staff did as long as the service users didn't give him any trouble.

"While you're here, we'll work on the rest of the case. If more people died, there must be a record. And can you give me the details of your dog? Do you have a photo?"

"Several hundred. I have no idea how to explain Teddy's disappearance to my daughter."

"Could you tell her he's at the veterinarian?"

"That might work for a day, but what about next week? And the week after?"

"We'll get him back; don't worry. I called Rania while you were taking Iris to her room, and she's gonna go and look for witnesses this evening."

"I already did that. Nobody saw a thing."

"She means *dead* witnesses. It's amazing what people see when nobody realises they're watching."

Dead witnesses. Of course. I really had stepped into the twilight zone. But if they helped to get Teddy back, did I really care where the information came from? Honestly? No.

Outside, it was still chucking it down, and the car park didn't just have puddles, it had a lake spreading across the bottom corner. A lone Renault Clio sat in the middle of the water, a shiny red island in the storm. As I watched, a couple of ducks swam past. Nobody was in the smoker's shelter to the side of the building, so I nipped in there with Nicole while we exchanged email addresses and I sent the information over—Teddy's pictures, my home address, and Laurel's too.

"If I had to name a suspect, it would be my wife. Tread carefully with her, though. She doesn't take kindly to being crossed."

"You're still married?"

"We can't finalise the divorce until we agree on the

custody arrangements and financial settlement, and so far, that's proving difficult. I want more time with my daughter, and Laurel wants everything."

Unfortunately, I wasn't joking. Her list of demands had included my wedding ring, a canoe, the treadmill she'd never once used, and a whole bunch of kitchen utensils she had no idea what to do with. With the amount of rain we were having, I'd be fighting her for the canoe, but she could have the wedding ring with pleasure. My time with Laurel had put me off marriage for life. Sometimes, it was hard to admit to yourself that you'd made a mistake, and I'd persevered for longer than I should have in the hope that we'd be able to go back to the way things were. But for that to happen, both people had to want it, and Laurel was more interested in her lifestyle than in me. Spa days, dinner dates with her girlfriends, yoga, Pilates, getting her chakras realigned. Towards the end, I'd basically been a cash machine, a babysitter, and someone who looked fitting on her arm at parties. She'd liked the idea of being Mrs. Doctor Marcus Hastings far better than the reality.

The life she'd chosen made her fake outrage at finding me in bed with another woman all the more insulting.

My phone vibrated, interrupting the bad memories, and I fished it out of my pocket. Unknown number.

"Do you mind?" I asked Nicole.

"Go right ahead."

I turned up the volume to hear over the rain and pressed the phone to my ear.

"Marcus Hastings?"

"Who is this?" If it was yet another person trying to

sell me an online investment plan...

"Sergeant Custer with the Hertfordshire Constabulary. I'm afraid I've got some bad news."

Funny how the bottom could drop out of your world in an instant, wasn't it?

"Has something happened to my daughter? Or is it my dog?" Teddy wore a collar with my name and phone number, plus he was microchipped with all my details. If he'd been run over or fallen down a—

"No, no, nothing like that. It's about your house."

"My house? I've been burgled?"

Thank goodness. There wasn't a whole lot left in the house. I'd sold the treadmill and most of the other stuff Laurel wanted on eBay to pay for my lawyer. The canoe had been listed for months now, but with the local roads more like rivers, I was strongly considering keeping it.

"Not many burglars out in this weather." The sergeant chortled, then seemed to catch himself. "Er, yes. It's actually a sinkhole that's opened up on the road right outside, and part of your driveway's collapsed. There's a structural engineer assessing things at the moment, but it's not safe for you to come home tonight."

"Is this some sort of joke?"

"No joke, sir. Do you have family you could stay with?"

"My mother lives in Spain."

And that was all the family I had left. No brothers, no sisters, and my last grandparent had passed away when I was seventeen. Mother would welcome me, but travelling to Costa Daurada was impossible given the goings-on at Lakeview. And now a sinkhole? Somebody up there was laughing at me.

"A friend, perhaps?"

Thanks to Laurel, I didn't have any of those left either.

"I'll sort something out. Any idea when the place'll be accessible again?"

"Afraid not. I'll ask the engineer to give you a call once he's taken a look."

Did anything else want to go wrong? At least I still had my car, although being six feet tall, folding myself into the back seat to sleep would be a tad uncomfortable.

"Bad news?" Nicole asked.

"Part of my driveway just fell into a sinkhole. Honestly, you couldn't make it up."

"No way! I heard something about that on the radio on my drive over here. Holes are appearing all over the area. The guy said developers keep building new housing estates on old mines without checking the ground properly first. You're not allowed home?"

"Not tonight, at least. I'll have to find a hotel."

"Rania and Will have a spare room if you need a place to sleep? The rest of us are already staying with them, so I doubt they'll notice one more."

"But they barely know me."

"No, but Iris does, and we trust her judgement."

"I wouldn't want to impose."

"It won't be an imposition. You're helping us out, and we should help you too. If there's one thing I've learned over the past six months, it's that a team can get much more done than people working alone."

Did I want to stay with these people? They were strangers, emphasis on the strange, but from a professional point of view, it could be fascinating. Two more necromancers... And they didn't seem to be dangerous. Even Iris herself had never done more than lash out with her sharp tongue. Plus I'd save money, money I didn't have in the first place.

"How far away is the house?"

"About forty minutes? Probably less for you. I drive real slowly. I had an accident a while back, and I still get nervous behind the wheel."

"If you're sure..."

"I'm sure. Give me a minute, and I'll call to let them know you're coming."

***

Three hours later, I pulled into the driveway of a rather nice bungalow beside Nicole's Prius. The driveway was pretty full already, and I had to block in an SUV.

"Will moved his car to RJ's," Nicole said, getting out and bleeping the locks. "The Mazda's Rania's, and Kimberly and Reed rented the SUV."

"Does RJ live nearby?"

She pointed to a tall brick house just visible through the trees at the back of the bungalow. "Right over there, in Tech Tower. We call this place the White House."

Normally, I never got nervous meeting new people, but the last few months had taken their toll on my body and my mind. I needed to practise what I preached to my patients and focus on the positives. Rationalise the negatives and understand that things weren't as bad as they first appeared. What was the worst that could happen? That they wouldn't like me. And what impact would that have? Possible discomfort for a few weeks until we got this Iris mess sorted, and then they'd be out of my life.

I could handle this.

Nicole had a key in her hand, but the front door opened before she got the chance to use it. A tall, blond-haired man filled the doorway, and a cold sweat popped out on the back of my neck. This guy could have stepped out of a Marvel movie. He stooped to kiss Nicole as she walked in, and I mean stooped. He was at least a foot taller than her.

"Marcus, this is Beck, my boyfriend."

Beck held out one massive paw. "Good to meet you."

Thankfully, he didn't try to crush my hand. "Likewise."

"Will and RJ went to interview a lawyer, and Shannon's at work, but the others are here."

"Who's Shannon?" I whispered to Nicole as we followed Beck further into the house.

"RJ's girlfriend."

"Does she know about the...er..."

"The ghosts? Yes, but they freak her out, so she prefers to pretend they don't exist."

I might not have met Shannon, but I identified with her more than anyone else in that house. "That seems like a remarkably good idea."

Nicole just laughed. "We all wish we could do that sometimes. But there are no ghosts here. Will bought the house as a surprise for Rania, but he researched it beforehand to check nobody died on the property."

There must have been more money than I thought in private investigation. If Will had bought this place, he couldn't have been short of a bob or two. Having spent weeks checking property prices before coming to the conclusion that I couldn't afford to buy anywhere for the foreseeable future—not when I was paying the mortgage on the house Laurel still lived in as well—I estimated that it couldn't have been worth much shy of a million. With that sort of money around, no wonder Nicole hadn't balked at Calvert's admin fee.

"Is your home haunted?" I asked Nicole, trying not to gawp.

"Not my current one. My old place had a ghost outside the front gate. Herman. I miss talking to him sometimes. And Kimberly has Margaret in her living room."

"Isn't that a little...intrusive?"

"Not really. We all like Margaret." She bit her lip. "If this Judge thing is true, we'll be sorry to see her go."

"*If* it's true? *You* think Iris might be lying?"

"I hope not. And it makes sense. We've always wondered why whoever created us didn't include some way of clearing out the older ghosts. Once their killers have died, we've got no way of righting the wrong, and the spirit world's getting really crowded. Did you know there are two soldiers standing in the parking lot at Lakeview? They've both got gunshot wounds."

"How do you know they're soldiers?"

"They're wearing uniforms."

"They keep them when they die?"

"The spirit form's like a freeze-frame of a person's final moment. They keep their clothes, their hairstyle, and any wounds they received. Every time I go out, I get a history lesson. Back in the thirties and forties, people never used to leave the house without looking their best, but now..." Nicole shook her head. "The other day, I met a girl who'd been run over outside a Walmart, and she was wearing pyjamas."

"Do they follow you around?"

"They can't. They're tethered to the spot where they died forever. Or sometimes an object, if it's big enough. A car or a bus or a plane. It's as if their energy interacts with the surroundings and forms some kind of bond."

A red-headed child toddled out of a doorway to Nicole's right, and I gave a start. Who was she? Nobody had mentioned children.

She pointed at me. "Who dat?"

Nobody got a chance to answer before a dark-haired lady strode out behind her and swung her up onto one hip. If I had to guess, I'd say it was Rania, and she regarded me with undisguised curiosity.

"You must be Marcus?"

"That's right. Rania?"

She didn't offer a hand, merely nodded. "Yes. And this is Aisling."

"Your daughter?" Hard to believe since they looked nothing like each other, but I hadn't met Will yet and genetics sometimes did unexpected things. Iris was proof of that.

"No, Shannon's daughter. I look after her when Shannon and RJ are out."

My breath hitched as Aisling reached out and grabbed my jacket sleeve, now damp from the rain. Her giggles reminded me of Cassie at that age. Damn, I missed my daughter. A day and a half until I could see her, and if my house wasn't accessible, I'd need to call Jacqueline and ask her to meet me at a café or something. She'd bitch about that, just like she bitched about everything.

"Where are Kimberly and Reed?" Nicole asked.

"In the kitchen."

Rania seemed to be a woman of few words. Guarded, that was the best way to describe her.

Not so with Kimberly. Two more different people, I couldn't imagine.

"This is Marcus?" she asked Nicole, hopping off the stool she'd been sitting on at the kitchen island. The man opposite her was chopping carrots, but he put the knife down as we approached.

I held out a hand, but she ignored it and stood on tiptoes to kiss me on the cheek. I didn't miss the instinctive flash of jealousy in the other man's eyes. Reed, presumably. But he quickly smiled.

"Marcus Hastings," I said.

Kimberly did the introductions, polite, practised, and I began to wonder if some of the money came from her. Her appearance said socialite, and her demeanour said heiress. "I'm Kimberly, and this is Reed Cullen. Good to finally meet you. How's Iris?"

"Holding her own. Has Nicole brought you up to speed on everything that's happening?"

"We had a discussion over dinner yesterday. Do you eat lasagne? That's what we're making tonight, but if you don't like it, we can find something else."

"I'm good with lasagne."

"And when Kim says 'we're making,' she means Reed's doing the hard work while she makes the plates look pretty," Beck said, eyes twinkling.

"I can cook if you want," she offered.

Reed shook his head. "Not a good idea, sweetheart."

"I burn things," she explained.

I'd worried about fitting in, but they made it easy.

Half an hour later, Will and RJ walked in through the back door, followed by flame-haired Shannon soon after that. Once I'd met her, there was no mistaking who Aisling belonged to. As well as the hair colour, the little girl shared her green eyes and her attitude with her mother. Although she called RJ "dada," I didn't see anything of him in her, looks-wise, and I wondered if he was her biological father. Earlier, Rania had referred to the little girl as Shannon's, but not as RJ's.

Relax, Marcus. Sometimes, I wished I could stop analysing people. It was a bad habit.

"How did it go with the lawyer?" Rania asked as Kimberly slid a plate of food in front of each person. Beck had been right about the presentation. The spread looked like something out of a magazine. I'd never met anyone who used a table runner in real life before. Even Laurel's mother made do with a white tablecloth and whatever place mats she'd decided were the fad that week.

"We hired him," Will said. "He's gonna request Iris's file from her old lawyer as soon as she signs the paperwork."

"Do you think he'll hand it over?" Nicole asked.

"Apparently, the Law Society guidance says he has to provide most of it—any correspondence sent to him while he was acting on Iris's behalf, and any letters or documents prepared at her expense belong to her."

RJ shrugged. "Even if he doesn't, we'll still get the stuff, so don't worry about it."

The way he said that, nonchalant, made me think that the methods he intended to use should the need arise perhaps skirted the bounds of legality. Did that bother me? A month ago, I'd have certainly said yes, but having seen the way Iris and my other patients were treated in Lakeview, I was no longer convinced that the guidelines provided for their care were adequate. And maybe that sketchiness applied to other areas of the law too.

"I just want to get her out of there," Kimberly said. "I hate the thought of her being locked in a room while we sit here eating dinner." She turned to me. "Is the food at Lakeview good?"

"It could be better."

"Can we take food in for her? What about other stuff? A phone? Can we give her a phone?"

"Residents aren't allowed mobile phones, and rooms are searched weekly. But you could add money to her commissary account."

"Then I'll do that. How?"

"Wait a second," Will said. "We want to keep this investigation quiet for now. Iris doesn't normally get visitors, and if you add a thousand dollars to her commissary account, somebody's gonna ask questions."

"Really?"

Reed squeezed Kimberly's hand. "Will's right, sweetheart. You're already paying towards the lawyer, and that's the best thing you can do to help her right now."

"I can get her snacks from the vending machine," I offered. Technically, eating in the meeting rooms was banned, but like so many things at Lakeview, nobody cared. "But I'm her doctor, so I can't be seen to be playing favourites."

Kimberly got up and fetched her wallet, then passed me a hundred pounds in crisp twenty-pound notes.

"Here. Buy snacks for all of your patients."

"You don't have to give me this." Pride made it difficult to take her cash, even though I needed it.

She just waved a hand. "Keep it. I just wish there was more I could do, but I'm not a detective or a genetic genius. Normally, I organise weddings."

Many revelations had surprised me over the past week, but that one didn't.

"You've already done more for Iris in three days than anyone else has done in years."

Chapter 23 - Marcus

"YOUR HOUSE FELL into a sinkhole?" Iris asked. "Are you kidding? I thought you said it was bad to lie."

"I only wish I was kidding. It wasn't my house, just part of my driveway, but I'm still not allowed to go home."

Now that I understood more about Iris's mental-health issues, or rather the lack of them, there wasn't a need to tiptoe around her psyche quite so lightly. Yes, she was still fragile from being incarcerated for years, but without medication unbalancing her and secrets to keep, she was just a regular—if somewhat unusual—person. And one I'd now need to deal with six days a week, as per the treatment plan I'd discussed with the nurse manager earlier. An experimental protocol, I'd explained, based on intensive short-term dynamic psychotherapy.

ISTDP aimed to help patients overcome internal resistance to experiencing true feelings, but the methods were controversial as they involved triggering painful or forbidden emotions in order to show the patients how to deal with them. Death threats were common. Indeed, some practitioners encouraged patients to describe their proposed methodology in graphic detail. I'd given Iris a briefing on what to tell other staff members should anyone question her on what we were doing, and she assured me she'd shout every so often and add in some tears to throw off any suspicion.

I'd also got change for one of Kimberly's twenty-pound notes and raided the vending machine, and right now, Iris seemed quite happy to munch on crisps and chocolate while we chatted.

"Wow. That's shitty. Part of our roof blew off in a storm once, but me and Mum put a tarpaulin over it as a temporary fix. And one of our neighbours was a roofer, so he fixed it at the weekends around his other jobs in exchange for babysitting and help with his garden. What will you do? Fill the hole in?"

"The landlord's looking into it." For the first time in my life, I was glad to live in rented accommodation. "He says he's got insurance, but given that it took him two months to get the gas safety inspection done, I don't hold out much hope it'll be fixed quickly. Plus there's heavy rain forecast for another week, and the council's worried about more holes appearing."

"They're probably scared of getting sued if someone walking along the pavement gets swallowed up. Do you think that could actually happen? How deep is your hole?"

"At least ten feet by all accounts. I haven't been back to look yet. And yes, it could happen. Bobby showed me a story on the internet about a chap in Florida whose bed fell into a sinkhole as he slept."

They never did recover the body, and Bobby had been entirely too cheerful about the whole thing. I only hoped the situation at my place didn't worsen. While I might have been willing to take a risk on myself, Cassie wasn't going anywhere near that house until it got the all-clear.

"Chap?" Iris said. "You're so posh. Did you go to a private school?"

"No, the local comprehensive."

"Really? So did I, but we didn't have 'chaps,' just dudes and fellas. Maybe it's because you're older. How old are you, anyway?"

"Does that matter?"

"Not really. Our souls are thousands of years old, so who cares about a decade? Does it still freak you out when I mention that stuff? I can stop if you want."

I smiled without thinking, then caught myself. Natural Iris was an idiosyncratic mix of sweet and headstrong, and talking with her made the fact that today's overtime was unpaid easier to bear.

"I'm getting used to it." Not only had I stepped into the twilight zone, I'd pulled up a chair and taken a seat. Last night over dinner, the others had spoken about the ghosts as if they were regular people, but apart from that, the group had seemed remarkably normal. "And I just turned thirty-one. That's eight years older than you, not a decade."

"More like seven. It's my birthday next week. Maybe you can get me one of those rubberised cupcakes from the vending machine?"

"I'd better not tell Kimberly. She'd probably try to send a three-tier affair with candles."

"You've met them all now, huh?"

"I stayed at Will and Rania's house last night. I was going to find a hotel room, but then Nicole offered, and that was where I ended up."

Iris fell silent and leaned forward, her face hidden behind her hands. Up until then, she'd been breaking off tiny pieces of chocolate and nibbling them, but now she stopped.

"What are you thinking?" I asked.

"Doesn't matter."

"I'm here to listen."

"You'll think it's stupid."

"I very much doubt that."

"It's just..." Iris glanced up at me, chewing her lip. She was much less guarded with her emotions now, and her eyes glistened. Shit. What had I said? "It's just you're there, and I'm in here. Those are supposed to be my people, and... Told you it was stupid."

Sadness and a little jealousy—both perfectly natural reactions. "It's not stupid in the slightest. They *are* your people, and they're working very hard to get you out of here." I took a deep breath. "We all are."

"But how? How can they do that?"

"I won't deny it'll be difficult. We'll have to prove you're well enough to live in the community with support and not reoffend, which given some of your actions—however justified—might be a struggle. It also takes time."

"How much time?"

"First, you'd have to spend a while on the hospital grounds with a staff member. Then on your own, and after that, you'd go out into the community with one of us. If that all went well, you'd be moved to a supported living facility. Each step would have to be approved by Mr. Calvert and the Ministry of Justice, and your final release would need to be agreed to by a mental-health tribunal."

"I can go outside again?"

Dammit, she looked so hopeful, and I hated to dash

those hopes.

"Not at the moment. I, er, I suggested that to Mr. Calvert several weeks ago, but I'm afraid he vetoed it for now."

From happiness to utter dejection in five minutes flat. Being with Iris sure was a roller-coaster ride.

"Don't give up, flower." Flower? Fuck. "We're not giving up. And he didn't say anything about inside. Want to go for a walk around the hospital?"

She raised her head slowly. "You'd take me?"

"Just try not to trip me up, okay? You seem somewhat..."

"Accident prone?"

"Exactly."

"Mum always used to say that too. I'd come through gymnastics practice totally unscathed, and then fall over the doorstep on my way into the house. Or the cat. Did you know I used to have a cat?"

I shook my head.

"He was called Screech because he used to make this awful noise whenever he wanted to come inside. We didn't buy him—he just turned up one day and adopted us. When I went into foster care, one of our old neighbours took him on, and I sent him treats every month until I got arrested. Did you find your dog? I should've asked earlier, but I'm not very good at this. Talking to people, I mean. I don't get much practice anymore."

Her honesty was refreshing. "No, not yet. But..." How much did I want to tell her? "But Rania snuck around the neighbourhood last night and found a... ghost? A spirit?"

"Either will do."

"Right, yes. She found a spirit in the alley behind my house, and we know who took him."

"Let me guess—your wife?"

I nodded. Rania had apparently conversed with a young lady murdered during the construction of the housing estate twenty years ago, something that hadn't shown up on any of my searches before I moved in. It wasn't the best area, I knew that, but I'd still been somewhat shocked at the news. The thought of walking down the alley to put the rubbish out gave me the chills now. Anyhow, the girl had seen a blonde woman open my back gate and tempt Teddy out with treats on the evening he'd disappeared. Her description fitted Laurel to a tee—thin with poker-straight hair, wearing stilettos even in the most inappropriate of situations. Laurel was five feet three, and her stature had always bothered her. Apparently, Teddy hadn't particularly wanted to go with her, but she'd slipped a lead over his head and dragged him. Even now, my blood boiled from thinking about it.

"If you know where she lives, can't you just go and get him back?"

"If only it were that simple."

"You *don't* know where she lives?"

Of course I did. I owned the damn house; I just wasn't permitted to live in it. "I do."

"Then go ask her for the dog back. She stole him."

"Firstly, she wouldn't keep him at her house. She knows that's the first place I'd look." Laurel was many things, but stupid wasn't one of them. Vindictive, spiteful, petty, but not stupid. "And secondly..." I might as well tell Iris. This discussion had already gone far beyond a doctor-patient relationship, and while I realised I should pull it back to a more professional level, I wasn't sure I wanted to. That thought scared me slightly. But not enough to stop. "Secondly, I'm not allowed within a hundred metres of her."

I could almost see the cogs whirring in Iris's brain. She wasn't stupid either. If I had to put money on it, I'd say she was actually smarter than Laurel.

"She has a *restraining order*?"

"She lied to get it. Stood in court and lied that I was violent and she was scared of me."

"Without any evidence?"

Unfortunately, no. "I went over to the house. There was an argument. She pushed me, I pushed her, and she fell against the table in the hallway and a vase broke. She told the judge I threw it at her, and her father plays squash with the judge's brother, so..." My turn to put my head in my hands. The court order was on my record now, which would make getting a new job even more difficult. Laurel was determined to leave me destitute. I'd always thought that was counterproductive, but if she had a rich boyfriend now, perhaps she simply didn't need my money anymore. "I'm not proud of what I did, not proud at all, but she's on a mission to make my life hell, and so far, she's succeeding."

Iris reached out and pried one hand away from my face. "Hey, don't get upset. If you get upset, she wins."

"I try not to. But she's already won every battle so far. She's taken my house, my job, my little girl, and now my damn dog."

"Karma's gonna kick her butt in the end."

"Does karma exist?"

"Honestly, I have no idea. That's beyond my remit.

But a lot of stuff happens that we don't fully understand, and I'd like to think karma's a part of that."

"So would I." I forced myself to focus, to turn the conversation back to something bordering on proper. "How about that walk around the hospital?"

CHAPTER 24 - IRIS

WOW. MARCUS'S LIFE was almost as screwed up as mine, and seeing as I was locked away in a psychiatric hospital, that was saying something. A restraining order? Seriously? Yes, I hadn't always been the best judge of character, but he wasn't a freaking monster, and it was obvious how much he loved his daughter. I was curious as hell about the details, but he clearly didn't want to discuss it any further so I let it lie.

For now.

How could she steal his *dog*? I got angry just thinking about it.

Calm, Iris.

This was the first time in I couldn't remember how long that I'd been allowed to walk somewhere other than to the shower or a meeting room. To anyone else, the hospital may have been full of stark white hallways and weird noises and nasty smells, but to me, it was an adventure. From the outside, Lakeview was a beautiful building. Some famous Victorian architect had designed it back in the days when asylums had been intended for recuperation and recovery. In another life, it could have been a posh hotel or luxury apartments, and one of the nurses—a lady long since retired—had told me that when it was first built, Lakeview had been home to a working farm, a bakery, and even a brewery.

These days, alcohol was banned, although one orderly kept a hip flask in his trouser pocket and swigged from it when he thought nobody was looking.

Inside, it was ugly as fuck, the cheap modern refurb done by somebody with no imagination whatsoever, but if you looked up, the old moulding still edged the walls, and occasionally, there was a ceiling rose that hadn't been replaced by strip lights. And then there were the cobwebs. Those probably hadn't been brushed away since the eighteen hundreds either.

"What's Rania's house like?" I asked as we walked, speaking quietly so nobody would overhear.

"Rather splendid, actually." That was good, but also depressing. Marcus gave me a sheepish smile. "Sorry."

"No, I want to hear about it." He didn't look convinced. "I'm a big girl. I can cope."

"Whether you like it or not, I'm still concerned about your welfare."

And I appreciated that. Really. Although nobody had cared for so long, his concern felt like a favourite jumper that had shrunk in the wash. Comforting, but at the same time, it didn't quite sit right.

"Please?"

He considered for a moment before coming to the right decision. "It's not huge, but it's a nice size. Lived-in rather than a show home. There's a little girl who comes over—the daughter of a friend of theirs—and the garden's full of her toys. There's even a swimming pool in a building at the back, but that's still being renovated. They only moved in last year."

A swimming pool? I hadn't seen so much as a bath in years. What I wouldn't give to float around on my back, staring up at the sky, doing nothing but whatever

I pleased.

"How long will you stay there?"

"Until I can find an alternative. They've been remarkably understanding about the situation. Rania said something similar happened to her in the past, so I suspect there's a touch of empathy at play."

"Tell me more about Rania and Kimberly?"

"Rania's quiet. She prefers to observe rather than speak. And Kimberly's the most outgoing of the bunch. Very organised. Did Nicole mention she works as a wedding planner?"

"A *wedding planner*?"

"Shhh."

I lowered my voice. "Sorry. That's just the last thing I'd have imagined her doing. But I never imagined she'd have a boyfriend either. That any of them would have boyfriends. Mum always said that it was impossible for us to have proper relationships."

"Why?"

"Because of the secrets we had to keep."

"She didn't tell your father about her abilities?"

"She didn't even tell my father her name."

When I was fourteen and getting old enough to understand about the birds and the bees in a non-horticultural sense, she'd sat me down one night over fish and chips—our weekly vice—and told me a little about my origins. She'd always known she needed to have a child to pass her Electi abilities to because she couldn't bear the thought of an unknown girl suddenly being lumbered with powers she didn't understand, but the traditional meet, date, marry route was out of the question. Outsiders couldn't handle our secrets, she always told me. But she'd wanted to give me a good start in life, so she'd gone on a mission to find me the best genes she could.

Nicole would have been proud.

In her younger days, my mum had been the adventurous type, and when she turned eighteen, she'd set off to see the world. Following in my grandma's footstcps, shc said. My grandma had perished under an avalanche in the French Alps at the grand old age of forty-three. Mum had spent one ski season in Zermatt, then headed for warmer climes, working her way from one destination to the next with a series of cash-in-hand jobs. Somehow, she'd ended up waitressing in a bar just around the corner from the stadium during the Commonwealth Games. More by alcohol than luck or judgement, she'd ended up doing the nasty with a member of the men's gold-medal-winning gymnastic team, and I was the result. From time to time, I'd looked my father up on the internet back when I still had a computer. He'd retired from competitive sport after an Achilles tendon injury, and now he spent his days advocating for action on climate change while working as a human rights lawyer. Nicole would probably laugh her head off if I told her.

"I'm sorry to hear that," Marcus said.

"Don't be. I doubt he'd have wanted me if he knew I existed."

"I'm sure that's not the case."

"I wasn't exactly planned." We turned a corner just as the sun broke through the clouds and shone through a window up ahead. I paused to let the sunbeam rest on my face, basking in the warmth. "What about your parents? Are you close to them?"

"My father died of a heart attack, which was

somewhat ironic considering he was a cardiac surgeon."

"I'm so sorry."

"It made for a difficult few years, but it happened almost a decade ago. I've had time to adjust. My mother sank into a depression, but I convinced her to take a holiday, one of those group tours, and she ended up marrying the owner of the hotel she stayed in. Love at first sight, she claims. I'm not sure I believe in that, but I'm glad she's happy again."

"Do you get on okay with your stepfather?"

"I've only met him a few times, and he barely speaks English." Marcus shrugged. "He seems nice enough."

Footsteps came in our direction, and Marcus straightened, moving back a couple of feet before a nurse came around the corner. I wrapped my arms around my body, straitjacket-style, and did my best to look unhappy.

"How are you feeling, Iris?" Marcus asked. "I realise this is a big step for you."

"Kind of...I don't know? Anxious? How long do I have to stay out?"

"If you feel overwhelmed, just let me know, and we can go back."

I recognised the nurse. Paula? No, Paulina. She'd brought my dinner a few times, and she always seemed friendly but nervous. No doubt my reputation preceded me.

"Afternoon," Marcus said.

She nodded and smiled, but stayed on the far side of the corridor. "Everything is okay, Dr. Hastings?"

"Yes, Iris is doing well today."

I breathed a sigh of relief as Paulina carried on past us. Not that we were doing anything wrong at that moment, but I was all too aware that Marcus was skirting the boundaries of what was appropriate, and I didn't want to get him into trouble. If he got into trouble, I'd be on my own again.

More than that, I'd be on my own *without him*. Lately, some of *my* thoughts had been skirting the boundaries of what appropriate as well.

"We'd better not stay out too much longer," he murmured. "I'd rather not invite difficult questions."

"Shall we head back?"

"We can take the longer route."

I followed Marcus away from the light, into a gloomy hallway I'd never been in before. He held a door open for me, shepherding me through with a hand on the small of my back. He didn't seem to notice he'd done it—probably just being gentlemanly, as usual—but shivers ran up my spine from the contact. Was it because I'd gone so long without a human touch, or... or...

"Wait," he said.

"What?"

"That's the prayer room."

"And? I'm...well, not exactly an atheist, but I've seen enough of the other side to know that all the major religions have got it wrong."

He pointed at a set of stairs right in front of us. "Mandy Horner's our first suspected victim, and Bobby told me she died when she fell down the stairs next to the prayer room."

Oh. "Then where is she?"

"She's not here?"

"Nope, this place is dead. Sorry, that was a terrible joke."

"So either her ghost somehow vanished, or she was never here in the first place."

"Ghosts can't just vanish. No way. It's impossible without one of us doing our thing, and we all say we didn't, so..."

"What about the Judge?"

"I don't think he can release them alone. Is there another prayer room?"

"Not that I know of. From what I understand, management pays lip service to religion the same way as it does to most of the other guidelines, which is why the prayer room is out in the proverbial sticks."

"Then Mandy died of either a genuine accident or natural causes."

I wasn't sure whether to be pleased she hadn't been bumped off or disappointed because our theory about the Lakeview deaths being linked didn't hold water.

"That's good news."

"Yes, it is, isn't it?"

"Iris, are you okay?"

"I don't know, I just... I was so sure this was all connected."

"Could it be that Lakeview just has a terrible safety record? If Jacinda Warren had been given an accidental overdose, would that still count as a wrongful death?"

"I guess, but what about Rylie? Someone came into the shower, smashed her head against the tap, then legged it."

"I can't explain that one."

"We need to check the others. Do you know where they died?"

"According to the newspaper, Lee Sorensen died in St. Anthony's Hospital, but as for the rest, I haven't got a clue. I only heard about Mandy by luck."

"Can you find out?"

"Subterfuge doesn't exactly run in my blood. I'm not sure where I'd even start. And if they died in their rooms, then we're scuppered. I can't just walk you in to visit another patient."

"But can you *try* to find out?"

Marcus sighed and looked down at me. "Yes, Iris, I can try."

CHAPTER 25 - MARCUS

WHEN I ASKED Jacqueline to bring Cassie some clothes suitable for horse riding, I'd meant a pair of leggings, not an outfit worthy of Charlotte Dujardin at the height of her Olympic career. Why did a six-year-old need to wear a show jacket and a hairnet?

Cassie seemed to feel the same way.

"I look stupid," she whispered as Jacqueline marched back to her car. "Nobody else in my lesson wears this stuff."

We'd met at Starbucks for the handover because I didn't want Jacqueline's negative energy anywhere near Will and Rania's home. *Negative energy.* I was sounding more like Iris every day.

"You look very smart," I told Cassie.

"Mummy says it's important to dress for the job we want." If that was the case, Laurel would be working as a mannequin in the Louis Vuitton store. "But I want to be an astronaut."

"I'm not sure astronauts ride horses."

"Why?"

"Horses can't go into space."

"Why?"

"There aren't any spaceships big enough."

She took a moment to consider. "Then I'll ride horses on my days off. Like you go running on your days off."

Originally, I'd only done that to get peace from Laurel, but I found I quite liked the exercise.

"That's a great idea, sweetie."

While Cassie climbed onto her booster seat in the back, I rummaged around in the boot of the car. All sorts of junk got shoved in there, and I hadn't had time to clear it out for weeks. Thank goodness—there was one of Cassie's sweaters, slightly grubby, but still better than a fancy jacket the other kids would laugh at. And they *would* laugh. I knew that because my mother had sent me to tennis lessons channelling Pete Sampras while the other kids wore football strips or tracksuits.

Kids didn't need expensive clothes to be happy.

I'd planned to take Cassie to the floodlit crazy-golf range after her lesson, but as we were walking to the car, the heavens opened, and that idea floated away into the gutter. What else could we do? Sit in a café? Find an indoor play centre?

"I'm hungry," Cassie announced.

"What do you want to eat?"

"Pasta. With cheese, the way you make it, but I don't want to go to your house."

"Why not?" Not that we *could* go, but I was curious.

"Grandma told me your house has a big hole in the garden, and if more holes happen, they could swallow me up." Cassie lowered her voice to a nervous whisper. "She said it's *dangerous*. I don't want you to get eaten, Daddy."

Gee, thanks, Jacqueline. I made every effort not to bad-mouth her and Laurel in front of Cassie, and she repaid me by scaring my daughter.

"It's just a little hole, sweetie. Not dangerous at all.

People are filling it in right now, but how about we go for pizza while they work?"

"I don't want pizza. Rupert made me eat pizza yesterday and it was yucky. The cheese had black bits in, and he said it was *mould.*"

She stuck her tongue out and gagged, and I thanked *The Bachelor's Guide to Cooking* that I'd managed to get at least one thing right. It also gave me a certain satisfaction to know that Cassie had inherited my dislike of blue cheese.

"But he said we can go to Disney in Paris for my birthday next year," Cassie continued. "And he'll buy me a princess dress and whatever food I want."

Dammit. I was fighting a losing battle, wasn't I?

It made my decision easier, though. If Cassie wanted cheesy pasta, I'd make her cheesy pasta. Somehow. I tapped out a message to Will.

Me: Any chance I could borrow your kitchen to make my daughter some dinner?

The reply was almost instant.

Will: The more the merrier.

Cassie's eyes widened when I pulled into the driveway beside Kimberly's SUV. "This house is almost as big as Rupert's. Did you buy it?"

"It belongs to a friend of mine. I'm staying here while the hole gets fixed."

"Can we go in?" She tried to get out of the car without undoing her seat belt, and in a move worthy of Iris, nearly face-planted into the gravel. I got her unravelled and let us inside. In an extraordinary show of trust, Will had given me a key this morning and told me to come and go as I pleased.

Someone was already cooking, and the smell of

bacon drifted through to the front hall. Cassie tried to run on ahead, wrestling with the door that led to the long kitchen-slash-dining room that took up one side of the U-shaped house, and I held her hand to save her from tripping.

"Can I have bacon in my pasta?" she asked.

Reed looked around from the stove. "You'll have to ask your dad."

Meanwhile, Cassie had stopped beside the dining table, transfixed by Kimberly. "Who are you? I'm Cassie."

"I'm Kimberly."

"Are you a princess? You're wearing jewels. I want to be a princess."

"I thought you wanted to be an astronaut?" I said.

"I want to be a princess astronaut."

Kimberly laughed and shook her head. "No, I'm not a princess. Would you like to try my necklace? It'd look real pretty on you."

"Yes!" Cassie turned to me. "Can I?"

"She's adorable," Kimberly mouthed from behind her, and I had a feeling I'd be second best for the remainder of the day. That hurt a little, but if Cassie was happy, then I couldn't complain.

"Sure, you can try the necklace on."

"Pancakes with syrup and bacon?" Reed asked. "I've made enough for everyone."

"Isn't it a bit early for dinner?"

"This isn't dinner, it's a snack, and it's never too early for bacon."

I had to concede on the bacon point. "In that case, why not?"

"If you've got a minute, RJ wants to speak to you.

He's in the study."

"Where's that?"

"Through the lounge, then take the hallway all the way around the house, past the bedrooms, and it's at the far end." He pointed out the window to the other end of the U. "Right over there."

"I can take care of Cassie," Kimberly offered, and although she was smiling, I thought I detected a hint of sadness in her eyes. "She looks just like you, doesn't she?"

In the study, RJ had set himself up at one of two desks arranged facing each other. His 'n' hers? Like the rest of the house, the study was bright and airy, with filing cabinets lining one wall and a large-scale map of the UK beside the door. A row of empty coffee cups graced the desk beside RJ as he tapped away at a keyboard, half-hidden behind a giant flat-screen. Another laptop sat open beside him. How long had he been working?

"Did you want me?"

"I've got a favour to ask."

After everything these people had done for me, I probably owed them one or two. "What kind of favour?"

"I need to get into Lakeview's computer network, but so far, none of the fish have taken the bait. Any chance you could help with that?"

It took a second for me to process the information. Maybe *I* was the one who needed coffee. "Wait. You're trying to break into Lakeview's network? What are you? Some kind of hacker?"

"I prefer cyber intelligence specialist."

He could give himself whatever job title he wanted,

but it still didn't change what he was doing. "Isn't that illegal?"

"So is murder, and that's what we're trying to prevent."

"You can't just go rooting through personal files." Our patient information was scanned in and backed up. Names, addresses, details of crimes, treatment plans, progress... All sensitive and all highly confidential. "Our service users are vulnerable adults, and we have to safeguard them."

"I'm not interested in their personal information. At the moment, we've got six questionable deaths and two concerns—what circumstances did these people die under, and did someone try to cover up the truth?"

His words made sense, but assisting him to access Lakeview's files still went against every oath I'd taken. I needed to protect my patients, and any secrets they'd told me in confidence needed to remain just that: secret.

But didn't I need to protect them physically too? I knew in my gut that six deaths in a year was too many for a facility like Lakeview. Whether they were due to poor treatment, negligence, or something worse, the situation couldn't be allowed to continue. Someone should alert the authorities, and with a sickening feeling, I realised that that person would most likely have to be me. None of the other staff seemed inclined to do anything. But first, I needed more facts. Nobody would start an investigation based on intuition and the word of a service user who'd stated in court that she spoke to ghosts.

Which brought me back to Iris. If she got injured and I'd stood by, knowing that there was something I could have done to help, no matter how morally dubious, I'd never forgive myself. I'd promised to help her, not spout indignation while she sat alone in her room, scared because she thought there was a killer on the prowl.

I'd already done a number of questionable things over the past week, and what was the saying? Go big or go home? I'd never thought that way before, but taking the moral high ground with Laurel had done me no good whatsoever. And what if somebody else died?

What if that person was Iris?

I leaned against the wall, wrestling with the decision, but I already knew there was only one answer I could give.

"What do you want me to do?"

Chapter 26 - Marcus

"TIRED?" I ASKED as Iris covered her yawn with a hand. The yawn was infectious, and I soon followed suit. "Do you want my coffee?"

"You look as if you need it more than me. Didn't you sleep either? You don't like the new house?"

"The house is fantastic. It's..."

I didn't need to burden Iris with my ethical dilemma. If I decided to breach Lakeview's network, that was for me to decide, not her, and any fallout was for me to deal with. She'd proven to be remarkably resilient considering everything she'd been through, but there were still cracks. The Leland Baker incident, for example. While I could in no way condone her running the man over, I understood her reasons for doing so, and I suspected she wasn't quite as calculating as everyone seemed to assume, even her. Years of seeing her mother trapped—a form of psychological torture for even the strongest-minded of people—had taken their toll on her, and she'd snapped. Perhaps there *had* been a moment of insanity. We all suffered from them. And in my professional opinion, she wasn't a danger to the public.

I forced a smile. "It's just that there was an owl in the tree outside that made a lot of noise."

"What kind of owl?"

"It was dark. I didn't see it."

"But they make different sounds. A tawny owl goes 'twit two,' a barn owl screeches, and a long-eared owl goes 'hoo hoo hoo.'"

They did? I had no idea, but listening to Iris try to make owl sounds was funny as hell. She glared at me when I laughed.

"What? Didn't you grow up in the country?"

"No, I grew up in Maidenhead."

"Where's that?"

"It's a town in Berkshire. Near—"

My phone vibrated in my pocket, which was notable because few people ever called me. Normally, I wouldn't touch it during a session, but this was Iris.

"Someone's calling me. Do you mind?"

"Sure. Can I call Nicole?"

Calls out were forbidden other than to pre-approved numbers. Who approved the numbers? Doug Calvert. There was a form to fill in, and apparently he denied more contacts than he okayed. Once, I'd assumed that was to maintain balance in the service users' lives—on occasion, we'd carefully controlled access at Deane Valley too—but now I suspected it was more due to the fact that he had something to hide.

"Yes," I told Iris. "But you'll have to do it quietly."

The call came from Lakeview's switchboard, and I groaned at the sight of the number. It must be something serious, or they'd have waited until I finished the session.

"Dr. Hastings?" The voice sounded panicked, breathless. "Matthew Simpson just went crazy. He hit a nurse, then ran off." Matthew Simpson was one of my patients. In the background, a siren blared as the place went into lockdown. "He screamed the 'power man' was after him. Do you know what that means?"

"Yes, it's part of—" I glanced at Iris. She didn't need to know the details of Matthew's repressed childhood trauma, and neither did the nurse. "Try to locate Simpson, and I'll come and speak to him. I'll need someone to sit with Iris McGivern in Meeting Room Three."

"I'll be fine on my own," Iris said once I'd hung up.

"I've broken more rules in the last week than I have in the entire rest of my career, so if you could help me to stick to one or two of them, that'd be good."

"Sorry." She looked contrite, but only for a second. "I'll behave; I promise. Does this mean I won't see you again today? Someone's escaped, right?"

"I'll slot you in somehow. It might be at the end of the afternoon. I'll bring coffee."

"You'll slot me in later? That sounds like something out of a Mills & Boon novel."

"Really? I wouldn't know." Except I did. My grandmother had been an avid reader. And lately, my thoughts where Miss McGivern was concerned had been veering into highly inappropriate territory. The innuendo might have been more than a slip, and I cursed myself for it.

"Just for reference, I like my coffee black," she said. "No milk, no sugar, no drama."

I couldn't hold back a smile at that. "Iris, you're the very definition of drama."

***

After two hours spent talking Matthew Simpson out of

a janitor's closet—a closet that should have been locked but wasn't—three consultations, and an emergency staff meeting to remind everyone of the proper procedures when moving patients through the building, I could barely keep my eyes open by the time I staggered to the break area. As I fed a pile of Kimberly's money into the vending machine, a new sign caught my eye.

From Monday 23rd September, all shellfish is banned from the building. For clarity, this includes shrimp, crab, lobster, clams, mussels, oysters, and scallops. Anyone caught with shellfish will receive a written warning, followed by further action for a second offence.

The notice had been signed by Doug Calvert, and a cluster of staff stood around reading it.

"What, they're gonna take the lobster thermidor out of the vending machine?" an orderly asked dramatically. "How will we live without it?"

"What about crab sticks?" a janitor whined. Fred, according to his name badge, but Calvert had called him Frederick when he'd scolded him in the meeting earlier. "I always have crab sticks for lunch."

"I don't think crab sticks have any crab in them."

"Why are they banning shellfish?" I asked. "Is someone allergic?"

"A new crazy," Fred said. "Coming on Monday."

"The term is 'service user,'" I reminded him, somewhat testily since he'd wasted hours of my time earlier. If Matthew hadn't gotten into the closet, he wouldn't have found the Stanley knife he'd threatened to harm both himself and me with.

"And the last time a service user had a severe allergy, he died," Glenda said from behind me. "Remember? So you'll have to live without your bloody crab sticks. Disgusting things anyway."

My ears pricked up. "Someone died? When?"

"Beginning of the year," the orderly said. "Peanuts, it was. Archie Majors. Collapsed in his room, and we called an ambulance, but he breathed his last in the corridor as they wheeled him out of the building."

"Whereabouts did he die?" I asked before I could stop myself.

Glenda narrowed her eyes. "What does it matter?"

"Right outside the woodwork room," Fred said. "Pissed himself, and it ran under the door and then under the workbench with the vices. Took three men to shift it so I could clean up."

"Thank you, Frederick. Don't you have work to do?"

"Bloody jobsworth," he muttered as he stomped off.

I had to agree, but between the three of them, they'd filled in one more piece of the puzzle. Archie Majors and a peanut allergy. The question was, was his death an accident or murder? Only Iris could find out.

**

"One black coffee." I slid it across the table towards her, together with a sheaf of paperwork. "And papers to appoint your new lawyer."

"I can't afford a new lawyer."

"Will and Kimberly are paying him."

"You think he's okay?"

"The lawyer? I haven't met him."

"No, I meant Will."

"Will? Yes, he's a good guy, and he selected the lawyer. I'd trust his judgement on that."

"Okay." She scanned the pages, signed, took a sip of coffee, then made a face. "It's terrible."

"Sorry. It's all there is."

"I used to have one of those fancy machines that took the pods. Who knows what happened to it? I expect the landlord put my stuff on eBay when I stopped paying the rent."

"When you get out of Lakeview, I'll buy you a coffee machine, how about that?"

What was I even saying? Participating in corporate espionage had left me frazzled, and I hadn't had time to gather my thoughts before I talked to Iris. Just prior to our meeting, I'd paid Becca, Calvert's PA, a visit on the pretence that I'd broken the lanyard for my ID badge, and while she went to find me a new one, I'd jammed RJ's thumb drive into the USB port on her computer. He'd assured me that's all it would take.

Iris managed a tired smile. "If I ever get out of here, it'll be me that owes *you* the coffee machine. Are we going to call Nicole now?"

"Actually, no. If you're up to it, we need to take another walk."

"A walk? To where?"

"To the woodwork room. We need to see a man about a peanut allergy."

CHAPTER 27 - IRIS

"HE'S THERE," I whispered to Marcus the instant we got around the corner.

Archie Majors—at least, I assumed it was Archie Majors since he wore a Lakeview tracksuit similar to mine—was leaning against the wall halfway along the corridor. As he heard us approach, he turned, and his expression changed from resignation to recognition.

"It's you!"

"Archie?"

"Yeah. What took you so long?"

"I only just got notified of your death. A peanut allergy, right?"

He nodded. "Someone put peanuts in the curry. I always said the food in this place would kill me, but I figured it'd be salmonella rather than anaphylactic shock. That asshole who runs the place swore they'd banned nuts."

"It might have been contamination at the factory," I said, trying to play devil's advocate. I was also second-guessing our theory after Mandy's absence. "You don't know it happened here."

"There was a whole damn peanut. In chicken curry. What kind of chicken curry has peanuts?"

"You ate it?"

"Before I realised what it was. Then my throat

closed up, and I hammered on the door for ages, but nobody came."

"What about your call button?"

"It was broken. This fucking place. I knew coming here was a mistake."

"A...mistake?" It wasn't as if we picked Lakeview out of a brochure. We got sent here. Do not pass go, do not collect two hundred pounds.

"I could've gone to a regular prison, but I heard what happens to fit blokes like me in there."

Archie smiled at me, cocky, his head angled as if posing for a non-existent photographer. Was he waiting for some sort of compliment? Because if so, he'd be waiting for a long time. What was the old saying? *Beauty is in the eye of the beholder*. Archie seemed to be rather fond of beholding himself.

In the end, I went with, "Right."

His wrinkled nose suggested I was either too blind or too stupid to see what was in front of me.

"My lawyer said these places were like holiday camps. That all I had to do was act crazy so they'd send me here, then when I arrived, say I'd had a breakdown and I was sorry, yadda yadda yadda, and the psychologist would see I'd 'recovered'"—he used finger quotes around the word—"and they'd send me home."

"What did you do?"

"Everything the asshole told me to do, but Calvert wouldn't even put my case before the tribunal. Said I was still a menace to the public. That's bullshit."

"I meant, what did you do to end up in court?"

"What? Oh. I shot my neighbour's dog. Damn thing kept barking in the garden all night. Dunno what everyone was so upset about—it was only a mangy thing he found on the street."

"You *shot* it?"

For once, I was in agreement with Director Calvert. "Menace" was a good word.

"With an airgun. Don't look at me like that. They're perfectly legal, and you'd have shot it too if you had to put up with that yap-yap-yapping."

Er, no, I wouldn't. Even the thought of hurting an animal made me physically nauseous. I felt the lightest touch on my arm, and I glanced across at Marcus.

"You okay?" he mouthed.

Far from it. How did he do this every day? How did he listen to idiots confessing their crimes without smacking them around the head with a chair? I attempted what I hoped was a smile.

"Fine," I muttered.

Marcus was wearing glasses again today, and he peered over the top of them. That shouldn't have made my blood run hot, but dammit, it did. "I know what 'fine' means, Iris."

I put a finger to my lips and turned back to Archie. I needed to get this done, but there and then, I vowed never to visit the woodwork room again.

"Couldn't you have asked him to keep the dog inside?"

"You think I didn't try that? The guy was a flip-flop-wearing hippie vegan, and he said it had the right to express itself. Look, I'm perfectly sane, okay? Calvert's just a self-serving prick, and so was my lawyer."

Well, we had that much in common. Archie Majors had been a really shitty human being, but his story did sound eerily similar to mine.

"Who was your lawyer?" I asked out of interest.

"Some court-appointed schmuck. Johnny Gibbs, esquire. Don't forget the 'esquire.' He never signed off an email without it."

Holy shit. Johnny Gibbs had been *my* lawyer too. I'd laughed at the "esquire" bit too, but it did seem strangely fitting for a man who insisted on wedging himself into polyester suits made for a man half his size. And the hair gel. Don't even get me started on the hair gel. He slathered it on every morning, and I'd never been able to make up my mind whether it'd feel slimy or crispy.

"Gibbs did that to me too."

"Did what?" Marcus asked. "Did someone else hurt you?"

"Shh. I'll tell you later."

"What are you in here for?" He pointed at the Lakeview logo on my sweatshirt. "Wait, wait—don't tell me. You got in trouble for trying to fulfil that crazy prophecy?"

"Crazy prophecy?"

"Some fog woman told me about it right after I died. That you're supposed to hunt down my murderer and kill them? Never heard anything so ludicrous in my life. Talking to dead people is one thing, but the idea of you being some sort of supernatural avenger? Don't make me laugh. How stupid do you think I am?"

Did he want an honest answer to that? Probably not, but his scepticism made my life easier.

"Yeah, that's a totally dumb idea. I've got no idea why they make up stories like that. No, I'm here because I tried to jump off an overpass. Sometimes life gets too much, you know?"

Archie nodded. "Good way to go. Cause plenty of

chaos on your way out. I like it."

Sick, sick, sick. Carefully, I reached out a foot and trod on Marcus's toe. Would he get the message? Yes, thank goodness. He checked his watch, then motioned along the hallway with his head.

"Iris, I'm afraid you need to leave your imaginary friend alone for today. It's time for your meds."

"But, Doctor—"

His voice was firm. "Sometimes the mind plays tricks on us, remember? We can speak more about this in our session tomorrow."

For Archie's benefit, I gave a what-can-a-girl-do shrug and a little wave. "It's been fun, but I gotta go."

"Oi, when are you coming back? I got no one else to talk to."

Never, if I could help it. I followed Marcus's lead and headed for the stairs.

***

In my room, Marcus closed the door behind us and leaned against the wall. He looked exhausted today, and I wondered if my conversation with Archie had taken more of a toll on him than it had on me. Changing his entire belief system couldn't have been easy.

Beside me, Jacinda stood and silently clapped her hands together. "Oh, yay! The hot doctor's back. Hey, hot doctor! You can give me an exam any time."

Good grief. "His name's Marcus, and he can't hear you. It's Jacinda," I told him, just in case he'd forgotten about my dead roommate.

"You can pass the message on, right?" she said.

"Wrong." Jacinda had seemed a bit prim when we first met, but now she'd been well and truly corrupted by reality TV. I picked up the remote and switched her goggle-box on. "Here, watch this."

"Woohoo! I love this show."

Marcus glanced at the TV, and his eyes bugged out. "What the hell...?"

"It's called *Naked Attraction*," I explained, turning back to face him. "The person with clothes on picks one of the naked people to go on a date with. They reveal more of their bodies with each round." Currently, the men were visible from the waist down, which may have explained Jacinda's enthusiasm. She really needed to get out more, but of course that wasn't possible.

"You can't watch that."

"Why not?"

"The channels available to service users are supposed to be screened. This is totally inappropriate."

"Why? Nudity's natural. It's not as if I haven't seen a guy's bits before."

"I... Er..."

Flustered Marcus was hilarious. He didn't know where to look or what to say. What would *he* look like naked? *Whoa, whoa, whoa. Hold that thought right there, Iris.*

"You thought I'd never had a boyfriend? I didn't get put in here until I was almost nineteen, and I was no choirgirl." Sex had been nothing to write home about, but I'd partaken from time to time. After my experiences with Terrence and George and whoever had molested me in the middle of the night, I wasn't sure I wanted to try it again, but I could deal with Jacinda's viewing habits if it kept her quiet. "Lakeview's changed me, though. I'm practically a nun now."

"I should have a word with management."

"No, don't." I took a step forward and lowered my voice. "If Jacinda doesn't get fed her daily diet of reality shows, she'll start talking to me again, and that really would make me feel suicidal."

Marcus glanced over my shoulder again, and judging from Jacinda's whoops, they'd just done another reveal.

"*Please*." I leaned in closer. "Don't ruin my life."

"Iris..."

Too close. We were too close. Bloody hell, I felt something twitch against my hip, and it wasn't a finger. Fuck! I leapt back as Marcus cursed under his breath.

"She's gonna choose the peanut guy!" Jacinda shrieked. "No, no, pick the salami."

For a second, my brain ceased to function and Marcus and I just stared at each other. Then I came to my senses. "Uh, speaking of peanuts..." Dammit, he didn't know what Jacinda was saying, did he? "Forget that part. We should discuss what Archie said. Archie's a psycho, by the way. He shot his neighbour's dog."

"Yes, yes, quite. The Archie. I mean, the murder. Was it a murder?"

"Someone killed him, for sure." *Breathe, Iris. Don't forget to breathe.* "There was a peanut in his chicken curry. I've eaten that slop many times, but never have I found anything remotely resembling a peanut in it." Or, in fact, any chicken.

I recounted the rest of the tale, from Archie's crime to his death to the fact that we'd both been sent to Lakeview by a slimeball stuffed into a cheap suit. Marcus seemed particularly interested in the last part.

"Why push you to come to Lakeview? Was it easier for him to do that than fight for a shorter prison sentence?"

"I don't know. At the time, he sold it as the best option for me, and I guess I didn't know any better. If I could turn back the clock, I'd pick prison for sure." Suddenly, emotions got the better of me. This afternoon had been a roller coaster. No, not a roller coaster—a spin dryer bobbing around on a stormy sea. A sob welled up and escaped before I could swallow it down. "Thank you for not judging me. I mean, I realise that you must be judging me inside, but thanks for not getting all sanctimonious like the other doctors."

"I understand why you did what you did. That doesn't mean I condone it, but I understand. And I also believe you were under great pressure at the time."

"I'm not a bad person."

"I know, Iris. And I'll do everything within my power to help you prove it. So will Nicole and the others."

"There've been three murders now, and I'm...I'm getting scared."

"I'll let Will know the situation. Now that you've signed the papers, your new lawyer can request your file, so hopefully we'll be able to find out your old lawyer's reasoning. You don't have any allergies, do you?"

"I'm allergic to assholes."

He chuckled at that. "Aren't we all, flower? Look, I wish I could stay longer, but I need to go. I'll come back tomorrow."

That was the first time he'd called me "flower" without getting pissed at himself afterwards. I kind of liked it. "What about Nicole? Will she come too?"

"She needs to set up another appointment via Calvert first. By the book, remember? So it'll be Monday at least, I'm afraid."

And today was Saturday. I hated waiting. I'd been patient for five long years, and now things were finally happening, I just wanted everyone to get a damn move on. But at least I wasn't alone anymore. I forced myself to take a deep breath. To calm myself. I wasn't alone.

"Marcus?"

"Yes?"

"Tell them to hurry up with whatever they're planning, would you?"

"Hang in there." He gave my hand a squeeze. Held on to it for a beat too long, then seemed to catch himself and dropped it as if I'd scalded him. "Tomorrow at two."

The door closed behind him with a quiet *click*, and I leaned against it until I couldn't hear his footsteps anymore. Today... Today had been weird. First the lockdown, then meeting Archie Majors, whose death I couldn't get too upset about. What kind of psycho shot a dog? If I'd met him in real life, I'd have bought him a whole packet of full-size Snickers bars. And then there was Marcus, and every minute I'd spent with him lately left me more confused. At first, I'd thought he was just another suit with a tick sheet, but now that he'd loosened up a bit, I realised he was different. I caught myself smiling as I remembered the way he'd squeezed my hand, then swore under my breath when Jacinda spoke in a stupid sing-song voice.

"Iris is in lurve."

"What?"

"With Doctor Hottie. You know that's against the rules, right?"

"Shut up."

"Bronwyn from my tapestry class got caught doing bad things in the prayer room with Dr. Sedgewick, and he got struck off. Struck. Off." She giggled. "Off with his head."

"Dr. Sedgewick? Eeuw."

"I know, right? He was, like, sixty." Since when did Jacinda talk like a sorority reject? Reality TV had a lot to answer for. "And Bronwyn was our age. She was sucking his—"

"Please, I don't want to hear the details. Uh, where did *you* hear the details?"

"From Bobby." She sat back on the bed, and I had to admit she'd gotten good at the floating thing. "Iris and Marcus sitting in a tree, K-I-S-S-I-N-G. First comes love, then comes marriage, then comes a baby in the baby carriage."

"Just stop, would you?"

"Sucking his thumb, wetting his pants, doing the hula, hula dance! He likes you too, you know."

"Can't we go back to talking about the Antichrist?"

"He's on vacation right now."

Please, somebody get me out of here.

CHAPTER 28 - MARCUS

SUNDAY REPRESENTED A fresh week and a fresh start. From now on, I vowed to maintain a sensible distance from Iris McGivern because what happened yesterday had been a wake-up call. If I hadn't been all too aware of the ghost watching us from the other side of the room, I might very well have been tempted to kiss her. And not only was she a patient, she was a scared, vulnerable patient, and to make any sort of move would be abusing my position and taking advantage of her in the worst possible way.

Thankfully, I had Nicole, Kimberly, and Rania to assist with the distance-keeping. They couldn't visit in person, of course, but I put my phone on speaker and held it in my lap out of sight so Iris could talk to her soul sisters, as she called them. The soul thing still boggled my mind, but when I compared Iris to Laurel, who didn't have a soul at all, I knew who I'd rather spend time with. Their other halves were a welcome surprise too, especially Reed and Beck. I confess I'd always avoided their type—guys who lifted all the weights at the gym with ease and exuded a confidence I only wished I had—but they were actually pleasant company. Last night, everyone had got together in the lounge with a movie playing in the background while we worked on our respective tasks—for me, that was writing up patient notes, and for the other three men and Rania, that meant reviewing various Lakeview-related files. Nicole spent the time on scientific research while Kimberly coordinated her wedding-planning assistants back in the US. I might have had letters after my name, but their collective intelligence left me feeling like the poor relation.

Opposite me, another tear rolled down Iris's cheek and plopped into her coffee. I passed her a handkerchief. They were good tears, an overflow of emotion rather than distress, so I wasn't too concerned.

"I sent your DNA sample to Professor Fairchild," Nicole said. "We've been going back and forth all night, and it turns out you have the same genetic marker as the rest of us."

"What does that mean?"

"Thousands of years ago, a virus inserted a DNA-based copy of its own RNA genetic material into our genomes, and it got passed down from our ancestors all the way to us. I've never seen it in anyone but the Electi, and it has two implications. Firstly, if one of us dies without an heir, then we believe our soul gets randomly reassigned, right?"

"Right."

"Except I don't think it's so random. I think that out there in the world, there are a few more people with this virus in their DNA. Backup copies, if you like. The Electi soul combines with the virus to create us."

Rania spoke up. "And potentially the Judge also has this virus?"

"That's my theory. There're a bunch of DNA databases in the world, and one of them might hold a clue if I can access them. Professor Fairchild's going to help. He has contacts. But you know what else it means?"

"What?" Iris asked.

"Have you heard of CRISPR?"

"Is that a brand of salad?"

Nicole burst out laughing. "No, it's a tool for editing genomes. CRISPRs are specialised stretches of DNA that act like a pair of molecular scissors. They can cut out chunks of the genetic code we don't want and replace it with new pieces. The technology's still in the early stages of use, but potentially we could modify our DNA, or our children's DNA, to turn off our Electi powers."

"But we can't! We're here for a reason. We have a purpose."

"Yes, but we can't fulfil that purpose anymore or we'll end up in jail."

"You mean I might be able to have non-Electi kids?" Kimberly asked.

"Possibly."

"No!" Iris said. "No way. I'm not being genetically modified. And you don't know that we can't fulfil our purpose because we haven't found the Judge yet. We might be able to get rid of all these trapped people, which is half of our job, even if we can't do the rest."

"Easy, Nicole," I warned. I didn't want Iris getting upset.

"Iris is right," Rania said. "Before we start tinkering with who we are, we should find the Judge. At the very least, he needs to be involved in the decision."

Nicole sighed. "It was just an idea."

"And a good one, but it's too soon. Can you focus on looking for the Judge? If you need access to the DNA banks, RJ can probably help."

"Okay, fine."

"We shouldn't argue," Kimberly said, her voice overly cheerful—for Iris's sake, I suspected. "Iris, what's your favourite colour?"

"My favourite colour? Why does that matter?"

"Because I'm getting your room ready at Rania's house for when you get out of that horrible place."

"A room?" Iris choked up a bit, and I wanted to reach out for her. But I stopped myself just in time. "I get a room?"

"Of course. You didn't think we'd just abandon you? You'll need somewhere to stay while we help you to get back on your feet."

Kimberly wasn't just planning to paint a room. I'd overheard her speaking to Will and Rania over breakfast this morning, and they'd decided to speed up the renovations on the pool house. And when I said "pool house," it was really a little cottage. Two bedrooms and a bathroom upstairs, plus a kitchen, living room, and dining area downstairs. The glass-roofed pool room joined onto one corner, forming an L shape. The pool was only eight metres long, but it came with swim jets for exercise, and there was a Jacuzzi at one end with a couple of sunloungers. Paradise in a small space. But I understood why Kimberly wanted to keep things low-key around Iris. No sense in making the place sound too fantastic in case things didn't work out as we hoped.

Iris wiped at her eyes, and it was the first time I'd seen her genuinely speechless. Finally, she croaked out, "Orange. I like orange."

"Orange?" Kimberly sounded somewhat dubious,

and I couldn't blame her. Orange walls were straight out of the seventies. "I guess we could go with apricot? Or peach?"

"Anything's fine as long as I have a door I can go in and out of. And no unwanted roommates."

"There are definitely no roommates. We checked."

"Then I can't wait to stay there."

***

Back at base that evening, I found RJ had got into Becca's computer—it seemed she never powered it down, just turned the screen off and went home—and information was already coming in.

"Iris was right about Archie Majors being a psycho."

"That's not actually the correct term."

"He didn't just kill his neighbour's dog, he shot his neighbour too. Blinded the guy in one eye before the police took him down with a Taser."

On second thoughts, "psycho" was a fairly accurate descriptor. I couldn't help thinking of Teddy—if Laurel had hurt him, I might be tempted to go full Archie Majors myself.

"Okay, I see where you're coming from."

"And the girl Becca Morten told you about? The one who was part of a study but didn't finish it? I think that must've been Libby Henkel. The study was some experimental thing with brainwaves, and halfway through, Libby stole a pair of scissors from the craft room and slit her wrists. At least, that's what this email says."

"Bloody hell."

"The study got cancelled after that, and the sponsor

was pissed because up until then, all the patients had been responding well. And Calvert was annoyed because the nurse who found Libby went on sick leave for a month due to the stress, and it messed with the schedules."

Every new snippet of information I heard about Lakeview made me hate the place more. "Have you found anything that'll help Iris?"

"Not yet, but I'm still looking."

***

On Monday, I spent a somewhat uneventful session with Iris—just a walk around the building with no dead people and no emergency lockdowns, and since I was careful to maintain a gap of at least two feet between us at all times, I managed not to do anything stupid. Nicole paid her two hundred and fifty quid to Calvert and came in after the session under the guise of taking follow-up samples, and the girls chatted for half an hour while I caught up on my notes. Thankfully, Nicole steered clear of DNA-related controversies, and Iris seemed happy when we left.

When I got back to Will and Rania's, I found Iris's new lawyer waiting in the lounge. He'd agreed to come to us for the initial meeting to save seven people from trekking to his office. Everybody had questions, and nobody wanted to be left out.

"Miss McGivern's file arrived remarkably quickly," he told us. "But now that I've been through it, I understand why. There's very little in it."

"You think Gibbs took stuff out?" Will asked.

"I think it's more that he didn't do much work in

the first place."

"Laziness?"

"Partly, but perhaps also an element of shrewdness. Gibbs came via Legal Aid, and those guys have too much work and too little time. They need to prioritise. I asked around, and while the judge in Iris's case has a reputation for handing down the harshest sentences possible, the prosecutor had historically shown a willingness to plea-bargain an insanity defence. The evidence against her was strong, as were the indicators of premeditation, so Gibbs had to make the choice between life in a mainstream prison or an indeterminate sentence at Lakeview. In his position, I might well have come to the same decision."

"We've heard it's not the first time he's done that."

"As I said, the prosecutor in the case appears to be surprisingly open to negotiation."

"When you say 'surprisingly'…?"

"Eleven cases in the last year. I'd say it's unprecedented, but when I began reviewing other files for that circuit, I found two other prosecutors with similar records."

"Doesn't that strike you as odd?"

"Yes, but the number of insanity pleas has been steadily increasing in the UK over the last decade, as has crime in general, and the judge's nickname is 'Lock 'em Up Leavitt.' It's possible that given Leavitt's notoriety, the prosecutors felt a modicum of sympathy for certain defendants, such as Miss McGivern, and decided to offer them what they saw as a better option."

"Are judges allowed to do that? Give everyone the maximum sentence?"

"I'm afraid it's at their discretion. Many of us feel

it's not a particularly fair system, but it *is* the system, and as long as they stick within the guidelines, there's nothing we can do about it."

"Can't we put in a complaint or something?" Kimberly asked.

"If no new evidence or facts have come to light, we don't have any grounds for an appeal."

Dammit. Before this meeting began, I'd had hope that the lawyer could spot some kind of loophole, but everything he'd said so far, as well as his general attitude—matter-of-fact but overwhelmingly negative—suggested he wouldn't be able to offer the miracle we'd all been hoping for. And this guy was supposed to be the best.

"I meant about Judge Leavitt. Surely he can't keep doing this?"

"As I said, he's sticking within the sentencing guidelines, albeit at the top end."

"So how can we get Iris out?"

"Her best chance of release is to prove that she's been rehabilitated. That she's no longer a danger to herself or the general public." The lawyer turned to me. "I understand you're her psychiatrist?"

"That's right. In my professional opinion, Iris McGivern is a suitable candidate for release, but Mr. Calvert—the director of Lakeview—refuses to follow the procedural steps to work towards that. He frames it as a need to maintain public safety, but many patients in similar situations have been successfully rehabilitated."

Albeit not at Lakeview. Rehab wasn't high on the list of priorities there.

"Is that unusual? For his opinion to differ with a psychiatrist's?"

"From what I've heard, no, it isn't unusual. He believes he knows best, even though he's not a medical professional. I realise it *is* unusual for me to meet with a patient's lawyer like this, but it's an intensely frustrating situation, and Miss McGivern is bearing the brunt of other people's bad decisions. Currently, she has nobody but us advocating for her. The court appointed somebody, but I haven't seen the lady while I've been at Lakeview."

"I left a voicemail," Rania said. "She hasn't got back to me yet."

"I see," the lawyer said. "Who runs Lakeview? Is there a dispute resolution procedure?"

"Hannity SP Limited," Will said. "It's a private company headquartered in London. From what I can see, they run five other psychiatric hospitals plus a network of care homes."

"And they pay lip service to the concept of dispute resolution," I added. "According to the staff handbook, we're meant to write a letter to head office if we have a problem."

"I see. Well, they must be regulated by somebody. Presumably, they're taking government money to care for these people, so there needs to be an element of oversight. I'll look into it."

"How long will that take?" Nicole asked. "Iris has already been attacked twice by staff, and we don't want it to happen again."

"Attacked by *staff*?" The lawyer seemed incredulous, and I couldn't blame him. We were meant to be taking care of Iris, after all.

I closed my eyes for a brief second, trying to compose myself. The more I thought about what had happened to her, the sicker I felt. "In the first incident, she believes she was drugged and raped. She never told anybody at the time, so there's no evidence available. The second incident was an attempted rape, but she was half-awake and fought back. The perpetrator lost part of an ear but claimed she lashed out unprovoked. It's his word against hers, and management failed to carry out a proper investigation. Both incidents took place before I began working at Lakeview."

The lawyer sucked in a breath. "I see how that ups the stakes somewhat. Do you believe her?"

"I do. She realises she has no recourse, but there's definitely residual trauma from what happened."

"Do something," Kimberly said, her words directed at the lawyer but meant for the rest of us too. "I don't care what it costs—we have to get her out of that place."

Chapter 29 - Marcus

ON TUESDAY, I had to break the news to Iris that the meeting with the lawyer hadn't gone quite as well as we'd hoped. I tried to stay upbeat, but understandably, she saw little reason to smile.

"I'm gonna be stuck in here for good, aren't I?"

Iris needed a hug, but I couldn't even offer her that. Cassie told me I gave the best hugs, although I'll admit she was most likely biased.

"We're doing everything we can. The lawyer's looking into the possibility of me making a complaint to the regulator about what's going on in here."

"*You* making a complaint. Wouldn't that have repercussions on your job?"

I took a deep breath. "Yes, quite possibly."

"But—" She leaned forward and traced a finger across my forehead. "You're getting worry lines. Dammit, this isn't just affecting me, it's affecting everybody I care about."

She cared about me? My heart swelled a fraction, then deflated rapidly when I realised that Iris wasn't *meant* to care for me. "I have to do this. It's not only you that Lakeview's management is screwing over; it's all the other patients too."

"I don't like seeing you stressed."

"It's not just because of the situation here. There's

the sinkhole at my house, and...and I have a custody hearing coming up for my daughter."

My own lawyer had emailed this morning, and he sounded remarkably similar to Iris's in terms of his optimism. Perhaps they were related?

"You're going for custody? That's...that's..."

"Unusual? Surprising? Ridiculous? I've heard it all."

"A little surprising, I guess, but from what I've seen, I'm sure you're an excellent father."

"Maybe I should get *you* to testify on my behalf. Everyone else is siding with my ex."

"I would if I could, but I'm not sure putting one of Lakeview's finest on the stand would help. Why are people siding with your ex?"

"Laurel plays dirty. She always has. I just didn't realise that until after I'd married her."

"The restraining order?"

"Among other things."

"What else did she do?"

"You don't need to be burdened with my problems."

"But you're burdened with mine. What is it they say? 'A problem shared is a problem halved.' And I think I'm qualified to listen. You have no idea how many reruns of *The Jeremy Kyle Show* I've been forced to watch over the last two weeks."

They gave her access to *The Jeremy Kyle Show*? Good grief. That alone should get the place closed down.

"Iris, you're my patient," I said, desperately trying to shift the session back onto a more appropriate footing. "We should be getting to grips with your issues, not mine."

I failed in my attempt the moment she smiled at me.

"I'm not talking about my issues today." She mimed zipping her lips together and throwing away the key. "I don't even want to *think* about my issues. So either we talk about your stuff, or I'll give you a blow-by-blow account of who got up to what with who on *Survival Island* last night."

"Surely you couldn't be that cruel?"

"Oh, I could. Debbi and Jayden got into an argument and—"

"All right! Enough. I surrender. You want to hear all the sordid details about my disaster of a marriage? It's really not that interesting."

"You're probably right. I mean, when I saw you had a tattoo, I was thinking you were a failed rock star or something, but then it turned out to be your daughter's voice. Uh, not that your tattoo isn't really, really cute, but it's hardly a skull with flames coming out of the eyes."

"No, that's on my back. And they're not flames, they're snakes."

"Oh, you're funny."

She thought I was joking? I wasn't.

"Laurel hated it. She wanted me to have it removed."

"You're serious?"

"Always."

Nearly always.

"Let me see."

"Flower, I can get away with bringing you flapjacks and coffee, but I'm not taking off my shirt in the middle of a counselling session. There's a viewing window in the door. Anyone could walk past."

"Where's your sense of adventure?"

"In the attic at my old house, along with my guitar and my leather jacket."

"Hold on... You *did* play in a band?"

"For a while."

Yet another thing I'd given up to try and make my marriage work. Playing in a rock band hadn't fitted in with the image Laurel wanted us to project as a couple —her words, not mine—and besides, I'd had no spare time with all the extra hours I needed to work to keep up with her spending habits.

"That's awesome. When I first came here, I was allowed to go to the music room, and I was teaching myself to play the guitar. Then it got broken, and that was the end of that."

"Broken?"

"Hey, for once, it wasn't me. Someone dropped it, and the neck snapped."

"If I ever manage to get my guitar back from my hopefully soon-to-be ex-wife, consider it yours."

"If I'm still in here, I won't be allowed it. Might strangle myself with the strings or something."

"Nobody's giving up on you."

"You're nice, you know. Maybe one day I'll be able to buy *you* a flapjack. As a thank you for making my life not quite so miserable."

Buy me a flapjack? Well, it wasn't as if she was asking me out to dinner. "Deal."

"So, now that we've established you have a tattoo, which makes you more interesting than you care to admit— Wait, do you have any piercings?" Er... "Oh my gosh, you're blushing. You *do* have a piercing. Where?"

"Iris, we are *not* talking about this," I said through gritted teeth.

"Oh, we so are. I mean, it's not in your ear. Nipple?"

"Shut up, Iris. I mean it."

"Why? What're you gonna do, *Doctor* Hastings? You're a dark horse, aren't you?"

I'd almost forgotten what it was like to banter with a woman, to spar back and forth in a form of verbal foreplay. Laurel's sense of humour had vanished around the time she got her first country-club membership, probably because she decided laughing would give her wrinkles. Despite the circumstances, my time with Iris had helped me to loosen up a bit, reminded me of the man I'd been before I became Mr. Laurel Burton.

Fuck. Why did she have to be a patient?

I leaned halfway across the table. "No, it's not in my nipple. Yes, it's where you probably think it is. No, I'm not giving you any more information than that. And if you mention a word of this to Jacinda, I'll ask the nurses to feed you nothing but soup for a month."

"The soup in here's disgusting."

"There's your incentive to keep your mouth shut."

"Spoilsport. Okay, so back to your old ball and chain... What did the shrew do?" Iris nudged me under the table with her foot. "Come on, vent all you want. You need someone to talk to as well."

Aaaaaaand, back to reality. "Yes, but that person isn't you."

I'd worn my glasses today because buying more disposable contact lenses was yet another thing on my list of things to do. I still hadn't been allowed back to my house, and right now, I was wearing one of Reed's shirts, which was too big, a pair of Will's socks, no boxers, and the same suit trousers I'd had on for days. Basically, I was one step above being a hobo, but at least I'd taken a shower.

Iris reached across for my glasses and slid them onto her own face. "Just call me Dr. McGivern. How do you feel, Marcus? Wow, these are blurry."

I turned my snort of laughter into a cough. "Give those back."

"The glasses suit you. Why do you wear contacts?"

"Less chance of them being knocked off by patients or my daughter. Or stolen by wayward ghost-hunters. Come on, give them back."

She peered over the top of them. "Are you gonna spank me if I don't?"

Her words and the innuendo behind them brought me back to my senses, and I moved my leg from where it was still resting against hers under the table. Iris McGivern made me lose my damn mind. Mentally, I poured a bucket of cold water over the heat building in the room.

"Flow—" No. Wrong. "*Iris*, we can't do this. I have rules to follow. Whether you like it or not, I'm still your doctor, and you're still my patient. You can't say things like that, even in jest."

Contrite Iris was almost as dangerous as dirty Iris, and I was careful to avoid touching her hand as she held my glasses out.

"I'm sorry," she said, eyes down. She was biting that damn lip again.

"We just need to keep our relationship on an appropriate level. Whether or not you want to admit it, you have some unresolved issues, and I think it would benefit you to work through them."

"What issues?"

"Some nasty things have happened to you in here."

"Yeah, but it's easier not to think about them."

Brilliant. Now we had sullen.

"Do you ever have unexpected memories pop up? Or do you get bad dreams?"

"Sometimes," she admitted.

"I really believe it would help you if we talked these things over."

"Fine."

Wonderful. We'd regressed to "*fine*." My mission to ruin her happiness was complete.

Dammit.

***

"How did it go at Lakeview today?" Will asked that evening. Reed and Beck had teamed up in the kitchen, and it smelled like we were having some sort of chicken. I'd volunteered to help, but Kimberly had shooed me out and told me to relax. Beck looked as if he wanted to shoo her out too.

"Lakeview was fine." Great, now I was at it.

"You're back there tomorrow?"

"As always."

"Good. What are the chances of you getting Iris into an unoccupied room on the first floor?"

Well, at least if we were walking around the hospital, she wouldn't be acting like an ingénue and I wouldn't be trying to hide a half-chub under the table.

"Why?"

"RJ found out where Libby Henkel died. Room 134.

According to the records, it's been empty ever since, and we need Iris to find out whether the death was a murder."

"How did she die? Do you know?"

"She stole a pair of scissors from the craft room and slit her wrists in the shower."

Bloody hell. Quite literally.

"Iris doesn't need to see that."

"Unless you can get Rania or Nicole or Kimberly inside, we don't have much of a choice."

I knew that, but Iris was still more fragile than the others realised. This afternoon, once we'd settled back into our doctor-patient relationship, she'd confessed how bad the nightmares about her attacks had been. She'd sobbed as she described the way she woke up unable to breathe as she imagined Terrence's weight pressing down on her, and her subconscious had filled in the gaps for the first rape and left her imagining the worst. I made a mental note to borrow another handkerchief tomorrow. For all her talk earlier, she was scared of having a sexual relationship. At one point, she'd called herself damaged goods and said she might as well stay at Lakeview. Obviously not an option.

"Every time Iris suffers through another trauma, it damages her a little bit more inside. I'll get her into that room, but you'd better get her out of the hospital while there's still something left of her to save."

Will looked as sick as I felt. "Understood."

Chapter 30 - Iris

"IRIS, IN HERE."

The orderly up ahead disappeared around a corner, leaving the hallway empty, and Marcus quickly bleeped open the door to room 134. Libby Henkel had died months ago, but the place still smelled like death. Probably something to do with the faint bloodstains that graced the floor. If it weren't for the fact that Claire Welby had knocked back a bottle of drain cleaner, I'd have suspected Lakeview didn't have any cleaning products at all. Management cut corners everywhere, and the grime was yet more evidence of that.

"Try not to touch anything," Marcus murmured, switching on the bathroom light so we could see better. Although the en-suite washrooms on the first floor had showers, they didn't have windows or extractor fans, and black mould lurked in the corners of the room, creeping closer and closer to the floor as if pulled by gravity.

"I'm trying, believe me."

A gasp escaped my lips when I spotted Libby, and my spine stiffened as I willed myself not to run right out of there. Jacinda and Archie—they'd looked reasonably normal, albeit dead, and although Rylie had a dented forehead, the water had washed most of the blood away and she'd been more bewildered than anything else.

Libby looked absolutely wretched.

She might have died in the shower, but the tap hadn't been turned on, and blood from the trails streaming down her wrists had soaked into her pale green Lakeview pyjamas.

"Just get the information, and we're leaving," Marcus said.

My steps faltered as I moved closer, my hands balling into fists at my sides. At that moment, the Electi blood surged through me the same way as it had when I aimed my car at Leland Baker and pressed the accelerator. I wanted to find whoever killed Libby Henkel, do my duty, and wipe them off the face of the earth.

But I couldn't exactly admit that in front of Marcus.

He took one of my hands and gently uncurled my fingers, then gave it a squeeze. I managed a shaky smile before I turned back to Libby. She was about my age. Was that why I felt such a strong connection?

"I'm here. I'm not going anywhere," Marcus told me, and I glanced heavenwards and thanked whoever sent him to help me. I couldn't have got through the last few weeks without him by my side.

I knelt on the hard tile as I put myself at eye level with another of Lakeview's victims. Libby was huddled into the corner against the tiled wall, curled as small as possible in what was already a tiny space.

"Hi," I said, keeping my voice soft. "You're Libby, right?"

"Do I know you?"

"I'm Iris. One of the Electi. And I'm so sorry this happened to you."

"The elected?"

"The Electi. Didn't a spirit guide visit you?"

Libby stared at me for longer than was comfortable. "Yes. Yes, she did. I remember now."

"I'm the person she told you about."

"Oh." Libby didn't seem to be quite all there, both physically and metaphorically speaking. She reached a hand towards me, and it passed through my arm. "You're glowing. Are you an angel?"

"Not exactly."

"You're so beautiful."

So had Libby been once. She was tiny, waif-like, with fine features and long brown hair, tangled and damp around her face. The end hadn't been kind to her. She'd been crying as she died. I felt a tear run down my own cheek, and Marcus pressed a handkerchief into my hand. The monogrammed initials said *WJL*, and a stupid giggle threatened to escape. Will monogrammed his hankies?

"You're beautiful too. Who did this to you, Libby?"

"Am I dead? I'm not sure. There was pain, so much pain, and then it went away." She held up one wrist, the deep slashes frozen in time. "I was bleeding, but then it stopped."

"I'm afraid you died, yes."

"Do you know if someone's feeding my cat?"

"Were they feeding your cat when you moved here?"

Libby paused for a moment, her head tilted to one side. "I think so."

"Then I'm sure they're still feeding it."

She gave a sad smile. "I miss my cat."

"Me too." Marcus squeezed my shoulder as if to say

"hurry up." Message received. I wanted to get out of there too. "Libby, do you remember what happened?"

"Happened?"

I motioned to her wrists. "In here. Somebody killed you."

Libby's eyes widened. "The scissors! There were scissors!"

"Who had the scissors, Libby?"

"She...she..."

She?

A soft squeak sounded, and I froze. I knew that sound. It was a nurse or maybe an orderly, although their footsteps tended to be slower and heavier. The squeak had been close by, which meant the nurse was too. Right outside room 134, in fact.

"Who's left the light on in here?" she muttered. A *bleep* told me she'd unlocked the door.

Shit, shit, shit!

I straightened and turned, ready to run or slam the door or jump out the window or *something*. I didn't know what. But what I actually did was trip over my own feet. Dammit! I lurched forward and slammed into Marcus, knocking the wind out of both of us. His reflexes were quicker than mine, and he caught me right as Nurse Glenda walked in. He should have let me fall.

Nurse Glenda took one look at me in Marcus's arms and her jaw dropped.

"What's going on here?"

Did I look as guilty as Marcus? I sure felt that way. *Think, Iris. Think.*

"Miss McGivern felt ill, so I brought her in here to use the bathroom. I thought that was better than having a mess to clean up."

Except he forgot to remove his arms from my waist before he spoke, which I'll admit looked bad. One hand was dangerously close to my ass, and I was still squashed against his chest, which in any other situation, would have been a very nice place to be. Nurse Glenda folded her arms, going full-on dragon lady.

"And that involved giving her mouth-to-mouth, did it?"

"What? Er..." Marcus's arms dropped away as if I'd burned him, and I rocked back onto my heels. "She tripped."

"Do you think I was born yesterday?"

"It's true," I told her. "I did trip."

She ignored me. "What are you doing, preying on young women? You should be ashamed of yourself. Don't think I haven't noticed how much time you've been spending with Miss McGivern. Sessions every day? We don't have time for that. When I saw her new 'treatment plan,' I said to myself, 'You'll have to watch that one, Glenda.'"

Oh, hell.

"But I really do feel sick," I blurted. I wasn't lying. To prove it, I lurched for the toilet, letting my hair flop over my face to cover up the fact that I had a finger down my throat. One quick touch was all it took. I'd had plenty of practice at puking up pills over the years, and I knew exactly how to do it. Marcus leapt forward to hold my hair back, but Nurse Glenda elbowed him out of the way with a low growl.

"You've done quite enough damage here today already. You should leave."

"Iris is my patient."

"Well, she won't be for much longer, I'll see to that." No. She *couldn't*. I vomited again, bile mostly, and this time, I didn't need any help. "Taking advantage of a vulnerable girl that way. It's disgusting."

I grabbed a piece of toilet paper and wiped my mouth, trying with the other hand to grasp Marcus as Nurse Glenda hustled him towards the door. "Stop! Please. It's not like that. I lo—"

Fuck. I'd been about to say I loved him, which would have been the worst move in the history of truly terrible moves. But I really did, and my whole chest seized with the revelation.

"You what?" Nurse Glenda asked. She was only two inches shorter than Marcus and a heck of a lot wider, and although he was probably stronger, he wasn't resisting as she pushed him.

"I've made loads of progress in my recent sessions. I feel like a different person now."

"I bet you do. What did he do? Brainwash you?"

"No!" If anything, it was the other way around. "I was doing intensive short-term dynamic psychotherapy." Did I remember that right?

"Sounds like something he made up."

"Actually, it's a recognised—" Marcus started, but Nurse Glenda cut him off.

"Save it for Mr. Calvert."

With one final shove, she bundled him through the door, and then she turned her beady eyes on me. I backed away because quite honestly, she looked a little maniacal.

"No need to be scared, Iris. I'm here to help you. Men are all the same, and one day you'll learn that.

They just can't keep their hands off no matter how many fancy bits of paper they have. But don't worry, we'll make sure *Mr.* Hastings can't hurt you again."

CHAPTER 31 - IRIS

WHAT WAS HAPPENING? Nurse Glenda had forced me back into my room despite my protestations and stomped off, no doubt to give Marcus hell. She didn't mean what she said about telling Director Calvert, did she?

"What's up?" Jacinda asked. "Why did that old bag bring you back instead of Dr. Hottie?"

"You don't want to know."

"No, I do. OMG, did you have a fight? Two women properly laid into each other this morning on Jezza. The fake blonde lost her false nails and the real blonde pulled the fake one's extensions out. The audience went *wild*."

Jacinda *really* needed to lay off the TV.

"We didn't have a fight, okay?"

I flopped onto the bed, and Jacinda didn't even have the decency to move over. She just rolled onto her side, head propped up on her elbow with her nose an inch from my face.

"Well, something happened. You look like someone ate your puppy, except you don't have a puppy, so...?"

"We got a lead on another dead person, so we snuck off to find her, and everything went wrong."

"Everything? Like what? Who was the dead person?"

"Libby Henkel. Do you know her?"

"Oh, she was weird."

Coming from Jacinda, that was saying something. "We snuck into one of the rooms on the first floor, and she was sitting in the shower with—"

"Wait—they have showers on the first floor?"

"You didn't know that?"

Jacinda shook her head. "Man, this place sucks."

"Why do you care? You'll never need to take a shower again."

"It sucks for you. Director Calvert's such an asshole. If I could move, I'd haunt the heck out of him." Wow, that was sweet of her. "Maybe—*maybe*—he's the new Antichrist. I mean, that evil soul had to go somewhere, didn't it? What if it hopped into Director Calvert and adopted him as its new vessel? You should kill him. That's your job, yes?"

Please, I really don't need this right now. "An interesting theory, but can we stick to the facts for today? And I'm not killing anybody."

She shrugged as best she could while lying down. "Just a suggestion. What did Libby say? Did she know who killed her? How did she die?"

"I'm not going into the gory details."

"Spoilsport. Who did it?"

"I'm not sure. I think Libby was about to tell me, but all she managed to say was that it was a 'she.'"

And the worst part? I hadn't even managed to tell Marcus that before we got forced apart. Which meant he couldn't pass the information on to the others, and they'd still be one step behind.

"A woman? Really?" Jacinda asked.

She sounded surprised, and to be honest, I was too.

I'd always assumed it was a man. Partly because it was a man who'd attacked me before, and partly because two of the deaths—Libby's and Rylie's—had an element of physicality about them. "I'm sure I didn't mishear. She must've been strong, though, the way she pushed Rylie over."

"Or driven. The Antichrist was bigger than me, and I still managed to get the job done. Why didn't you get more details? Then we wouldn't have to sit here and speculate."

"Because Nurse Glenda walked into Libby's room and caught us in the bathroom, and now she thinks I'm having an affair with Dr. Hastings."

Jacinda burst out laughing, and I wanted to shake her. "Well, you are, aren't you?"

"No!"

"Seriously? You should. He's dreamy."

"Are you crazy?"

"That's what the judge said."

"I'm worried he's gonna get into trouble. Nurse Glenda's like Mussolini in Crocs, and she was really, really pissed. What can I do? What if they fire him?"

"What can you do? Nothing. You think anyone would listen to a word you had to say? We're just vermin to them, so you might as well kick back and enjoy an episode of *Survival Island* with me."

"You think I want to watch TV at a time like this? Dr. Hastings is probably getting yelled at by Director Calvert as we speak, and it's all my fault."

If I hadn't been able to see ghosts, if I hadn't agreed to talk to Libby, if I hadn't tripped and fallen right into Marcus's arms... I was a one-woman disaster zone.

Jacinda morphed smoothly into a cross-legged

position. Had she been practising that? "You're right. I'm sorry. I should try to be more understanding because we're friends now, aren't we? So tell me about your problems. I've been watching *Dr. Phil*, so I'll be dead good at giving advice."

On second thoughts... I reached for the remote and turned the TV on.

***

Nobody would tell me anything. While Jacinda watched TV, I paced the room—five steps up, five steps back, five steps up, five steps back—alternately freaking out about Marcus and racking my brain for clues to our culprit.

Half of the staff at Lakeview were women, perhaps even more than half. And thanks to Marcus's request, I'd had nothing but female nurses, female cleaners, and even female orderlies. It was as if the universe was torturing me. Was one of the people who'd served me dinner or brought me sleeping pills or mopped my floor secretly plotting my death? Apart from Glenda, nobody gave off bad vibes, and hers were more obnoxious than creepy.

Scary though it was to contemplate a murderer being on the loose, that was actually preferable to beating myself up about Marcus. If he could have got a message to me, he would have, of that I was certain. Which meant whatever had happened after he left Libby's room was bad. Really bad. On Thursday, grains of hope slipped through my fingers like sand when a nurse pumped me full of pills, and on Friday, they trickled away to almost nothing when an orderly took the TV away. Jacinda's shrieks of outrage made me wish for earplugs.

"It's just a damn TV," I told her.

"The finale of *Survival Island* is tonight!"

"How about *my* survival? Can't we worry about that instead?"

"But—"

"Put it this way—if I die, you won't just have no TV, you'll have no one to talk to either."

That got her attention, and she sat up straighter on the bed. "Do you have paper? You should make a list of names."

***

Even with radio silence from Marcus, I held on to the thinnest thread of optimism that he'd just taken Thursday and Friday off, as per his regular schedule. That thread snapped on Saturday morning when an orderly escorted me to my first psych appointment in four days. My heart thud-thud-thudded all the way down in the lift, and I had to force myself to breathe as we walked along the corridor to Meeting Room Three. But instead of Marcus, a woman sat under the sign reminding me of the many, many rules he'd broken for me.

I'd seen her once or twice in the hallways, but I had no idea who she was. I put her in her mid-forties with strands of grey hair among the brown, wire-framed glasses, and a distinctly unamused expression when she looked up at me.

"Iris McGivern?"

"Yes. Who are you?"

"I'm Dr. Kelley, your new psychiatrist."

"Where's Dr. Hastings?"

"Dr. Hastings no longer works at Lakeview." My world? It stopped spinning. Stopped *dead*. Which was what I'd be soon if a certain member of Lakeview staff had anything to do with it. "I understand there was an incident on..." She consulted her notes. "On Wednesday. Perhaps you'd like to talk through that? I understand it may have been uncomfortable for you."

"I don't want to talk to you. I want to talk to Dr. Hastings."

"I'm afraid that's not possible."

"We had sessions scheduled. He can't just leave like that."

"Between you and me, it wasn't his decision."

They *had* fired him. Those absolute bastards. "Why did they push him out? Was it because of what happened on Wednesday? I already told Nurse Glenda she had that all wrong, but she wouldn't listen. It was the fish. I felt sick because of the fish I had for lunch. Did you try it? The chef should be fired, not Marcus. I mean, Dr. Hastings."

Dammit.

"These fibs are part of the problem, Iris. I'm only sorry nobody spotted this issue sooner."

"There is no issue."

"No one blames you. None of this was your fault. Dr. Hastings abused his position, and we've ensured he can't continue to do so with you or any of our other residents. You don't need to keep covering for him now. He can't hurt you anymore."

"But—"

"I've reviewed your file, Iris. Dr. Hastings

scheduled almost twice as many sessions with you as with any other service user, and procedures have been tightened up to ensure nobody else has such unfettered access to patients."

"What about Dr. Bordais? I was part of a study. She said she could help me."

"Thankfully, Mr. Calvert has agreed with me that you're not a suitable candidate for her research at this time. We're better off sticking with the tried and tested methods to support your mental health, not experimenting." She glanced at the papers in front of her again and sucked in a breath, speaking almost to herself when she continued. "And as for your medication... I don't know what Hastings was thinking."

"I don't need more medication. For the last few weeks, I've felt great, but the nurse gave me extra pills yesterday, and now I'm all groggy again."

Dr. Kelley gave me a condescending smile. "Iris, you need to trust me. I've been a psychiatrist for nearly two decades now, and medication can be very beneficial in situations like this. Now, tell me, have you ever heard of Stockholm syndrome?"

Stockholm syndrome? Ah, *that* was what it was called. Bloody hell. I was fucked.

***

"Dr. Kelley's a patronising old biddy," I slurred to Jacinda on Sunday. "She doesn't listen to a word I say."

"I told you that. Didn't I tell you that?"

"And she says I need even more pills."

"The pills aren't so bad. If you take enough of them,

you might even forget you're in here."

Today had been one long pity party for Jacinda and me. She was lamenting the loss of the TV, and I'd been crying over the loss of my new friends. Yes, I cried, okay? The medication messed with my tear ducts as well as my mind. I used Will's hankie to wipe my eyes, which was yet another reminder of what might have been. The only thing I had left of Marcus was his fancy silver pen. In the daytime, I hid it behind the bedside table because it wasn't as if anyone would move that to clean, and at night, I slept with it under my pillow.

Beside it, I also had the list of names I'd been working on with Jacinda. We'd written down everyone we could think of on the back of an old garden design plan, and when she wasn't plotting Glenda's murder, we talked over the possibilities. But so far, we'd drawn a blank. Sure, we'd crossed off a few names because they hadn't been working there for all the killings— Archie's was the first that we knew of, and that was almost a year ago—but beyond that... Perhaps I should have spent more time watching *CSI* and less time gardening.

When Jacinda got distracted and rambled on, I thought about Marcus. Where was he? What was he doing? Would he find a new job? From what I'd seen of Nicole and heard about the others, I didn't think they'd abandon him, so he wouldn't be homeless, but how would getting fired affect his custody fight?

Some of those questions, I wasn't sure I wanted to know the answers to.

At night, I dreamed of him, of his smile, those all-too-brief touches, the glimpses of the dirty mind I'd seen when he dropped his guard. His tattoo. A hidden piercing...

Then the demons would visit. Terrence and George and an unknown presence, pressing down on me. Harder, harder... I'd wake up sweating, screaming sometimes, and if I was lucky, Jacinda would murmur a few words of sympathy.

I began to think that maybe being dead wouldn't be so bad, after all.

CHAPTER 32 - MARCUS

A WEEK. A fucking week had passed, and I was losing my mind.

"She's on her own in there," I muttered as I paced the kitchen. "This is impossible."

Beck leaned back in his chair and stretched. Over the past seven days, the house had turned into one giant office. RJ had wedged another desk into the study alongside Will and Rania, Reed and Beck were at the dining table, and Nicole was in the living room with Kimberly. Kimberly had taken delivery of four giant whiteboards, and I'd spent this morning screwing them onto the walls. Now the two women were transcribing every significant fact we'd found, but there was still an awful lot of blank space.

So far, we knew that Archie Majors's death had been blamed on the company that manufactured the curry he ate. They'd denied it, of course, but since Lakeview didn't actually make any of the swill they served, merely reheated it, the kitchen didn't contain any peanuts and therefore management claimed the incident couldn't possibly have been their fault.

The circumstances of Rylie Draper's demise were also interesting. RJ found a sworn statement from Sandra Morris, the nurse who was meant to be watching her, describing how she'd been sitting attentively on the seat outside the shower room, waiting for Rylie to come out, when she'd heard a shriek and a "sickening thump." When she ran inside, she found Rylie gasping for breath on the floor, too far gone from her head injury to be saved.

What wasn't mentioned in the statement? Sandra's trip to the break room, the pasty she'd stayed there to eat, or the phone she spent all day, every day engrossed by.

Still, the authorities had bought the story, and Rylie's death was written off as a tragic accident, nothing more.

Lee's, Claire's, and Libby's deaths had been declared suicides, and Jacinda's was natural causes—a cardiac arrest in her sleep, if you could believe that. None of us did, obviously. But how could we contradict the official findings? The bodies were long since buried, or in Libby's case, cremated.

Every day, the glimmer of hope I'd started with grew ever dimmer, but we had to keep looking.

RJ's girlfriend, Shannon, had taken over the cooking, and she seemed to be a big fan of bread and potatoes. Although I didn't feel much like eating, I forced myself to take a few bites each mealtime because I needed the energy. I'd also started running for half an hour or so in the mornings. It was the only time I left the house. Although I wanted to spend the whole time poring over files, I knew I had to release the pressure somehow or I'd give myself a stroke.

"Not impossible," Beck said. "Just difficult. But we're good at this. We found Iris in a sea of seven billion people, didn't we?"

True. I was trying to stay optimistic, but it wasn't

easy. "How *did* you find her, anyway?"

"It was a team effort. Originally, I started researching the Electi four years ago, so we had a head start, and—"

"Wait... I thought you only met Nicole earlier this year?"

"I did, but I'd been looking for her for a lot longer than that."

I shook my head, trying to sort my jumbled thoughts. Clearly, I was missing something. "Can you start at the beginning?"

"Nobody told you? Damn, I thought Nicole would have. When I was an Army Ranger in Afghanistan, I got shot up pretty bad, and I died on the operating table back at base. Just for a few minutes, I saw what they saw."

"*You* saw ghosts?"

"Yeah, I did. And the spirit guide. It was her who told me about the Electi and their job." Beck closed his eyes for a moment, but in the instant before he did so, I glimpsed a whole world of pain in them. "Before I met Nicole, a friend of mine got murdered, and when I realised she was trapped in the ruins of her house and only the Electi could free her..."

"A close friend?"

"We were dating. It was a casual thing, but my ex didn't see it that way. Fucking psycho crazy bitch," he muttered.

He had a psycho ex too? Beck came from a different world to me, but it seemed we had that much in common. "Hell hath no fury like a woman scorned. Or in my case, a woman who thinks she's been scorned."

Beck winced. "Your wife?"

I nodded, but I didn't want to talk about Laurel. Or think about her. Not then, not when we had bigger concerns. "So after your experience, you started looking for the Electi? You thought one of them could free your girlfriend?"

"I did. But I found Nicole by accident. People talk about fate... There's definitely a higher power in play here. Planets aligning or something, I don't know."

"Did she...?" Surely not. I couldn't imagine Nicole killing anybody, let alone hunting down a woman and executing her in cold blood.

"Nicole? No, no way. It's a long story, but Anna's still trapped in California. I thought there was no hope, but then Iris mentioned this Judge... We need to find him."

"How do you know this *thing* even works? That the girls can free the ghosts? That the Judge can?"

"It's been tested several times." Beck's voice had hardened, challenging me. His tone left no room for doubt.

Several times? "By who?"

"All of them. The ghosts definitely vanish." He folded his arms as if to ask, *What are you gonna do about it?*

For a moment, I was shocked into silence. Rania, I could perhaps imagine killing a person—she definitely had an edge to her, and Nicole had said as much. But Kimberly and Nicole? Then I thought back to Iris. If I'd met her outside of Lakeview, I wouldn't have said she was capable either, and yet she'd ploughed into Leland Baker. At first I'd struggled with that, but as I got to know Iris, I'd made peace with what she'd done. Whether she admitted it or not, she'd been under great stress, with little help to process what had happened to her mother. Pile on the pressure of being a member of the Electi and Baker getting out of prison, and she'd cracked.

"I don't really know what to say."

"Then say nothing. Right now, Iris takes priority."

Damn right she did. Whatever the other girls had or hadn't done, I had a degree of confidence that their actions would have been at least somewhat justified. None of them struck me as irrational or overly impulsive. The details could wait.

"How *did* you find Iris?" I asked again.

"Back when I first started looking, I bookmarked a newspaper article about Iris and her mom, but it wasn't until we got organised and began working together that we were able to go through each possibility and come up with a shortlist."

"How many on the list?"

"Iris was the eleventh girl we visited, and definitely the most challenging to speak to."

"How did you know it was her? I was there for the meeting, and Nicole seemed to realise right away. So did Iris."

"Apparently, the girls glow, but only they and the spirits can see it. Nicole's blue, Rania's white, and Kim's pink, which figures."

"What about Iris?"

"Orange, so Nicole says."

Fiery. That figured too. Damn, I missed Iris. I'd given up even trying to pretend that what we'd had was a doctor-patient relationship. In some ways, I was angry at myself for screwing up my career, but it had already been in the toilet thanks to Laurel. Doug

Calvert had merely flushed. At Lakeview, I'd still been within my six-month probation period, so all he'd had to do when Glenda complained was say things weren't working out and then show me the door, muttering about inappropriate behaviour and rocking the boat as he did so. I'd heard whispers of a government inspection coming up, so it didn't shock me that he wanted to bury bad news. Kimberly had been furious on my behalf and consulted with the lawyer, but we had no recourse. Again, no surprises.

I'd already researched employment law when I left Deane Valley, and my own lawyer was of the opinion that I could make a case for wrongful dismissal there, but Cassidy had to come first. If I sued the hospital where Laurel and her father worked, she'd paint me as a vindictive ex-spouse out for revenge, and she already had enough firepower to use against me without adding more ammunition to the pile. I'd decided to back off to improve my chances of getting custody.

At least, that had been my original plan. By getting fired from Lakeview, I'd just handed Laurel a fucking cannon.

Perhaps I *should* file a wrongful dismissal complaint after all? At this stage, I had little to lose, and I needed to pay the rent somehow. Rent for a house I couldn't even live in. Someone from the council had accompanied me back to the place for long enough to pack some belongings, but there was a crack in the front facade and a good chunk of the driveway was gone. My life was currently sitting in half a dozen borrowed suitcases in Will's semi-renovated pool house. And a small room on the second floor of Lakeview Secure Hospital.

"What else can I do to help?" I asked.

"There's more security camera footage that needs viewing."

Tracking down a killer without being able to speak to any potential witnesses, or search the crime scenes, or examine the bodies was a near-impossible task. Reed and Will were both cops turned private investigators, and I heard the weariness in their voices each time Kimberly or Nicole demanded an update. Usually Kimberly.

RJ had used the backdoor I'd loaded onto Becca's computer to ferret around in Lakeview's network, and that was where most of our information had come from so far. With Iris's safety at stake, my morals had taken a back seat. We had three lists—the victims, the remaining residents, and the employees. One by one, we were going through them for any possible links. We knew for certain that we had four victims—Archie Majors, Libby Henkel, Jacinda Warren, and Rylie Draper—because Iris had spoken to them. There were still question marks over Lee Sorensen and Claire Welby. They'd both died following incidents at Lakeview, but had they been killed?

A further complication was that each victim had died in a different manner. An allergic reaction, slit wrists, a potential overdose, and an "accident" in the shower, plus a second overdose and an apparent suicide by drain cleaner if we took into account the two possibles. The deceased had little in common. Apart from the fact that they'd been at Lakeview and they'd all either killed or seriously injured people, we couldn't find a connection.

According to Will and Reed, the overdoses and the

allergic reaction indicated a woman's touch, as females statistically liked to utilise hands-off methods, but the other three... We were either talking a man or a hell of a lot of pent-up anger. If it was the latter, the culprit hid it well. None of the staff at Lakeview came across as cold-blooded killers, but then again, if you'd asked me when I first met them, I'd never have guessed that Kimberly or Nicole would be capable of taking a life either.

What a mess.

At the end of this, I could see myself needing the services of a psychiatrist.

CHAPTER 33 - MARCUS

ANOTHER GLOOMY MORNING, another fifty files of security camera footage.

We'd been able to estimate each victim's time of death from the autopsy reports RJ found on the system, and even allowing a tolerance of three hours each way, no member of staff had been scheduled to work during all six deaths. Narrowing the focus to just Archie, Libby, Jacinda, and Rylie, there were seven crossovers according to the staff rota—two orderlies, one psychiatrist, three nurses, and a cleaner—so Reed and Rania were focusing on researching their backgrounds.

But the rota didn't necessarily mean much—when I'd worked overtime, it wasn't listed on there, for example, and there was nothing to stop staff members from coming and going as they pleased. Hence the reason I was going square-eyed staring at a computer screen.

Lakeview's management had cheaped out on everything, it seemed, not just patient facilities. The CCTV system worked when it felt like it, which was to say, not very often. Around half of the cameras seemed to be on the blink at any given time, and when the hard drives filled up, the software simply overwrote the earlier footage. RJ had retrieved shreds and snippets from the backup system, but there were still great chunks missing. Reviewing it was like trying to do a jigsaw puzzle where half the pieces had gone astray.

The access control system recorded each time somebody opened a door, but it didn't record who that somebody was. At the moment, Kimberly and I were trying to match up the door movements via the camera footage to see who went where, a time-consuming task made all the more frustrating by the fact that we'd had no news about Iris for two days. The last update to her patient file had been on Tuesday when they'd increased her dose of haloperidol, a drug I'd taken her off because she simply didn't need it. Seeing those words on the screen and imagining what she must be going through made me want to slam Calvert against a wall and shake him until he understood the damage that Lakeview's policies—policies that he was responsible for—inflicted on the residents.

RJ wandered into the kitchen, rubbing his eyes.

"Have you ever picked at a thread on a sweater only for the whole thing to unravel? And has anyone made coffee?"

"I'll make coffee," Kimberly offered. "I need a break."

"What's happened?" I asked.

"Will was trying to find out how many patients are at each of Hannity SP's hospitals, so I dug out their management accounts because they go into more detail than the financial statements filed at Companies House. The P&L lists expenditure for each facility line by line, and in the last year, Lakeview spent half a million pounds on patient enrichment."

I thought back to what I'd seen during my time

there, or rather, what I hadn't seen. "No way."

"There was even a note in the board minutes about it. The directors said the costs were too high, and Calvert argued that a full range of activities was necessary in order to provide a fulfilling patient experience, whatever that is. But Nicole said Iris never got out of her cell?"

"She didn't. Not until I got there."

"The board asked for further information, and Calvert provided a list of activities by patient." RJ consulted his phone. "Iris goes swimming on Fridays, takes a dance class on Sundays, does basket weaving on Mondays, and on Wednesdays, she's learning to play the piano."

"That's utter bullshit. The swimming pool's closed off, there are no dance classes, Iris got banned from basket weaving, and the only musical instrument she can play is the guitar."

"So where the hell is the money going?"

We stared at each other for a second.

"Calvert," we both said at the same time.

It fitted. He was in a position of responsibility, and he had expensive hobbies. Plus he'd been at Lakeview for eight years, according to his biography on the hospital's website, which was plenty of time for him to cook the books and garnish them too. Five hundred grand a year? They weren't even spending half of that.

"But how?" I asked. "Expense claims need to be approved. Calvert himself signed off on mine..." And he'd bitched like hell about the gym mat I ordered for Iris. "But it stands to reason that someone higher up checks his. They may not be good at patient oversight, but they sure like to keep an eye on the money."

I'd overheard one of my colleagues in the break room the other day, grumbling because she'd been forced to buy sanitary towels for a patient with her own money after Lakeview ran out of supplies. Apparently, Calvert had refused to reimburse her because she didn't seek his approval first. I screwed my eyes shut because I didn't want to think of what Iris was going through, then realised that didn't help in the slightest and opened them again. See no evil, hear no evil, speak no evil—that was the Lakeview philosophy. At first, I'd thought it was mere incompetence that tarnished the place, but if Calvert was deliberately diverting funds from the patients...

Reed made his way over from the dining area. "I had a case like that once."

"A hospital?"

"A construction company. I was undercover, and even now, I can still build one hell of a brick wall. Took me a month of snooping, but I worked out the manager of one of the sites was submitting false invoices for goods and services they never received."

"Like, say, for music lessons that never took place, or pool maintenance that never happened?"

"Exactly. RJ, can you find invoices for all the activities that went into the P&L account?"

"I can try. In a company that size, they'll have an accounting department at head office, and I'll need to get into their files. Kimberly, can you bring that coffee through to the den?"

"Sure, and I'll even bring cookies too."

***

Luckily for us, it turned out that Lakeview's data security was about as good as its physical security. Apparently, they'd set the system administrator's password to "administrator" and now RJ had access to everything. Including folders and folders full of scanned invoices for everything from basket cane to guitar strings to a massage therapist. Kimberly and I had put our efforts with the camera footage on hold to look up the suppliers on the internet, and so far, around three quarters of them didn't appear to exist. A handful were registered at Companies House, but their annual accounts—if they'd filed them at all—gave little information, and their websites were generic, single pages with no contact details beyond an enquiry form. Others appeared to be sole traders, with no official footprint and no evidence of trading other than a few cut-and-paste reviews on Yell.com.

Interestingly, half of the dodgy invoices had been added to the purchase order system by an admin clerk and the other half by the PR lady Calvert was reputed to be screwing around with, before being countersigned by Calvert himself. Purchasing woodwork tools didn't fall under the remit of any kind of PR I knew, but it seemed she was excellent at multitasking.

"JR Art Supplies," Kimberly said. "The closest company I can find that's actually selling products is JB Art Supplies, and they're at a completely different address."

Reed grinned from the other side of the dining table. "JR's fake. They borrowed their logo from a defunct Canadian stationery supplier, and the registered office is a derelict building. Add it to the list, sweetheart."

The list took up half of one whiteboard, and although it was getting longer by the hour, I still had one burning question. "What are we actually going to do with this information? Calvert's dirty, yes, and I want him removed from his position at Lakeview as much as you do, but how does that help Iris? Even if they replace him and she gets access to the greenhouse again, she's still stuck there."

"Maybe the new person will be more willing to follow the proper procedures?" Kimberly suggested. "Like evaluating her for release?"

"Firing Calvert, installing a new manager, getting Iris through the system... That'll take months, if not years, and she's in imminent danger."

"We're going as fast as we can, buddy," Reed said. "If I could click my fingers and get her out of there, I would."

Honestly, I was beginning to think that Nicole's idea of busting Iris free might be the way to go. The delay was interminable. Couple that with the wait for Cassie's court date, and I was tempted to write myself a prescription for a little something to take the edge off.

But I couldn't. Thanks to tiredness and eye strain, my vision was already blurry. The email address at the top of Calvert's approval to purchase a new, non-existent piano swam in front of my eyes. The second part of Calvert's email had changed from .com to .co. I squinted, but the *m* was definitely missing. Strange.

"Reed, does Calvert have two email addresses? I thought we'd only found one?"

"I've only seen one."

"Then there's something odd about this authorisation email."

Everyone had a .com address, including me when I worked there. I typed the .co address into my web browser and got a domain parking message. What was going on?

Reed leaned over my shoulder. "Yeah, that *is* weird. I'll send a message to RJ. Maybe we missed an account? Thinking about priorities, do you want to go back to looking at the camera footage? I can handle the invoices with Kim, and once Nicole gets off the phone with Professor Fairchild, she can lend a hand."

My stomach dropped as I thought of watching daily life at Lakeview once again, but at the same time, I knew we needed to catch the psycho roaming the hallways—and I wasn't talking about a service user.

"Sure, I'll pick up where I left off."

But first I needed more coffee.

Chapter 34 - Iris

I STARED AT the squirrel through the glass, elbows on the windowsill. He had acres and acres of countryside to roam in, and that was where he decided to sit?

"Dude, you must be so bored."

"Join the club," Jacinda muttered from behind me. "Can't you ask for the TV back?"

"I tried." Believe me, I'd tried. Jacinda hadn't given me a moment's peace since it got removed, and I was so sick of her talking that I'd resorted to stuffing toilet paper in my ears again. Of course, then Dr. Kelley assumed I must be hearing voices—which was true, just not in the way she thought—and gave me extra pills. Some of them were even fun. The big pink tablets, for example. Right after I took them, the room went all floaty.

"You should try harder." Jacinda leaned forward as far as she could, trying to look out the window. "That squirrel's evil. Do you think he's a messenger? Maybe this is a sign."

Huh? "How is he evil?"

"His eyes are weird."

They were just little black squirrel eyes. Nothing strange about them at all. "His eyes are perfectly normal. He's cute."

"You're weird. Squirrels are basically rats with

bigger tails. Tree rats."

Jacinda thought a squirrel on the windowsill was a sign of evil, and *I* was the weird one? I turned a wonky cartwheel and landed in a heap on the floor, my bum aching where I hit the cold tiles. Life at Lakeview had gone back to the way it was before, in the pre-Marcus days, except somehow, it was worse. Why? I had the same dull routine, the same zombifying medication, the same slop to eat. Why, why, why? Was it because I'd known *more*? Yes, that must be it. I'd had a friend, two friends, and now they'd gone. Poof. Vanished. Disappeared into the ether like leaves on the wind.

Or birds. A red kite and a blue jay, soaring towards the horizon until they flew out of my life altogether. Actually, wrong metaphor. What happened to Marcus was more akin to getting blasted out of the sky by a farmer holding a grudge and a shotgun.

I stretched out, arms above my head, and in that position, I could touch both walls. The ceiling had a water stain shaped like Brazil. Or was it Argentina? I never was very good at geography. The furthest I'd travelled was Manchester, so perhaps that wasn't surprising?

"Have you ever been abroad?" I asked Jacinda.

"How did we get from tree rats to going abroad?"

I pointed at the ceiling, and she looked up.

"Argentina," I said.

"That's Peru."

See?

"Have you been there?"

"No, just Spain, France, Belgium, Croatia, Canada, New York, Madeira, Barbados, the Canary Islands, and Florida."

"What, did you win the lottery?"

"No, my dad was an airline pilot so we got cheap tickets. At least, we did until he left Mum for a member of the cabin crew. After that we stayed at home. I remember Mum asking him what Alex had that she didn't, and it turned out to be a penis."

Ouch. "I'm sorry."

Jacinda shrugged. "Everything happens for a reason. If Dad had paid his child support, we wouldn't have had to move to a smaller house. And then I wouldn't have met our new neighbours and cleansed the world of the Antichrist."

Well, there was that.

"You also wouldn't have come to Lakeview and died."

Jacinda shrugged. "I have a purpose here."

Other than to get on my nerves? "What purpose?"

"I'm not sure yet."

The door lock bleeped, and I looked up to see Nurse Hazel standing over me with a tray. Smelled like Teen Spirit. Only kidding. It smelled like week-old dog vomit with top notes of cabbage.

"What are you doing on the floor, Iris?"

What did it look like? "Lying down."

"Up you get. It's dinner time."

"I'm not hungry."

"You need to eat something or you'll end up as skin and bone."

"I ate breakfast."

She didn't bother to answer, just sighed before backing towards the door. "Suit yourself. I'll be back in an hour with your medication."

At least that would zonk me out for the night. Once

Nurse Hazel had gone, I rolled onto my knees and checked out the tray. Cottage pie with green stuff. Or maybe shepherd's pie. Someone once told me there was a difference, but I didn't know what it was. In Lakeview, I didn't want to know. I staggered to my feet and scraped the whole lot into the toilet so at least I wouldn't have to look at it anymore.

"Are you on a hunger strike?" Jacinda asked.

"Nope."

"A diet?"

"Nope."

I'd have sold my soul for a flapjack. Or one of those giant cookies with the chocolate chips. Or a packet of Revels, even the coffee-flavoured ones.

"Hey, Jacinda. Next time you speak to your guy, can you ask him how much he'd pay for my soul?"

"I'm not sure he buys souls."

Gah. I flopped backwards onto the bed to wait for my meds. Day 1,945 at Lakeview. Or was it 1,946? Was it a Monday? My mind just wouldn't *think*. At least in an hour, I'd be dispatched to sweet oblivion, ready to dream about Marcus and freedom and endless flapjacks dipped in chocolate.

I closed my eyes and tried to block out Jacinda as I counted down the seconds.

Three thousand six hundred, three thousand five hundred and ninety-nine, three thousand five hundred and ninety-eight...

Chapter 35 - Marcus

ON TUESDAY MORNING, Will walked into the dining area holding a printout and a croissant. "Iris had another psych appointment."

I nearly snatched the paper out of his hand.

"What happened?"

"Not a lot. She refused to speak unless someone gave her a flapjack, so the psychiatrist sent her back to her room."

That was my Iris.

"Nothing else?"

"Apparently she's talking to wildlife again. One of the nurses heard her having a conversation with a squirrel."

A squirrel who was most likely named Jacinda. I breathed a long sigh of relief because at least Iris was okay. Alive and obstreperous, and I wouldn't want her any other way.

"I deposited two hundred pounds into her commissary account," Kimberly said. "Why won't they let her buy her own flapjacks?"

"Because they're probably skimming off the commissary accounts too," Will pointed out.

Six days we'd been at this, going through invoices, and there was no doubt in any of our minds what was happening and who the guilty party was. Doug Calvert was running Lakeview as his own personal piggy bank. We'd begun preparing a report detailing the hundreds of fake invoices, dates, and amounts, ready to go to Hannity SP's Board of Directors. I wanted to go to the police as well—theft was theft, after all—but when Kimberly consulted with the lawyer, he said it would be a civil case unless Hannity's board wanted to press charges.

A blow, but at least we could get rid of Calvert. Perhaps his replacement would allow Iris to have visitors again? I had to think positive.

"Coffee, anyone?" I asked.

There were murmurs of assent, and I was just about to take a turn at making drinks when Will's countenance morphed from cheesed-off to concerned. I followed his gaze, turning to look over my shoulder, and saw RJ standing in the doorway. His expression... Was that excitement? Or horror? Or shock?

"Mate, what happened?" Will asked.

RJ's voice came out as a whisper. "I didn't just unravel the sweater this time, I unravelled the whole damn sheep. Guts are gonna spill."

The atmosphere charged in a second. Everyone went rigid.

"And?"

"I got into Calvert's second email account. Fuck, I don't even know where to start..."

"At the beginning?"

"Which beginning? The one where he bribed the medical examiner to change Lee and Jacinda's causes of death? The one where he's been taking kickbacks from the drug companies based on the volume of product Lakeview uses? Or the one where Hannity SP's been bribing prosecutors and a certain judge we're all familiar with to send them patients, or as they call them, 'revenue-generating units'?"

Will just stared at RJ, along with the rest of us. "I'm sorry, what?"

"The second email address Marcus found? I bet Calvert used it by accident that day. It's his... Hmm, what to call it? His blackmail bank? His dastardly alter ego? Whenever he needed to do something underhanded, he used it instead of his regular account. It's basically a confession."

Five minutes later, all nine of us were clustered around RJ's computer, even Shannon since Aisling was taking a nap. Who cared about coffee anymore? I was wide awake and sick to my stomach.

There was a chat group. A fucking chat group on an instant messaging service. Presumably, they'd picked that particular app because it was encrypted and therefore safe from the prying eyes of outsiders, but Calvert had been screen-shotting conversations for years and sending them to himself for safekeeping.

"Grifters gonna grift," Beck muttered.

Will shook his head. "This is beyond grifting."

"Criminals gonna crime."

"Bet he kept this as his get-out-of-jail-free card. If the directors ever came after him for the invoices, he'd fire back with this little lot."

"A crooked crook—who'd have guessed?"

RJ was right. Where did we start?

With Archie Majors, it seemed. That was as good a place as any. Surprise, surprise, they'd lied about the peanuts. Before the health and safety people visited, they'd cleared the Snickers bars and the peanut M&Ms

out of the vending machine and removed any offending items from the kitchen. The catering company had gone bust from the fallout, but rather than feeling guilty, one of Hannity SP's directors had sent a "Phew, that's us off the hook" message.

And it got worse.

A panicked paragraph from Calvert shortly after Lee Sorensen's death informed the others that Lee had been sweating and vomiting right before he died. The doctor suspected an insulin overdose, but Lee wasn't diabetic. What should they do?

The CEO personally assured him that he'd take care of the problem, and the very next day, it turned out that Sorensen had died of a diazepam overdose, as certified by the newly appointed medical examiner. Did these people realise how much diazepam it took to kill a man? Simply hoarding a few pills as they'd claimed wouldn't cut it. He'd have needed hundreds.

Was that why the same medical examiner had gone with heart failure for Jacinda? I recalled a comment Iris had made in one of our chats, that Jacinda looked sweaty with dilated pupils. Those were both symptoms of—you've guessed it—an insulin overdose.

Fuck. All it would take was one needle, one little prick, and Iris would be gone.

Then I breathed again as I recalled the insulin at Lakeview was under lock and key, and only a few members of staff had access. Were the previous deaths the reason why? As with the shellfish allergy signs, were they shutting the stable door after the horse had bolted?

Will rose to his feet, knees cracking. "Guys, I hate to say this, but we need help."

"I've been telling you that for years," RJ quipped.

"Oh, very funny. No, I mean this has gone beyond expense fraud and into criminal territory."

"We already knew that," I pointed out.

"But we only had Iris's word for it. Now we have proof."

"So what are you suggesting we do? Call the police?"

"I think we have to," Will said.

RJ shook his head. "We can't tell them where we got this evidence, and none of it would be admissible in court."

"And what if the police mess up?" I asked, thinking back to my restraining order. The constables who came to the house had done zero investigation, just listened to Laurel's teary sob story and thrown me into a cell for the night. "It wouldn't take much for Calvert to delete this entire email account."

"Or for someone from head office to start scrubbing incriminating evidence from the network." RJ rubbed his temples. "From the IP address, it looks as if the server with the emails is located at Lakeview. Easy enough for a person to carry it out of the building."

"There must be hard copies of those invoices, and they're probably at Lakeview too. What if they get shredded?"

"Then what do you suggest?" Will asked. "We can't raid the place ourselves. This is a government-approved hospital, not a crime boss's house in California."

The way he spoke, it almost sounded as if they *had* once raided a crime boss's house in California.

"A what?" I asked.

"Long story. Anyhow, my point is, we can't do this alone."

RJ scrubbed a hand through his hair. The others seemed to be leaving the decision to the Brits, probably because England wasn't their usual stomping ground.

"Can you think of anyone we could trust?" RJ asked Will.

I didn't know a huge amount about Will's past, but from snippets I'd heard here and there, I gathered he'd left the police force under as much of a cloud as I left the medical profession. A vindictive by-the-book asshole with an expertise in paperwork had been mentioned, and it seemed Will's former colleagues had been as supportive of him as the mental-health team at Deane Valley had been of me. Which is to say, they'd kept their heads down to save their own skins.

With that in mind, it struck me that Will would want to avoid involving the police if at all possible, so for him to suggest calling the authorities... Yes, this was serious.

Will thought for a few moments. Everyone else was watching him, and I felt a little sorry for the man. No pressure.

Finally, he spoke. "There is one person. I'll give her a call and sound her out."

***

After lunch, Will, RJ, and I faced Detective Joanne O'Dowd across the dining table. The Americans had made themselves scarce for the time being—Will didn't think the British police would take too kindly to having their jurisdiction trampled all over—and Rania didn't like law enforcement.

O'Dowd was a slight brunette who wore glasses and a vaguely cynical expression. I couldn't say I blamed her. Will had been spectacularly vague on the phone earlier, just saying that he had a case that could make her career if she played her cards right. Now, she folded her arms.

"Well? You got me here on my day off, so this had better be good."

Will did the talking. "We've got fraud, corruption, and even a few potential murders to liven things up a bit. What do you know about Lakeview Secure Hospital?"

"That place on the hill where the crazies go?"

I wasn't sure I liked her. "They're not crazies, they're people suffering from mental illness. And I'm not convinced all the residents are even ill."

She adjusted her glasses. "And you are?"

"Dr. Marcus Hastings. Until a few weeks ago, I worked at Lakeview."

"I see."

"No, I don't think you do. The—"

Will held up a hand to stop me. "Let's start from the top, shall we? Jo, you know I don't bullshit. The last time I handed you a case, you got a promotion out of it."

"And a headache from trying to explain to the superintendent where my tip-off came from."

"Details, details... Three weeks ago"—was it really so little time? It felt like a lot longer—"Marcus came to us with concerns over the treatment of his patients. They're locked up in their rooms pretty much twenty-four-seven, drugged most of the time, and a number of them are being treated for illnesses he doesn't believe they have."

"That sounds like more of a civil matter. Isn't there an ombudsman for these things?"

"Yes, and that was our initial plan—to file a report. But the ombudsman route's slow, and while we were digging around, we found some accounting irregularities. Costs in the financial statements for patient activities, for example, that don't match up with what Marcus saw at the facility. So we dug deeper, and it looks as though the hospital director's skimming from the company."

"Again, that's a civil matter. There'll be a board of directors—"

"We haven't got to the best part yet."

"Go on."

"In the process of our evidence gathering..." Will avoided looking at RJ. "We found that bribery makes the world go round at Lakeview. The people at the top are paying off Judge Leavitt and several of his prosecutors to send them patients, and since procedures aren't followed, the chances of those patients getting out alive are slim. Each patient's worth £450 in revenue per day to Lakeview's parent company, charged to us the taxpayers. £165,000 per patient, per year," he added for emphasis.

"Lock 'em Up Leavitt? Are you serious? He's Mr. Law and Order."

"Except when he's flouting it, it seems. He went so far as to alert the board of Hannity SP—that's Lakeview's parent company—that he's got a whole bunch of potential revenue-generating units coming their way, and they responded by refurbishing a new wing. It's ready and waiting."

"Bloody hell." O'Dowd sighed, hopefully because she was starting to realise she wouldn't be getting much sleep over the next week or two. "And what do you mean by getting out alive? You mentioned murder?"

"In the past year, six patients have died at Lakeview, which is excessive. In the last large-scale study done, 271 vulnerable patients died over the course of six years across 136 NHS bodies. That's an average of two each, *over six years.* Extrapolating Lakeview's track record, they'd have thirty-six fatalities during the same time period. Thirty-four extra deaths. That number alone indicates a problem, but we also found documents suggesting that Hannity SP paid a medical examiner to change the cause of death for two patients. The other four? If they weren't murdered, it indicates a lack of care so staggering it borders on involuntary manslaughter."

"Okay, you've got my attention. So where's this evidence?"

"The trouble is, we may have cut a few corners in obtaining it."

Detective O'Dowd rolled her eyes. "How did I guess?"

RJ spoke up. "In terms of above-board information, we can provide an analysis of Leavitt's sentencing record showing he's way out of step with other judges. Plus there're the statistics Will just mentioned. And Marcus here will tell you what he saw at Lakeview. We can show you other stuff, but that'll be off the record. It'll be up to you to work out how you can use it to get a warrant."

"I'm not sure—"

My turn. "With the state of play at Lakeview, I've got little doubt somebody else is going to die soon. Do you want their blood on your hands? Because if we can't get the director removed and proper procedures put in place, that's what's going to happen."

"Hey, don't you go putting this on me."

"You're the police. We're reporting to you that there's a serious problem. We can hardly march in there and get the place shut down ourselves. You'd arrest us."

That got me a flicker of a smile. "That's true enough. Go on, then. Show me this evidence you're not meant to have."

When she got up to leave, Detective O'Dowd looked ten years older than when she'd arrived. Her parting words?

"Leave it with me. I'll see what I can do."

Just hold on, Iris.

Chapter 36 - Iris

MONDAY, TUESDAY, WEDNESDAY, Thursday, Friday, Saturday, Sundaaaaaaay. What day was it? I didn't know, and it didn't matter anyway. Every day was the same now.

"The squirrel's back," Jacinda said.

"Yeah."

I didn't like the squirrel anymore. It had walnuts, and I didn't. And Jacinda was right—it *did* have weird eyes.

This evening, my room stank of fish. Nasty, slimy fish that had tasted worse than it smelled. I'd asked Nurse Glenda to take it away as soon as she brought it, but she'd shaken her head, said rules were rules, and left it on my desk. My *desk*. Why did we have desks if we didn't have any work to do? Jacinda said she'd had a set of paints once, but when I asked if I could have one, Nurse Hazel said the art supplies were no longer available due to funding issues.

Funding issues. Yeah, right. My room overlooked the car park, and Director Calvert had just gotten a new Bentley. Guess there were certain things they found the money for.

Speaking of Nurse Hazel, she bleeped the door open and walked in holding a tray. Hurrah. Time for the day's final dose of medication. Dr. Kelley seemed to be treating me as a science project, and the pills changed nightly. It was pot luck whether I fell unconscious in an instant or lay awake for hours with what felt like ants crawling under my skin. *I'll take door number one, Monty.*

"You didn't like your dinner?" Nurse Hazel asked.

"How did you guess?"

"Dr. Kelley says you're losing weight. You really should eat more."

"I'd love to, but it tastes like it's been digested already."

She chuckled as she tidied my blankets. "So you don't want me to pass your compliments to the chef?"

"I'm pretty sure you don't have a chef. You have a microwave."

"No, we have a chef. He's been here since Lakeview opened."

"Then he should have been sacked long ago."

Nurse Hazel's smile faded, and she tutted a bit. "Manners cost nothing, Iris. Would it hurt you to be polite?"

"Letting me out of my cell costs nothing. Would it hurt you to take me for a walk every so often?"

Take me for a walk, like a dog. All I needed was a bloody leash.

"Not my decision, I'm afraid. You'll need to speak to Dr. Kelley about that."

"I already did." Care to go out on a limb and guess what she said?

"Well, there's your answer. Time for your pills, Iris."

It was like being in *The Matrix*. A red pill and a blue pill, except lucky old me got to take both of them. Okay, so the red one was more pink, but Marcus would still have been jealous. Was he watching a movie tonight? Who with? Did he even remember who I was? The thought that he might have forgotten depressed me more than I could bear.

"What have I got today?"

"Asenapine to stabilise your mood and zolpidem to help you fall asleep."

"My mood's just fine as it is." Apart from being miserable, anyway. I needed happy pills. Something to mellow me out. One of my former housemates had sworn by cannabis, but when I tried smoking a joint, I coughed so hard I nearly brought up my lungs, my guts, and everything in between.

"Please, Iris. I don't want to have to call Dr. Kelley again."

She'd done that last week, and then I'd got an injection that left me zonked for days afterwards. No way did I want to go through that again. I swallowed the pink pill, then reached for the blue capsule.

"She's got it wrong," Jacinda said.

Who'd got what wrong? I couldn't exactly ask for clarification, not with Nurse Hazel watching me. I managed a half-shrug.

"That's not asenapine. Asenapine's little white pills you dissolve under your tongue. I took them for years."

I stared at the capsule in my hand, sky blue with one transparent end that let me see the powder inside.

"Uh, I think you picked up the wrong pill," I said.

Nurse Hazel shook her head. "No, that's what Dr. Kelley gave me."

"Then *she* got it wrong."

"Iris, it's almost the end of my shift. Stop being silly

and take your medication."

"I took asenapine before, and this isn't it."

"Sometimes they change the packaging."

Jacinda jumped in again. "Four years, and it never changed once."

"Can't you just call Dr. Kelley?"

Nurse Hazel grabbed my chin with unexpected strength and squeezed. What the...? My mouth popped open—from surprise or from pain, I wasn't sure—and before I could clamp my jaw shut again, she'd rammed the blue capsule down my throat.

And then I realised.

Nurse Hazel was Lakeview's killer. In an instant, her eyes had gone from blue and twinkly to dark and glittering, and she forced me backwards onto the bed, pinning me in place with her bodyweight. And people said *I* was the crazy one? I tried to scream, but she clamped a hand over my mouth.

Jacinda had no such problems. "It's the Antichrist," she shrieked. "He's back!"

She was back. I had to concede Jacinda was half-right.

"Swallow," Hazel ordered. She didn't deserve the "nurse" title anymore. What happened to the caring profession? "Swallow, swallow, swallow!"

No, no, no.

"Get rid of it!" Jacinda yelled.

What did she think I was trying to do?

But even as I fought to spit, gravity was working against me. Then Hazel backhanded me, a hard slap, and the damn pill slipped down my throat.

She grinned triumphantly when she realised what had happened, rocking back on her knees to stare at me.

"There, there, it'll all be over soon. Don't worry."

"Why?" I choked out.

"You really have to ask that? You killed a person, Iris. You killed a person, so you don't deserve to live."

"You killed six people. *You* don't deserve to live."

"Eight, actually, but it's my job. Somebody needs to get rid of the broken people before they can do more damage." She reached out to stroke my hair, almost tenderly. "It's nothing personal, Iris. It's not your fault you're sick in the head."

Her job? *No, love, it's* my *job*.

And if I didn't get on with it, I was going to die, and then my soul would be left to find a new host. There would be no gradual transfer of power. A baby would be born seeing spirits, and a whole world of trouble would await.

But what could I do?

My call button was too far away to reach. I tried to roll off the bed, but Hazel leaned forward, pressing onto my chest, and held me there. How long for? A minute? Two minutes? Ten? Time slowed to a ponderous *tick, tick, tick*. What had she given me? Dammit, I didn't want to die, not in a shitty room in a shitty hospital because a shitty nurse had lost her fucking mind.

I'd never see Marcus again.

Marcus, Marcus... The only man in the last five years who'd treated me like a human being instead of a pest. Marcus, Marcus... Such a pretty face. Maybe he'd plant a garden one day, and my ideas would live on even if I didn't. My ideas. All those pictures I'd drawn...

The pictures I'd drawn.

The pictures...

I scrabbled under my pillow, already drowsy and weirdly calm, and with the last of my strength, I grabbed Marcus's fancy silver pen and jabbed it at Hazel's face as hard as I could. Did I hit her? Everything was blurry now.

I tried to roll off the bed again, and this time, she didn't stop me. My fingers found their way into my throat, and I retched, bringing up a pile of fishy yuck and a mushy blue mess. Was it gone? The pill? And what about Hazel?

I struggled onto my side in time to see a black soul rise above my bed and then scatter like dust to every corner of the room. Next to Hazel's lifeless body, Jacinda barely had time to wave before she faded away.

My cheeks felt damp. Was I crying? I was crying. I rubbed at my eyes and then wished I hadn't because Hazel's face was right in front of me, Marcus's pen protruding from her right eyeball. What had I promised him when he gave it to me? Oh, yeah... That I wouldn't stab anyone in the eye with it. He was gonna be pissed. Sooooo pissed.

I giggled. And giggled, and giggled, and giggled, and then I fell asleep.

"JO, WHAT'S HAPPENING?"

The phone had only rung once before Will switched it onto speaker, and I paused mid-stride in the kitchen. I was surprised I hadn't worn a track in the floor. We'd been waiting almost two hours for an update, and every second had felt like a decade. RJ had been checking Twitter obsessively, and when he didn't find anything concrete, Kimberly had threatened to drive over to Lakeview and take a look until Reed confiscated her car keys.

Tonight was the night of the raid, a coordinated effort between several police forces that Detective O'Dowd and her colleagues had managed to organise in little more than a week, driven by concern over the atrocities happening within the hospital walls and the knowledge that any cock-ups on their part would make the news.

Lakeview was their primary target, but they were also hitting Doug Calvert's home, Hannity SP's headquarters, and two more hospitals that a team of forensic accountants had identified as anomalous. The past week and a half had been like peeling an onion—every layer made us want to weep more.

But at least Iris was hanging in there. According to a file update this morning, she'd lost half a stone over the last month, but she was still alive. By tomorrow, she'd be safe, and by next week, we should have a better idea of how to get her out of there.

"You're not gonna believe this," O'Dowd said. "We got inside okay, then found the fuse box and cut all the power except to the door locks as planned, but when the team got to the second floor, they found another dead body."

Every atom in me froze. The second floor? Iris's room was on the second floor.

"Whose body?" Will asked.

Don't let it be Iris. Don't let it be Iris. Don't let it be Iris.

Perhaps that was selfish of me, to wish for someone else's death, but not one other person in that place lit up my life the way she did. Sure, she was awkward and stubborn and she liked to talk back, but she was also sweet and funny and no matter how much I'd tried to deny it, I wanted to shuck her out of her clothes and carry her to bed.

"That girl you mentioned," Detective O'Dowd said. "Iris McGivern?"

I don't know exactly how, but I ended up on my knees. My legs just buckled. Iris? She'd gone? Dammit all to hell, we'd been so close. *So* close. And the worst part? She died alone, thinking I'd abandoned her. Something came out of my mouth, but it wasn't words. More of a wail, and then Kimberley was beside me, quick with a hug.

"The body was in her room with a pen sticking out of its eyeball," the detective continued. "McGivern was sleeping on the floor next to it. Who knows how I'm gonna explain this one to the super."

"It wasn't her," Nicole whispered, crouching next to me and squeezing my shoulder. "It wasn't Iris."

It wasn't? I fought against the shutters that had slammed down on my world. Iris was alive?

Somehow, Will kept his voice steady. "Any idea what happened?"

"Right now? Not a scooby. This mess is gonna take days to unravel."

"Where's Iris now?"

"Under arrest at Deane Valley Hospital. She seems out of it. Woke up long enough to mutter something about going to a proper prison this time and then passed out again."

"If she killed someone, it was in self-defence. Trust me on that."

"We're still going through the scene. It's secured; don't worry."

"Take care of her, okay?"

"There's a guard on her door."

"You need her. She's not the lunatic Hannity'll try to make out. She's smart, she's sane, and above all, she's a victim in this."

"Noted. Lawson, I've got to go."

"Wait—did you find the server?"

"There's a box in a closet in Calvert's office that seems like a good possibility. The super's waving me over—speak later."

Had Iris really killed somebody else? Just when we thought things couldn't get any worse...

"I'll call the lawyer again," Kimberly announced. "I think we'll need him."

CHAPTER 38 - MARCUS

"I'M NOT SUPPOSED to be here."

Detective O'Dowd glanced furtively behind herself as she slipped through the front door of the White House, her small black hatchback tucked out of sight beside Kimberly's SUV.

Will just laughed. "We won't tell anyone. Something to drink?"

"Nothing alcoholic—I'm driving."

"Coffee? Tea? Cola? Water? Orange juice?"

"I won't say no to a cup of tea."

"You wouldn't be a proper copper if you did."

Twenty-four hours after the raid on Lakeview, we still had precious little information, just a few snippets from Joanne plus whatever the reporters camped outside the front gates had managed to ferret out. As Will predicted, the case had made the headlines, the media hungry for a scandal in what had previously been a slow news week. A juicy raid on a secure hospital, of all places, quickly bumped the story of two minor celebrities who'd escaped from *Survival Island* to tie the knot in Vegas down to the inside pages.

Iris's current lawyer was with us too. Lance Benton was a younger chap than I'd expected—no older than thirty-five—whose comedy socks were at odds with his made-to-measure suit and serious expression. Apart from the medical staff at Deane Valley and the police, he was the one person who'd been allowed to speak to Iris so far, and since he'd only arrived two minutes before Detective O'Dowd, I hadn't had a chance to quiz him yet.

Yes, I recognised the need for patience, but I most certainly didn't have to like it.

Shannon offered to make the drinks, and the rest of us headed to the living room. The sofas seated eight, so Nicole perched on Beck's lap and Reed carried in a couple of dining chairs so nobody had to sit on the floor. Finally, everyone was comfortable.

"Been a hell of a day," Joanne said. "Where do you want to start?"

Wasn't it obvious? "How's Iris?"

"Physically, she's making a good recovery, but she's shaken."

"Hardly surprising," Benton said. "Somebody tried to kill her."

"That's still under investigation."

"Oh, please. She didn't swallow enough heroin to kill a horse all by herself."

Gasps came from the girls, and even the men looked shocked. Me? I felt lightheaded for a moment. Iris had come painfully close to death, and I hadn't been there to protect her.

"Heroin?" I asked, just in case I'd somehow misheard.

"From what I understand, it was stuffed into an Adderall XR capsule and forced down her throat. I take it you photographed her defensive wounds?"

"Of course we did," O'Dowd said. "Where did you get the information about the Adderall capsule?"

"Does it matter?"

"Yes, because we shouldn't have leaks like that."

Benton gave a smug little grin. "If it helps, I don't think she'll be leaking to anyone but me."

O'Dowd put a hand over her eyes. "Tell me you haven't been corrupting the crime scene techs again?"

From the way she said it, resigned but not angry, they'd clearly crossed paths before.

"I'm going to plead the fifth."

"We're in England. We don't have a fifth to plead."

"Shall we get back to the discussion at hand? A young woman who's been unfairly incarcerated is far more important than my extracurricular activities."

"Fine." O'Dowd folded her arms. "When we found Miss McGivern, she was alive but unresponsive. A paramedic recognised the signs of a heroin overdose and used a NarcoCheck ampoule to test the pool of vomit next to her for its presence. It came back positive, so they administered naloxone. That's a medication used to block the effect of opioids," she added for the benefit of everyone in the room who hadn't had the pleasure of dealing with drug misuse in their professional lives.

"What about the dead person?" Will asked.

"Hazel Waters. A nurse."

Hazel? Really? But she'd always been so friendly. So smiley. Happy to help out if you had a problem, and one of the few staff members who'd gone above and beyond to help the patients. Bloody hell. *Hazel*? If that was true, she'd been a true wolf in sheep's clothing. I thought back to RJ's favourite analogy—seemed we'd unravelled the sheep and found the devil herself inside.

Benton took over again. "My client says the nurse

tried to trick her into taking the wrong pill, and when she refused, Nurse Waters forced her to swallow it. Iris realised there was a serious problem and struck out with a pen in an attempt to save herself, with unfortunate consequences."

"I'll concede that fits with the evidence we have so far."

"Too damn right it does. And that incident wasn't an isolated one. Heads are going to roll for this, I can promise you that much."

"Between you and me, they deserve to." O'Dowd's demeanour softened. "My little brother has learning difficulties, and sometimes he acts out. The thought of him in a place like that, drugged to keep him quiet while bastards in suits rake in the cash..." She glanced at Benton, who hadn't even taken his tie off. "No offence. It makes me sick."

"We've all got the same goal here," Will reminded her. "Put the bad guys in prison and let the good guys go free."

"If you're talking about Miss McGivern, she did kill a man previously."

"And she's done her time, don't you think?"

"It's not up to me to decide that." She let out a long sigh. "But there were men from the government at Lakeview today. The blowback on them's gonna be huge, I bet, and they were talking about getting an emergency team in to re-evaluate the residents. Check they're on the right medication, that sort of thing."

"All we're asking is that they follow their own procedures," Benton said. "My client's former psychiatrist"—he waved a hand in my direction —"believes she should have been considered for reintegration into society years ago. Have you got contact details for these people?"

Another sigh. I couldn't blame Detective O'Dowd— she'd had the mother of all cases foisted on her with no notice, and it had to be taking its toll. "I'll do what I can."

"Need any help with the server?" RJ offered.

"Wish I could take you up on that, but I'm having a hard enough time keeping your names out of this as it is. The superintendent isn't fond of anonymous tips, even when they lead to busts like this one."

"Fair enough. Want another cuppa?"

"What I need is sleep. I'll be able to pay off my mortgage with the amount of overtime this case is gonna generate." She paused, then gave a smile. "But thanks. I've never given a press conference before, and the chief constable knows my name now."

"Always welcome, Jo," Will said. "Same time tomorrow? Keep us updated, won't you?"

"As long as you promise to stay out of the way."

***

Once Detective O'Dowd had left, talk turned to strategy. I had to concede that Kimberly had found a good lawyer to represent Iris. He may have worn a made-to-measure suit, but underneath, he was a terrier —scrappy, tenacious, and he didn't let go.

"What now?" she asked. "Re-evaluation's good, right? But how long will that take? Can we see Iris?"

"One question at a time, Ms. Jennings," Benton said.

"Kimberly, please. How soon can we get Iris out of

there?"

"Anything the government gets involved with tends to take more time than we'd like, but in light of the amount of time Miss McGivern has already spent in what's effectively solitary confinement, I'll be pushing for a speedy resolution. The longer she's held, the higher any compensation will be."

"You think she'll get compensation?" I asked.

"If we can prove she should have been reassessed and wasn't, we've got grounds to fight for it. Then there's the fact that she almost died at Lakeview, plus two alleged attacks by staff members other than Hazel Waters."

"They happened."

"That'll be difficult to prove, but we can certainly include them in our claim. You'll most likely have to testify if Miss McGivern gives you permission to speak about your discussions. There was certainly negligence on Hannity SP's part by failing to ensure her safety, and quite possibly the government's too, since they awarded the contract to run the hospital and it also passed their inspections."

The inspections they'd comprehensively dropped the ball on.

"Can we see her?" Nicole asked. "She's on her own."

"Detective O'Dowd's right on that count, I'm afraid. It would be wise not to broadcast your involvement, any of you, but especially Mr. Hastings. Speaking to Iris could be construed as you coaching her on what to say. You can be sure Hannity SP's going to fight this, and we don't want to hand them the weapons to do so."

"But—" Kimberly started.

"What I'd suggest is that we ask for an independent

psychiatrist to be appointed. Somebody not connected to you, Hannity, or the government. They can assess Iris and make a recommendation regarding her care."

Even Kimberly stayed quiet. She knew it was the right thing to do. We had to play the long game on this one because it was the only way to win.

"Can I make one suggestion?" I asked, and Benton raised an eyebrow. "If you get any say in who they appoint as Iris's new psychiatrist, there's a lady I'd recommend. I used to work with her at Deane Valley before she left to set up a private practice. I haven't spoken to her in several years, but she specialises in PTSD, and she'd be a good choice for Iris."

"I'll see what I can do."

"What you can do," Kimberly said, "is sue the asses off those people. They need to pay."

CHAPTER 39 - IRIS

"IRIS, MY NAME'S Detective O'Dowd. I'm here today because we need you to make a formal statement regarding what happened last Friday evening at Lakeview. Do you understand?"

Lady, I'm crazy, not stupid. But because I was meant to be behaving myself, I nodded.

"Could you speak for the tape, please?"

"I understand."

"Present are Detective Joanne O'Dowd, Iris McGivern, and Lance Benton. Shall we begin?"

My lawyer nodded. My new lawyer, and he sounded as if he actually knew what he was talking about. I'd met with him twice over the last three days, and he'd promised they were doing everything they could to get me out of there. Plus he'd seen Marcus.

Marcus. When so long passed without hearing a word, I thought he'd abandoned me, but now I understood he was there in the background, fighting alongside my Electi sisters. Above everything else, that knowledge kept me going as I lay alone in the hospital, handcuffed to the freaking bed.

He'd sent a message with Mr. Benton: Iris, *behave.* If I screwed my eyes shut, I could imagine him peering over his glasses as he said it, and that made me giggle, but I made sure not to do it when Detective O'Dowd was there.

Marcus had also sent flapjacks. My hero.

With Mr. Benton interrupting every so often to clarify points, I told the tale of my stay at Lakeview, from my arrival, through the time I thought I'd been raped in my sleep, solitary confinement, the attack by Terrence, the drugs, so many drugs, all the way to Friday night. Hearing myself describe what happened, detail by painful detail, was actually worse than living through it. When Nurse Hazel tried to kill me, the adrenaline had been flowing, combined with what I now knew to be heroin, and I'd just reacted. Now? I wanted to bury that bitch deep down in my mind and never think of her again.

I did change one tiny detail at the end though— when I mentioned the asenapine, I told the detective it was *me* who'd taken it in the past, not Jacinda. I'd been on so many kinds of medication, what was one more? Better to blame the realisation on Lakeview's suspect record-keeping than a dead woman. When Marcus said to behave, he also meant "don't mention the bloody ghosts."

Detective O'Dowd seemed happy with my story, anyway. So did Mr. Benton. Apparently I'd have to sign something, but it was over, for now at least. It wasn't as if there'd be a trial.

But I did have one question.

"Why did Hazel do this? I mean, she was a nurse. She was supposed to look after me."

Detective O'Dowd looked at Mr. Benton, who nodded. "If you don't tell her, I will. She deserves to know."

"Is she...?" the detective asked.

"Strong enough? You've seen that for yourself, surely."

Normally, I didn't like lawyers, but I decided to make an exception for Mr. Benton.

"Okay, Iris. We've dug into Hazel Waters's history, and it seems she hasn't always been called Hazel Waters. Before she got divorced, she was Hazel Benedict, and her young son and cat got murdered by a man suffering from paranoid schizophrenia. We believe this was her revenge. It fits with what she told you about it being her job. It seems that after she split up with her husband, bitterness pushed her to target people similar to her son's murderer. And with your diagnosis..."

"I get it."

And I honestly did. Nurse Hazel hadn't been all that different from me, had she? Not really. The only difference was that I had to live with what I'd done. And also with what I was meant to do. My birthright. *My job.*

I had plenty of soul-searching to do, and I didn't mean hunting them down, Electi-style. Judge, jury, and executioner. I meant contemplating the whole reason for my existence.

Detective O'Dowd mistook my thoughts for something else.

"It's over now, Iris. She can't hurt you anymore." Thank goodness. "But I'm afraid I do have one piece of news you might not like."

"What news?"

"The doctors here say you've recovered enough to be transferred back to Lakeview."

That little bit of relief I'd felt? It forced its way

down my throat and punched me in the stomach.

"*What*?" I croaked.

"It won't be like it was before," she assured me. "Director Calvert's gone, and the government's installed an emergency replacement. You'll have a new psychiatrist, and any staff in direct contact with you will be thoroughly checked first." She glanced at Mr. Benton. "Your lawyer's insisting on that."

"*All* the staff should be thoroughly checked," he informed her, somewhat snottily. "Iris isn't the only person to have suffered at their hands."

"They will be, but there's a lot to get through. A *lot*," she repeated, seemingly to herself. "We're going as fast as we can."

I believed her. The dark circles under her eyes didn't lie, and I knew first-hand what an utter clusterfuck hid behind Lakeview's front door.

"I'd better wish you luck," I said. "You'll need it."

There was no amusement in her chuckle, no mirth in her smile. "That I will."

Once she'd exited, I was left with Mr. Benton, a lukewarm cup of tea, and my snazzy handcuffs.

"Is it true?" I asked. "Director Calvert's really gone?"

He nodded. "Along with half of the nurses, most of the orderlies, several psychiatrists, and the entire management team. I understand they kept the majority of the cleaning staff on."

"Wow."

"I realise going back to Lakeview isn't appealing, but you can't take up a bed in here, and since all of Hannity SP's hospitals are—"

"What's Hannity SP?"

"The company that runs Lakeview. Or rather, *ran* Lakeview. All of their hospitals are under investigation and being operated by an emergency government team. Some patients have had to be moved to different facilities, so there just aren't any other free places. You'll have a new room, and trust me when I say that you wouldn't be returning there if I thought there was any chance you'd be in danger."

"What about the new psychiatrist? I don't want a new psychiatrist. I want my old one back. Marcus got fired unfairly, so can't they reinstate him or something? He didn't deserve to lose his job because I tripped over and some nosy old nurse lied. Did she get fired? Glenda?"

"I'm not sure about her, I'm afraid. But Marcus doesn't want his old job back, even if it was offered."

"Oh. He doesn't like me anymore?"

Shit, how high-school-playground did that sound? The bloody words just slipped out, but the sentiment was true. Marcus didn't want to be my psychiatrist again? That hurt.

It was Mr. Benton's turn to chuckle, and unlike Detective O'Dowd, he *did* seem amused. "No, Iris, that's not the problem at all. In fact, I think he likes you a little too much."

"I don't understand."

"Principle 2.1 of the Royal College of Psychiatrists' Code of Ethics states that psychiatrists mustn't engage in an inappropriate relationship with a current patient. GMC guidance frowns on sexual relationships with former patients too, and one of the deciding factors over whether they take any action is the length of time since the professional relationship ended."

Oh. His words gradually sank in. *Oh.* "You're saying Marcus wants an inappropriate relationship with me?"

I rather liked the sound of that.

"He hasn't stated so explicitly, but I've learned to read people over the years, and I very much suspect that's where his thoughts are heading. I didn't mention that to you, by the way."

"I didn't hear a thing. So, a new psychiatrist, huh? I guess I can learn to live with that."

"Marcus suggested the lady in question. Apparently, she was his supervisor many years ago, so she's certainly competent. And when you get back to Lakeview, the wheels have been set in motion for you to have a full psychological evaluation with a view to release if that's deemed appropriate."

I sagged back against the pillows. "Thank goodness. When do I leave here?"

"Transport's been arranged for this afternoon, but before you go, I need to speak to you about our next steps."

"Next steps? What next steps?"

"What happened to you at Lakeview was... I barely have the words for it. *Appalling.* And you deserve to be compensated for everything you've suffered. In the interests of full disclosure, I've also agreed to represent the families of Jacinda Warren and Rylie Draper, because they should still be here with us and they're not, plus Ellie Thomas."

Who? "Ellie Thomas?"

"Another patient. When the emergency team went in at the weekend, they gave each resident a thorough health check. Ellie Thomas was found to be five months pregnant. She's been non-verbal since she arrived there, so quite apart from the fact that staff shouldn't be having sex with patients, there's no way she gave consent to anybody."

Holy fuck. It hadn't just been me.

"Who did it?"

"That's still under investigation. The police are waiting for the DNA results to come back. Currently, all male members of staff have been barred from having any contact with patients. Someone will be checking in with you every day, Iris."

"Can I have a phone?"

"The rules still prohibit you from having a phone of your own, but you'll have access to the hospital payphone. Kimberly's added enough credit to your commissary account for you to spend the rest of your life calling premium-rate numbers. Not that we plan on you being at Lakeview for the rest of your life," he added hastily.

I still couldn't get Ellie's fate out of my head. Pregnant with her rapist's baby? That didn't bear thinking about.

"Poor Ellie," I whispered.

"We're getting her help too. And financial assistance, which is what my question for you involves. Marcus has assured me you're capable of making your own decisions."

My heart skipped again. Was that what love felt like? I thought it might be. "Go on."

"We have two choices—to take Hannity SP and the government to court and go for the maximum amount of compensation we can possibly get, or to push for an out-of-court settlement. By going that route, the amount would most probably be lower, but you'd have it sooner, and we'd avoid a circus of a trial. I believe there's also a strong likelihood of Hannity SP going bust over this, so if they draw the litigation out, there may not be any money left to collect."

Wow. "You really think I might get some money from them?"

"Most definitely. You don't have to make a decision right now, but we haven't got forever."

"What about the people who ran Lakeview? Will they get off scot-free if we don't go to trial?"

"They'll still be facing criminal charges. This is purely a civil action."

Then it wasn't a hard choice at all. "Go for the out-of-court settlement."

"Are you sure?"

One hundred percent. I didn't want to be a reality TV star—I'd seen enough of that shite to last me a lifetime without being a part of it. And it wasn't just me I had to consider. Marcus and the others would be dragged through a trial alongside me, and Marcus had a daughter to think of too.

"I'm positive. More than anything, I want to be free. Any money is a bonus."

"For what it's worth, I think that's the right decision. I'll get the paperwork drawn up." He flashed me a smile. Yeah, I liked this guy. "Do you have any message for Marcus?"

As it happened, I did. "Tell him I'm looking forward to testing the GMC's boundaries with him."

CHAPTER 40 - MARCUS

WILL AND KIMBERLY turned to stare when I burst out laughing. Hardly surprising—Iris's message was the only splash of light in an otherwise dark day.

She wanted to breach GMC guidelines with me? Thank goodness. All these weeks, I'd been worrying I'd imagined what was between us, but her words made my heart jump. And another part of my anatomy, but thankfully I was sitting down so nobody noticed.

Even over the phone, I could hear the smile in Lance Benton's voice. "Thought you might find that amusing. You were right about Iris, by the way. She's sharp as a tack. I'd say her previous lawyer should be disbarred, but if it weren't for him, she'd be doing life in HMP Bronzefield right now."

"I'm certain she's not a danger to the public. She had a brief reactive psychosis triggered by seeing her mother's killer on the street, and she's aware that what she did was wrong."

"I understand that. Hell, in her position, I'd probably have done the same thing. We'll get her out. And she made the choice you thought she would regarding the out-of-court settlement."

"Good. That's good."

A tiny part of me had feared she'd want justice at any cost, but the toll that would have taken on her psyche... She'd made the right decision. And I was somewhat relieved I wouldn't have to testify again on her behalf. Once in the criminal trial would be quite enough. I'd spent the past three days at the police station, being questioned as a witness to the events that had transpired at Lakeview. Everything from the multitude of deaths to the solitary conditions to the overuse of drugs was now recorded for posterity. Whether I'd ever work as a psychiatrist again was another question—I'd already been blacklisted from most places thanks to Laurel's father, and now even the most cowboy of practices would be unlikely to touch me.

But I'd survive.

Will and Rania had offered me room and board for as long as I needed it, and when I went to pay the latest instalment of *my* lawyer's bill, I found somebody had already cleared the whole thing. No one would admit to it, but my guess was Kimberly with an outside chance of Will. I was more grateful to them than they'd ever know. To everyone in the White House.

I hung up with a sigh and stared at the wall opposite. Iris's life was on its way to being sorted out, but mine was still an utter disaster. She might have wanted me, but how could I give her everything she deserved?

"What's up?" Will asked. "I thought you'd be happy with developments."

"I am. Don't think for a second that I'm not. I guess... Now that Iris's case is heading in the right direction, I have to tackle the situation with Laurel and Cassie. And Teddy, of course. I know he's only a dog, but..."

Damn, I missed that mutt, even his hot breath huffing all over me first thing in the morning.

RJ wandered into the kitchen, heading for the fridge.

"Did somebody mention a dog?"

The house was quieter today. Shannon was at work, Rania had taken Aisling to the park, and Nicole had flown back to California yesterday with Beck. They'd both wanted to stay, but Beck couldn't get any more time off work until Christmastime and Nicole had a big project with a tight deadline to finish—a money project, she'd called it—plus her research on the Electi to continue. Reed didn't have an urgent need to return, and Kimberly was spending her nights organising weddings from afar because she wanted to stay too, but today, they'd gone to the furniture store to order sofas for the pool house. Kimberly was determined to have the place ready for Iris when—not if, *when*—she got released.

"My dog's still missing," I said. "I called the local shelters to no avail, and even if my ex-wife dumped him further afield, he's microchipped. I should've been notified if he was found straying. Unless she just gave him away."

RJ shook his head. "When you first said he was missing, I set up alerts for his description on all the usual free-ad sites. Preloved, Gumtree, that sort of thing. Shannon's been keeping an eye on them, and he hasn't turned up."

My first instinct was to be relieved, but if Teddy hadn't been foisted onto an unsuspecting dog lover, then where was he?

"Then I'd wager on Laurel having hidden him away

somewhere. A boarding kennel, perhaps."

She had to spend Cassie's child support money on something, didn't she? Her new boyfriend seemed to be buying all the toys. Before the raid on Friday, I'd taken my daughter out for a quick lunch, and she'd insisted on bringing along a plastic horse, complete with equestrian Barbie and a Ken doll dressed like a douche. Apparently, they'd been gifts from Rupert bloody Horton.

"Now that we've got more time, we'll start calling around. How's the divorce going?"

I grimaced. "Slowly. Laurel's been dragging it out because she wants to keep living in the house. I'm not kidding myself that I'll get full custody of Cassie— Wallace and Jacqueline Burton would never allow that —but I want more than an afternoon a week with her. She can't even stay overnight at the moment." I gave myself a mental slap as I realised where I was. "By 'at the moment,' I mean when I had a house with space for her."

"She can stay here if you want," Will said. "Rania loves kids. We'll sort something out space-wise."

These people... I barely knew them, yet they'd taken me in and treated me as one of their own. I know I was meant to be good with emotions, always calm in a crisis, but tears prickled and I had to grab a handkerchief and pretend to blow my nose to cover up the fact that I was wiping my eyes.

"Thank you. That means a lot."

"Wallace and Jacqueline Burton?" RJ asked. "Who are they?"

"My in-laws. Wallace is also my former boss, hence the reason I got fired from Deane Valley."

"Deane Valley Hospital? Wallace Burton... Hmm... I've seen that name recently."

"Seen it where, mate?" Will asked.

"I'm not sure. Leave it with me."

"Marcus, what else do you need? Is your lawyer on top of things?"

"As on top of things as he can be when I've been fired twice and accused of adultery. Laurel's trying to paint me as an unfit father, and she's doing a good job of it so far."

The pair of them looked at each other. "Adultery?" Will said.

I knew exactly what was going through their minds. If I'd cheated on Laurel, how could I be trusted to do right by Iris? I couldn't blame them for being suspicious, and I was actually glad they were. It meant Iris had people looking out for her.

"I didn't cheat. It's just... It's a long story. Our marriage was on the rocks long before the incident that ended it, and I'm not sure Laurel even believes what she accused me of, but— I'd better start at the beginning, hadn't I?"

"Seems like a sensible idea."

Okay, here goes...

"Laurel...she was very demanding. She didn't start out that way, but over the years, our interests changed, our friends changed, our world views... I stayed for Cassie's sake, but with hindsight, I should have ended things a long time ago. Anyhow, that night, we went to a party. I'd just finished a twelve-hour shift at the hospital, and the last thing I wanted to do was stand around making small talk with a bunch of people I didn't like much, but if you knew Laurel... It was easier to go than to argue."

"Sounds like my mother," Will muttered. "Most of the time, I don't know how my father puts up with her."

"Sometimes, it's easier just to stay. Anyhow, once everyone had a few drinks in them, I snuck upstairs to one of the guest bedrooms and crawled under the covers. Laurel was busy with her cronies, and I figured nobody would even notice. Except I woke up to her screaming, and there was a half-naked woman lying beside me."

RJ snorted. "Nice work."

No, it really wasn't. "I had no idea who she was, and she scuttled out of there like her heels were on fire when Laurel started bashing me with her handbag. I'd unbuttoned my shirt because the house was stiflingly hot, and... Yes, I realise it looked bad. Everyone was staring..." I could still see them now, clustered around the doorway with shocked expressions on their faces and glasses of wine in their hands. I was the evening entertainment. "So I left. I drove home and started packing. To cut a long story short, Laurel arrived to continue the argument, and when I didn't back down, she called the police, lied, and now she has a restraining order against me. The only saving grace is that Cassie slept through the whole drama."

"Cassie was in the house?" Will said. "Oh, man."

"Laurel yelled at the babysitter to fuck off the moment she stormed through the door. Poor girl."

"The babysitter witnessed Laurel's behaviour?"

"Yes, but not the actual fight. My lawyer said that's the part that mattered."

"What about the woman from the bed? Couldn't she refute Laurel's version of events?"

"Possibly, but she reeked of alcohol and I can't find her anyway. It was a large gathering, and none of those so-called friends will speak to me anymore. Laurel and her family have significant influence as well as deep pockets." Another sigh escaped. "Full custody is a pipe dream, I understand that. Right now, I just want to get the divorce finalised with the best visitation schedule the judge will allow, and carry on with my life."

"With Iris in it?" Will asked.

"If she'll have me."

"Then we'll do everything we can to help. Iris is Rania's family, which means she's our family too."

RJ made me jump when he suddenly snapped his fingers. "I just remembered where I saw Wallace Burton's name."

Will raised an eyebrow. "Where?"

"Remember how Calvert's blackmail bank detailed all those kickbacks Hannity was receiving from big pharma to use their drugs?"

"From Mayer Healthcare?"

"I might have had a poke around in Mayer's servers too, and Hannity's directors weren't the only people they were bribing. I found two dozen names, and one of them was Wallace Burton of Deane Valley Hospital."

Bloody hell. Wallace holier-than-thou Burton was dirty? I thought back to my time at Deane Valley, all the "discussions" we'd had over treatment plans. The times he'd overruled me on my own patients.

"When I worked there, he always encouraged me to use more medication than I thought was strictly necessary. At the time, I put it down to the fact that he was old-school and that's how psychiatrists used to do things thirty years ago, but now..."

"Wouldn't it be a shame if that list leaked?" RJ said, eyes gleaming.

Will grinned back. "I know a reporter or two. I'll make some calls."

Chapter 41 - Iris

I PLUCKED A dead leaf off one of my plants as I digested the latest piece of information Dr. Call-Me-Meg O'Brien had given me. Terrence was the father of Ellie Thomas's baby. In all honesty, that wasn't a surprise, but it still disgusted me. I should've bitten off more than just his ear.

Dr. Meg preferred to have our "chats," as she called them, in my room rather than one of the meeting rooms. She wanted me to be comfortable, she said, and the meeting rooms were still being refurbished by the interim management team. I didn't mind. I liked my new room on the first floor. I had a shower, a view over the woods, and the squirrel even showed up occasionally. Plus I'd gotten to keep my plants and Acting Director Adams let me have the gifts people sent too. A guitar and a "How to Play" book that could only have come from one person even if he didn't put his name on the card, a bunch of art supplies from Kimberly, books from Nicole, and a new TV from Rania.

I was monitored a lot more closely now. People checked on me at all hours of the day and night, but I didn't mind because they were much nicer than before. And now that Jacinda had gone, I wasn't going to get caught talking to myself. In a strange way, I missed her.

Not her TV viewing habits, but she'd turned out to be okay most of the time.

I liked Dr. Meg too. She was very different to Marcus, but then again, Marcus and I hadn't exactly had a conventional doctor-patient relationship. I'd be kidding myself if I tried to claim otherwise. Dr. Meg was older, in her early sixties at a guess, with a soft Irish accent and kind grey eyes that matched her hair. She dressed conservatively, always in a twinset and knee-length skirt, but she did like her jewellery. Today's necklace was silver with a pendant made out of twinkly blue stones.

The only person I didn't like? Nurse Glenda. The old battleaxe was still there, as I'd found out on my second night back. Had somebody had a word about her attitude? Her smile looked forced, more of a grimace, but she followed it up with, "How are you this evening, Iris?"

Each word was pronounced carefully as if it pained her to ask.

"Alive, no thanks to you."

"I wasn't on duty the night Hazel lost her mind. That was nothing to do with me."

"That particular incident, maybe, but Dr. Hastings was worried by the number of deaths, and when he tried to look into the problem, you had him fired. That's complicity."

"Now, now, there's no need to be rude. I reported him for behaving inappropriately, as you well know. My job is to protect the residents, and that includes you."

"He wasn't being inappropriate!"

"He had his hands all over you."

I wished. "He caught me when I tripped. I *told* you

that. What was he supposed to do? Let me fall on the floor and hit my head? Don't you think there was enough negligence going on?"

"I didn't see any negligence."

"Then you've got a problem with your eyesight. Seeing things that didn't happen, not seeing things that did... I've got no idea how you still have a job."

"I've only ever wanted what's best for the service users."

"Well, you've got a funny way of showing it."

"You were in an empty room with him."

"I already told you—I felt sick. It wouldn't surprise me if Hazel had put something in my food. Did you hear she poisoned Archie Majors with a peanut?"

"That's a rumour."

"My lawyer seems to think it's true."

"You met with Dr. Hastings every day. That's excessive."

"It's called patient care. I meet with Dr. O'Brien every day she's here—do you think she's trying to molest me too?"

"Obviously she isn't, but—"

"There are no buts. You lied, and a man lost his job because of it." I rolled over on the bed, turning my back on her. "I'm done talking to you now. Do whatever you have to do and leave."

Rude? Perhaps. But I was sick of being walked all over. Nurse Glenda didn't come back after that, thankfully.

Which left me with Dr. Meg.

"How does the news about Terrence make you feel?" she asked.

How *did* it make me feel? I blew out a long breath.

"Relieved, I guess. Happy that people can't keep saying I imagined things. Well, that particular thing."

We'd had the conversation about the ghosts. About Leland Baker and my "brief reactive psychosis" as Dr. Meg called it. I accepted now that the apparition of my mum had all been in my mind—or so I said because I knew it was my only chance of getting out of Lakeview —and I realised what I'd done was very, very wrong. Honestly, I was still on the fence regarding that part. Five and a half years ago, I'd been convinced I was right, finally doing my duty, but Hazel Waters had made me wonder whether it was that clear-cut. What made the two of us so different?

I wanted—*needed*—to talk to the others about it, but although I was able to phone them now, and did so every day, the calls were recorded and we had to be really careful what we said. For that reason, I'd barely spoken to Marcus either, just a few words when he snuck onto a call with one of the others to check I was okay. No names. Nothing more than small talk. Mr. Benton said we needed to avoid each other until the police had all the information they needed and the civil suit was well underway.

I didn't like it, but I put up with it.

A year ago, I'd probably have told Mr. Benton to get lost, but I'd done a lot of growing up in the last few months. I realised that for once in my life, I had to do what I was told because it was my only chance of freedom. As well as a new outlook on life and weird little shivers that ran through me whenever I thought of him, Marcus had given me something else: hope.

Dr. Meg smiled encouragingly. "Those are perfectly normal reactions."

"I also feel guilty, though. What if I'd made more of a fuss after the first time? I *knew* someone had attacked me, even if I couldn't prove it. Would that have helped Ellie?"

She made a face. "Honestly? Having seen what I've seen of the previous management, I don't believe it would have made any difference to Terrence or Ellie."

"What'll happen to the baby?"

"It's too late to consider a termination, so Ellie will have to carry it to term. There's a team supporting her, and since they've cut down her medication, she's begun talking." Dr. Meg rolled her eyes halfway before she caught herself. "Apparently, nobody had any idea she could speak before."

"Has everyone had their medication cut down now?"

Her answer was careful, and she'd told me before that she couldn't discuss individual cases that weren't public knowledge. Ellie's *was* public knowledge because her parents had done an interview with the BBC, and they'd also asked Mr. Benton to keep me fully informed.

"I believe many patients have."

"Good. I turned into a different person after Dr. Hastings cut out most of my pills." Always Dr. Hastings in front of Dr. Meg. Never Marcus. It felt weird being so formal now. "Although I guess that's not always a good thing."

Dr. Meg laughed. "It's a balance, to be sure."

"I heard you used to work with Dr. Hastings?"

"For several years, yes. He's an excellent doctor."

"It sucks that he got fired."

"That it does. It was bad enough the first— Forgive

me. I shouldn't talk about things like that."

"Like what?"

"His previous tenure."

"I already know he got sacked from there too. Something to do with his wife?"

"Who told you that?"

"My lawyer." The lies were easier when they were small.

"Aye, the nepotism was strong with that one. A nasty piece of work. We all had to pretend to like her because of who her father was. Between you and me, I'll never understand why Marcus married her."

"People change. I've changed."

"That you have." She put her pen down and straightened her necklace. "Is there anything else you want to talk about today?"

"Not really."

"Nothing about Terrence?"

"I'd rather focus on the future now. We've done the past to death." I clapped a hand over my mouth. "Sorry, that sounded terrible."

Another chuckle. "In that case, I'd better go and write up my report."

CHAPTER 42 - IRIS

A CHILL WIND blew through my sweatshirt as I climbed out of Mr. Benton's car on a freezing Friday evening, but I didn't care. Not one bit. Why? Because I was finally free.

Acting Director Adams, a mental-health tribunal, and the Ministry of Justice had all approved my release, just in time for the last shopping weekend before Christmas. We almost didn't make it—the final approval got stuck in somebody's email outbox and frantic phone calls ensued—but Mr. Benton had stayed late to take me to my new, albeit temporary, home. Ordinarily, a girl like me without two pennies to her name would have ended up in a hostel, but thanks to Will and Rania, I had a place to stay. As a condition of my "reintegration into society," I still had to see Dr. Meg once a week, but that was fine by me. By then, our sessions were more "coffee with an old friend" than deep dives into my psyche, and I could go to her office in future instead of Lakeview.

The front door opened. The White House, Kimberly had told me it was called, but the plaque beside the doorbell said Hopewell Place. *Hope*. There was that word again.

For weeks, I'd been imagining what it would be like to meet my soul sisters, but nothing had prepared me for the sight of their white, blue, and pink glows all intermingling, nor for the incredible wave of belonging that washed over me. *These were my people.*

My ears rang with Kimberly and Nicole's squeals as they ran towards me. Rania didn't squeal, she just smiled as she embraced me with the others.

"Welcome home," she whispered.

I burst into tears.

Dammit.

I felt a handkerchief being pressed into my hands, and I tried to blink away the blurriness. Marcus. It was Marcus. I managed to disentangle one arm and wrap it around him, pulling him into the hot mess of women blubbering and sniffling. He didn't seem to mind, just curled an arm around my waist and kissed my hair.

He kissed my freaking hair.

"Hey, she's ours," Kimberly told him.

"You'll have to fight me for her."

"You can borrow her later. We've been waiting hundreds of years for this."

He just laughed, properly laughed, and let them pull me away.

"Later," he whispered in my ear before he took a step back, and those little shivers I usually got from the sound of his voice turned into a full-on shudder. One word, but it had been so full of promise. *Later.*

"Are you staying for dinner?" a brown-haired guy asked Mr. Benton. Will. I recognised his voice.

"Can't tonight. I haven't even started my Christmas shopping yet."

"Thanks for bringing Iris."

"Any time. I always like a happy ending."

Three more men materialised and unloaded my

belongings from the boot of Mr. Benton's car. The two giants were Reed and Beck, I presumed, which meant the smaller guy was RJ. They picked up all of my stuff between them—not that I had much, just my plants, guitar, art stuff, and the clothes I didn't want but was given anyway—and the girls herded me into the house. Wow. Being in a real home was strange after so long. I paused to peer at a picture, an abstract piece of art in pink, blue, white, and orange, and Nicole squeezed my hand.

"Reed painted that."

"Is it us?"

"Our auras, yes."

For so long, the only pictures on the walls had been Lakeview propaganda, and even that had been stripped back to bare white over the last month. This place... I belonged, and I'd only just walked in the door.

"It's beautiful."

"What do you want for dinner?" Kimberly asked. "We could go out? Or order something in?"

"Can we stay here?" I'd only just arrived; I didn't want to leave straight away.

"Of course. We could get Chinese takeout, or Indian, or pizza. There's no Mexican or Japanese nearby." She made an exaggerated sad face. "We have to drive for miles to get those."

"Pizza? I haven't had pizza in years. With pepperoni?"

In Lakeview, I'd been practically vegetarian, the meat tasted so bad. What I wouldn't give for a good steak, but that could wait. Everything could wait. I had the rest of my life to look forward to now.

Barking came from further in the house, followed

by the scrabble of nails on a hard floor and a pale streak hurtling towards me. Before I could brace, a medium-sized dog hit me square in the stomach, and I flew backwards, narrowly missing a Christmas tree and a white side table before landing in Beck's arms.

"Oof."

"Teddy!" Marcus scolded. "Iris, are you okay? I'm so sorry. He's forgotten how to behave."

"You got him back?"

His grin spread from ear to ear. "Two days ago. He 'escaped' from a shed at Laurel's boyfriend's place with a little bit of help."

"Otherwise known as Beck and Rania," Kimberly said. "And Laurel can't very well say anything because then she'd have to explain why he was in the shed in the first place."

"They kept him in a *shed*? No wonder he's got so much energy." Once I'd caught my breath, I knelt on the floor, only to get assaulted with doggy kisses. "He's so cute! Hey, Teddy Bear, do you know how to sit?"

And just like that, life began to return to normal. I'd worried I might not fit in, that the others would think I was weird when they met me in person, especially since we all came from such different walks of life, but nobody looked at me funny or gave me a wide berth or talked in hushed tones or rolled their eyes when I did something clumsy.

"He does know how to sit," Marcus told me. "He just chooses not to for the most part. Teddy, *sit*."

Teddy did a lap of the hallway while I scrambled to my feet, then leapt on me again. This time, it was Marcus who caught me, and he didn't let go. I rather liked the feel of his arms around me. *Thanks, Super*

Ted.

"I'm so glad you got him back."

"We all are." Kimberly smoothed down her skirt. "So much has happened in the last few days."

"What? What's happened?"

"Don't worry; it's mostly good. We didn't want to distract you from your assessments, so we figured we'd wait until this evening for a catch-up."

"But I didn't know until this morning that I'd be released."

"Honey, no way would you have failed those tests. There's nothing wrong with you. Now, this house only has four bedrooms, and we want you here with us to start with, so Marcus has offered to move out to the cottage for now. Reed, can you get Iris's stuff? I want to show her the bedroom."

"What cottage?"

Kimberly tugged me out of Marcus's arms and led me through a door to the left, into a cosy lounge. I say "cosy" not because it was small—it wasn't—but because it had that feel about it. A real fire blazed in the grate, shielded from Teddy by a fireguard, the squashy sofas were adorned with cushions and blankets, and Christmas music was coming from somewhere.

"The cottage is over there." She pointed out the back window, and I saw a small L-shaped building in the far corner of the garden, two compact storeys to the main house's sprawling one, and super cute. Through the downstairs windows, I glimpsed peach-painted walls and another Christmas tree. "Originally, we thought you might want to stay there for a while, but then Marcus ended up a bit homeless, and..."

"Absolutely, he needs somewhere to live."

And he was so close.

"Here's your room."

It had the same peach walls as the cottage, and the paint smelled fresh. I still couldn't believe they'd redecorated for me. That was...that was... I choked up just thinking about it. The huge double bed was bigger than anything I'd ever slept in, and there were two wardrobes for all the stuff I didn't own. A dressing table, a flat-screen TV on the wall, more pictures, even a vase of irises on one bedside table.

More tears rolled down my cheeks, and I wiped at my face with my sleeve because I'd lost Marcus's hankie somewhere.

"I don't know what to say."

"You don't have to say anything. Just smile."

That I could manage. "Thank you. Thank you so much."

Kimberly gave me a long hug. "We're finally together, just like we were always meant to be. I'll go and order that pizza."

I had a moment of peace to take in my new surroundings. To breathe. To relax. But only a short moment because Marcus slipped through the door.

"Hi."

I almost threw myself into his arms, but I caught myself just in time and managed a rather restrained hug instead. Our first proper hug. I never wanted to let him go. He squeezed me back, and then his lips brushed against my ear.

"How are you feeling?" he murmured. "And I ask that as a friend, not as your psychiatrist. Because I'm definitely not your psychiatrist anymore."

"I missed you."

"I missed you too, but that doesn't answer my question."

"Happy. For the first time in years, I feel happy."

I also felt as if I wanted to kiss him, but I'd never had a boyfriend who lasted longer than a month, and I desperately didn't want to screw things up before they even started. So I settled for burying my face in his shoulder instead. Outside of work, he'd chosen well-worn jeans paired with the softest jumper, and I decided I liked new, casual Marcus.

"That's a good answer, flower. I know this is a big day for you, so if you feel stressed at any time, just let me know and I'll fix it."

How did I explain that the only thing stressing me out was how to act around him? I couldn't, so I shook my head instead. "Everything's fine. No, not fine. Great. Everything's great. I've missed having people around."

"Even Jacinda?" he asked, eyes twinkling.

"I never want to watch another reality show in my life."

"How about a movie? These people sure like their movie nights."

"I love movies."

And I loved them even more when I got to watch them from a comfy sofa with Marcus's arm around my shoulders and a pizza box balanced on my lap. I didn't even mind when Teddy drooled on my foot, his gaze fixed on the last slice of pepperoni with extra cheese.

"Can he have it?" I asked.

Marcus smiled. "Yes, but we'll have to take him for a long walk tomorrow. If you want to, that is. Otherwise, I can take him on my—"

"I'd like nothing better than to go for a walk with the two of you."

"You'll have to take your walk in the afternoon," Kimberly said. "Don't forget we're going Christmas shopping in the morning."

"Nobody could possibly forget," Rania said. "You remind us every five minutes."

"Iris didn't know. You're coming, right?"

"I don't have any money for shopping, but I can help you to carry stuff."

"You have money. We opened a bank account for you, and I put a little bit in there."

"What? I can't spend your money."

"Call it a donation from my father. He..." The atmosphere in the room suddenly chilled, and Marcus's arm tightened. "He... When he found out about my mother's abilities, he had her committed. She died in a place not all that different from Lakeview. Until I met Nicole and Rania, I never spent a cent of my trust fund because to me, it's dirty money. But if it can help you guys... We're meant to work together. Look after each other."

"What about you?"

She tried a smile, but it wasn't a cheerful one. "Don't worry about me; I have other income."

"Just take it," Reed mouthed from behind her. "Please."

I swallowed hard and nodded. "In that case, thank you." It couldn't be much money, right? Maybe in time, I'd find out more about her past, but I wasn't going to push her. "So, what's the other news?" I asked in an attempt to change the subject. "You said a bunch of stuff had happened?"

Now she grinned properly.

"It's the *best* news. Laurel's father got fired."

"*What*?" I seemed to be saying that a lot lately.

"He was caught up in the same scheme as Hannity, taking bribes from drug companies in return for using their medication. The more Deane Valley used, the more cash he got. And unlike Hannity, where the entire company was infected with filth, Wallace Burton was pocketing the cash personally. The trustees at the hospital had no idea until a reporter pointed it out to them."

"That's just... Wow." I seemed to be saying that a lot too.

"Right. And rumour says the police are going after everything Doug Calvert owns under the Proceeds of Crime Act."

"It's more than a rumour," Rania said. "Lance Benton heard it from the inquiry team. Plus Judge Leavitt and three prosecutors are about to be struck off."

Kimberly got to her feet. "We've got champagne chilling in the fridge. Shall I open it now?"

"What's the bad news first?"

"The bad news?"

"You said the news was *mostly* good."

"Uh, let's not worry about that tonight."

"I want to know." No more being kept in the dark.

It was Marcus who spoke rather than Kimberly. "I have a court date for the custody hearing. It's not all bad news—at least I can finally get the divorce finalised."

"What about custody?"

"Laurel's being...difficult. It's not unexpected. The

hearing isn't until January, so let's just enjoy Christmas in the meantime, okay?"

He leaned in to kiss me on the cheek, and I might have sighed. Okay, I'd enjoy Christmas before I started worrying on his behalf.

Chapter 43 - Iris

KIMBERLY WAS SUCH a bullshitter. A little bit of money? She'd put fifty freaking grand into a bank account and then given me a debit card. I tried to hand it back, but she folded her arms and refused to take it.

"Please, Iris. Just spend it. Seeing you happy makes me happy."

I hugged her instead. What other choice did I have? One day, I'd pay her back, but for now, I needed money to live on. It turned out the wardrobes in my bedroom were full of clothes and the en-suite was fully stocked with toiletries, but little things like bus tickets and plant food and treats for Teddy—I had to buy those. And a swimsuit, apparently, because it turned out there was a swimming pool in one wing of the cottage. An actual swimming pool, not an oversized paddling pool like my roommates had set up in the concrete yard of my old house when things got a bit hot in the summer.

I also got a haircut and spent a few pounds on Christmas gifts for everyone. It was the least I could do, even if they were rather generic because I didn't know my new family very well yet. By that logic, Marcus should have been the easiest to buy for because I knew him best, but it turned out the opposite was true. I agonised over what to get him for ages before a light bulb finally pinged.

And walking Teddy in the countryside took more out of me than I thought it would. In Lakeview, I'd been able to stretch in my room and do bodyweight exercises, but the stamina that came with a good bout of cardio had escaped me. By the time we'd covered three miles, my feet ached, and I was panting harder than the dog.

"You okay?" Marcus asked as he helped me over a stile.

"Fine, just really, really unfit." He was a runner, or so Rania had told me. Every morning at seven a.m., even if it was raining, until this week at least. "I need to get out more."

"Teddy's never going to say no to a walk."

"Can I take him if you're not around?" Did he trust me to do that?

He gave my hand a squeeze. "Any time you want."

He *did* trust me. My heart swelled.

Back at the White House, we found the counters laden with food. Bowls of nuts and crisps, a fancy box of chocolates, dried fruit, and a note that there was cottage pie plus bread-and-butter pudding in the oven. Unlike Lakeview's offerings, the cottage pie here actually smelled edible.

"Shannon," Marcus told me. "She likes to cook, but everything's heavy on the carbs."

"I love carbs. What's the difference between cottage pie and shepherd's pie? Do you know?"

"No idea, flower. Does it matter?"

"Nope. Not one bit. Should we wait for the others to show up before we eat?"

"Nobody stands on ceremony here. Everyone just mucks in—somebody cooks, and people eat whenever they fancy."

"I think I'm going to like staying here. I mean, *really* like it. I'm worried I won't want to leave."

"Between you and me, I feel that way too. But nobody seems in a hurry to kick us out, which is a good thing because my landlord's still dicking me around over the house."

"He's making you pay rent?"

Marcus nodded. "He says because my stuff's inside, the house is still mine. Never mind that a second sinkhole opened up in the garden and now I'm not allowed anywhere near the place."

"Can't you stop paying?"

"I have a feeling he'd get nasty, and quite frankly, I don't have the energy for a third court battle at the moment."

I couldn't blame him, not in the slightest. One fight had left me drained, and I never wanted to speak to a lawyer again. Unless it was Mr. Benton stopping in for dinner on occasion. That I could cope with.

"Do you have the energy to swim with me this evening? I know it's late, but I really want to try out the pool. There are lights, aren't there?"

Five years without more than a shower had left me craving water. This morning, I'd sat in the bath until it turned cold, and I would have refilled it if Kimberly hadn't been shouting at everyone to hurry up. In a terribly nice way, of course, but the urgency was there.

Marcus smiled and pulled me in close. I loved the way we fitted together, my softness against his hardness. I stood on tiptoes, wanting more, but I'd barely pressed my lips to his when he drew back. What was wrong? Didn't he want me as much as I wanted him?

He answered even though I hadn't spoken out loud. "I do want you, don't doubt that for a second, but this is too important to rush. Most of the time we spent together was in a far from ideal situation, and you need to be sure about your feelings before we take things further."

"I'm sure."

He chuckled and kissed me on the forehead. "Yes, I'll swim with you this evening."

When I said "swim," I meant "float." The pool room had a glass roof, and we held hands as we bobbed around with a pool noodle under our necks, kicking lazily every so often so we didn't sink. The only problem with staring upwards was that Marcus was beside me. In a pair of swim shorts. And that tattoo was under the bloody water. I'd glimpsed it earlier, but I wanted to have a really good look. And possibly a lick. I appreciated his concern about my feelings, don't get me wrong, but at this rate, we'd spend several weeks on foreplay and I'd self-combust before we got to the good bits.

"We're in water. You can't self-combust."

Shit. "Did I just say that out loud?"

All those years in a room on my own, and I'd got into bad habits. But dammit, that spot between my legs was practically liquid, and if my heart skipped much more, I'd end up in the hospital, hooked to an ECG machine.

Marcus only chuckled, rolled, and brushed his lips over mine. "I don't think I can hold out for weeks, flower."

***

"Can we go for a drive today?" I asked Marcus over breakfast on Sunday morning.

"Just a drive, or do you have somewhere in mind?"

"I need to run some errands. Please?"

"As if I could ever say no to you."

"You did say no. Last night, remember?" When I'd been gagging for it and he walked me to my room with nothing more than a sweet kiss. The only part of Marcus that hadn't been entirely under control was his dick. It was hard to miss it in swim shorts, but although I'd studied the outline as closely as I'd dared, I hadn't seen any evidence of a piercing. Where the hell was it?

"And it was the hardest thing I've ever done."

"It wasn't the hardest thing I've ever done, because you wouldn't let me."

Marcus pushed back his stool. "I'll get my car keys."

"There's no hurry."

"Yes, there is, because if you keep talking like this, the only place we'll end up is in my bedroom."

I hopped up to follow him. "I'm not seeing a problem with that."

Before I could blink, he'd backed me up against the fridge and his mouth was on mine. Hard. I gasped as he ran his tongue along the seam of my lips, and they parted automatically, a sigh escaping when he tangled his hands in my hair and tugged gently. Bloody hell, I'd never been kissed like that before, with such passion, such fierceness. If this was what he could do with his mouth, then how would I handle the rest of him? I wasn't sure I was ready to find out, but at the same time, I *needed* to.

I inhaled the scent of his aftershave as he deepened the kiss, and his hands switched from my hair to my sides, running gently down my waist with a feather-light touch that made me squirm and giggle and press into him. Oh, holy hell, the kiss wasn't the only part of him that was hard. And there was still no sign of a cock ring. Had I guessed wrong? That would be oh-so-disappointing. To make up for the lack of jewellery, I grabbed his ass and squeezed, relishing the feel of his muscles tightening.

"Fuck," he choked out. "I really need to get the keys."

"No, you don't. You don't need to get the keys."

He leaned in again, and this time his fingers skirted the top of my waistband. *Do it, do it, do it.*

Then somebody cleared their throat, and it wasn't either of us.

Bollocks.

Cue red faces from me, Marcus, and Will. Only Teddy seemed unperturbed.

"Uh, I think the dog needs to visit the garden."

I leapt for the leash. "Sure, I'll take him. Absolutely no problem."

Oops.

CHAPTER 44 - IRIS

"TAKE THAT LEFT turn," I said. "The one where the red car's coming out."

We'd eventually made it into Marcus's Volkswagen, although his habit of kissing my knuckles at traffic lights was doing nothing to cool my libido. Did he carry a fire extinguisher? Because I'd need one if he kept that up.

I hadn't visited Highcross since the day I got arrested. Judge Leavitt had refused to grant me bail—probably as part of his "get them into Lakeview" strategy—so I'd languished in a jail cell for six weeks until I plea-bargained my way to Lakeview. But today, I was going back. On the way, we'd driven past the spot where my mother died, and I'd breathed a heavy sigh of relief when I saw she was indeed gone. Until that moment, there'd always been the tiniest doubt at the back of my mind, a niggle that wouldn't go away. But my fears were unfounded. The Electi's gift, as Kimberly called it, worked perfectly. At least, it did as long as a girl didn't get caught.

Another mile, and I pointed at a dilapidated semi four doors along from the Blackwood Arms.

"That's where I lived when I was eighteen. After I finished in foster care."

We'd spoken about those months during our time

at Lakeview. None of my foster parents had been bad people, but they weren't my mum. Nobody could ever replace her. I'd never connected with any of them, and as soon as I turned eighteen, I'd hightailed it out of my final foster home and jumped on the bus for the fifteen-mile journey back to Highcross. I couldn't wait to get back to the village I still called home.

"It looks...er..."

"Don't say 'nice.' It was a dump. But my roommates were okay—stoned half the time, but okay—and I like this area. Turn left up here. There, by the old water pump with the little roof."

Two minutes later, we drew to a halt outside Rosemary Cottage, the place Mum and I had escaped to when we left London. A family lived there now, judging by the playhouse in the front garden and the two cars wedged into the driveway. They'd tiled over what had once been my asparagus bed to make both vehicles fit. And the old apple tree was gone. It had been a bit wonky, so that didn't surprise me, but its absence still made me sad. They'd made changes to the house, too. Gone were the old leaded light windows, replaced with double-glazing, and the front door was PVC rather than wood. Probably more economical for heating, but not so good for the cottage's character. Some things never changed, though—the ghost of Hermione, a girl who'd been run down by a careless horseman in 1832, was still sitting on the front wall. I gave her a little wave, and when she realised who I was, she grinned and waved back.

"It's...different," I said.

"Good different or bad different?"

"Just different. More modern, less...less..." I

struggled to find the words.

"It's lost some of its charm?" Marcus suggested.

"Yes, exactly."

"I know who hasn't lost her charm."

"That's so freaking cheesy."

"What's wrong with cheese?"

Nothing. Nothing was wrong with cheese. I leaned over and kissed him, and we didn't come up for air until there was a knock on the window. I looked up to see a grey-haired man on a bicycle peering in at us, and my cheeks heated for the second time that day.

"This isn't one of those dogging spots," he said. "You'll have to go to the car park by the duck pond for that."

Oh, good grief, I'd almost forgotten about that. When Mum and I first moved to the village, we'd had no idea and got the shock of our lives when we decided to take a walk that way one evening.

"Er, thanks," Marcus said, winding down the window. "We'll bear that in mind."

I took a closer look at the man outside. Was it...? Yes, I recognised those whiskers. "Mr. Hendry?"

He practically stuck his head through the window, squinting. "Young Iris? Is that you?"

"Yes, it's me."

"Well, what are you waiting for? Get out and give an old man a hug. I promise not to tread on your fella's toes."

I remembered to undo my seat belt before I scrambled out—I'd learned my lesson after I forgot once and ended up on my ass. Mr. Hendry lived three doors along on the other side of the road, in a tiny white cottage with gnomes lining the driveway. A quick glance showed his collection had expanded into the garden and up the front steps.

Mr. Hendry hugged me tight, then held me at arm's length, studying my face. "You look well, love. They finally let you out?"

"They did."

"Good job too. You should never have been locked up in the first place. That Baker chap deserved everything he got."

"The judge didn't see it that way."

"Damn law enforcement. Corrupt, the lot of them. Did you see the news last month? Crooked lawyers, crooked judges, crooked doctors taking bribes. They're the ones that should be in prison."

I glanced across at Marcus. He'd got out of the car, and he was regarding Mr. Hendry with a mix of amusement and bemusement.

"Marcus, this is Mr. Hendry. He ran the Highcross Horticultural Society."

"I still do run it, missy, but it hasn't been the same since you left. Nobody grows runner beans like our Iris."

Okay, it was true. My beans were awesome. The trick? Plant perennial clover between the vegetable beds. Nodules in the clover roots fixed nitrogen in the soil, and voila, fertiliser. Plus the bees liked the clover.

"Mr. Hendry, this is Marcus, my...my..." My what? I could hardly introduce him as my ex-psychiatrist, could I?

"I'm her boyfriend," Marcus said, holding out his hand.

Boyfriend. Yes, I definitely liked that better.

"Have you come to pick up Screech?"

"Screech is still alive?"

"Mrs. Sylvester's been taking care of him. That cat's got more than nine lives, the way he runs out into traffic. Reckon she'll miss him when he leaves."

"I... I..." I hadn't thought for a moment he'd still be around. Mr. Hendry was right. Screech did have a death wish. The fact that he'd made it to twelve years old was perhaps the most surprising revelation since the oh-so-satisfying downfall of Laurel's father. "I should stop by and see her."

"You'll want to hurry up—it's the church luncheon at one o'clock."

We bade Mr. Hendry goodbye, then Marcus found a place to park the car. Not at the dogging spot, I hasten to add.

"Do we have a cat now?" he asked as we climbed the steps to Mrs. Sylvester's flat. She lived on the second floor of a converted house, a home she'd moved to after her husband died two decades previously.

"Does Teddy get on with cats?"

"I have no idea."

"Honestly, I think Screech is better off staying where he is. Highcross is his home, and I don't know how long we'll be at Will and Rania's. Moving him from pillar to post isn't fair."

Thankfully, Mrs. Sylvester agreed with me. After a hurried tray of tea and cakes, during which Screech purred on her lap and ignored me completely, we decided he was her cat now, but I'd send treats and drop in for the occasional visit. That seemed like the best solution for everyone.

"Are you coming back to the village?" she asked as I helped her with the washing-up.

I glanced at Marcus. "I'm not sure yet."

"Well, we'd love to have you. Too many young people leave for London and never return. Can't see the attraction myself."

"Me neither. No way am I going back to London. Not enough green space."

"All concrete, isn't it? Well, we've got plenty of green space around here. Shame I don't have a garden anymore, really, but at least I've still got my pot plants."

"She means *potted* plants, right?" Marcus whispered as Mrs. Sylvester went to refill Screech's dish with kitty kibble.

"No, pot plants. They live on the bathroom windowsill, but she swears they're for medicinal purposes only."

"I didn't hear that. Tell me you don't smoke it with her?"

"No, it makes me cough."

"I didn't hear that either."

"Oh, lighten up. I thought you were a rock star? Or were you too busy getting your cock pierced to smoke a little doobie? It *was* your cock, wasn't it?"

Mrs. Sylvester bustled back in. "There we are, dearie, he won't go hungry now. I made the mistake of buying him salmon flavour instead of chicken last month, and now he turns his nose up at the chicken."

Dammit, I'd been so close to getting an answer.

"Salmon, got it. I'll buy him salmon treats."

"Stop by anytime you want. If the door's locked, I still hide the key in the same place."

Blu-tacked to the bottom of the milk caddy. I'd told her a hundred times not to keep it there, but she said nobody would rob an old lady like her. Still, at least she locked the door now. I'd just have to keep nagging.

"Don't you have a lunch to go to?"

"Oh, goodness, I do. Look at the time—I'm late already. See you soon?"

"Definitely."

I'd have to work out the bus route because I didn't want to spend Kimberly's money on a car, and it would feel weird asking Marcus to play chauffeur, but tea with Mrs. Sylvester was something to look forward to. She was like the grandmother I'd never had.

Back in the Volkswagen, Marcus reached over to cup my cheek.

"It's funny seeing you with people you knew before...before..."

"Before I killed Baker. It's okay, you can say it. I did that to death with Dr. Meg as well as the PTSD stuff. She said I'm more resilient than she thought."

"You're more resilient than I initially thought too." Another knuckle kiss. "Does that sweet old lady seriously smoke pot? Tell me you were joking."

"She rolls joints any stoner would be proud of. And I notice you avoided my question in there."

"What question?"

"Oh, don't play innocent with me."

He hesitated a moment, a moment that stretched into a good half minute. What was running through his mind? I let him think. He'd come to the right decision. He always did. Finally, he took my hand and guided it down, down, right into his lap. My fingertips brushed over two little steel balls nestled at the root of his cock.

My eyes widened. "There? I thought it'd be at the end."

"Dare to be different, babe."

"Babe?"

"Rock star, remember?"

A giggle burst out of me. He had a freaking piercing. "It's just...decorative?"

"With the barbell? Yes. But if I put something meatier in, you'll soon find out why it's there."

"Tell me you've got something meatier."

"One of the few things I picked up from the other house." He closed his eyes for a second. "Even then, I was thinking of you. Of us."

"Is it too soon to say I love you?"

"Yes, but say it anyway."

This time, I took his hand and kissed *his* knuckles. "I love you, Dr. Hastings."

"Fuck," he muttered under his breath. "I love you too, Miss McGivern. We had a mountain to climb, but we're halfway to the summit, and we'll go the rest of the way side by side."

I embraced him in a rather weepy hug, holding him until I couldn't stand the gear knob poking in my side any longer.

"So damn cheesy."

"Next thing you know, I'll be writing a song about you. But not here. The car's starting to steam up, and I don't want the police to knock on the window next time. Where to now? Any more errands?"

"Just two, but we can't do the second until it gets dark."

"Why does it have to be dark?"

"Uh, I'll tell you later. I can go by myself if you want."

"If you think I'm letting you run around in the dark

by yourself, you've got another think coming. Whatever it is, we'll do it together. Do you want to get lunch first?"

"Are you going to take me on a date, doctor?"

I ran my tongue over my top lip, and he groaned.

"If you want to run these errands, you'd better stop that or I won't be responsible for the consequences."

Of course, I did it again.

"Iris, bloody hell," he growled, half to himself, then started the engine and mashed the car into gear. "We're getting lunch."

CHAPTER 45 - IRIS

AT THAT POINT in my life, a day of highs wouldn't have been complete without a low or two. The dark moment came after our first official date, two hours spent in a quiet corner of the Blackwood Arms, nibbling on a shared platter of tapas while we talked about everything and nothing and a bunch of stuff in between.

"We need to go to the garden centre next. It shuts at four. Or it did five years ago, anyway."

"Is that the place where you used to work?"

"Indeed it is."

Except when we pulled up outside, it was obvious Oak Acres hadn't been open for a very long time. Weeds grew through the tarmac in the car park, half of the panes of glass in the greenhouses were shattered, and the little wooden building that had once housed the shop was closed up and dark. Worse, Percy's cottage looked derelict, with a hole in the roof and broken windows at the front. Tattered beige curtains poked through the jagged shards and flapped in the breeze.

"It's gone," I whispered, my stomach sinking. "Percy's gone. Everything's gone."

I wanted to believe he'd moved away or even gone to a care home, but in my heart, I knew that wasn't true. He always said they'd have to carry him out of

Oak Acres feet first. A tear rolled down my cheek, cooling fast on my skin.

"I'm so sorry, flower. I understand how much you loved this place."

"I just wish… I didn't even get to say goodbye."

"You don't know for sure that Percy's passed away."

"I do. Believe me, I do. This place was his home. He'd never have left voluntarily."

"Seems a shame the place has gone to ruin. Wonder who owns it now?"

"His son, I expect. He's a banker in Paris. Or a stockbroker, something like that. He's too busy flying around on jets and dining in fancy restaurants to worry about this place."

He hadn't cared much for Percy either. Poor Percy. That had been the worst part of going to Lakeview. I'd just been uprooted from my life with no opportunity to tell people where I'd gone or what I was doing. Any information the people of Highcross got came from the news, not from me, and I'd always been too embarrassed to even contemplate writing a letter.

But enough of the pity party. I had a new challenge.

"Uh, I have a small problem."

Marcus raised an eyebrow. "Oh?"

"I need a trowel for my final errand. I planned to borrow one from Percy, but now he's not here, and the next nearest garden centre is twenty minutes away. They'll close before we get there."

"A trowel? You need to plant something?"

"No, I need to dig something up. Hmm… If Percy died, I bet nobody moved his tools." The gates were padlocked, but it only took me a second to vault over the top. I turned back to Marcus. "Are you coming?"

"Iris, you're trespassing."

I held out a hand. Marcus pinched the bridge of his nose, then gave his head a small shake and scrambled over the gate after me.

"What if we get caught?" he asked.

"Easy. We'll just tell them we got lost on the way to the dogging spot." I strode towards the potting shed I knew stood in the tangle of trees beyond the greenhouses. "Keep up, *babe*."

***

"I thought you said we were going to visit someone," Marcus said.

"We are."

"This is a cemetery."

"We're here to visit my mother."

"With a trowel?" Marcus buried his head in his hands. "Tell me you're not planning to dig her up? I might be able to cope with a little breaking and entering, but grave robbery?"

I burst out laughing. Honestly, he was so sweet but soooo melodramatic.

"Of course not. But I left something with her for safekeeping, and now I need it back."

Five and a half years ago, she'd been the only person I trusted completely, and I'd always feared I'd get caught when I killed Baker. Call it luck, call it fate, but those days hadn't been kind to me. Now? Now I had a partner in crime, quite literally, one who followed me out of the car and eased his door shut gently while I tightened my scarf. It really was cold out, that damp kind of chill that seeped into your bones, but thankfully the ground wasn't frozen solid.

"Shh," I warned, gesturing at the light in the cottage next to the church. "The vicar's a really light sleeper."

"I don't want to know how you know that."

I gripped Marcus's hand as we tiptoed between rows of headstones, some plain, some works of art with carved angels and flowers. The spirit of a genuine grave-robber hovered in place with his spade, his head bashed in because someone had caught him mid-act. I'd never stopped to speak to him, even though he shouted every time he saw me. Tonight was no different. I ignored his pleas and then the insults he hurled when things didn't go his way.

Mum's grave was in the far corner near an old oak tree, its boughs bare at that time of year, twisted branches reaching for the moon. Some kind soul had been tending to the spot while I was away—Mr. Hendry, if I had to guess—and the narrow plot was edged with winter pansies.

"Hi, Mum," I whispered, even though I knew she couldn't hear me. Her soul was in a new body somewhere, and I hoped she was happy. "Missed you."

Only the trees whispered back.

Marcus held the torch while I dug around at the foot of the headstone. A few inches down, the plastic-wrapped package lay where I'd buried it the night before Baker's death, slightly frayed around the edges now, but when I held it up, moonlight still glinted off the treasure inside.

I shook the gold piece out into my hand.

"What is it?" Marcus asked. "A necklace?"

I nodded. "Part of the Electi legend. I'm not sure exactly what it does yet, but Mum always said it was important."

"It's quite something. Want me to put it on?"

"Would you?"

I held my hair back while he fastened it around my neck, and then it was time to go. I patted the grass down, then waved goodbye to what was nothing more than a symbol of a life lived and lost.

"Bye, Mum."

The stars twinkled from a clear sky as I backed away, tripped over a raised plaque, and squealed as the trowel flew out of my hand. Said trowel flew through the air and clattered against a metal watering can someone had left half-hidden behind a copper vase.

Another light went on in the rectory.

Shit.

"Who's there?" the vicar shouted. "Clear off, ye varmints. I'm calling the police."

Marcus grabbed the trowel with one hand and my wrist with the other. "Run."

I took off beside him, but I was laughing as we sprinted between the headstones. Why? Because I was alive again.

CHAPTER 46 - IRIS

ON MONDAY, I woke up feeling complete for the first time in over five years. My necklace was back in its rightful place, and I stared at myself in the mirror for a long while before I climbed into the bath. Boy, I'd aged during my time at Lakeview. I may have only just turned twenty-four, but I had faint creases on my forehead, and my eyes spoke of a time I'd rather forget. I needed new memories, like last night's nocturnal jaunt with Marcus. There, that was better. Laughter lines sure beat worry lines.

And bath wrinkles were okay too. I must've spent an hour in the tub, listening to music on the phone and speaker that had magically arrived from somewhere. Floating in the mass of bubbles helped to wash away some of yesterday's disappointment at finding Percy gone. When we got home, Will had checked on the internet for me, and the obituary said he'd died of a short illness almost four years ago. Secretly, I'd been hoping to get my old job back someday, so I'd need to have a rethink on that. Maybe I could do something with water? Bath-bomb tester, perhaps?

When I eventually made it to the kitchen, Marcus was sitting at the kitchen island with a plate of half-eaten toast in front of him, staring incredulously at his phone.

"Everything okay?" I asked.

"Uh, yes. I think so."

"Who was it? You don't have to tell me if you don't want to."

"Fred Adams."

"Who?"

"The acting director at Lakeview."

A chill ran through me. "Did I do something wrong? The vicar didn't install CCTV, did he?"

Marcus barked out a laugh. "No, nothing like that. It now seems that I didn't do anything wrong either. Apparently, Glenda Simmons admitted she might have been mistaken and changed her story."

"Changed it? To what?"

"Something closer to the truth. You spoke to her?"

"Weeks ago. I just told her to stop pretending to be nice to me when she'd basically ruined your life and put me in danger. I may have been a tiny bit upset after you left."

"Well, it seems she did some soul-searching and decided to do the right thing."

"What does it mean for you? Anything?"

He took a swig of his tea before answering. "Adams offered me my old job back."

Wow. Never in a million years did I think Nurse Glenda would recant. I'd just been letting off steam, angry at yet another injustice in the world. But now Marcus's reputation had been restored, at least in regard to his time at Lakeview.

"Will you take it?"

"I don't want to. Yes, I'd be happy to work with the service users again, but I'd rather scrub septic tanks with a toothbrush than deal with more fallout from

Hannity's mess. That's not what I trained for. But..."

"But what?"

"I still need to earn a living, Iris. Nobody's hiring over Christmas, and if I can't find a job in January..."

"You'll find something. Don't go back there if you hate it."

"Not having an income will count against me at the custody hearing."

"Have you applied for other jobs?"

"Several dozen, but my record isn't exactly glowing. Laurel's father saw to that."

"His record isn't exactly glowing either."

"Unfortunately for the recruiters, two wrongs don't make a right."

"Do you have to make a decision straight away?"

"I've got a couple of weeks."

"Then let's enjoy Christmas and think about the heavy stuff afterwards, okay?"

Marcus hooked one arm around my waist and pulled me close. With him on the stool, I was an inch or two taller, and I laid my forehead against his. Would I ever get used to acting so normal? Every tiny contact with him felt special.

"Okay," he murmured.

Footsteps clattered on the tile, and I looked around, guilty, even though there was no reason for me to feel that way. Was that habit? At Lakeview, if something had felt good, it probably meant I shouldn't have been doing it.

"Oh my gosh!" Kimberly squealed. "Your necklace—you got it back. Where was it?"

"You don't want to know," Marcus muttered.

"Yes, I do."

"I buried it at the cemetery with my mum."

"Not in her actual casket?"

"No! Beside her headstone."

Kimberly reached out to touch the shimmering gold as Nicole and Rania walked in. They made a beeline for me too. Four of us, all wearing the relics of an ancient curse, a gift, a...a *magic*.

"It's smaller than I thought it'd be," Rania said. "There's going to be a gap in the middle."

Nicole tilted my gold piece towards the light, and sparkles danced over the cupboard opposite. "The Judge must have one."

A good theory, but I wasn't sure it held water. "He might not."

"What do you mean?"

"My mum didn't know what happened to the original Judge's gold piece after he and the Electi... Uh, you really don't know this?"

"None of it," Rania said. "All we know is that we can kill people and scatter their souls. What happened?"

"The original Electi...they were executed for witchcraft, and the Judge too. In the late fourteenth century or maybe the early fifteenth. It was the 1300s when Pope John XXII issued decrees identifying sorcery with heresy and pacts with the devil, and the witch hunts began. Our ancestors got rounded up and convicted in one of the early trials, but the moment they died..."

"Their curse got passed on to their daughters," Rania whispered.

"Exactly. Except the Judge didn't have a son, so his soul could have ended up anywhere. The girls were young, too young, but perhaps I was the oldest because

I've remembered more of what I was told? We got scattered to the four corners of the earth to grow up with people who could keep us safe until the time came."

"Until the time came for what?"

"Who knows? To meet again, I guess, and here we are. Four of us, at least."

"Four of us, the world's a mess, we can't find the Judge, and we're meant to clean it up?"

"Something like that."

When Rania put the problem in such stark terms, the idea of us solving it did sound slightly farfetched. Plus I'd already learned my lesson with Leland Baker— I wasn't cut out for this job. As well as the memories of him bouncing off my car bonnet, stabbing Nurse Hazel in the eye with a freaking pen still gave me nightmares, vivid nightmares where I woke up gasping and sweating. I'd considered asking Marcus whether he could somehow get me more sleeping pills, but I didn't want to admit my mind wasn't quite as healed as I might have led the medical tribunal and Dr. Meg to believe.

Rania wore her talisman on a leather cord, and now she lifted it over her head. "Then I guess we should get started. What do we do? Put the pieces together?"

"Wait a second. I'm not risking another prison sentence."

"We can't carry on as we are. We should try the pieces."

Marcus stood, his arm still around me and the toast forgotten. "No way. Iris has been out of the hospital for less than four days. You have no idea what might happen, and she's not ready for this."

"Have you seen what's going on out there? Lakeview's just another symptom. Too many dark souls mean prisons are overcrowded, which is why the government contracts outfits like Hannity to open more of them. The public sector can't build facilities fast enough. And all the bad vibes from the trapped spirits affect people's minds. Did you know they give off electromagnetic radiation? One spirit on its own doesn't have much effect, but there are thousands of them now. Maybe even millions."

"Tens of millions," Nicole pointed out. "Think of all the genocide. There was Leopold in the Congo, the colonisation of the Americas, the Holocaust alone cost six million lives, and then we have the wars in Iraq, Afghanistan, and Syria. Maybe even hundreds of millions."

"Rania and Nicole are right," I said quietly. "So many people have been killed. Some of those deaths were justifiable, but most weren't. The Judge should have been releasing the older spirits, plus the thousands who were either bumped off accidentally or whose murderers have already been punished by the authorities. But he hasn't, and they're piling up. And the more recent, unsolved cases—those...those are meant to be ours."

"I realise that," Marcus answered. "I'll admit I still struggle with the concept from time to time, though I understand you have a purpose to fulfil. But you still can't kill anyone."

Kimberly put her hands on her hips. "I'm not killing anyone else either."

"Or me," Nicole said.

Rania huffed a bit. "You think I enjoyed shooting

people? In Syria, it was war. I didn't have any choice if I wanted to live."

I wriggled out of Marcus's grip and went to Rania. She'd had the hardest life out of all of us, even tougher than mine. Growing up as a refugee in Syria, seeing her mother murdered, selling herself as she travelled across Africa before finally managing to smuggle herself into Europe. Claiming asylum had been an arduous process, and she was still working her way towards British citizenship.

"I understand. We all understand, but Marcus is right as well. It's too soon. Please, just give me a few weeks to get used to living in a house again before we try to save the planet?"

"Six hundred years have passed," Nicole said. "Another month or two won't make much difference."

"We can't avoid this forever."

I squeezed Rania's shoulder. "And we won't. Two months. Can you give me two months?"

Finally, she smiled. "We can wait two months."

CHAPTER 47 - IRIS

ON TUESDAY, I pushed Electi business, Lakeview business, Laurel business, and everything else bad to the back of my mind because I was determined to enjoy Christmas. Christmas Eve had traditionally been a source of chaos in the household while I was growing up—we'd had everything from a burst pipe to a car breakdown to Mrs. Sylvester slipping over and breaking a hip. Oh, and then there was the time Mum thought she'd save money by ordering a turkey direct from the farmer, only when it arrived, it was still clucking. Neither of us could bring ourselves to wring his neck, so we called him Wilbur and spent Christmas Day building him a little house in the garden.

But this Christmas Eve, I took Teddy for a walk with Marcus in the morning, and then Kimberly decided we were going to Winter Wonderland, which was basically a giant, Christmas-themed fair with as many adults as children eating candy canes and playing games for prizes. I felt a bit sorry for the man running the shooting gallery when Rania, Beck, and Reed wiped him out, but Marcus offered to carry my giant cuddly polar bear so I still had my hands free for hot chocolate.

The only shadow over the day came from what—or rather, who—wasn't there. Cassie. Marcus missed her desperately. I saw it in his eyes every time he glanced at

Shannon and RJ and their little girl, but it wasn't his turn to see his daughter until Friday, still three long days away. He'd tried asking his wife if she'd swap for Boxing Day, but of course the bitch said no.

All I could do was try to make him smile. Would a distraction work?

"Want to go ice skating?"

"Can you ice skate?"

No, and I didn't mix well with roller skates either. "Surely it can't be that difficult? Can you?"

"I haven't been for years."

Of course, we ended up on our arses, but I didn't care one bit. Marcus was laughing, so I'd make a fool out of myself all afternoon if that was what it took.

"Is it too early to say 'I love you' again?" I whispered as he half carried me off the ice.

He leaned in and snatched a chaste kiss as he set me on my feet. "I love you too, Iris."

Only one person didn't look happy about our public display of affection. Will.

"Hey, stop that," he murmured.

"Why?" I asked. He kissed Rania in public all the time.

"Because there's a guy over there watching you."

"Where?"

"By the popcorn stand. Green jacket, woollen hat. He's backing away now. How dirty is your wife likely to play with this divorce?"

See what I mean about something always going wrong on Christmas Eve?

"Laurel has the ethics of a sewer rat," Marcus said. "Fuck."

I took a step back, tears prickling at the corners of

my eyes. "She's going to use me against you, isn't she? Say that Cassie shouldn't be with you because of me."

I could just see it now. Her solicitor arguing that a young child shouldn't come into contact with a convicted murderer, especially one who was crazy. I tried to drop Marcus's hand, but he gripped it tighter.

"We shouldn't..."

"Iris, I'm not pretending that you don't exist or that we're not seeing each other. Custody's a long shot anyway."

"But just for a month..."

"If it doesn't come out now, Laurel would just haul me back to court at a later date. She'll always be watching. Don't let her spoil our day, flower."

But she already had. Marcus was tense, I was miserable, and even Kimberly treating us to dinner at a fancy restaurant didn't cheer me up. Nothing short of a miracle would have made me smile, because as the evening wore on, I realised what I had to do. There was only one option open to me.

Walk away.

I couldn't let Marcus risk his visitation rights for me. Our relationship was still young, and it was better to end it now than later when he'd truly dug his way into my heart.

Oh, who was I kidding? He already had.

I stewed about it the whole way home in the car, but when Kimberly asked me if I was okay, I forced a smile.

"I'm fine. Everything's fine. Thanks for dinner."

"You know we're all here if you ever want to talk?"

"Yes, I know."

And I appreciated it, but some decisions I had to

make alone.

***

The living room light in the cottage was still on at midnight, and every so often, I saw Marcus walk past the window. Couldn't he sleep either? I'd curled up on the sofa in the conservatory at the back of the house, almost invisible in the dark. The room was chilly, frost already lacing the windows on the outside, but better to be cold than fidget constantly in bed.

At half past twelve, Marcus's silhouette shadowed the window once more, and I could take it no longer. Why put off the inevitable? Why spend another day falling deeper in love when I knew it couldn't last?

The low hoot of a tawny owl startled me as I crept across the garden, determined to get the most horrible part over with. Mum had always told me not to procrastinate. "It only makes things worse in the end," she said.

Marcus opened the door a few seconds after I knocked, and he looked like I felt. Tired, haggard, utterly miserable. He had a piece of sellotape stuck to his jumper, and I reached out to pick it off before I caught myself. That wasn't what I was there for.

"Marcus, I—"

"Forget it."

"Huh?"

"I know why you're here, and the answer's no."

"Why am I here?"

"You've come to break up with me because you're worried about the court case."

How did he know me so well?

"It's for the best. Cassie's your daughter, and she needs you as much as you need her. I grew up without a father, and yes, my mum was amazing, the best in the world, but there were days when I wished he was around. All those times I had to sit on the sidelines for the father-daughter race on sports day. Every year at primary school when the others in my class made Father's Day cards. The day I won my first gymnastics competition. I missed him, even though I never knew him."

Marcus gently cupped my chin, forcing me to face him instead of looking at my feet.

"It's a different situation, flower. Circumstances may keep Cassie and me apart, but she's a smart kid. She knows I'll always be there for her."

"She should get the chance to have you all the time."

"Have *us* all the time. There's no me without you anymore."

How could he say things like that and expect me not to cry? Tears leaked out, and of course he had a clean hankie waiting.

"Don't do this," I begged.

He waited until I'd dried my eyes before he carried on. "Okay, I'll let you break up with me on one condition."

"What condition?"

"You look me in the eyes and tell me you don't love me."

I tried. I really tried to meet that intense gaze of his. "I... I... I can't."

He closed the gap between us and kissed me, and all I could do was kiss him back, inwardly cursing myself the whole time. What happened to staying strong? This man was my weakness.

I barely murmured a protest when he dragged me over the threshold and slammed the door behind us, and two seconds after that, we were tearing at each other's clothes. Suddenly, I wasn't cold anymore.

"What happened to taking it slow?"

"I'm not waiting for your pretty blonde head to come up with any more dumb ideas. After everything we've been through, you think we don't belong together? You're wrong. The way I feel... It's not something I can turn on and then turn off again."

"I'm turned all the way on."

He was too. I could feel his hardness pressing into my stomach, and I reached behind his waist and hooked my thumbs through his belt loops, pulling him closer. When his cock jumped, I knew he was mine. And I was his. I gasped as he cupped my ass and lifted me, squeezing hard as he kissed me with an intensity that bordered on desperate. I matched him all the way. Tongues, teeth... He nipped at my bottom lip, and heat flooded between my thighs.

It had been a long while since I'd got naked with a man, but I never remembered feeling like this. So wanton and needy that I'd tear my own clothes off if Marcus didn't do it fast enough. I dragged his jumper over his head, and his shirt too, then lifted my arms for him to return the favour. Only when I was standing there in my bra did he pause.

"Iris, shit, we should've talked about this beforehand. Lakeview... Terrence..."

"Don't mention his name."

"But—"

I pressed a finger against his lips. "Yes, bad things happened, but I don't remember the worst of them. Actually, the most invasive part was when the doctors insisted on testing me for *everything* just in case he had some sort of disease, but it came back clear."

"I know that feeling," he muttered.

"Laurel?"

"Laurel was good at projecting. If she accused me of sleeping with someone else, the chances were that she'd done it herself." He kissed me softly on the lips. "But everything came back clear, and I don't want to talk about that anymore."

"Shit. I don't have a condom. Tell me you have condoms?"

"I do, but...I've also had a vasectomy."

"What?" The words came out as a strangled sob. "But I...I..."

A vasectomy? That shouldn't have changed everything, but it did. I loved Marcus. More than anything, I loved him, but I'd always imagined a future with a little girl in it. My little girl.

"You want a baby?" he asked softly.

"Not now, but someday. I have to pass this gift on, which means I need a daughter, a biological daughter, and—"

"Shh." It was his turn with the finger. "I'll get it reversed."

"You'll have a baby with me?"

"When the time's right." He gave me a soft smile. "I love kids. But for now..."

"Let's go and make a mess."

He carried me up the narrow staircase, bridal-style, and for the first time, I saw the room that Kimberly had originally decorated for me. Three magnolia walls and the fourth with floral wallpaper opposite the bed, tiny orange irises on a lilac background. Lilac curtains framed two dormer windows that looked out onto the garden, and my feet sank into soft peach carpet when Marcus set me onto the floor. The room wasn't as big as my one in the main house, but it was cosy and homey and I loved it.

I loved the man in it too.

Once, being naked in front of a guy had been an awkward affair, something to be rushed with the lights off, but when Marcus laid me back on the bed and tugged my bra down so my breasts bulged over the top, I looked on in fascination rather than horror. A low groan escaped when he sucked one nipple into his mouth, then ran his tongue around the hardening peak before he gave the other equal treatment. Little zings of electricity sizzled through me, the sparks shooting south to my core.

My back arched off the bed as Marcus kissed his way across my stomach, and I lifted my ass when he unzipped my jeans and tugged them down my legs. My knickers soon followed, and as he dipped his head and softly blew across my mound, I realised I was half wearing a bra and he was wearing an awful lot more.

"Wait."

He stopped in a heartbeat. "What's wrong, flower?"

"You've still got trousers on." I knifed up. Reached forward for his belt buckle. "That's not fair."

He knelt above me, one leg either side of my stomach as I pushed his slacks over his hips. Oh, holy hell, he'd gone commando and he had that ring in, a chunky silver hoop with a small sphere at the bottom. I wasn't sure whether to lick it, flick it, or stick my damn finger through it. In the end, I settled for stroking the solid shaft that jutted out below.

"Mine," I whispered.

"Always."

He wrapped his hand over my smaller one, both of us stroking. A small bead of pre-cum appeared, and I spread it over the head of his cock with my thumb. Fuck, I wanted to taste it, but I wanted him inside me more.

"Please, just do me."

His smile turned into a wide grin. A filthy grin. "I love a lady who doesn't mince her words."

"Then what are you waiting for?"

Nothing, it seemed. He slid inside me bare, and the little sting of pain at being stretched further than ever before only sweetened the pleasure. One gentle thrust, and he stilled and gave me room to adjust.

"Okay?" he asked, punctuating the question with a sweet kiss on the tip of my nose.

I nodded, and okay turned into oh-my-gosh-I'm-dying-of-sensory-overload as he stroked deep inside me, and the ring bumped and ground and sent me to a place I never even knew existed. The pleasure built and built, and when I couldn't take any more, I cried out as he buried himself with a soft grunt.

"What the hell was that?" I choked out once I could speak again.

Mind blown, I flopped back on the bed, panting, struggling to work out which way was up as little waves of sensation continued to ripple through me. I...I...I felt as though every atom in me had been blown apart then put back together again, but in a good way. New me felt complete.

Marcus stared at me, wide-eyed. "You've never had an orgasm before?"

"Was that what...? Holy shit, no."

Now he smiled that dirty smile again, all cat-that-got-the-damn-cream, and he deserved every drop of it. "Well, I'm glad we fixed that."

"I need more."

"Flower, I want to give you everything."

He did, twice more that night, but at some point in the early hours, exhaustion got the better of us and we passed out in each other's arms.

Happy Christmas to me.

***

Hammering on the front door woke me up—loud, insistent knocking—and I shook Marcus awake.

"Someone's downstairs."

"Huh?"

Oh, he looked adorable in the mornings, all messy hair and sleepy eyes with enough stubble to burn if he kept kissing me the way he had last night. My chin was still a bit tender.

"Shall I see who it is?"

"No, I'll go." He felt around on the bedside table for his glasses and slid them on before rolling out of bed. "It's cold—you stay here."

Like I was going to let him deal with problems on his own. Once he'd pulled on a pair of pyjama bottoms and jogged down the stairs, I slipped on the shirt he'd been wearing yesterday and hugged it around myself. I'd pulled it off him the lazy way yesterday—over his head—and a couple of the buttons were missing.

I got to the top of the stairs in time to hear Will's panicked voice.

"Iris is missing. She's not in her room, she's not in the house, Nicole's freaking out..."

"Uh, I'm not missing."

Both men turned to look at me as I made my way down the stairs, and Will's face turned bright red.

"I see, yes..." He backed away and tripped over the pot of orange pansies Kimberly had left by the steps. Marcus leapt forward and grabbed him before he tumbled to the bottom. At least it wasn't just me who was clumsy. "Well, I'll see you at dinner. Congratulations, both of you," he muttered before practically sprinting across the garden.

I couldn't stop giggling as Marcus closed the door. "His face..."

"Guess the cat's all the way out of the bag now."

"Do you think Kimberly'll be mad that she decorated the big bedroom for me and I only slept in it a handful of times? I won't be sleeping in it, will I?"

"Kimberly won't be mad in the slightest, and no, you won't be sleeping in it."

"I love you."

"I love you too."

I caught sight of myself in the little mirror beside the front door and nearly screamed. Flippin' heck, I could've been an extra in a horror movie. My hair was sticking out in a hundred directions, and the mascara Kimberly had carefully applied for me before we went out yesterday was smeared across my cheeks.

"How can you stand to see me like this? I look like the love child of an eighties pop star and a zombie."

"Because you look freshly fucked, and I did that, so..."

"I need a shower."

"Give me fifteen minutes to finish wrapping Cassie's presents, and I'll join you."

I looked past him into the living room, where toys and paper and sellotape lay on the floor. That was what he'd been doing last night? I loved that he loved his daughter so much.

"I'll help you. Mum was terrible at wrapping, so I used to do it all. Then we can try shower sex." I stood close to him, then raised one leg and hooked it over his shoulder. I'd always been insanely flexible, and stretching in my room at Lakeview had kept my muscles supple. "Does this work?" I murmured in his ear.

"Bloody hell, woman. You're gonna be the death of me."

CHAPTER 48 - MARCUS

BY SOME MIRACLE, I made it to Friday alive, no thanks to Iris. Mind you, if I was going to die, having my heart give out while making love to a human pretzel wasn't a bad way to go. Nicole had given Iris an e-reader for Christmas, and by the time we staggered back to the cottage that night, full of mulled wine and eggnog and turkey dinner, she'd downloaded a copy of the Kama Sutra. We were a quarter of the way through already.

Oof. I tried not to let the pain show as Cassie barrelled into me. Jacqueline had tried to call the visit off because she didn't want to drive in the snow, but the thought of another week passing without seeing my daughter had made me push for my allocated Friday, plus today I got the whole day because she was off school. Hence why Jacqueline was currently picking her way down a frozen driveway in fur-lined boots that probably cost a fortune. And now that I knew where that fortune had come from, every step she took disgusted me more.

"You'd better not bring her back late. This was your idea," she said, gesturing to the black clouds above. "Don't say I didn't warn you."

The roads were well-gritted, and I'd borrowed Kimberly's SUV. She'd returned the rental and bought an Audi to keep at Will's house because with Rania and Iris both in the UK, she said she planned several visits a year and owning a vehicle there made sense.

"I'll be on time." The roads weren't the only thing that was gritted. My teeth were too. "How are you going to take her back to Laurel's if you won't drive?"

"Laurel's staying here. We're having a *family* Christmas, no thanks to your interruption."

I didn't need Cassie to hear any more of the bile that Jaqueline spewed. The woman had never met a person she didn't criticise. You should've heard her at parties. Oh, darling, how are you? Haven't I seen you in that dress before?

Cassie ran ahead of me to the car and scrambled onto her booster seat in the back. Once I'd checked she had her seat belt securely fastened, I pulled out slowly into the road. At least there was no traffic today.

"You got a car for Christmas, Daddy?"

"No, I borrowed this one from Kimberly."

"Pretty Kimberly? I like her."

"I like her too, sweetie."

"Is Kimberly your girlfriend?"

"No, she isn't." I took a deep breath. "But Daddy does have a girlfriend now. Her name's Iris."

We'd agonised over whether or not to tell Cassie about our relationship, and Iris had offered to make herself scarce for today's visit, but what was the point in waiting? Iris wasn't some flash in the pan, a fling I'd move on from in a week or two. In just a few short days, my feelings for her had eclipsed anything I'd ever felt for Laurel, and I didn't even want to contemplate a life without her. It was only fair that I share her with Cassie.

"Iris." Cassie tested the word out. "Is she pretty too?"

"She's very pretty." More than pretty. Beautiful. Beautiful in a way that made me pinch myself every morning I opened my eyes and found myself beside her. And she wasn't only beautiful on the outside. The inside matched. "Would you like to meet her?"

"Yes!"

I knew that would be Cassie's answer. She'd always been outgoing, able to walk into a room and charm every adult in the place. I'd encouraged her sense of adventure, whereas Laurel muttered about injuries and paedophiles and tried to keep her at home as much as possible. Yes, there was always a risk with any activity, but what was life if you didn't live it? It had taken Iris to remind me of that fact.

"Did you have a good Christmas?" I asked Cassie.

"Nuh-uh."

Oh? It wouldn't have surprised me if Laurel and Rupert had somehow gift-wrapped a pony.

"What happened?"

"I made a cake with Grandma, but Mummy threw it at Rupert."

Marcus, don't laugh. I held back for Cassie's sake, but didn't that woman ever learn? Believe me, I'd got good at ducking over the years.

"I'm sorry about your cake, sweetie."

"I didn't even get to eat any of it." Cassie sniffled, and I prayed it wouldn't turn into full-blown tears because I couldn't hug her while I was driving. "And then Rupert left, and Grandma says he's not coming back."

Cassie hiccuped a sob, and I reached back to

squeeze her hand, thankful that Kimberly had bought an automatic so I didn't need to worry about shifting gears.

"Does that make you sad?"

"Sort of. Rupert was boring, but he promised I could have a pony and now Mummy says I can't."

Dammit, why did Laurel always do that? Get Cassie's hopes up and then let her down? Two years ago, she'd done the same thing with a hamster, only to suddenly realise that hamsters were rodents and she hated rodents. She'd cancelled play dates in favour of spa days, a pantomime trip to go to the opera... The list went on.

I wanted to cheer Cassie up, but no way could I afford a pony, and I didn't know how to make a cake.

"How about next week, we eat cake after your riding lesson?"

The stables were closed for Christmas, unfortunately.

"Okay. Can I have chocolate cake?"

"I'm sure we can manage that."

Back at the White House, Iris looked more nervous than I'd ever seen her when Cassie rushed through the front door. In a weird way, I liked that. It meant she cared.

Cassie hugged each of the girls she already knew—Kimberly, Nicole, and Rania—then stopped in front of the love of my life.

"Are you Iris?"

"I am."

"Daddy was right. You *are* pretty."

Oh, Cassie. She was better at breaking the ice than any adult. Iris knelt on the floor and smiled at my daughter.

"You're pretty too. I love the bow in your hair."

"It's because I'm practising to be a princess. A princess who rides horses and shoots fuckers."

Horrified gasps came from all around. Bloody hell. I was careful not to swear out loud around Cassie but someone else obviously hadn't been.

"Where did you hear that new word, sweetie?" I asked.

"From Grandpa. He said some fucker ruined his life."

"That's a bad word, Cassie. You mustn't say it again."

"But Grandpa said it."

I pinched the bridge of my nose. *Give me strength.* I'd always refrained from criticising Jacqueline and Wallace because Cassie didn't need negativity around her, but at that moment, I wanted to punch the fucker in the mouth.

"Call those people potato heads instead," Iris said. "Bad potato heads."

"Potato heads?" Cassie asked doubtfully.

"Yup." Iris blew out her cheeks and crossed her eyes, which sent Cassie into a fit of giggles. "Potato heads. A princess who rides horses and shoots potato heads is awesome."

"Potato heads! Potatoes, potatoes, potatoes!" Cassie sang as she galloped around the living room. "I'm gonna shoot potato heads."

I squeezed Iris's hand as I helped her to her feet. Did she ache as much as me after our nighttime exertions? "Thank you," I mouthed.

"The first time I called someone an arsehole, I was

eight, and Mum told me to call him a potato head instead," she said softly. "It lasted until I was fifteen, and then I figured I was old enough to graduate to real swear words."

Fifteen. When Leland Baker had killed her mother.

I leaned in close. "I love your mouth, filthy or otherwise."

"That's good, because you're stuck with it. Did the pickup go okay? They don't know you're the fucker that ruined Grandpa's life, do they?"

"Apparently not." RJ and Will had been very careful not to mention my name when they blew the whistle on the drug scandal at Deane Valley, and secretly, I liked being a fucker outside of the bedroom as well as in it. "Jacqueline was her usual prickly self, but over Christmas, Laurel managed to split up with Rupert, trash Cassie's home-made cake, and renege on a promise to buy her a pony."

"I can't help with the pony, but I could make cupcakes with her. We've got flour, eggs, butter, and sugar. I mean, only if you want me to. It's your day with Cassie."

Just when I thought I couldn't possibly love Iris more, I managed it. Once, I'd told her she wasn't all that special. I'd lied.

"Hey, Cassie. Do you want to make cupcakes with Iris?"

She cantered to a halt in front of us, tossing her head and whinnying. "Yes, cakes!"

"Cakes *please*."

"Yes, cakes please."

"There's your answer, flower."

***

Of course, I'd known Iris was a gymnast. She'd told me. But until that Friday, I hadn't realised quite how good of a gymnast.

She'd clearly spent some time baking in the past too because the Nutella butterfly cakes she'd made with Cassie were delicious. I'd loved watching them together in the kitchen, and now my face ached along with the rest of me. I'd never over-smiled before.

The afternoon found us in the garden, the presents opened, hot drinks in hand. I'd bought Iris a coffee machine for Christmas, plus several hundred coffee pods. The promise I'd made to her at Lakeview three long months ago as we sipped the vending machine's terrible offerings hadn't been forgotten.

Our snowman stood five feet tall with a carrot for a nose and black olives for eyes, and my clothes were damp where both of my girls had pelted me with snowballs. I didn't even care.

"Let's make snow angels," Iris said.

"What's snow angels?"

Unsurprisingly, Laurel had vetoed playing in the snow due to an irrational fear of pneumonia. I'd explained many times that pneumonia was an infection, and that in a healthy child dressed in appropriate clothing, simply breathing cold air wouldn't cause it, but Laurel always knew best. Hence no snow angels.

"Like this."

Iris lay down in the snow to demonstrate, brushing her arms and legs back and forth until she'd made an angel shape. Cassie copied her, squealing, and then Iris leapt up and turned a cartwheel, out of sheer exuberance, it seemed.

Cassie clapped her hands. "Again, again."

Iris obliged then walked a few steps on her hands, which of course delighted Cassie, before backing up into the corner by the patio, taking a deep breath, and flipping her way across the garden. She ended by the cottage with a somersault that had me holding my breath. Holy shit.

Cassie's tiny mouth dropped open.

"Iris is *magic*."

In so many ways. "Yes, sweetie, she is."

She was also patient and kind, and she spent twenty minutes teaching a well-wrapped-up Cassie to do a cartwheel of her own in the soft snow. Cassie's attempt was slightly wonky, but she was smiling and that's all that mattered. It made the past four months of strife worth it. Then Shannon came out with Aisling to watch, and soon we had toddler snow angels and giggles too.

The afternoon went far too quickly, but I'd learned everything I needed to know. Someday, Iris May McGivern would make a great mother, and I'd give her as many little girls as she wanted.

WHAT WAS WRONG?

Last night, we'd been celebrating Marcus's new job —only three days a week, but since Will and Rania would only accept one pound a month in rent for the cottage, it was enough. An old friend of Dr. Meg's had called out of the blue. She needed a psychiatrist to provide maternity cover at her private practice for the next year, and would he be interested? Dr. Meg thought he might be available and had provided a recommendation.

But now, he'd gone from happy to horrified in one phone call, and I didn't even know who he was speaking to.

"Yes, yes, I understand. If you can send me the file, I'll make other arrangements." Then when he hung up, "Shit, shit, shit!"

"What's happened?"

"My solicitor just had a heart attack."

Oh, shit, shit, shit indeed. The custody hearing was five days away.

"Is it bad?"

"The funeral's next Wednesday. I guess I should send flowers, but *fuck*."

"Now what? Can you delay things?"

"After Laurel's endless shenanigans, the judge said

no more delays, and even if I could, I wouldn't know where to start with the request. The solicitor handled all that."

"Then you need a new solicitor."

"The last guy was recommended by an old gym buddy. I don't know anyone else who's got divorced recently, and I don't even have a gym membership anymore."

"I'll call Mr. Benton."

"He's not a divorce lawyer."

"But he's a *lawyer*, and he must know other lawyers."

"I'm not sure I can afford the rates of any of Lance's lawyer friends."

"If I call him and there's nobody suitable, we haven't lost anything."

Marcus kissed my hair, but he was buzzing with stress. "You're right as usual, flower."

We hadn't seen Mr. Benton for almost two weeks. Lance. He kept telling me to call him Lance, but it didn't feel right, even though we'd had our last meeting over coffee in the living room at the White House. Apparently, he was a member of the same golf club as Will and RJ, so they met up for drinks from time to time.

In the meeting, he'd told me that things were progressing nicely with Hannity SP, but they were lowballing. The government's people were slower, apparently because they didn't know their arses from their elbows. Chin up, he'd said, but his advice was hard to take at that moment.

I dialled his number, still slightly in awe of my new smartphone. When I went into Lakeview, I'd had a chunky thing with all the buttons, while this one did everything but make the tea.

"Mr. Benton?"

"Lance, please. You must be psychic, Iris. I was just about to call you."

Really? "What for?"

"It's better if we speak in person. I was hoping to swing by your place on my way home this evening."

My place. *Our* place. I'd never get sick of hearing that.

"I'll be here. Uh, Marcus also needs a new divorce attorney. The fact-finding hearing's on Monday, and his solicitor just freaking died."

"Ah. I see how that could be a problem."

"Do you know of anyone? We don't have the biggest budget."

"Let's talk about that this evening, okay?"

I gulped in a breath, trying to quell the rising panic. So much to do, so little time. "Okay."

"I can get there for five."

"Five. Thank you."

***

Holy. Fuck.

We'd still been reeling from the morning's news when Mr. Benton arrived, this time wearing Garfield socks and a broad smile. The others were out, but I'd mastered my new coffee machine and managed to make three passable cappuccinos with chocolate sprinkles on the top. When the small talk was over, he'd slid a letter in my direction. I recognised the logo of Hannity SP's solicitors at the top.

"Two million pounds?" Was I seeing things again? I blinked, but all the zeroes were still there. Had I misread the legalese? I gripped Marcus's hand, and he squeezed mine back. "Is this a joke?"

"Hannity's first offer was a joke. Half a million? No way were we settling for that. I told them you'd make far more from the talk-show circuit and a book deal."

"What? I'm not going on talk shows!"

"But they didn't know that. And no, you're not now. As part of the settlement, you'd agree not to participate in any interviews or publish any books, written, ghostwritten, or otherwise."

Oh. My. Gosh.

"What about the others? Jacinda's and Rylie's families? Ellie? Have they got deals too?"

"Similar to yours."

"Are they taking them?"

"The Warrens and the Drapers are. The Thomases have opted for public shaming instead."

I meant what I'd said to Dr. Meg all those weeks ago. I wanted to focus on the future and let the past die.

"Marcus?" I whispered.

"Whatever you want to do, I'm behind you, but it sounds like a good settlement to me. Two million pounds." He gave a low whistle. "You'll be a wealthy woman, Iris."

"*We'll* be wealthy. No me without you, remember?" I turned back to Mr. Benton. "I just want to put this behind me and move on."

"Then you'll take the deal?"

"It's the best we can get?"

"From Hannity? I believe so. They're running out of money fast. The government amount, when it comes, will be much smaller, but it'll pay for a nice holiday."

"In that case, where do I sign?"

"I've drawn up the papers right here."

Two million pounds. I scribbled my signature on the dotted line with Marcus's new fountain pen, the one I'd given him for Christmas. I figured it was the least I could do after I ruined his old one with Nurse Hazel's eyeball.

"At least we can afford to pay a divorce lawyer now. Uh, did you think about one of those?"

"Yeah. You're looking at him." Mr. Benton sighed and leaned back against the sofa. "I was meant to spend a long weekend sailing, but my buddy with the boat had another fight with his wife, and guess what? They're getting a divorce. I figured it was fate that I'm free for the next four days. This may be blowing my own trumpet, but you won't get anyone better at short notice."

"But...but you're not a divorce lawyer."

"I was until six years ago. The constant bickering got to me, and you wouldn't believe how many vindictive wives think it's okay to proposition a member of their legal team. So I switched to corporate. But I'm up to date on the relevant laws and regulations, and I can handle a fact-finding hearing."

"Are you serious?"

"Will's done me enough favours over the years. Just keep the coffee coming."

***

Talk about bickering... On Sunday evening, Marcus and Lance—I'd finally given in and started using his first name since I'd ended up doing his freaking laundry yesterday—were still arguing over tactics.

"It's an insane idea," Marcus said, pausing his pacing for a second to glare at Lance. "We're not taking Iris to court with us."

Lance stretched his arms above his head, his feet propped up on the coffee table. He'd opted for Star Wars socks today. How many pairs of comedy socks was it possible for one man to own? I'd never seen him wear the same ones twice.

"You want custody of Cassidy, don't you? It's the only way we'll win."

"Iris has been through hell for the last five years, do you understand that? Stress won't help her recovery. And you've never even met Laurel."

"No, but I've met hundreds of women just like her. Bring Iris with you, and Laurel'll lose her shit, guaranteed."

"Think of another way."

"Iris is stronger than you think."

"Hey!" I inserted myself between them. "Don't I get a say in this?"

Marcus wanted to say no. I could practically see the word hovering on the tip of his tongue, but he stayed silent. Lance did the smart thing and kept his mouth shut too.

"I'm coming. If there's the slightest chance of Marcus getting more time with Cassie, then I can take whatever shit Laurel slings at me for a morning."

"Iris—" Marcus started.

"That's my final answer. You can thank me afterwards."

CHAPTER 50 - IRIS

DESPITE WHAT I'D said to Marcus and Lance, I still felt utterly, utterly sick as I took a seat in the public gallery behind them. Like, to the extent that I'd lined my handbag with a plastic bag in case I got the sudden urge to puke. I wasn't being called as a witness, I was just there for moral support, but even so... And Rania had come as *my* moral support.

It was the first time I'd set eyes on Laurel Hastings, and my first impression was that I'd go out of my way to avoid her. Not only because of what she'd done to Marcus, but because she just looked like a bitch. Snooty expression, cold eyes, red-soled pumps with spindly little heels to draw attention to how much money she had. Her lawyer looked like a ball-breaker too. The body of Aunt Spiker mixed with the charisma of Aunt Lydia. *James and the Giant Peach* versus *The Handmaid's Tale*. Aunt Splydia. Sort of like Chlamydia, but without the fun parts.

Lance had gone for Pac-Man socks, and Marcus was giving him a run for his money in the suit department. Whatever happened, the consolation prize was that I'd get to peel him out of it later.

Today's session was for both sides to present facts and evidence ahead of the final hearing, which would decide how custody of Cassie would be split, as well as

Marcus and Laurel's finances. Before Christmas, Laurel had submitted a long, long list of allegations, most of them so heavily embellished they were fast heading for fictional, and Marcus's solicitor had drafted a response. This was the judge's chance to cross-examine both parties and hear from witnesses before deciding whether or not the incidents had happened as stated. The problem was, Marcus had so few people on his side. Following Wallace Burton's suspension from Deane Valley Hospital, two of Marcus's former colleagues had agreed to act as character witnesses despite incurring Laurel's wrath, and the babysitter who'd witnessed Laurel's temper on the night Marcus left her was coming, but she hadn't seen much. Will and Rania had managed to track down the girl Laurel said Marcus cheated with, but firstly, she barely remembered the party let alone being in the bedroom with him, and secondly, she'd just been admitted into rehab.

Things weren't looking great.

The judge arrived along with a court reporter, and a man I recognised from the papers as Laurel's father slid into the seat behind his daughter. He took a moment to glower at me before the judge announced the commencement of proceedings.

Of course, the first thing Aunt Splydia did was try to upset the apple cart.

"Your Honour, with your permission, we'd like to call an extra witness who has some rather pertinent information that's just come to light."

"Their name?"

"Cassidy Hastings."

Marcus got halfway out of his seat before Lance

yanked him back down. "Hell no."

The judge fixed him with a stony stare. "Mr. Hastings, please refrain from interrupting in my courtroom."

"She's six years old."

"Mr. Hastings, be quiet."

Laurel glanced in his direction, and I caught the triumphant gleam in her eyes. Bitch.

The judge peered over his glasses. "What is the nature of this information?"

"My client's husband is believed to be cohabiting with a convicted murderer."

Stay calm, Iris. We knew they'd go there, but calling Cassie to prove Marcus had moved on? That was a low move. I was sitting in court for crying out loud. We weren't exactly trying to hide the fact that we were together.

Lance stood up. "My client is happy to acknowledge this relationship without calling Cassidy into court."

Aunt Splydia argued back. "It's not only that the relationship exists, it's the nature of the relationship that concerns us. On recent visits to the property Mr. Hastings shares with Miss Iris McGivern, Cassidy's life has been put in danger on more than one occasion."

What the actual hell?

Marcus's fists balled up at his sides, but he managed to bite his tongue. He knew he couldn't afford another outburst.

"Mr. Benton?" the judge asked.

"The allegation is ridiculous, but without knowing what it is, we have no way to refute something that didn't happen."

"Cassidy's waiting outside with her grandma, Your

Honour."

The judge sighed. "Very well, I'll allow it. But as Mr. Hastings so kindly pointed out, Cassidy Hastings is only six years old, so let's keep it brief, shall we?"

My heart went out to Cassie as her grandma led her in and lifted her onto the wooden seat by the judge. Her legs dangled in mid-air, and she fidgeted as she waited for her grilling. What was Laurel thinking? She didn't care about her daughter. She simply wanted to score points off Marcus.

I smiled at Cassie, willing her not to be scared, but she didn't smile back.

Aunt Splydia spoke first. "Cassidy, do you remember visiting your father two days after Christmas?"

"Yes, I got presents."

"And who else did you see on that visit?"

"Iris and Kimberly and Nicole and Rania and Will and Reed and Beck and RJ and Shannon and Aisling." Bless her, she'd remembered all our names. "Aisling's younger than me, and Kimberly's a princess."

The judge appeared confused for a moment and looked to Marcus for clarification.

"Kimberly wears a lot of jewellery."

"Ah. Carry on."

Aunt Splydia consulted her notes. "Do you remember what you did while you were visiting?"

"We made cakes! Cakes with chocolate spread, and I ate three."

"I see." The woman made it sound like a bad thing. Lighten up, lady. "And after that?"

"We played in the snow. We builded a snowman and made snow angels. Daddy said I made the best one." Of course he did. "And then Iris showed me how to do cartwheels."

Aunt Splydia turned to the judge. "There you have it. In the course of one afternoon, Mr. Hastings put the daughter he claims to care for at risk of hypothermia and allowed his new girlfriend to teach a young girl reckless acrobatics. When Cassidy arrived home that evening, she attempted another cartwheel at her mother's house and hit her head on a table."

"I see. Mr. Benton, would you care to ask any questions?"

Lance held a muttered conference with Marcus before standing up.

"No questions. Cassidy's been through enough already. But on the twenty-seventh of December, she was wearing a padded, waterproof snowsuit her father gave her as a Christmas gift, so there was no risk of hypothermia. Miss McGivern is a qualified gymnastics coach, so she's more than capable of teaching a child to turn a cartwheel, and if Cassidy had an accident in her mother's home, then perhaps she should have been more closely supervised."

I could have kissed Lance for that. I'd almost forgotten I'd mentioned the coaching thing in one of our early chats at Lakeview, but it was true. After Mum died, I'd signed up for the coaching program in a desperate attempt to keep myself busy, and I had a Level 2 qualification from British Gymnastics by the time I left school. I'd worked Sundays at the garden centre to pay for it.

"Okay, Cassidy, you can step down."

She looked so vulnerable as she took a seat between her grandparents. Why didn't they take her home? Was this the way they wanted her to remember her parents? Arguing in court?

The next three hours went about as expected. Laurel tried to assassinate Marcus's character in every way possible, and she even brought up his freaking piercing. Apparently, it was yet more evidence of his foolhardy character and his inability to think things through. What did the damage was the police report, though. I was watching the judge when Aunt Splydia showed photos of the bruises on Laurel's wrists and produced a copy of the restraining order, and he didn't look impressed.

Finally, he nodded to himself, seeming to come to a decision.

"Having considered the evidence presented, I believe it's best that we stick with the current arrangements for the moment. Mr. Hastings, you'll see Cassidy on Friday afternoons each week, and for the full day during school holidays. Now, shall we go on to the finances?"

Marcus's shoulders slumped, and I felt devastated for him. Twelve more years without being able to take a holiday with his daughter. Without going to her birthday parties or having her stay overnight. Even if we had a baby together, there'd always be a gaping hole in his life.

But with all that, Laurel still wasn't happy.

"Are you kidding?" she snapped. "Was there something you didn't understand? She..." Laurel pointed one manicured finger in my direction. "Is a murderer. A psycho. I refuse to let my daughter go anywhere near her."

Aunt Splydia tried to quiet Laurel as she addressed

the judge. "We'd like you to consider supervised visitation."

"No, Miss Sprague, I've made my ruling quite clear."

"He's not having her!" Laurel yelled. Then just in case she hadn't been clear enough, she swivelled to face Cassie. "Cassidy, you're not going to your father's house while *she's* there."

Cassie burst into tears, but still Laurel wasn't done.

"I demand a retrial," she told the judge.

"This isn't actually a trial," Lance pointed out.

"Shut up! Nobody asked you."

Now Marcus tried. "Laurel, sit down. You're causing a scene."

"Don't you tell me what to do, you cheating bastard!"

Cassie's cries grew louder. "Don't yell at my daddy," she sobbed, then she tried to get off the seat and run to him, but Jacqueline grabbed her arm and yanked her back. Cassie yelped in pain, but somehow she wriggled out of her cardigan and escaped her grandmother's grip. Once she got to Marcus, she clung onto him, and then they were both crying.

Bloody hell, I needed popcorn.

Laurel was incandescent with rage as she stormed in our direction. Aunt Splydia tried to body-check her, but she barged her out of the way and carried on. Oh, shit. I glanced at the judge, but his mouth was hanging open as he looked on, frozen. Guess stuff like this didn't happen often in family court.

"Don't hurt my daddy again," Cassie squeaked. "Don't hurt him."

Should I wade in? I was fairly certain I could take

Laurel, but I'd promised Lance I'd be on my best behaviour. Socking the competition probably wouldn't be a good move.

Luckily, Lance came to life and grabbed the wailing nutcase in a bear hug, Rania vaulted over the wooden rail to grab her kicking legs, and the judge banged on his desk with the gavel.

"Bailiff! We need some help in here."

Laurel was still screeching as a pair of policemen handcuffed her, and Wallace Burton had his head in his hands. I couldn't stand the man, but at that moment, I did feel a little sorry for him.

Finally, Laurel was subdued and reseated between two burly coppers. And she said *I* was the psycho? Marcus wasn't wrong when he said she projected. The judge was still a bit red-faced, but he took a sip of water and adjusted his glasses.

"Right, shall we try this again? I realise I may have made an error in my earlier judgement."

"See?" Laurel said, triumphant. "I was right."

She just didn't get it, did she?

The judge leaned forward and beckoned to Cassie. "Can you sit up here again? Your father can join you if you'd like."

Marcus carried her to the front and sat her in the chair again, but this time he crouched beside her, holding her hand as the judge asked his questions.

"Cassidy, just now, you said you didn't want your mummy to hurt your daddy again. Can you tell me when she hurt him before?"

Aunt Splydia tried a weak, "Objection. The witness is only six years old."

The judge practically rolled his eyes. "That didn't

seem to bother you before." Then to Cassie, "Please answer the question."

"Mummy was yelling, and Daddy was putting things into a suitcase. Then Mummy hit him on the head with flowers, and there was lots of glass."

Marcus's soft, "Oh no," broke my damn heart. Cassie had seen the fight? He thought she'd been asleep.

"You saw your Mummy yelling?"

"It was loud, and I was scared, so I got out of bed to find Daddy."

"What happened after you saw the glass?"

"I was scared Mummy might hurt me too, so I ran back to bed."

"Has your Mummy ever hurt you before?"

"Not with glass."

"In any other way?"

"Sometimes she smacks me if I'm naughty."

Marcus hugged Cassie, and she burrowed against him, holding him tight. That poor, poor little girl. She didn't deserve to be in the middle of this, but the judge still had one more question.

"What about Iris? Has she ever hurt you?"

Finally, a tiny smile. "No, Iris is fun. I love Iris."

A tear rolled down my cheek, and this time, it was Lance's turn to be on handkerchief duty. That little girl loved me? My heart swelled so big I thought it'd burst clean through my ribcage.

Another heavy sigh from the judge. "From today, custody of Cassidy Hastings is granted to Marcus Hastings. I'll allow one supervised visitation session per week for Laurel Hastings. We'll adjourn the financial discussion until next week. Miss Sprague, I trust you'll have managed to calm your client down by then?"

"I'll do my best, Your Honour."

"Then this hearing is adjourned."

***

We were both still in shock when we exited the courtroom with Cassie between us. Wow. Lance was wearing his I-told-you-so grin, and it was totally justified.

"Is it unprofessional to hug your lawyer?" I asked.

"Who cares?"

I squished him as tight as I could. "If it weren't for the fact that I'm very much in love with Marcus, I'd kiss you."

"I couldn't even be mad about that," Marcus said, laughing.

"What about me?" Cassie asked. "I want a hug."

Marcus picked her up, and she ended up squashed between the three of us, giggling, while Rania went to fetch the car. We'd won. We'd bloody won! Even the dead guy yelling at me from the other side of the courtroom steps couldn't dampen my mood. Judging by the number of holes in him, he'd been the victim of a drive-by shooting. I ignored him. Talking to dead people wasn't on my to-do list today.

Of course, the victory brought other challenges—we had a little girl now, and because we didn't want to jinx things, we hadn't bought any new stuff for her. All she had was her Christmas gifts and the bits Marcus had retrieved from his old house. The landlord had at least agreed to stop charging rent thanks to a strongly worded letter from Lance, but Marcus still wasn't allowed in to pick up the rest of his belongings. New bits of the housing estate fell into holes every week.

Eventually, we managed to disentangle ourselves, and Lance picked up his briefcase.

"Gotta go. I have a date tonight, although after that spectacle, I think I might turn gay instead."

"Can't say I blame you. I mean, I knew Laurel was unhinged, but that..."

"Seen it before, buddy. When the spoiled princesses don't get their own way for the first time in their life, they lose their sh—" He glanced at Cassie. "They lose their marbles. I'll call you tomorrow about the financial side of things."

"I don't care about the financial side. There was only one thing I ever wanted."

"Maybe so, but we'll still get you an appropriate settlement. There's equity in the house, and you don't want Laurel getting those talons on your pension plan."

"Can we have pancakes for breakfast tomorrow?" Cassie asked. "I love pancakes."

"Sure, sweetie." Then to Lance, "Make the call after ten, would you?"

Lance nodded, chuckling as he backed away.

In the car, the three of us piled into the back while Rania drove. None of us wanted to be separated. I still couldn't quite believe where I'd ended up. Six months ago, I'd had no hope of leaving Lakeview alive, and now I had three sisters, a boyfriend, and a beautiful little girl to spend time with. A ready-made family. Plus a whole bunch of friends and enough money to live on for the rest of my life if I was careful.

"Rania, would you mind stopping at a mall on the

way back?" Marcus asked. "Cassie needs clothes, toys, everything really."

"No, she doesn't."

"Yes, she does."

"No, she doesn't. Me, Kimberly, and Nicole went shopping before they left for the US, and you know Kimberly..." I was beginning to get the picture. "It was all we could do to talk her out of buying a pony. Will's going to be glad to get the garage back."

"But we didn't think we'd win," I said.

"*We* did." I caught Rania's smile in the rear-view mirror. "Have faith, sister."

EPILOGUE - IRIS

"I'D LIKE ME a pair of those mouse ears," Darlene said as we cleared away the dessert dishes. "But they'd fall right through me, wouldn't they?"

"I'm afraid so," Nicole told her. "How about we get you some Disney DVDs?"

"That might be nice. I saw an ad for a Disney movie on the TV the other day. The one with the mermaid. What's she called again?"

"Ariel."

With Laurel undergoing a court-mandated residential anger-management program after throwing a legal pad at the judge in the final court hearing, we'd decided to take a quick vacation to visit Nicole and Kimberly before Marcus started his new job next week. Wallace and Jacqueline had tried to claim Laurel's weekly visitation rights, but the judge figured that any six-year-old would prefer a trip to Disneyland, so there we were in California. We'd spent five days in Los Angeles before driving up the coast to Nicole's adopted home city of San Francisco. Since she and Beck only had two spare rooms, Professor Fairchild had offered up his home for the rest of us, and Cassie had flaked out upstairs just after eight o'clock. Two days at Disney followed by a trip to the beach had left her exhausted.

Darlene, the professor's wife, had died in the dining

room, the unfortunate victim of a robbery gone wrong, but rather than staying bitter, she smiled constantly and gave tips on how to bake the perfect apple pie. Having all four of the Electi over to visit had left her thrilled, but after dinner when we told her about the Judge and the possibility that he could release her, she went quiet.

"But I like being here," she said after a moment. "In my eyes, Geoffrey's still my husband, and if I didn't remind him to do the laundry and change the sheets and pick up the dry cleaning, he'd never get anything done."

She meant via Nicole, of course. She and Beck visited at least once a week, and Nicole wrote Darlene's instructions on a whiteboard beside the television.

"We don't know if it's even possible yet," Rania said. "Leaving might be optional."

"How will you find out?"

"Someday, we'll put our four gold pieces together and see what happens. We might not even be able to find the Judge."

"When will you try it?"

"When the time's right."

The comment started me thinking, and even when the conversation turned back to lighter subjects, I began to wonder whether the time would ever truly be right. I had a family to consider now, and I wouldn't do anything that would risk the life I had with them. We had a future to look forward to, and a new home waiting for us when we got back. Well, not a new home, exactly. It practically needed to be rebuilt.

Once my money came through from Hannity, I'd got Will to ferret out the contact details for Percy's son in Paris. He'd accepted my offer for the old garden centre, and as soon as we arrived back, I'd sign the contract and it would be mine. *Ours*. Marcus would chip in once his old home was sold—the judge had awarded him half the equity. As well as the plant nursery, we planned to open a café with a craft area to give the villagers of Highcross somewhere to meet and chat. Sometimes, the older residents got lonely on their own.

The place even had a paddock out the back for Cassie's eventual pony, although we hadn't told her that yet, and if I remembered rightly, there was an old brick-built stable block hidden in the undergrowth behind Percy's cottage. *Our* cottage. The place was called Mayfield, and since my middle name was May and my mum's had been too, there was something poetic about that.

But that was a project for later.

In San Francisco, the professor spent most of his life in the dining room—because of Darlene, no doubt—and after the plates had been cleared, I curled up on one of the sofas next to Marcus with a glass of wine. I'd found bliss. More new friends, a good merlot, and tomorrow we were going on a cruise to see the Golden Gate Bridge.

Which was why his next words shocked me to my core.

"I think it might be time."

"Huh?"

"For the four of you to try this thing. We're settled, you're strong, and it might be months before everyone's together again."

"Cassie's asleep upstairs," I reminded him.

"Thanks to you, Cassie's always going to be asleep upstairs."

Silence fell. I'd expected a debate or possibly even an argument, but then I understood. The men were leaving us to make the decision ourselves. Marcus had planted the seed, and it was up to us whether or not to water it.

"I'm in," Nicole said. "I want to know how this thing works. I've been scanning DNA databases for months and found two possible lines for replacement Electi, but nothing yet for the Judge. Every piece of information helps."

Rania nodded. "I'm in too. Kimberly?"

"Honestly, I don't want to do it, but I have to, don't I? The world's only getting more dangerous, and if this Judge can do anything to help, we should try to find him."

"No matter what the cost?" the professor asked softly.

"Yes. That's what we're here for. The decision's made."

She undid her necklace and slid the chain out of the middle, leaving just the gold piece flat in her palm. The rest of us followed suit.

"Now what?" I asked. "We put them together?"

Rania shrugged. "I guess so."

Each of us put a puzzle piece down on the coffee table. Mine fitted neatly between Nicole's and Rania's, with a hole left in the middle for the Judge. Slowly, slowly we slid them closer until they touched, and... nothing. Zero. Zilch. Not one single thing happened. I'd expected a glow at least, maybe a few sparks. Some kind of magic-magic.

This was... It was disappointing. But in another way, also a relief. If we couldn't work out how to activate the full Electi team, then I could go home and start hacking back brambles. Digging them out was a pain in the ass, but—

"Perhaps we need the Judge's piece for it to do anything?" Kimberly suggested.

That didn't make a whole lot of sense. "The four of us are meant to be able to find him if we work together. If we already had his gold piece, we'd know where he was, wouldn't we?"

"Are you sure these things didn't come with instructions?"

"You know everything I know. Maybe the symbols mean something we don't understand? What if they're an instruction manual?"

Rania stated the obvious. "Then we'll never understand this curse."

Marcus picked up my piece and turned it over in his hands. The back was plain. A shiny gold mirror. Even after thousands of years, it didn't have so much as a scratch on it.

"I don't know about the smaller symbols, but the holes and the lines connecting them? They look like stick figures the way Cassie draws them. Heads and arms, viewed from above. What if you try sitting in a ring and holding hands?"

That all sounded a bit playground-ish, but okay. Marcus slotted my gold piece back into place, and we assembled cross-legged on the floor.

"I need a cushion," Kimberly said, and Nicole giggled.

Rania frowned. "Wait, Nicole needs to swap places

with Kimberly so we're in the right order."

Finally, we got ourselves sorted out, and Marcus gave my shoulders an encouraging squeeze.

"Is this where you say 'trust me, I'm a doctor'?" I asked.

"Something like that."

Okay, here goes. My heart sped up because this really was our only hope. If this didn't work, our gold pieces would merely be pretty pieces of jewellery with an interesting story behind them.

Nicole and I were the last to join hands, and then... I felt it. Just a tingle at first, but the tingle quickly turned into a rush of energy, and suddenly we weren't in San Francisco anymore. A rocky landscape lay ahead, dull and barren save for the occasional scrubby tree. A narrow valley. Long shadows extended from a sun that hung low over the mountains in a clear blue sky.

And the eyes I was looking through weren't my own.

As I began to adjust to the strange sensation of seeing what wasn't in front of me, I realised our host wasn't alone. Ahead, a quartet of spirits lounged on a rock, soaking up sun they couldn't feel as blood dripped from their wounds. One had a large chunk of his head missing. They didn't react to our host, just carried on chatting amongst themselves. To them, he wasn't special.

Could he see the spirits? Or was that just us, channelling our abilities through him? He scanned the rocky vista, and when his gaze lingered on the group for just a beat too long, I realised he *could* see them.

Which made him the Judge.

This was how we found him. We saw *through* him.
Holy fuck.

Rania realised at the same moment I did. I couldn't
see her, but I could feel her—her thoughts, her
emotions, her fears, plus the grip of her hand on mine.
Then Nicole, and finally Kimberly.

The Judge glanced down, and I saw his hands.
Strong, weathered hands, but that wasn't what startled
me. No, it was what he held in them that was
important. In his right, a pistol nestled in his grip, and
in his left, he clasped a smaller hand with long, elegant
fingers. A woman's hand. He turned to speak to her,
but I didn't understand his words.

"It's Farsi. I understand a little." Rania translated
through her thoughts. "The men are behind them,
getting closer. They have to run."

Easier said than done. The woman wore a long,
flowing burka that covered everything but her eyes, and
when she moved, the wind blew the billowing fabric
against her. Was she...pregnant?

Then the gunfire started.

I felt giddy. Faint. I'd never been so scared in my
life, and I wasn't even there. Kimberly screamed, and I
wasn't sure whether that was just in her mind or in real
life, but I felt a squeeze of my shoulders, a touch from
another world, and I realised Marcus was still with me
too. Nicole's palm was sweating as I clung to her hand,
and I thought I should loosen my grip, but I couldn't.
Only Rania stayed calm, and her strength got us
through the initial shock.

Far away from us, the Judge and the woman ran.

Go, go, go! I willed them on, feeling every trip,
every stumble. The Judge raised his pistol and fired at a

shadow ahead of him, and a man crumpled to the ground. No black soul rose. Either the man had never killed anyone in his life—hard to believe considering he was in his thirties or forties and holding a rifle—or the Judge couldn't dispatch souls in the same way the Electi could. We were learning more about us in the worst possible way.

Nicole's thoughts echoed mine. "This is like a mutant science project."

The woman yelped as she fell, but the Judge hauled her up and kept on going, half carrying her now as they headed for the other end of the mountain pass. That chink of light was their only escape route unless they were world-class climbers. But as they got closer, more men with guns appeared, blocking the way.

They were trapped.

No, no, no. Don't kill them.

We'd got so close. So close to finding the Judge, and now we were meant to watch him die? Fate had a really warped sense of humour. Kimberly started crying, and fear gave way to helplessness as the men surrounded the Judge and the woman. Who was she? What was she to him?

One of the men snatched her away. *One of the potato heads.* I choked out a sobbing laugh as I recalled chiding Cassie for using a bad word, and that day seemed a hundred years ago now. Another body, another world.

The leader barked out a command at the Judge in guttural Farsi.

Drop the gun.

He didn't have much of a choice, did he? It fell to the ground with a clatter.

On your knees.

This was the end? The Judge was about to be executed, and we had to watch. I didn't want to see, but at the same time, I couldn't look away. I glared at the leader as he raised his gun, and I cursed his band of merry men, wishing looks could kill.

Die, motherfucker.

Kimberly took up my plea: *Die, die, die!*

Then Nicole: *Die, you asshole.*

And finally Rania: *Die.*

The leader's gun paused, halfway up, and his eyes glazed. His body seemed to wage an internal battle as his black soul struggled to free itself, and then it sort of popped out and burst, like a balloon blown too big and then pricked with a pin. The other souls behind him rose as well—eight, ten, twelve of them—and little tatters of darkness scattered to the edges of the valley as their former bodies crumpled to the dusty ground. Only one man stayed standing, the youngest of the bunch, little more than a boy, and after a few moments staring in dumbfounded horror, he threw his gun to the ground and sprinted away. Puffs of dust hung in the air behind him.

The Judge cursed under his breath in English. "Holy fuck. What just happened?"

Then the girl in the burka was screaming, Kimberly was screaming, Nicole was crying, and my brain was jammed full of confusion as I tried to work out what had just happened.

Men had died, their souls banished without us so much as touching them. But how?

Everything changed. In a heartbeat, I was back in the professor's dining room, and Beck was holding a sobbing Nicole while Reed tried to comfort Kimberly. Marcus clutched my gold piece in his hand, the circle interrupted, the spell broken. I threw myself into his arms.

"What the hell happened?" Will asked Rania, who rose to her feet, impassive. "You were all in some kind of trance, and Kimberly was hysterical. We didn't know whether to stop it or not, but then Marcus made an executive decision."

How did Rania stay so calm? I wanted to be like her when I grew up.

"What happened?" she said. "A dozen men just died, and I think we killed them."

"Is that true?" Marcus asked me.

"I-I-I think so. I don't know. I don't understand. They just... They just *fell*."

Reed swept the gold pieces off the table and into one hand. "If it *is* true, then these things are dangerous."

"No!" Kimberly made a grab for him. "Leave them!"

"Give me one good reason why I should."

Nicole finally found her tongue, her voice thick with fear even though the four of us were safe. "Because the Judge is in trouble, and we need to help. These..." She uncurled Reed's fingers from our amulets while Kimberly hung on to his wrist. "These are the key to finding him."

WHAT'S NEXT?

The Electi series concludes in *Judged...*

When Ro Keyes quit the military, he was looking forward to a slower pace of life. A chance to pursue his love of learning as part of an exchange program with Kabul International University. But you know what they say? You can't escape your past. Or, as it turns out, your birthright.

As a woman in Afghanistan, Ziya Khalizai has no choice but to marry the man chosen for her. Perhaps it won't be so bad? He did promise to protect what was left of her family, after all. But promises get broken, and futures get destroyed. Ziya's spirit? Luckily, she still has that.

Haunted by their pasts plus several unruly ghosts, Ro and Ziya set out to save lives, but around them, people are dying. How? Why? And more importantly, will they be next?

For more details: www.elise-noble.com/judged

And if you also enjoy romantic mysteries without supernatural elements, why not give my Blackwood series a try? The story starts in *Pitch Black*...

What happens when an assassin has a nervous breakdown?

After the owner of a security company is murdered, his sharp-edged wife goes on the run. Forced to abandon everything she holds dear—her home, her friends, her job in special ops—she builds a new life for herself in England. As Ashlyn Hale, she meets Luke, a handsome local who makes her realise just how lonely she is.

Yet, even in the sleepy village of Lower Foxford, the dark side of life dogs Diamond's trail when the unthinkable strikes. Forced out of hiding, she races against time to save those she cares about. But is it too little, too late?

Pitch Black is currently available FREE.
For more details: www.elise-noble.com/pitch-black

If you enjoyed *Demented*, please consider leaving a review.

For an author, every review is incredibly important. Not only do they make us feel warm and fuzzy inside, readers consider them when making their decision whether or not to buy a book. Even a line saying you enjoyed the book or what your favourite part was helps a lot.

WANT TO STALK ME?

For updates on my new releases, giveaways, and other random stuff, you can sign up for my newsletter on my website:
www.elise-noble.com

Facebook:
www.facebook.com/EliseNobleAuthor

Twitter: @EliseANoble

Instagram: @elise_noble

If you're on social media, you may also like to join Team Blackwood for exclusive giveaways, sneak previews, and book-related chat. Be the first to find out about new stories, and you might even see your name or one of your ideas make it into print!

And if you'd like to read my books for FREE, you can also find details of how to join my review team.

Would you like to join Team Blackwood?

www.elise-noble.com/team-blackwood

END OF BOOK STUFF

A month before release date, and I'm sitting here late on a Friday night (because my life is *that* exciting), thinking about how things change, sometimes for the better, sometimes for the worse. Guess I'm being kind of morose. I think I need gin.

A bunch of years ago, I worked for a marketing company. Not selling stuff, but doing the techy-geeky stuff in the shadows. Back then, I used to read a lot, but I hadn't written a word of fiction since GCSE English classes (which, incidentally, I hated). And I was kinda bored. I signed up for evening classes—Arabic and, for some inexplicable reason, bricklaying—but I still needed more of a challenge. So I quit my job for one that paid much less *but* it meant I could go to business school. Sometimes you've got to take a step sideways to go forward, right?

I qualified as a chartered accountant. I got a promotion at my new job. I bought a whole lot of designer handbags and fancy shoes. But I also learned more about what was important to me, and I realised that no job title or bonus is as important as being happy. People matter, animals matter, stuff doesn't. I like the new me a lot better.

What set off all this thinking? Today, I went to a funeral. My old boss died. The world lost a great guy, one who frustrated me at times but also a kind man who taught me to think outside the box and see my own and others' potential. And I saw a bunch of my old colleagues, people I hadn't seen in years. Some of them have changed. Some of them are still exactly the same. One lady I used to work with also went back to school, and now she's a pastry chef. I'm so freaking happy that she followed her dream.

During those years since I left, I also started writing and found it's not only me who has to adapt to change. My characters change too, but in the microcosm of a novel. As an author, I can transform a whole bunch of lives. How cool is that?

Where will I be in ten years time? I have no idea. Where do I *want* to be? On a beach in Tahiti, sipping cocktails.

Kidding.

I'm not even sure, but I think I'd get pretty bored on that beach. The last ten years have been as much a surprise to me as to anyone else. I write books. Who'd have thought it? Certainly not my teachers, lol. At school, I had fun extracting DNA on my lunch breaks. At university, I spent a year researching the surface energy of diamond-like carbon coating. Last week, I learned about the hardships of being a woman in Afghanistan and also how to swear in Japanese. Life is a roller coaster. I suppose the one thing that's stayed with me through it all is my love of learning. Give me new facts to stuff into my brain and I'm happy :)

What's next in my book world? Well, it's back to Blackwood for Nickel, Sloane and Logan's book. Emmy and Ana make an appearance too. And there's a cat.

And for this book, I have some thank-yous... Firstly,

to my lovely friend Rachael, who's a social worker here in the UK. Thank you for eating pizza with me while I questioned you about your job, and also for reading the rough draft to check it wasn't totally unrealistic and that it (hopefully) wouldn't offend anyone. Thank you, as always, to Abi for magicking up a cover and to Nikki for editing. And also thanks to my beta team for the early feedback—Jeff, Renata, Terri, Lina, Musi, David, Stacia, Jessica, Nikita, Quenby, and Jody.

Thought for the year: Don't get stressed over bullshit.

Elise

Lithium
Carbon
Rhodium
Platinum
Lead
Copper
Bronze
Nickel
Hydrogen (2021)

The Blackwood UK Series
Joker in the Pack
Cherry on Top (novella)
Roses are Dead
Shallow Graves
Indigo Rain
Pass the Parcel (TBA)

Baldwin's Shore
Dirty Little Secrets (2021)
Secrets, Lies, and Family Ties (2021)
Buried Secrets (2021)

Blackwood Casefiles
Stolen Hearts
Burning Love (TBA)

Blackstone House
Hard Lines (TBA)
Hard Tide (TBA)

The Electi Series
Cursed

Spooked
Possessed
Demented
Judged

The Planes Series
A Vampire in Vegas
A Devil in the Dark (TBA)

The Trouble Series
Trouble in Paradise
Nothing but Trouble
24 Hours of Trouble

Standalone
Life
Coco du Ciel (2021)
Twisted (short stories)
A Very Happy Christmas (novella)

Books with clean versions available (no swearing and no on-the-page sex)
Pitch Black
Into the Black
Forever Black
Gold Rush
Gray is My Heart

Audiobooks
Black is My Heart (Diamond & Snow - prequel)
Pitch Black
Into the Black
Forever Black

Gold Rush
Gray is My Heart
Neon (novella)